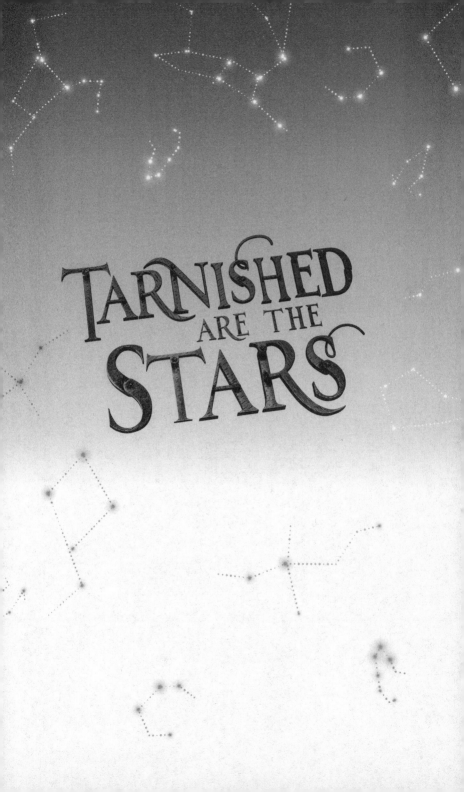

TARNISHED ARE THE STARS

TARNISHED ARE THE STARS

ROSIEE THOR

SCHOLASTIC PRESS | NEW YORK

Library of Congress Cataloging-in-Publication Data available

ISBN 978-1-338-31227-0

10 9 8 7 6 5 4 3 2 1   19 20 21 22 23

Printed in the U.S.A.   23

First edition, October 2019

Book design by Yaffa Jaskoll

FOR MOM AND DAD

(I GUESS YOU CAN FINALLY READ THIS ONE)

CHAPTER ONE

There was nothing quite like the first *tick* of a new heart.

The silver TICCER stuttered to life in Anna's palm, its metal pulse a metronome moving in time with her own clockwork heart.

Tick. Tick. Tick.

Grandpa Thatcher threw down his instruments with a clatter.

Anna's gaze snapped to the surgical table, where their young patient lay motionless, chest open. "What is it?"

"His condition is more severe than I thought." Thatcher leaned forward to get a better look. "Glasses."

Hands shaking, Anna pushed Thatcher's spectacles up the bridge of his nose. Complications in surgery were more common than not, but her grandfather's desperate tone still hit Anna at her core. She set her teeth at the memory of the last time this boy before them had gone under her knife. She'd held the scalpel steady but pressed too hard, splitting skin, severing arteries. Warm blood ran over her fingers, and Thatcher's voice boomed across the table as he pushed her away, reclaiming control.

The boy had lost an arm that night, and Anna had lost her nerve.

She blinked the memory away.

Thatcher pointed a gloved finger at the boy's chest cavity. "Tell me what you see."

The old man's wheelchair required a short operating table, so Anna, who stood taller than even the boys her age, had to stoop to see properly, struggling to look past the wavy hair and upturned lips that made the boy more human than patient. She squeezed her eyes shut, then opened them on rigid valves and a thickened heart muscle.

"It's enormous!"

"We're surgeons, Deirdre-Anne. *Enormous* is not an appropriate medical term."

Anna inhaled through her teeth. "It's hypertrophic."

"Good." Thatcher's fingers danced across the instrument tray. "And what does that mean?"

"He needs a TICCER, as you suspected."

Thatcher grabbed the cauterizer in acknowledgment of her correct answer.

He wouldn't ask her to help.

She didn't want him to.

He'd taught her everything he knew, but Anna wouldn't cut. She hadn't even considered it for years—not since her first surgery, not since the incident with the boy's arm. She was used to holding someone's life in her hands, pulling apart and piecing together the delicate machinery of TICCERs, but that was metal.

Flesh was different.

Flesh was fragile.

The TICCER rattled from her hands onto the instrument tray, her fingers shaking too hard to hold it. "I need to go."

Thatcher shook his head and tutted. "Don't be foolish. Your work here isn't finished."

Anna froze, her feet poised to flee. "Well, *I* am."

"Once made, a mistake cannot be *un*made." He glanced at the instrument table, drawing her eyes with his; silver steel stared back. "To turn your back on this—all this good you could do—is childish."

Anna let out a long, loaded breath. "I *was* a child. What did you expect from a twelve-year-old?" The memory of a scalpel whispered in her hand.

"It's been six years, Deirdre-Anne. You were Roman's doctor then, too." Thatcher indicated the boy on the table with his chin. "*He*'s a child, and there's only ever been space for one in my operating room."

For a moment, Anna held his gaze. She didn't speak. She didn't breathe. The only sound came from the ticking of their young patient's new heart.

Anna's eyes met her boots. "Then you won't be needing me."

Thatcher didn't look up, but his words chased her out the door: "Don't run from this, Deirdre-Anne. Our fears always catch us in the end."

Anna's breath overtook her, ragged and consuming, as the door swung shut in her wake. She peeled off her gloves and plunged her hands beneath the tap, breathing slowly to match the meter of her heart as water spilled across her skin. She scrubbed and scraped, washing away every trace of their argument with antiseptic before stepping into the kitchen, where Roman's mother waited for news.

The older girl sat slumped over the table, dark curls spilling over her brown skin, chin propped on tired hands. Anna doubted Ruby had moved at all since she'd been planted there with a mug of peppermint tea, Thatcher's signature comfort. Ruby had looked downright wild the night prior when she'd appeared at Anna's doorstep carrying an unconscious Roman. Now she looked worn, her deep brown eyes tired with sleepless anxiety.

Anna had seen her fair share of beleaguered loved ones waiting for news, good or bad. She'd sat with new widows and orphans, but Ruby gave her pause. Only six years had passed since Ruby had adopted the infant with one arm. Ruby's eyes had been sleepless then, too, but at least she'd had Dalton, her late husband. How unfortunate that her son fell ill so soon after her husband's death. Tragic, some might have called it.

But in Mechan—their hidden seaside village of outcasts—tragedy hung in the air like fog; it was their maker, their neighbor, their constant companion.

"How's Roman?" Ruby's voice cracked.

"Thatcher's still working on him." Anna wished she had more comforting news and a gentler tone to offer her best friend, but making promises, as Thatcher always said, wasn't a surgeon's business. Anna snatched Ruby's empty mug and filled it with water. "Here. You need to stay hydrated."

Ruby took the mug and pulled out the chair beside her. "Would you sit with me?"

Anna picked at her fingers; she'd cleaned them thoroughly, but she couldn't shake the feeling that a spot of blood lurked beneath one of her nails. "He's in good hands, Ruby. Thatcher's the best."

That was true: Thatcher *was* the best. His invention, the TICCER—Tarnish Internal Cardiac Clockwork-Enabled Regulator—had saved the lives of every citizen of Mechan. With steel and a scalpel, he mended all their hearts. He gave each patient who crossed through his operating room a chance to survive, and he'd given Anna a chance to learn.

Anna balled her shaking fingers into fists. Roman was in good hands—the only hands that could save him.

"Stay with me." Ruby grabbed Anna's wrist, her touch humming with frantic, desperate energy. Four years Anna's senior, Ruby was usually the calm to Anna's storm, the shield to Anna's sword.

Not today.

Anna glanced out the window to see the beginnings of light. "It's almost dawn. If I don't leave for the market soon, I'll be late."

Ruby's face fell. "Why don't you stay home today? I could use the company, and the Celestial Market is dangerous."

"You know I can't."

Though Ruby had never been to the Celestial Market—never even left the protection of Mechan—she'd certainly heard plenty about the Settlement. The convergence of so many people planetside was enough to make anyone in Mechan nervous. Residents of the Settlement knew better than to leave their walled city, but the annual fair brought double the officer presence. If one of them stumbled across the secret village, hidden though it was in the crook of rocky cliffs miles away from the Settlement, it would be the end of their carefully protected refuge.

Ruby rested her head against Anna's side. "I thought you might reconsider. That new decree—"

"What new decree?"

The crease in Ruby's forehead deepened, her dark skin wrinkling in waves. "The runners brought it back yesterday." She withdrew a crumpled bulletin from her dress pocket. "The Commissioner's calling you out, Anna."

The long-awaited thirty-fifth Tech Decree had been penned in familiar, thin letters:

Anna gulped. She'd lasted three years, running her business carefully and quietly outside the Commissioner's notice. She'd paid, blackmailed, and begged for silence, but it seemed someone had finally broken. Or perhaps the Commissioner had known all along, choosing now to strike, certain the Celestial Market would lure her out.

"I'll be okay." Anna waved off Ruby's concern. "This is only a formality. If he had anything on me, he wouldn't have used my alias."

Ruby pursed her lips. "I don't like the idea of you wandering about with a bounty on your head, especially with all those officers around."

"The officers won't know me from any other merchant, I promise." Anna's voice played assertive, but she tugged her copper braid with her free hand. "I've been running tech into the Settlement for three years now. If the Commissioner hasn't caught me yet, I doubt an official warrant will do much."

"Stay. *Please.*"

Anna shook her head, prying Ruby's fingers from her arm with difficulty.

"Just come back, all right?"

Staying to comfort Ruby was the safer option, but Anna couldn't fix Ruby's pain with nuts and bolts. She'd take her chances with the officers. Evading them would be easier, if more dangerous, and her clients needed her help, both in the Settlement and at home. She and Thatcher made do with what the runners could steal from the Settlement, but with the coin Anna earned from the market, she could stock her grandfather's operating room for a month without breaking the law. Well, without thievery, anyway.

"I'll be fine, and so will Roman." She fought hard to keep a grimace off her face. She wasn't supposed to make promises like that.

As Anna reached the door, she took one last look at Ruby, face pressed against the table, eyes closed in sleepless rest. Anna would be fine, like she said. She always came back.

The sun's yellow face greeted Anna outside. Its rays sprinkled golden light up the cliff face, tangling with the silvery threads spider-webbing across the rocks. Veins of cold metal turned ethereal in the early morning sun, almost as if the town mined gold instead of iron and zinc. Soon the inhabitants of Mechan would wake and fill the street with morning bustle, and she preferred to avoid the whispers and stares of her neighbors, the disapproval seeping through their words.

Ducking into her workshop behind Thatcher's house, Anna collected her cart before heading toward the mossy ridge overlooking the secret town below. Leaving behind a cluster of small homes, built with mismatched materials like patchwork quilts rising up from the earth, she pulled her cart onto the elevator and started the crank. When she reached the top, Anna couldn't see a single chimney, the entire town shrouded in the shadow of the cliff.

Mechan had grown at an uneven rate. Nestled between a cliff and the rocky shore, there was no room for farmland. The townspeople's supplies were limited to their small gardens, the ore they mined, and whatever the runners could smuggle out of the Settlement.

Anna trudged along the winding path, past the crag jutting out of the ocean like a jagged finger, toward the Settlement's red waterwheel. A large astronomical clock shone bright against the highest tower, sunlight reflecting against numerals etched in gold. The severe geography of the island served as Mechan's shield from the Commissioner's prying eyes, separating their coastal village from the flat farmland surrounding the Settlement. Though Mechan was only an hour's brisk walk from the Settlement gates, not a single officer had stumbled upon their village. The Commissioner had sent them, to be sure, but the people of Mechan could not be found so easily. Or maybe the Commissioner's officers were just incompetent.

The Settlement's city gates swarmed with people when Anna arrived. She longed to slip among the shadows and sneak into the Settlement like she usually did. Her fingers itched for the rope ladder hiding in the ivy along the clock tower, but there was too much security today, and her cart would never make it over the wall. She counted a dozen officers dressed in the Commissioner's maroon and gray, and half as many in icy blue—the Queen's colors. Perhaps Ruby had been right to worry—but no, the precautions made perfect sense with the influx of visitors.

"Papers," barked a youthful officer as Anna approached.

The officer held out a hand for Anna's documents, complete with her fake identity—a farmer's daughter from just around the bend—and the Commissioner's forged signature. The guard took one bored look at it and waved her through, more concerned with the crowd of Orbitals than a simple farm girl.

For most of the year, the Orbitals stayed confined to the Tower—the cylindrical space station where most of the population, including the Queen, lived. But on the day of the Celestial Market, the Tower's most illustrious (and irritating) came down from their palace in the sky to walk among their earthly subjects, complete with security detail.

"Visitors must submit to a screening upon entering or exiting the bullets," shouted one of the Queen's soldiers in the formal accent of the Tower, hollering over the crowd and pointing her stern finger at the large, metal vessels in the western field. They shone in the sunlight, a glittering horizon of silver pods. "Please be advised: Importing and exporting without a permit is illegal, and all Orbitals will be subjected to scanners upon returning to the Tower."

Anna ignored her and brushed past the Orbitals dressed from head to toe in silver-and-gold costumes, enormous hats with bells and feathers adorning their rather inflated heads. Beneath a canopy across the dusty street, actors from the Tower recited poetry in grand tones. Their leader announced to the rapt audience that they'd weathered the perils of space to bring the planetary colonists a "singular historical experience." Anna found their performance to be a singular torment.

Though Tech Decree Eighteen proclaimed the Celestial Market a celebration of culture to honor the memory of Former Earth, and to remember its demise at the hands of technology, Anna couldn't imagine anyone among the crowd presented a true, historical portrayal—except perhaps the planetary citizens who gawped openmouthed at the Orbitals' descriptions of death and doom. Their horrified reactions were real, just as the Commissioner would want them to be. After all, with tech to fear, they would have no room for dissent.

None of the Orbitals' hyperbole or the officers' thinly veiled anti-tech rhetoric served so well a reminder of the true danger she faced as the wooden gallows set at the very heart of the market. A freshly hanged body spelled a reminder of the fate awaiting her if she were caught, its metal leg on display for all to see. Two stone slabs towered above on either side of the forbidding stage, engraved by hand with all thirty-five Tech Decrees—including the newest addition—to drive the warning home. Subtlety had never been one of the Commissioner's strengths.

Anna shuddered and turned from the sight, edging her cart in between a flower vendor and a candy stand where she couldn't quite see the gallows. With any luck, Anna would disappear into the background between two high-profile booths, noticed only by those who knew what to look for. She quickly changed from her soft linens into her market costume—a monstrous entrapment of brocades—and unpacked her wares onto her makeshift, rickety table, placing each locket carefully on the once-white tablecloth. Her intricate designs of interlocking gears would go unexamined by most of the marketgoers, who would ignore her in favor of more garish vendors.

A smiling older gentleman, whom Anna knew only as Mr. Second Tuesday Evening, approached, velvet purse in hand. He was one of her oldest customers, but still he used her secret code, circulated among her trusted patrons before each market day.

"You look ever so familiar." He winked. "I do believe I know your aunt Edith."

Anna smiled at him, the scripted exchange of pleasantries rolling off her tongue. "Any friend of my aunt's is a friend of mine."

"These are lovely." Mr. Second Tuesday Evening gestured at the lockets in an unnecessary, but still appreciated, display of overacting. Since the inception of her business, he had spread the word of her workmanship to several of his high-powered friends, serving as a middleman for those customers who couldn't afford the same risks he took. "A dozen should do it."

Anna chose twelve lockets, scribbling notes onto small slips of paper, denoting the details of their meeting in the form of a riddle. She carefully placed each note in its corresponding locket and secured all twelve latches before handing over her merchandise, the chains already beginning to tangle in her fist.

Mr. Second Tuesday Evening dropped a handful of coins into her palm and disappeared into the crowd without further ado. Over the next year, Anna would see to the mechanical needs of Mr. Second Tuesday Evening's friends, mostly fixing knickknacks for those secure enough to harbor tech in their own homes, but if she was lucky, he'd bring her a mechanical limb or an eye to fix. Though she relished working with metal of any kind, she preferred to fashion useful accessories from it as opposed to the purely decorative sort surrounding them in the market. Even if she couldn't mend everything and everyone, each bolt and cog she tightened against the skin of her clients brought her closer to redemption, closer to forgiving herself for destroying Roman's arm years ago.

The next hour brought few visitors her way, leaving Anna with nothing to do but twiddle her thumbs. She tried not to watch the theater troupe's finale, which culminated in a haunting rendition of "Tech, We Worship Thee" as they drowned in poisonous sludge and gas, their exaggerated performance a nevertheless effective reminder of Former Earth's fate at the hands of humanity's over-reliance on technology, however vague the surviving histories made it out to be. No one would leave the Celestial Market with any doubt tech was responsible for destroying the planet that Earth Adjacent was meant to replace.

The audience, which had enthusiastically clapped and whooped throughout, meandered away amid hushed whispers and furtive glances, evidently deeply moved. Anna watched them go, following the crowd's progress from her cart.

"Hello, miss!" A squeaky voice, louder than Anna would have preferred, brought her attention back to her own stall. "I'd like to make an appointment."

"I'm sorry," Anna said quietly, hoping to bring the girl's register down. Her new customer looked to be about Anna's age, and she stood unevenly, like one of her legs was longer than the other— perhaps the effect of an ill-fitting prosthesis. Anna hadn't seen the girl before, but new customers weren't uncommon, so she prompted her. "I only sell trinkets here. Perhaps you're thinking of my aunt?"

The girl's green eyes lit up, and a blush spread across her cheeks. "Yes, yes! Edith!"

Anna didn't trust the sudden churn of her stomach, but whether her discomfort stemmed from the girl's clear disregard for caution or the way Anna's skin warmed when the girl smiled, she didn't know. Anna took the girl's coin and wrote out a riddle, but as a young man approached the cart, the girl stammered a half-formed excuse before scuttling away, leaving both her locket and money.

Anna's eyes lingered a moment on the girl's golden hair before turning to her new patron, a clear-eyed boy about her own age with limbs too long for his body and a hat that added inches to his already considerable height. Her muscles clenched as he leaned across the cart, fingers brushing against the lockets. She kept her papers blank until point of sale for this very reason, but the girl's abandoned locket wasn't empty, and it would be far from innocuous if this new patron took it. It was too late to hide it within her skirts, so Anna lifted her eyes to greet the newcomer.

"What can I do for you?"

"Good morning, miss." The dandy offered her a hesitant smile with not a single tooth missing. Though his extra-large hat and well-tailored coat suggested wealth, his accent grounded him. Had he been from the Tower, his pronunciation would have been tighter and clipped over the vowels. "These are charming."

"Thank you, but certainly *charming* is not elevated enough for a gentleman like yourself." It was a gamble, but he had lily-white skin, unmarred by sun, that could belong only to a merchant or noble.

"Not at all!"

On the surface, he sounded elite, but a hitch in his voice marked the end of each sentence, and he carried his shoulders off-kilter as though an invisible force pulled on his left side. Something about him—his walk—no, his smile—no, his rhythm—was familiar.

"I rather prefer art that celebrates the roughness of the world."

Anna clenched her teeth. From extracting the ore and creating the steel alloy to melting the metal down and pouring the molds, her lockets were no more than a vehicle for her true business dealings. She had never thought of her craft as art, but neither did she think her lockets were particularly rough. The word ground against her insides like two mismatched gears.

He dug into his pocket and produced a gold coin, the sort no one in Mechan would have any use for, let alone change. Before Anna could protest, he looped his fingers through the chain of the silver locket she'd prepared for her last customer. "I'll take this one."

"No!" Anna grabbed wildly for the locket, but it swung out of reach. "It isn't finished." The lie felt hollow, like lukewarm tea—a mistake the moment it hit her tongue.

He held the locket just out of her reach, coughing a little as he surveyed it. "I like it. There's beauty in something incomplete." He bowed, tucking the locket into his pocket and pressing his palm against his chest. "You have a good day, miss."

"Don't bow. You look ridiculous," Anna scoffed, speaking without thinking. The dandy's brow furrowed at the insult, but she plowed on. "At the market, we shake hands."

He took her hand in his and she flinched, neither intending nor expecting him to take her at her word.

"Nathaniel." He pointed to himself.

A sharp rhythm beat against Anna's palm.

"Anna."

In the wake of their introduction, the stillness pulsed with the impossible *tick, tick, tick* of a heart that wasn't hers.

CHAPTER TWO

Nathaniel's chest pounded with the effort of every step. The uphill trek through the market district, crowded with vendors and canopied carts, taxed his weak lungs more than it had on the way to the Celestial Market. Though the crowds thinned as he entered the residential district, homes squeezed together like the bellows of an architectural accordion, the cobblestone streets turned upward. The closer he got to his home, the steeper the incline. As he crested a hill, a fit of coughing erupted, burning his throat with each convulsion.

But the market had been worth all the pain and the risk he took disobeying his father. The Celestial Market wasn't just a gaudy display; it was history—his own history. Nathaniel told himself he went only to keep an eye out for illegal tech, but more than the possibility of busting a tech-trading ring, the market gave him an odd sense of belonging.

Nathaniel never thought he'd see the market's silver skyline, glittering vessels dotted against the horizon like stars. But the moment he set foot among the ancient tech, he knew he wasn't alone. Even if they belonged to a faraway past, out of reach and out of time, for a single day, the market positively sparkled with forbidden steel and the assurance that somewhere, at some point, the device living in Nathaniel's flesh wasn't wrong. Though the market had brought him no answers, he hoped if he just looked closer, asked the right person the right question, they could explain to him what his father would not.

But that would mean telling. And Nathaniel was not allowed to tell. Of the many rules governing Nathaniel's life, it was the oldest and most important.

Earth Adjacent saw tech only when it was brought down by visitors from the Tower; none was permitted to develop organically within the bounds of the Settlement. Earth Adjacent would flourish, free of the tech that brought about Former Earth's demise— or at least that was the hypothesis of the Queen's experiment. With no planetary home to return to, she had terraformed Earth Adjacent and sent a contingent of her people to the planet's surface to rule themselves without tech. If it worked, Earth Adjacent could become humanity's new home. Nearly forty years had passed, however, and Nathaniel, who'd spent all eighteen years of his life planetbound, had no idea if the Queen considered her test successful.

Even in the privacy of the Commissioner's manor, tech was to be spoken about only in the past tense, but Nathaniel heard its whispers every day, intensely present in his ears, in his mind, and in his heart. Cold metal tattooed shame across his chest—a silver reminder that he would never be his father's perfect heir, kept alive by the very tech his father strove to eradicate.

When he arrived at home, Nathaniel mounted the marble stairs as quickly and quietly as he could. Though his father's council was scheduled to be in session all afternoon, it would not do for the Commissioner to find him as he was, dressed for the market and with contraband lining his pockets.

Nathaniel reached the top just in time, peering over the banister to see the council flooding into the foyer, gathered in a cluster at the foot of the staircase. The Commissioner led the party, dressed in full uniform, complete with gold epaulets. In his hand was a small holocom projecting a miniature blue hologram of a woman draped in veils. He could not see her face, but Nathaniel knew her immediately: Queen Elizabeth, their skybound monarch. Though Nathaniel's father presided over Earth Adjacent, her presence sent ripples of cold down Nathaniel's spine.

Nathaniel inched away from the banister, intending to make himself scarce. Politics were better left in the hands of the experts below, but the rickety voice of Councilor Ming pulled Nathaniel from his hiding place and into the fray.

"Junior!"

Nathaniel froze. He wasn't dressed properly to receive company—a slight his father, if not the councilors, was sure to notice. Composing his expression into a well-mannered smile, Nathaniel descended the stairs. He would be charming and gracious, the perfect son his father could be proud of. "Councilors. Commissioner." Nathaniel nodded to the assembly and bowed to his father, who promptly clicked off the holocom. The Queen's projection vanished in an instant.

A middle-aged councilor reached out to shake his hand. "So good to see you, Nathaniel. A pity you couldn't join us."

"Yes, you really ought to start sitting in," a long-haired woman added. "As your father's successor, you should get all the exposure you can."

Nathaniel doubted very much that any of them had noticed his absence until that moment, but he was grateful just the same.

Perhaps his father would see merit in their suggestion and finally invite him to join their meetings.

"Nathaniel has been quite busy with his studies—without a basic understanding of our government and objectives, he will glean very little from our sessions, I'm afraid," the Commissioner said, giving Nathaniel the slightest of unreadable glances before continuing on. "Perhaps once he has shown a more thorough understanding of the Settlement and its laws, he might join us."

The councilors chorused their approval, but Nathaniel didn't dare speak.

Once the *yes yes*es, *good good*s, and *quite right*s had died down, the councilors said their goodbyes. As soon as the door closed behind them, the Commissioner turned on Nathaniel, his words as cold as his eyes. "You're home."

Nathaniel withered under his father's gaze.

His father knew—of course he knew. All Nathaniel's efforts to conceal his trip to the Celestial Market had been wasted. His father always knew.

"You were to remain in the manor, Nathaniel. That was our agreement." The Commissioner's tone was firm as iron. "How can I trust my only heir to uphold our family's legacy if he disobeys me?" The Commissioner paced around Nathaniel in a circle, the crisp tap of each step echoing through the halls. It was an interrogation, not a welcome.

Nathaniel stared at the floor. "Would you prefer me dead like Mother?" The words slipped out before he could swallow them.

Nathaniel shrank back against the banister, but the damage was already done. They did not discuss Nathaniel's mother—not for years. Other than the solitary headstone hidden in the corner of the garden, the manor bore no sign that Isla Fremont had ever lived there. Nathaniel should not have spoken of such things. He should not have spoken at all.

Instantly, the Commissioner spun Nathaniel around with practiced force and grabbed him by the shoulders, forcing eye contact. "What did you say?"

Nathaniel's lungs constricted, panic building in his breath. "I . . . I'm sorry." The words were barely coherent through his asthmatic breathing.

"How *dare* you," the Commissioner growled, a strand of hair falling out of place in his fury. "I built this colony up from nothing— for *you*. My predecessor would have let the Tarnished run wild, spreading their tech—their ruinous lifestyle—throughout the Settlement. I cleaned up the mess—all for *you*—so you might inherit at an easier time than I!"

"I know," Nathaniel murmured, and he wilted, staring down at their evenly squared shoes. But even toe-to-toe, Nathaniel would never truly be a match for his father. It did not matter how tall he grew, how bold he turned. He would never reach his father on his lofty plinth.

The Commissioner loosened his grip on Nathaniel's shoulders. "You'll be Commissioner one day, and I won't have anyone but the very best carry my title." He took an even breath and smoothed his hair, letting his tone drop. "Are you ready to take on that responsibility?"

Nathaniel nodded, not trusting himself to speak, or even breathe.

"Should I abandon any notion of our dynasty?"

"No." Nathaniel had meant to speak with the conviction and confidence befitting his father's heir, but the word came out as a squeak.

"Should I give up on our legacy?"

Nathaniel squared his shoulders and stared at the Commissioner's chin, unable to bring his gaze to meet his father's cold glare. "No."

"Actions speak louder than words, Nathaniel Fremont." He took a harsh step forward. "Don't ever lie to me again."

Nathaniel's gut twisted. Lies formed the soft blanket keeping the warmth around him, lies made up the golden shield keeping danger at bay, and lies upheld the very framework of his existence. But they protected him, kept his metal heart secret from the rest of the world. They were not duplicitous or disobedient, not like the lies he'd spun to go to the Celestial Market.

The Commissioner smacked Nathaniel across his cheek.

Nathaniel was practiced at taking his father's blows, but his foot caught on the stair behind him. As he stumbled backward, the metal in his chest clicked painfully. He clamped his jaw shut, stifling a groan, and folded in on himself.

"You and your tech are an embarrassment to our family—to my position!"

Nathaniel deserved that. He'd lied, crossed the one man who was supposed to love him. He should never have left the manor. Not even the small feeling of belonging the market had granted him was worth his father's disappointment, especially not the tech that made him so inadequate, so embarrassing.

Nathaniel crumpled to the floor. The contents of his pockets scattered around him, but the force of his fall—or perhaps simple necessity—brought his heart back to a normal rhythm. Scurrying on his hands and knees to collect his possessions, Nathaniel's fingers found the locket he'd purchased earlier that day.

He stared a moment at its intricate craftsmanship: Gears and tiny spirals of metal had been painstakingly welded together by an attentive but imperfect hand. Nathaniel spun one of the gears with his thumb, and the locket began to open. He quickly snapped it shut and buried it in his fist.

"You are not permitted to leave this house." The Commissioner crossed his arms. "I've worked too hard, climbed too high. If you were caught, if the wrong people saw you—"

"The wrong people?" Nathaniel asked, too distracted by the gears in his hands to think twice about his words.

"We have enemies, Nathaniel." The Commissioner heaved a sigh. "Enemies who would use our secrets against us. If the Tarnished discovered you, it would mean chaos—riots and uprisings. We could lose everything . . ." He trailed off, drumming his fingers against the gold button over his heart. "Remember, no one can know."

He placed a hand under Nathaniel's shoulder and helped him to his feet. Nathaniel let him, dragging his eyes up to meet the Commissioner's icy stare.

"You are capable, my son." He withdrew a square envelope from his breast pocket and handed it to Nathaniel. "Even your fiancée has no complaints. The girl is completely besotted."

Nathaniel took an involuntary step back. "E-Eliza?" It had been weeks since he'd heard from the Orbital girl. They'd been formally betrothed for years, exchanging letters as regularly as communication through space permitted. Was his father in contact with her? Or had he simply intercepted the letters? Nathaniel flushed, thinking of his unpracticed flattery and clumsy penmanship. That, too, would surely be an embarrassment to his father. He made a mental note to do better.

The Commissioner frowned at his son's stutter. "Perhaps her lack of complaint is simply because she has yet to meet you."

The insult stung worse than the mark on his cheek, but Nathaniel reached up to take the proffered letter, pocketing it before the Commissioner could change his mind.

"Insecurity is an unattractive quality, Nathaniel. If you believed in yourself and paid a little more attention to the things that matter, you could be a passable Commissioner one day." The Commissioner narrowed his eyes, sizing him up. "Though it's often hard to tell, we are cut from the same cloth, you and I. Never forget that."

Nathaniel was not likely to forget. He was not Nathaniel; he was the *young Master Fremont*. And whatever he did, for better or worse, it would reflect on the Commissioner.

As his father's steps clicked a farewell against the stairs, Nathaniel stared at his own polished oxfords. When at last he was alone, he unclenched his palm. The locket had left grooves imprinted into his skin, tattooing him with its detailed design. He fiddled with the gears on the locket's silvery face until it sprang open.

Inside, Nathaniel found a crumpled slip of paper. He smoothed away its wrinkles to reveal words printed in precise purple ink:

The Technician thanks you for your patronage.

Nathaniel's heart raced impossibly against its metal prison. He knew only too well of the Technician, the worst—and greatest—of the Tarnished, tech users living outside the law.

The Commissioner and his officers did everything in their power to quash the use of tech inside the city. During Oliver Fremont's tenure as Commissioner, he had shut down the Tech District, originally designed to better regulate tech users—now the Tarnished—within the Settlement; imprisoned dozens of collectors, some of whom were threats to society, and more of whom were not; and dissolved the complex web of underworld black market dealers that rose up in the wake of the District's demise. The Tech Decrees made it nearly impossible to legally engage in tech-related activities, except during the Celestial Market, when tech was permitted for historic education. The Commissioner's laws had eradicated all technology, dangerous or not, from the Settlement— until the Technician brought it back.

For three years the Technician had been a thorn in the side of the Commissioner's government, funneling tech into the Settlement through what Nathaniel could only guess was a complex network of black market brokers. Nathaniel had imagined the villain as a burly, mustachioed man with perhaps a mechanical eyeball or limb. The girl at the market must have been a lackey, not the true criminal. No, the real Technician would not venture out in public so soon after the Commissioner's new Tech Decree calling for his arrest.

Nathaniel flipped the paper over.

For your tech-related inquiries, see a consultant when the moon sleeps and the kettle sings. It is a long four to the short nine.

Nathaniel almost laughed as he read the note. A riddle! How peculiar. But as he stared at the complex web of metal in his hand, he couldn't shake the notion that the riddle inside held the key to finding the most wanted criminal on all of Earth Adjacent. And if he could find the Technician, hunt him down, and turn him in— bring his father the Settlement's most wanted outlaw . . .

What would his father think of him then?

CHAPTER THREE

Eliza knew how to make an entrance. Some days, she sought to turn heads with an arch of her brow or a flash of her smile. It was the brightness of her skirts, the swing in her step, her carefully curated laugh. A good weapon, she found, needn't draw blood to be effective. A controlled target was better than a dead one.

But today, Eliza didn't need to make an entrance; she needed to escape.

The Queen's gallery—a balcony of sorts with a ceiling-high window looking out at the vast sea of stars around them—hummed with a chorus of voices, bursting at the seams with courtiers vying for the spotlight. Certainly, they'd exceeded occupancy twice over. In the case of an emergency, they'd all perish, blocked from the exit by a stampede of crinoline and frantic fools.

Eliza could not endure the indignity of a death by petticoats.

A party of any kind was the surest cover for misconduct, however, and though mischief might go unnoticed by most, Eliza was better than the majority. Not that the other nobles would agree, hardly bothering to acknowledge someone of such humble roots. It was for the best, of course. One among their number had broken the rules, and Eliza had been given the honorable task of discovering who, though it was easier said than done. Squashed between Lady Beatrix's enormous gown and Lord Farley's sharp elbow, Eliza was hard-pressed to see properly around the gallery to identify her target, let alone pursue them, whoever they were.

"Quite an uncivilized lot, I daresay," Lord Farley quipped in an inept attempt to return Eliza's gaze to him.

She nodded but never looked his way. The courtiers of the Tower had truly become insufferable. Though the Queen granted them nobility, not one of them was a lord or lady of anything in particular; the Tower had no need for a ruling class, and what was a landed title without any land? But the lot of them had seen the green grass and blue sky of Earth Adjacent now, and Eliza would have to tolerate the injustice.

"They are too much," Eliza replied, loosening her hold on the lord's arm slightly.

"No, no!" Lord Farley smiled, his goatee twitching. "I meant the Planetaries, my dear."

Eliza transformed her grimace into a delicate cough. Though Lord Farley boasted only two years in age her senior, he never missed an opportunity to belittle. She would enjoy unleashing her full array of weapons on his ego. But for now, it served her more to let him play the lord and she the charity case, untitled and un-assuming. To him, and the rest of the courtiers, Eliza was only a poor, unfortunate soul, orphaned and abandoned, on whom the Queen had taken pity.

It was better this way. As the Queen's Eyes, she needed to learn everyone's truths, not spill her own. Behind closed doors, she'd make them bend to her. And someday, she'd make them *bow* to her.

Lord Farley's brows knitted. "Are you quite all right, Miss Eliza?"

Miss Eliza. The slight rolled off her like a bead of water. It was, of course, the proper way to address her. She had no family name—she had no family at all—but the lord knew as well as she that to call her by her given name was to imply an affection they would never share.

No matter, she would do her best to exploit his mistake.

"Only a cough, my lord," Eliza said through her fingers, eyes lingering on the glistening champagne flutes at the end of the gallery. If only she could get the lord to release her arm, she could attend to her real duties—finding whoever set off the sensors and recovering whatever they'd brought on board.

To her delight, Lord Farley followed her gaze. "Pardon my manners. Let me fetch you a refreshment."

Eliza relaxed, but the attentive Lord Farley did not let go. Instead, he dragged her with him, through the sea of other courtiers, before handing her a chilled glass.

"Now, Miss Eliza, if you will permit me, I will resume my story."

Story was a generous term for it, but Eliza feigned interest and pretended to sip. She could not afford a clouded head this afternoon, but the intoxicants might still serve her well. Spirits made the best tongues loose, and Eliza had no other interest in Lord Farley's.

"The Planetaries, as I was saying—such odd creatures. The natural oxygen has done something to them, I'm sure. They run about, you see. Sometimes without shoes or coats—and they hold such pride in their little markets. Pathetic, really, when you compare our lives with theirs. Why the Queen wants to relocate, I'll never understand. I'll be glad if they never fully terraform the planet. At least not in my lifetime. It's all rather too . . . earthy."

If there were two things Eliza could not abide, they were courtiers complaining and anyone who dishonored the Queen. Lord Farley had now accomplished the first and come devilishly close to the second. She dearly wished to skewer him upon her words, but it would not do to offend him before his value expired.

"Surely there must be something of merit to a planetary life, my lord, else the Queen in her wisdom would not point us there." She arranged her expression into wide-eyed optimism.

"Hardly a thing to recommend planetary life, I'm afraid. All they have, we can simply import or re-create. What need have we for natural gravity when we can create our own? And live-stock? The smell alone, I tell you—" His gaze turned thoughtful, or maybe it was simply a gaseous disturbance of the digestion. "But, Miss Eliza, I fear I have troubled you with too harsh a recollection."

At least he had gotten that much right, though Eliza was loath to say it in so many words. Instead, she fluttered her eyelashes, adopting an innocent tone. "It is only that I'd hoped to see the planet up close someday—but perhaps it is not for me." If she couldn't get him to leave her alone, she would compel him to talk. She cast her eyes over his shoulder toward the massive window, gaze landing on the blue-green orb.

Earth Adjacent nestled below them, a pop of color in a starry sky. The planet took up nearly a third of the window's area, its oceans staring back as though observing them in equal judgment. It was the dream of all Orbitals and their forbears: Find a new planet, terraform it, and begin anew. Someday it would be their home. They would all get what they wanted.

Except Eliza. Eliza didn't care about planets and terraforming. She cared about secrets and scandal. She didn't want a new home on

Earth Adjacent; she wanted to find her target and enact the Queen's judgment upon them. She wanted to complete her mission.

"It is a disappointment, to be sure," Eliza continued, nodding toward the planet. "Seeing it from here, I thought it would be more . . ." She paused for effect, dragging her eyes to meet his in a practiced stare before laying down her challenge. "Impressive."

The word had its desired effect. Lord Farley's jaw tightened, and his cheeks flushed almost as though she'd insulted him rather than the planet. He needed only an ounce more goading by Eliza's measurements. The temptation to impress her, lady or no, would be too much.

"But if you say so, my lord, perhaps visiting Earth Adjacent is not so high an honor after all." She would not allow him to mistake her remarks for anything but taunts.

"It isn't all so bad, my lady," Lord Farley rushed to say.

My lady. Truly, if Lord Farley had forgotten to demean her, she had him in her reach. She needed only to decide if he was worth her claws. "Isn't it?"

"Come, let us take a turn, and I will show you the only worthwhile thing the earthly planet has to offer."

Eliza let him lead her from their perch by the refreshments— though did it count as leading if it was she who'd guided him to the decision? "What, pray tell, do you intend to show me, my lord?" she asked as they made their way from one end of the monstrous window to the other.

"First, you must promise to keep this our secret."

"A secret? I love secrets!" Though she said the words in a breathy, high voice enriched with false excitement, they were the truest words she'd spoken all day.

"With any luck, this will be the first of many secrets we may share." Lord Farley paused, steering her into the shadows of the sloping hallway beyond, resting his hand far too comfortably at her waist.

She would make him regret it all too soon, but first she needed to confirm he was, in fact, her intended target. "You have me quite intrigued, I must say. I sincerely hope it's worth all the fuss."

Lord Farley chuckled. "It's only a little something I brought back from my voyage, but—"

Eliza's face fell. "A trinket? Please, sir, if all you have to show me is a bauble from the market, tell me now. Any one of our friends in the gallery could fulfill *that* curiosity." She took a small step back—a simple trick but effective nonetheless as his expression grew desperate. "But you, Lord Farley, are not so ordinary, are you?" Now she leaned forward, one hand toying with her ringlets— another trick, this time a diversion—while she slipped her other hand into the deep pocket of her skirt. "You led me to believe it was something more . . . thrilling."

He grinned. "You're a sharp one, Miss Eliza."

"You have no idea."

"Let us say, my little souvenir would not be to the Queen's liking." He beckoned her forward, out of the other courtiers' lines of sight. From his breast pocket, he withdrew her prize, and Lord Farley outgrew his use to her.

"Quite the transgression, my lord." Nothing of the innocent tone remained in her voice, her tone acidic and dry. "The Queen will be interested to know what you've been up to." She shoved him square in the chest, pushing him back around the bend of the hallway, far from sight.

Lord Farley stumbled and hit the wall, an ill-formed mask of rage covering his panic. "What was it you planned? To get me alone and use your wiles to get me to talk?"

Eliza advanced, and Lord Farley retreated. "Not my wiles, no." She had him pinned now.

"Then I'm afraid you've miscalculated. I'm twice your size and twice your better. You'll earn no favors with the Queen by angering me—but if we were to join forces, I could promise you protection, and perhaps even elevation."

"I don't need protection." Sometimes a good weapon didn't draw blood, and sometimes a good weapon was a sharp blade. Eliza withdrew hers from her pocket, fingers wrapped around the hilt of the short dagger. The blade was etched with a light dusting of stars, and the pommel boasted a singular silver eye.

"Of course." Lord Farley sighed, closing his eyes in resignation. "I should have known you would be the Eyes of the Queen."

"And ears. I have many uses."

"You can't kill me! I'm a lord! The Queen would never stand for it. I am of the noble cla—"

Eliza swung, crashing the pommel into the side of his head, and he crumpled to the floor.

Today, the best weapon was the one that could draw blood but didn't.

Lord Farley wasn't wrong—killing him served little purpose. Though Eliza couldn't care less, the Queen, despite all her wisdom, preferred to keep her nobles breathing. Besides, Lord Farley wouldn't talk. Insufferable gossip he might be, but even he knew better than to cross the Queen—or her Eyes. He'd said so himself, he was twice her size. No one would believe she'd bested him, if his pride permitted him to admit it'd happened at all.

Turning her attention back to Lord Farley's hands, Eliza admired the solitary red flower resting between his fingers. Its vibrant petals curled up and out—an invitation, beckoning, luring, promising.

She snatched it up, and pain bloomed against her skin. Eliza yelped, letting the flower fall to the ground beside Lord Farley's unconscious form. A single drop of blood followed as Eliza ripped the thorn from her finger.

She swore under her breath, stooping to retrieve her prize. The Queen would want to see what she'd found and devise a proper punishment for Lord Farley. Perhaps the headache he'd have when he awoke would be punishment enough. He was a fool, not a felon. Still, the distinction didn't change his crime. He'd brought a terrestrial artifact onto the Tower without the Queen's approval, and without the proper decontamination, such a *souvenir*, as he'd called it, could be dangerous—even deadly.

Eliza took extra care to place her fingers between the thorns this time. Lord Farley wasn't *all* wrong; just as he'd said of Earth Adjacent, the flower was charming at first glance, with an ugliness underneath. But perhaps all pretty things had thorns.

The best things, at least, most certainly did.

CHAPTER FOUR

When Anna arrived in Mechan, after doubling back twice to make sure she hadn't been followed from the Settlement, she found Ruby tending the hearth as though it were her own. The scent of fresh basil filled the room, and brightly colored vegetables sat on the polished wood counter.

"You're just in time. I'm making stew." Ruby waved her over without looking up from her work, sweat beading at her temple. Though her voice was steady, her hands shook.

"Do you want to sit down?" Anna suggested. She'd been gone for hours, and Ruby didn't look as though she'd slept at all.

"No, no. I'm fine. Someone has to tend the pot." She wiped her forehead with the back of her hand. "Thatcher will be done soon, I'm sure. Want to make sure he's got a bowl of stew waiting when it's over."

Anna paused with her hand on the chairback. Surgery wasn't quick, but she'd thought her grandfather—and Roman—would be out by now. No wonder Ruby had taken to the pantry. Without any news, Anna doubted she'd have lasted, either. What was taking so long?

"He's still working," Ruby murmured, following Anna's gaze to the operating room door.

Over the years, Anna's neighbors, friends, and foes had waited in that very kitchen for news of a sister, a brother, a nephew, not all of whom survived.

But Roman would. He had to.

Anna bit her lip. "It's surgery. It takes time."

Ruby's fingers slipped, spilling yellow carrots. "Oh no! I'm sorry." Her voice wobbled as she dove for the floor, tears dotting her cheeks.

Anna knelt beside her, glad to have something to do other than watch worry move across Ruby's face like hands on a clock.

"Are you all right?" They were the wrong words, but they were the only words she had.

"Just clumsy." Ruby rocked back on her heels and pulled her hair into a knot. The effect left her hairline severe, but her eyes remained tired, unfocused. "Waiting is the worst part."

Anna's fingers twisted around the last of the spilled vegetables, remembering the thick lining of Roman's chest, the enlarged heart muscle that could barely keep up with his boyish energy. "If something was wrong, Thatcher would have finished already." She wished the words unsaid as soon as they left her lips. It was true, though. As long as Thatcher was still operating, there was still hope.

"Don't coddle me." Ruby fixed Anna with a foggy stare. "I know it's not in your nature, so just tell the truth. You don't have to pretend for my sake."

Ruby knew her well. Anna didn't know what her nature was, exactly, but it certainly wasn't this. She wanted to be the person Ruby needed, but she didn't know how.

Anna was saved the agony of a reply by the operating room door, which swung open to reveal Thatcher, stubble shadowing his jawline where none had been that morning. Tired eyes found Anna's for a brief moment before disappearing behind his hands. She forgot, sometimes, how old he was. Streaks of color still stained his graying hair, and his wrinkles were not half so bad as Ruby's, whose worry lines in her forehead were becoming a permanent fixture on her young face. But now, slumped in his chair with his spectacles askew, his age hung across his shoulders.

Ruby stood quickly, stew forgotten. "How is he?"

Thatcher swallowed. "He's resting now. I don't expect him to wake for a while yet, but you can sit with him."

Ruby knocked a chair to the ground as she rushed around the table. She paused a moment, backtracking to grasp Thatcher's hand. "Thank you."

Thatcher cast his gaze at the floor. "Just doing my job. Go on—go see your son."

"Anna." Ruby waved at her to follow.

Anna stood, tripping over the chair leg on her way up.

As she and Ruby approached the door to the spare bedroom, Anna's skin prickled. Inside, Roman would be sleeping, wounds held together with string and hope. Ruby had waited all night for this, but Anna . . . Anna had left. She didn't belong there.

"Are you sure you want me here?" Anna pulled her arm from Ruby's grasp, unsure which discomfort she'd rather face: the reunited family that wasn't hers, or the family in the kitchen that was. "He's your son. Don't you want a moment alone first?"

"Don't be silly. Roman will want you there when he wakes up." Ruby pushed open the door, her shoulders slumping and smile faltering.

The seven-year-old boy, usually bursting with joy and energy, lay still against the pillows. Thatcher had done his best to hide the incision with gauze and bandages, but the effect made Roman look even sicker.

Ruby rushed to his side, taking his pale hand in hers. "Roman," she cooed. "I'm here. I've got you, my darling boy."

Warmth spread to Anna's fingertips as she looked on, seating herself at the foot of the bed. The love Ruby had for that little boy—at least Anna knew she'd done right by him, bringing Ruby into his life all those years ago. Ruby had been newly engaged to Dalton then, and too young to think of children. But she'd never hesitated, not once. Finding a home for an orphan in Mechan wasn't impossible; neighbors looked out for one another, and children who lived were as common as children who died. But Roman's injuries were Anna's fault, not simply the cruel way of the world. She wanted more for him, better than the cold distance she shared with her grandfather. Ruby was the closest thing to family Anna knew—a woman overflowing with love—and Roman deserved nothing less.

Thatcher might have mended Roman's arm and given him a working heart, but Ruby gave him a home and a life. It was Anna— only Anna—who had failed him.

She looked away, the warmth gone. Thatcher had done what Anna could not. Thatcher was the real hero of the day, and it was he, not Anna, who should have been sitting there with Ruby. Anna couldn't even make it through a few hours of surgery.

"He looks all right, doesn't he?" Ruby pushed back his fluffy hair, so blond it was almost white, like a cloud.

Anna nodded. "Thatcher's good at what he does. If Roman wasn't all right, he wouldn't have let us see him."

That wasn't exactly true. If the surgery hadn't worked, wouldn't Thatcher have sent them in anyway, to say goodbye? At that thought, Anna flew to Roman's side to feel his pulse.

It was steady.

She let out a breath.

"He's strong." Anna sank back onto the bed. "Now we just have to wait. We'll know for sure in a few days, but there's no sign he's rejecting the TICCER yet."

Ruby nodded, reaching across Roman's body for her hand. "I hate waiting. I know it's just how surgery works, but it's the worst part."

Anna squeezed Ruby's fingers. "With any luck, this will be the last time."

Ruby's face fell, and she averted her eyes. "Maybe."

"Ruby! Don't think like that. If Roman pulls through, he won't need another surgery."

"I didn't mean Roman." Ruby dropped Anna's hand and hugged her middle. "I wasn't going to mention it until I was further along."

Anna's mouth hung open, and she didn't care to close it. "You—you're—"

Ruby nodded, her eyes overflowing with tears. "I didn't even get to tell Dalton."

Anna remembered the day as though it were yesterday. She'd been playing with Roman when the runners arrived back from another trip into the Settlement. As they'd been plotting a daring make-believe rescue, a commotion sounded outside. The runners had formed a semicircle around Ruby, who had fallen to the ground, her eyes blank, mouth wide in a whisper of a sob as they gave her the news.

Anna had stayed in Roman's room that night, there for him when his mother couldn't be. She caught Ruby throwing up sometime before dawn. She'd assumed it a result of grief or dehydration. Crying had that effect on some people, as Anna herself had discovered firsthand the night she'd botched Roman's surgery.

Anna should have known then. The symptoms were there, the clues laid out for her to see. Thatcher would scold her for such thinking—a diagnosis was not just a collection of symptoms but confirmation of cause. Ruby was her best friend, though; Anna should have known.

"How far along are you?" It was the clinical thing to ask. She ought to have inquired how Ruby felt or what she needed. Those were the things a friend would ask. But it was easier to be the Technician who dealt only in facts, not feelings.

"I'm not sure. A few months, I suppose." She laid her head down next to Roman's. "This is what I wanted, Anna. I wanted a family . . . but not like this."

"He has you—they'll *both* have you. That's more than some. I don't have parents at all, and I turned out fine." Anna picked her nails. *Fine* was one word for it. Thatcher might disagree.

Ruby looked up. "That's not what I mean. I'll miss Dalton every day of my life—Roman might, too, if he remembers all this—but my children will be okay without a father. I'm talking about this world where we have to fear for our homes, for our lives. I don't want to sit in your kitchen again, waiting for your grandfather to put metal into another one of my children. I don't want to worry that one day . . . that one day they just won't come home." She hiccuped, tears streaming from her eyes.

Anna's mouth felt dry. She swallowed, but no words came to her.

Roman saved her the trouble of responding. "Mama?" he whispered, voice rough and cracking.

Ruby sprang up to touch his hand. "I'm here, baby."

Anna fetched a glass of water Thatcher had left bedside, turning to give herself a moment to recover.

"You're going to be just fine," Ruby whispered against his hairline.

Roman drank with difficulty, but when he finished, he had a smile for them both. "Can we play a game?" he asked.

Ruby smiled back at her son. "When you're healed and strong again, we can play any game you like."

Roman nodded slowly, his eyelids fluttering with sleep. "Pirates," he said. "I want to play pirates."

Ruby fell asleep next to Roman soon after, and Anna couldn't help but feel she was intruding. She retreated to the kitchen, where she found her grandfather.

"He looks good. The TICCER seems to be working."

"Looks can be deceiving." Thatcher stared fixedly at the mug in his hand. "Your faith in technology may be misplaced, Deirdre-Anne."

Anna sat beside him. "That's rich, coming from a mechanic."

"I'm a doctor, not a mechanic." He sipped his tea. "I don't like installing tech on patients so young. There's too high a chance for failure."

"But it didn't fail."

"But it could have."

"You mean like last time." Anna rubbed her arm, trying to block out the memory of steel slicing through skin.

"No, I mean *every* time. The younger the patient, the more possibility for complications. And since he's not yet done growing, the TICCER isn't a perfect fit. He'll need maintenance all his life."

"It couldn't be helped. You saw it—the Tarnish was too far advanced. You saved his life, giving him a TICCER now."

"Perhaps." Thatcher pursed his lips. "I would have much preferred to wait another five years before opening his chest."

"You gave me mine when I was an infant." Anna's hand drifted to her heart, soothed by the cyclical ticking of blood through her veins.

"You were different. You were the first. I hadn't perfected the design yet, so I had to improvise."

"I don't know why you don't just use this same design on everyone. Old Reliable here works just fine." She patted her chest.

Thatcher shook his head as he poured more hot water. "Most of our neighbors here aren't mechanics like you and me. Think about how much maintenance you have to do; none of them could keep up with that. We'd be tied up here all day fixing machinery instead of saving lives."

Anna was a trained mechanic. She was a *good* mechanic. Most everyone else in Mechan needed tech to live but preferred to be ignorant of its functionality. Maybe it was better they didn't know the fragility of their clockwork hearts. He wasn't wrong. But he wasn't exactly right, either.

"Fixing machinery *is* saving lives."

Thatcher placed a mug of fresh tea in front of her. "Is that how you justify it?"

Anna pushed the mug away, the smell of peppermint stinging her nostrils. "Justify what?"

Thatcher withdrew the new Tech Decree from his breast pocket and laid it flat on the table. Ruby must have left it in the kitchen. "What in that blasted city is worth risking your life? *All* our lives?"

Anna drew back. "The people of Mechan aren't the only ones worth saving, you know. There are those in the Settlement who need my help."

"They choose to live within those walls, under the Commissioner's laws. If they want our help, they should leave."

"Are you telling me you'd never help anyone in the Settlement? Not even if they were desperate?"

Thatcher grabbed her wrist, shooting her an appraising look. "Not if my life depended on it. It isn't worth risking all the lives I've helped to build here."

"Then we have a problem." Anna stood, reaching for the satchel she'd carelessly discarded earlier.

"We do, indeed." Thatcher leaned back in his chair, looking at her squarely for the first time that day. "I've tried to be patient with you, Deirdre-Anne, but I can't sit by and let you throw away everything I've worked for. I'm afraid I have to forbid you from going to the Settlement from now on."

"That isn't fair! Being the Technician—that's my livelihood! You taught me to tinker and make things with my hands. You can't just take that away from me. I have nothing else!"

Thatcher sighed, setting down his mug. "You and I have a relationship complicated by our work, I know. I'm your teacher, and I want to see you learn and grow, but I'm also your grandfather, and I must think about what's best for you. Now sit down and drink your tea."

Anna stared at him, dumbfounded for a moment before she regained her nerve. "I'll be in my workshop. You don't have to choose between being my grandfather and my teacher—you won't have to be either."

Thatcher's gray eyes watched her, unblinking. Avoiding his gaze, Anna slung her bag onto her shoulder and turned her back on him. As the door swung shut behind her, she muttered, "And I hate tea."

Thatcher's words trailed after her, whispers in her mind, but her blood pounded too loudly, too intently. She didn't care what he thought. She *shouldn't* care.

But Thatcher wouldn't help anyone from the Settlement, even if his life depended on it. Those words proved far more worrying than any of his warnings.

She could still feel the mechanical tick of the dandy's pulse, beating against her hand, unnatural, impossible. If Thatcher had told the truth, then another rogue mechanic had installed the TICCER—had *built* it. If the boy, proper though he seemed, could unravel her riddle, she could ask him herself.

Of course, there was always the possibility Thatcher was lying.

CHAPTER FIVE

Nathaniel woke with the Technician's cryptic note on his mind. The allure of breakfast paled in comparison to the riddle in his vest pocket. Giving his father's stack of assigned reading a wary look, he crossed the room to his discarded clothing from the night before and retrieved the locket and folded letter from Eliza.

What would Eliza think of his exploits at the market? In all their correspondence, Nathaniel had never broached the topic of illegal tech, afraid of what she'd think of the metal around his heart—afraid of what *he* thought of it himself. Still, he'd need to get it off his chest, as it were, and quickly; after all, they would be married soon.

He set the locket aside, breaking the seal on Eliza's note.

Dearest Nathaniel,

I hope you're well. Word has reached us that Earth Adjacent had a very wet spring. I've been led to believe this is quite the horrid turn of events, but I must confess, the idea of rain bewilders and bemuses. What must it be like to feel the droplets on your skin?

The letter went on, detailing Tower politics and Eliza's take on relations between Earth Adjacent and the Tower. Eliza's outrageous stories of being one of the Queen's ladies never failed to capture Nathaniel's attention, but he liked the end best.

> *It is with a heavy heart and hand that I must set down my pen to return to my work. I do hope this letter finds you in good spirits, and if not, that it may serve to liven them. I await your reply, and hope we may exchange words in a more intimate setting soon.*
>
> *Ever yours,*
> *Eliza*

Nathaniel's chest swelled every time he read those words—not the sign-off. *Ever yours* was as common as they came, and he never really wanted her to be *his*. No, Nathaniel cherished the prospect of meeting Eliza when they would *exchange words in a more intimate setting*.

There was, of course, the chance he wouldn't be what she expected when they met. She might not like him as he was, marred with metal, less eloquent out loud than he could be on paper. He could conceal so much behind the written word, but he wasn't sure he could hide from her in person. He wasn't sure he wanted to.

At least they were even. All he knew of her was inked onto parchment. Her words had brought him comfort, but also at times great unease. She was his betrothed, but he couldn't be certain he wanted to marry her. He didn't truly understand what it would mean. Doubt burned at the pit of his stomach. He had no answer. With any luck, she wouldn't expect one.

It didn't bear worrying over yet, or so he tried to tell himself. He had something much more pressing to investigate anyway.

Turning his attention to the locket, Nathaniel withdrew the note and smoothed out the crease, letting his thumb drag along the purple letters.

For your tech-related inquiries, see a consultant when the moon sleeps and the kettle sings. It is a long four to the short nine.

It was a riddle, but to what end? If a game for children held the key to finding such a dangerous criminal, Nathaniel had only to decode it.

When the moon sleeps obviously meant during the day, and he could guess *the kettle sings* meant teatime, so roughly the afternoon—although he didn't know if common people served tea with the same punctuality as the highborn.

"A long four to the short nine," Nathaniel said aloud. It was complete nonsense, perhaps included to throw him off the trail. No, the Technician had given him a time but not a place. If he could decipher the Technician's code, he could find the outlaw. And if he could find the outlaw, he could bring him in.

There was only one thing for it. He needed the Technician case file.

Nathaniel made his way downstairs to a part of the house he never visited: the servants' wing. Greeted by a flurry of questioning looks followed by bows and curtsies, he had to ask for directions to the laundry room, where he found a stack of neatly folded uniforms—maid, valet, and, finally, officer.

Donning the maroon and gray, Nathaniel looked every part the soldier. Though he possessed neither strength nor confidence, his tall frame made him appear commanding. Not a soul who saw him walk by would suspect for a moment that he wasn't a fully trained officer. Besides, it had been a long time since he'd made an official public appearance, and he looked less like his father than most people said. They were trying to be polite, of course, but the resemblance lived only in the subtleties of his bone structure. Nathaniel wondered, not for the first time, which pieces of his face belonged to his mother, gone before he could commit her to memory.

Science had killed his mother—an accident of alchemy, his father told him when he was old enough to understand—not rebels with knives, but it was easy to draw the line from one to the other. The Tarnished would not heed his father's laws meant to protect them all, and the Technician brazenly thwarted them. Bringing the criminal to justice wasn't revenge, but in some small way it felt like action when all his life there'd been nothing he could do.

Nathaniel took one last look at his reflection before exiting the manor through the servants' entrance. The path from the manor wound through the back gardens and along the iron fence surrounding the manor grounds for a quarter mile before meeting with the bunker wall.

He entered the bunker to find the halls bustling with officers—officers who worked for Nathaniel's father. Nathaniel couldn't help but retreat into the shadows, avoiding gazes. He wasn't strictly forbidden to be there, but if anyone recognized him and told his father . . . Well, Nathaniel could imagine how his punishment would play out.

The archives were at the end of the hall, past the mess hall, several training rooms, and a single holding cell with thick metal bars. Nathaniel edged along the wall, eyes glued to the floor. With a furtive glance over his shoulder Nathaniel dipped inside the archives, letting the door click behind him. Shelves ran in evenly spaced rows, files upon files waiting to be read. Nathaniel slid his finger along a shelf, dust billowing in his wake.

He caught sight of a label halfway down the first row that said *Open Cases*. He took quiet steps, casting his gaze around, but it seemed he was alone. With any luck, he'd remain undetected.

His finger brushed against the letter *T*, and with a swift motion, Nathaniel removed the file labeled *Technician* and flipped it open. It was alarmingly sparse, with only a few pages inside. The first page listed the case information and contents:

> *Case Name: Technician*
> *Status: Open*
> *Active Officer: Benson*
> *Documents Enclosed: Coded instructions detailing date, time, and place for meeting (2)*

The front page was the only full-size page in the entire file. Behind it were two smaller slips of paper.

As Nathaniel read the words scrawled across the next document in snakelike writing, his stomach clenched.

The Technician thanks you for your patronage.

They were the same words. If his father's officers had already followed this lead, what good would it do Nathaniel to try? But even as he berated himself for his foolish diversion, Nathaniel flipped the note over, unable to tear his eyes from the page.

For your tech-related inquiries, see a consultant when the
moon last smiles to the east and the bacon burns. It is a long
eight to the short eleven.

There, among the Technician's thin letters, a different, heavier hand had penned small notes in the margins. Someone had written the word *morning* just above the word *bacon*. This fell in line with his own conclusions, but as he scanned through the second scribe's annotations, he saw the officer had circled the word *moon*.

Of course—the lunar calendar would tell him what he needed to know. A time of day would do him absolutely no good without a date. It seemed so clear now, but of course a trained investigator had found the truth before him. As Nathaniel read on, his eyes found the last annotation just above the words *smiles to the east*. It read *last week*. The officer had been too late, and the note had expired.

Nathaniel had time. His note was very much still in play; he'd snatched it right off the cart of one of the Technician's men—or, in this case, women. He'd simply plucked up the gear-woven locket without waiting for the girl's approval. He'd managed what his father's officers could not, but only by accident.

Replacing the annotated note where he'd found it, Nathaniel retrieved the next.

The Technician thanks you for your patronage.
For your tech-related inquiries, see a consultant when the moon
shines brightest and the embers glow. It is a long six to the short two.

That meant the full moon in the late evening—perhaps even after nightfall. Officer Benson's annotations seemed to confirm the theory, but the location still stumped him.

Nathaniel was unfamiliar with the island's geography. He'd never been allowed to leave the manor house, let alone the Settlement, and it had never been important before.

Officer Benson, it seemed, had enjoyed little luck in parsing the location, too. There were no notes on the latter part of the riddles. The only other marks on the page were two sets of lines—triangles. One was a wide V, the other . . . an arrow of some kind?

Nathaniel held his fingers up to make the shape in the air, glancing from the page to his hand and back again. One mark, he could write off as a mistake, but two—the officer had worked through the clue at least one step further, and Nathaniel would not leave until he understood at least as much as his father's investigators.

He glanced back over the riddles.

> *Long eight to the short eleven.*
> *Long six to the short two.*
> *Long four to the short nine.*

If not for the machine regulating it, Nathaniel's heart might have skipped a beat.

It was a clock.

He held up his hand again, positioning his fingers just so—the long hand to the short hand: 11:40, 2:30, 9:20.

But it didn't make sense for the Technician to include specific times when he'd already given a date and a time. No, the numbers meant something else. Were they points on a map? Longitude and latitude? But that required more numbers, and the Technician had given him only two.

"It is a long four to the short nine," he whispered, maneuvering his fingers to form a wide angle. It wasn't a time; it was a direction—and a duration.

That was all he needed.

"It is twenty minutes to the ninth hour." The nine on a clock would be to the west, and per the note, he would find the Technician twenty minutes from the Settlement.

The riddle solved, Nathaniel snapped the file closed, but with it poised to slide back into its place on the shelf, he thought better of it. He might still need the file. Probably, no one would miss it. With a few flicks of his wrist, he undid the buttons on his jacket and placed the file against his chest. Warmth spread out from his center, as if the paper itself gave him hope.

CHAPTER SIX

Time was a powerful tool. That was the first lesson Eliza had learned from the Queen. Sometimes it was a gift; sometimes it was a curse. Today it came in the form of a weapon Eliza was determined to wield.

The Queen circled her, blade in hand, a confident strength in her steps. They sparred on the Queen's terms, on her terrain. The Queen's office served a poor training ground, asymmetrical with a desk and bookshelves instead of padded floors and walls, but it was more *realistic*, or so the Queen insisted. Eliza was unlikely to fight anyone while wearing a bodysuit and kneepads, and hadn't trained with them in years. Besides, the Queen had taught her fashion was as sharp a weapon as her blade. She could wear bright colors to attract, dark colors to impress, or no color at all to disappear. Every color, every cloth, held meaning, whether or not the wearer or the observer understood its message.

The Queen held the advantage, projecting power in deep navy satin and a shoulder-length mourning veil to match, and yet she held back, waiting. It was a trap, of course, designed to lure Eliza into striking first. They'd been through this training exercise countless times over the years, yet it always ended the same: Eliza on her back, the Queen's knife against her throat.

Today would be different. Eliza took small steps, keeping her center of gravity low and her blade neutral—the better to block the Queen's attack when it finally came. It did not matter how long the Queen waited; Eliza would wait longer.

"You've been my Eyes nearly three years, is that right, Eliza?"

A distraction. The Queen sought to disarm her with conversation, but it wouldn't work. Eliza had spent the better part of her youth training under the Queen, and she knew her style inside and out.

"Yes, Your Majesty, and your student for six," Eliza said evenly, not taking her eyes from the Queen, searching for any indication of her next movement. If there was to be an attack, it would come from the Queen's chest, moving her center before her arm. With any other opponent, Eliza would simply look to the eyes for the telltale flicker of intention, but the Queen's veil prevented such tactics.

Eliza had never seen the monarch without the veil, worn in mourning for their lost planet. She would remove it only once they migrated to Earth Adjacent—*if* they ever did—so the Queen's face was as much a mystery as her motives or her methods. The more Eliza understood the latter, the more she hoped one day to see the former. How ironic: Eliza was the Queen's Eyes, forever sworn to see everything except the Queen herself. Was the veil weapon or armor, meant to pierce or protect? Eliza had not yet learned that lesson.

"I didn't know when I began your training you'd be such a quick study, such a valuable asset." The Queen quickened her steps, circling faster. "I suspected, I hoped—but I was not sure. Until now."

This was it—this was the conversation Eliza had hoped for all these years. She'd thought it would be with a desk between them, not knives. All the same, the Queen had been both mistress and mother to Eliza, who had no family before the Queen took her under her wing. Eliza had always thought if she worked hard enough—if she waited long enough—the Queen would finally acknowledge her, finally accept her as the daughter she'd never had, the heir she deserved.

Eliza knew the Queen had a son, but no one ever spoke of him except in whispers and rumors. He'd been sent to Earth Adjacent long ago, banished from the Queen's palace in the sky. The Queen, who could trust almost no one, certainly could not give her mantle to him, which left Eliza a particularly attractive substitute.

But all the power in the world, with all the skies under her command, was not half so important as the Queen's trust, the Queen's—dare she think it—love.

With every subtlety the Queen had taught her about body language, Eliza projected uncertainty. She held her breath, letting her grip on the knife falter, slowing her steps to an uneven rhythm.

The Queen slowed to match her, shoulders squared. "It's time for you to play the part you were trained for."

Eliza fought a smile. "I'm ready," she breathed.

The Queen's knife came from above, and Eliza dodged just in time, the Queen's knuckles grazing her shoulder. She should have been faster. She'd lured the Queen into the attack, after all, but better knuckles than a knife.

Rolling to the side, Eliza gathered herself and lunged for the Queen's leg. For once, Eliza had the upper hand. But the Queen's foot met the blade, kicking it from Eliza's grasp. Eliza hit the ground, the Queen's boot pressed against her chest.

Eliza was unarmed, and the Queen remained undefeated. She'd failed the test. Again.

Burying her frustration, Eliza did her best to mask her disappointment. "I yield." Though the Queen always won their sparring matches, Eliza had yet to master the art of losing.

The Queen stepped back and placed her dagger on her desk. "You must be more diligent. Remember your lessons and be conscious of your tells."

Eliza picked herself up and brushed the Queen's boot print—a badge of her failure—from her bodice. "Of course, Your Majesty." She would have to spend more time studying her form in the mirror to find the weakness the Queen exploited.

"Still, I do think you're ready." The Queen motioned for Eliza to sit across from her. "This mission is unlike any other, and it will take all your skills to see it through."

Eliza sat dutifully, crossing her legs and leaning forward. If she could not best the Queen with a blade, she'd at least perform a gracious resignation. Besides, from the sound of it, Eliza was about to win much more than a fight.

The Queen's voice turned from airy to sharp. "Earth Adjacent is a peculiar place. I've not been in many years, but I hope I'll live long enough to see our people migrate."

Eliza began to protest, but the Queen held up a hand.

"No, my dear. Though I am getting on in years, I do not want your sympathy, only your utmost dedication to this mission."

Eliza nodded, signaling for the Queen to continue.

"The goal has always been thus: Find a suitable planet, terraform it, and bring humanity to this new world. My people will flourish, and I will be remembered as the Queen who made the world." She paused, though whether lost in thought or for dramatic effect, Eliza didn't know. "I'm very close to finalizing those plans—*so very close*."

Another pause, this one surely for drama. The Queen had once spent an entire afternoon teaching Eliza the art of the well-placed pause. Eliza's pulse quickened in anticipation, and this time she took the Queen's bait. "But something is preventing you from moving forward," she surmised, breaking the cultivated silence.

The Queen gave a slight nod in approval. "Some*one*. You see, I've lost the cooperation of the one man I trusted to help me accomplish my goals."

Eliza sat straighter. There was only one man it could be—only one man who could hurt the Queen in such a way.

"The Commissioners of Earth Adjacent have not always been our allies, but whoever has held the position, they've known what was at stake. Now I find myself with an adversary on the ground— an enemy of my own flesh."

Eliza's breath caught. The Queen had never spoken of such things before, preferring to leave familial matters in the past. Surely she couldn't mean . . . "Th-the Prince?"

The Queen shook her head. "He lost the right to that title when he crossed me. I won't have him disgrace my legacy, not when he already seeks to claim it for his own."

Eliza longed to ask what betrayal he'd committed but thought better of it. The Queen would tell her only what she needed to know, as she always had.

The Queen rummaged in her desk drawer and withdrew an envelope, wax seal already broken, with Eliza's name scrawled across the front.

Eliza gulped. Part of her—perhaps the only truly innocent part of her left—had hoped the Queen would name Eliza her heir on the spot. She'd proven herself time and time again, sacrificing everything in the name of the Queen. What more would the Queen ask before finally granting Eliza this reward?

Serving the Queen is reward enough.

That was what Eliza told herself, repeating it every day since she'd been named the Queen's Eyes. She would see no other recognition than the job the Queen had granted her three years ago. She was the Queen's Eyes, and a spy's work always went uncelebrated. It would be selfish indeed to expect more.

"Going forward, you will no longer be Eliza, the Eyes of the Queen," she said, holding up the envelope. "You will be Lady Eliza—demure, pleasant, and unassuming, betrothed to the Commissioner's heir." She held out the letter.

Eliza's stomach pitched. She'd known this would catch up with her eventually, but she'd thought it a distant future, a problem for tomorrow's Eliza. But tomorrow's Eliza was today's Eliza, it seemed.

Engaged Eliza.

The Eliza she embodied when she wrote her letters was a cultivated version of herself, pieced together with careful penmanship. She'd revealed nothing she did not want her betrothed to know—so she'd revealed nothing at all.

With a shaking hand, Eliza took to the envelope, running her finger across her name, penned in a nervous hand. Nathaniel Fremont had been a diligent correspondent, writing to her often. But to marry the boy would be to give up her future, even though Eliza's future no more belonged to her than her present.

Still worse, marrying Nathaniel Fremont now, before the Queen and her courtiers descended to Earth Adjacent, meant leaving the Queen's side. It meant becoming a Planetary, falling further from the seat of power she sought.

"It's a silly exercise, marriage," the Queen was saying, "bound more in tradition and custom than any real exchange of power. Yet it has its uses. I've led the Commissioner to believe this engagement will appease me, and just now he wants to circumnavigate my wrath. It will make him feel confident; it may make him careless."

Eliza curled her fingers around the envelope and nodded. She knew this tactic well, taught by the Queen herself. *Convince a fool they've done you a favor, and they'll never see your blade coming*, the Queen told her once. *Gratitude is as strong a disguise as any mask.*

"And his heir?" Eliza asked, her throat suddenly tight.

"Once you have arrived and gained the boy's confidence, then we will plan the next steps. I find myself in need of better intelligence, and you are primed to infiltrate Earth Adjacent's highest circles." The Queen stood and offered her a silver holocom. "Do this for me, and you will prove beyond shadow of doubt you deserve to be my granddaughter-in-law."

Eliza reached for the metal device, weighing it in her palm. This would be her only tie to life on the Tower, the only tie to the Queen. It pained her to think of leaving, but the Queen had given her an order—a mission—and Eliza would not disobey, she would not disappoint.

A mission was an opportunity to show her worth. And if that failed, well, she was Eliza, fiancée to the Commissioner's son, and the Commissioner was the Queen's son. Though it certainly wasn't the way she'd expected, or the way she'd wanted it, Eliza was about to become royalty, and that, at least, was something.

With a deep curtsy, Eliza turned to go, but the Queen called her back.

"Aren't you forgetting something?" She inclined her head, and Eliza followed its direction.

The dagger still lay on the floor, discarded from their sparring match. Alone on the stark white tile, the blade looked inconsequential and small, not a grand symbol of Eliza's duty to her Queen.

Eliza darted forward to retrieve it. Cold steel sent a shock through her, as though she'd regained a piece of herself when her fingers closed around the hilt. From the moment the Queen had placed it in her palm, she'd never gone without it. The blade was a reminder that Eliza had been chosen above all the others—she'd *beaten* all the others.

All but the Queen.

In a flash, Eliza turned, ready to strike. The Queen caught Eliza's dagger with her own and twisted the blades to disarm Eliza once again, leaving Eliza's hand as empty as her heart.

"A sloppy attempt," the Queen said, returning Eliza's blade to her. "You'll try again tomorrow."

Eliza knew a dismissal when she heard one, but she couldn't bring herself to leave. "What is it?" she asked instead.

"What is what?" The Queen had already returned to her desk, her own holocom in hand.

"My tell—how you know when and where I'll move."

The Queen, busy with the blue light from her holocom screen, did not look up.

Eliza ought to have known better. The Queen liked her secrets, after all. But as Eliza turned to leave, the Queen's voice chased her out the door.

"It's your eyes. You always look where you plan to strike."

Her *eyes*. Eliza shut them, pausing on the threshold. It was the one lesson the Queen had never taught her. *Of course*. The Queen, who saw all but was seen by none. She had no use for the fluttering of eyelashes or the subtlety of eye contact. This was one last lesson Eliza would have to teach herself.

Perhaps veils had their uses after all.

CHAPTER SEVEN

Nathaniel had never left the Settlement before. He doubted many had, with Tech Decree Thirty hanging over their heads. No one was permitted to leave without express permission from the Commissioner's office. The farmers who worked the land just beyond the city were granted special passports, allowing them to pass freely through the gate, but the rest were to stay within the city's walls, safe from harm. Though exactly what sort of harm that was, Nathaniel didn't know.

The Settlement wall seemed a shield, a stone embrace around the city. From Nathaniel's bedroom window, the wall had always made him feel safe. He'd never needed to worry about anything beyond. He'd never needed to worry about much at all.

As Nathaniel made his way through the streets, still bustling with vendors and visitors for the final day of the Celestial Market, he felt trapped. The manor was spacious enough, with a vast perimeter, but the rest of the city hardly resembled the home Nathaniel knew. Here, everything was cramped and squeezed together. Though the buildings stood straight, he felt as though they leaned toward him, casting judgment instead of shadows.

Perhaps the wall *did* protect them, but so, too, did it keep citizens penned like animals. The Settlement's population had never been large—several thousand, perhaps, no more than ten—but the walls had not been constructed with growth in mind. There was nowhere for them to build but inward, nothing for them to do but cannibalize their own city, dividing it up into smaller and smaller fragments.

Nathaniel had been given far too large a piece of far too small a city. And still, the Settlement was not *his*. The Commissioner had made himself perfectly clear: Nathaniel was not free to do as he wished, to go where he willed. Nathaniel would never have his father's permission to leave the Settlement. And so, Nathaniel's father could never find out.

Nathaniel paused a few yards from the gate. He'd snuck out of the manor easily enough, where few officers roamed the grounds. But two guards flanked the gate, eyes focused, alert. There was nothing to be done for it. Nathaniel needed to leave the city, and they were in his way.

He froze. What if they recognized him? If his father had told the guards of his directive to Nathaniel, it would be mere moments before the officers hauled him back to the manor and his chance to meet the Technician would be gone forever.

A flurry of Orbitals passed by him on either side, chatting animatedly in their tight accents. The officers made way for them as they approached, letting them pass single file through the gate.

Nathaniel glanced down at his clothes. He wasn't dressed in the same avant-garde manner. The guards wouldn't believe for a moment that he belonged. Scanning the aisle of pop-up shops, Nathaniel spotted the perfect disguise: a tall hat covered in metallic stars. Nathaniel snatched the hat from its stand, placed it atop his head, and swept through the crowd as covertly as possible.

The officers bowed as the outermost Orbitals flashed silvery identification cards. Nathaniel kept his eyes forward, feet moving. With any luck, the officers wouldn't realize that one among the crowd didn't belong.

It worked. For once, Nathaniel's propensity for invisibility came in handy. No one stopped him to check his nonexistent identity card, and the Orbitals didn't seem to notice. As soon as they were far enough from the gates, Nathaniel peeled off from the group. He'd done it. He'd left the Settlement.

Getting back inside, of course, would be another challenge altogether, but Nathaniel could worry about that later—he had an appointment to keep.

Outside the Settlement, farmland stretched in one direction, and in the other, rolling green hills. He'd never seen so much green in his life. The gardens outside the manor didn't compare to the unbridled nature that overtook the horizon. Long grass, colorful flowers, and insects he couldn't name brushed at his ankles as he walked, heading west.

But twenty minutes later, Nathaniel had found nothing and no one. The farmland spilled back toward the Settlement in his wake, and ahead of him he could see only a rocky coastline.

The Technician wasn't there.

Nathaniel threw his embellished hat to the ground and stomped his foot, crushing the velvet brim beneath his boot. Then he whirled to check that no one had seen his childish outburst, but Nathaniel was alone with the wind, which promptly lifted his stolen hat and whisked it away.

With a sigh, Nathaniel jogged after it. No use in wasting a perfectly good chapeau. The hat, plastered as it was with metallic embellishment, was hardly wearable for every day, but it was all he had outside the Settlement gates. The Technician might have stood him up, but Nathaniel could still retain some scrap of dignity, even if it was a spectacularly garish scrap.

He caught it, eventually, but not before it took him several yards down the coast. Placing the hat firmly on his head, Nathaniel lowered himself gracelessly onto a rock to catch his breath. He pressed a hand against his chest, which throbbed as his heart thundered beneath his chest plate. At least his little clock came through for him now, even if it had let him down so thoroughly before.

Had the Technician known he meant harm? Perhaps the girl at the market had told the outlaw not to come. But no—she'd looked him in the eye and shaken his hand, not afraid of his status, or his tech, if she'd even been aware of either.

Long four to the short nine. Had he misunderstood the riddle? Had he somehow miscalculated, or misread the clock? How could something so close to him, so ingrained in his being it was embedded in his skin, steer him so wrong? Nathaniel's fingers crept up to his cravat before he stopped himself. What sort of gentleman would he be if he disrobed out in the open?

A desperate one, that's what.

And Nathaniel *was* desperate. But what would the clock on his chest tell him that a clock in his mind's eye couldn't? Nothing— and he'd be hard-pressed to read it upside down anyway.

Upside. Down.

Was it possible? Yes, it was—probable, in fact. It wasn't just anyone who'd created life out of metal and saved Nathaniel all those years ago. It had been the Tarnished, people who used tech on their own bodies. Abominations, according to his father. But no matter how depraved and dangerous they were supposed to be, one of them had saved Nathaniel's life when he was only a baby, and that was worth something. Maybe it hadn't been the Technician himself, but someone of the same creed, the same world, had sewn the metal into his chest. And, more than likely, there were others just like Nathaniel. Surely the Technician would know that.

Pushing off from the rock, Nathaniel retraced his steps across the farmlands, dipping away from the Settlement gates to avoid attention, and then east through grassy fields. If he ran, maybe he could still make it. Maybe the Technician would wait for him.

All his effort was finally rewarded when he climbed over a crest, lungs exhausted with asthmatic breathing, to see a building overcome with ivy and uncut grass. In the doorway stood the girl from the market, red hair bright against the expanse of green around them. Surveying him with a smug smile and sharp eyes, she said, "So you found me after all."

Nathaniel's stomach sank. He'd found her all right, but she was only the girl from the market, not the Technician he sought.

CHAPTER EIGHT

Anna's final customer of the day was late. The clock in her chest made her relentlessly punctual, but it also ticked an irksome reminder. The longer she waited, the more likely she was to get caught.

Defying Thatcher had been easy, but as the afternoon wore on with still no sign of the boy from the market, Anna wondered if perhaps her grandfather's fears hadn't been so far-fetched after all. The dandy boy from the market had cheated—taking her locket and its contents without her password. With any other customer, she would have left by now, but curiosity gnawed at her insides, the rhythm of his heart ticking a metal memory against her skin.

Leaning against the doorframe, Anna watched the horizon for any sign of movement. If any officers appeared, she'd see their maroon and gray first and begone out the side door before they arrived.

But just as she began to lose hope, Anna saw a figure in the distance, moving down the hill with an uneven gait. It took only a moment before she saw the silver glint of stars on a ridiculous navy top hat.

"So you found me after all," she said when he was close.

The dandy—Nathaniel—stared, his eyes growing wide. "I—uh—honestly wasn't certain I would." He cast his gaze around, eventually landing back on Anna. "Where's the Technician?"

Anna pressed her lips together, unsure whether she should tell him the truth. If he was only ignorant, there was no harm, but still, her anonymity had served her well. To this day, fewer than half of her clientele knew she and the outlaw were one and the same.

"The Technician only handles the truly complicated cases." She stood straighter, letting the lie fall from her lips as naturally as leaves from a tree. "I'm to assess your particular case first. Then the Technician will determine whether or not you're . . . *interesting* enough to tend to personally." She beckoned to him, watching something—disappointment, perhaps—flash in his eyes. "Why don't you come inside?"

He approached with an expression of confused awe, which she found both unnerving and endearing. He removed his ludicrous hat when he stepped over the threshold to reveal a thicket of wavy brown hair.

He was striking, but in an unusual sort of way—or perhaps unusual in a striking sort of way. His coloring was soft, but his features sharp and angular. The dandy had been charming when she'd met him at the market, though she didn't recall him having such a pleasant face.

"An odd meeting place."

Anna cocked her head. "I like it."

"Isn't it rather obvious? I'd have thought an open field or a forest would be less overt."

"Obvious?" Anna considered a moment. "No, I don't think so." She'd chosen her rendezvous points with care, after all. No one who wasn't meant to find her ever had. She'd thought at first the Commissioner simply wasn't trying hard enough, but this boy wasn't the first legitimate customer of hers to struggle with her riddles.

"Aren't you at all worried? A building in the middle of nowhere isn't exactly hard to find."

Anna tipped her chin down and raised an eyebrow.

"I-I mean," the boy stammered, averting his eyes as though his difficulty finding her was a secret he could hide. "It's just that it would be so easy for someone to stumble upon this place—to find you merely by accident."

Anna considered again for a moment. He wasn't entirely off; it was risky to pick something so easily marked. But the abandoned building suited her, first and foremost because it *was* abandoned.

"Did you see the overgrowth on the way in?" she asked, unsure if a boy from the Settlement could truly understand what it meant to be outside the city—to simply *be*. "This place hasn't been touched by the Commissioner. It's completely free of human disruption. No one else comes or goes, not since the Settlement built its walls and closed its gates."

Nathaniel looked down and crossed his arms. "Th-that's quite remarkable." His voice shook.

Perhaps she'd been too honest for his sensibilities—or not honest enough. "The Settlement and the Tower adorn themselves with pieces of culture and history like they're accessories. They pick and choose the ones they like and cast away the rest without a care for why or how they came to be. This place doesn't have to pretend to be anything it's not—this place *is* history."

"History," Nathaniel murmured, eyes still downcast.

He looked positively overwhelmed, and with his late arrival, Anna was already behind schedule. It was time to drop pretense and get to work.

"Enough pleasantries. Why don't we discuss why you're here?" She took a hesitant step toward him, desperate to see his tech up close, to inspect the craftsmanship. Perhaps if she could see the other mechanic's handiwork, she could get a better read on this new player in her game.

"I'm sorry." He picked at his immaculate fingernails. "I never thought I'd have the chance to ask, well . . . I'm not actually sure what. I find I don't know where to begin." He slid his too-long arms into his pockets, forcing his shoulders into a shrug.

Anna nodded slowly, taking in his defenseless manner. Was it all a ruse, or was his confusion legitimate? Whether she could trust him or not, he needed her help. Of that, she was certain.

"Begin at the beginning." Anna pointed to his chest. "Where did you get your TICCER?"

Nathaniel raised his eyebrows. "My what?"

Anna tapped her chest where her own TICCER worked beneath her clothes, and comprehension dawned on his face.

"Is that what it's called?"

"Tarnish Internal Cardiac Clockwork-Enabled Regulator. A TICCER." She frowned—how could he possibly not know, unless his mechanic failed to inform him? "Who installed yours?"

"No idea. I've had it as long as I can recall." Nathaniel's eyes snapped up to meet hers.

Anna took several more steps toward him, undoing the latch on her satchel. "That's not possible."

But it was—she was the living proof of that. Thatcher had told her he'd only ever installed a TICCER on one infant, that her tech

alone was unique, designed to expand through external maintenance as she grew. Though Tarnish took root in children, Thatcher
usually refused to install TICCERs earlier than puberty; it was too
risky. At seven years old, Roman was one of the few to receive a
TICCER so young.

She paused inches from Nathaniel, stopping herself. He was a
new client, a patient. He wasn't the enemy. "I need to take a closer
look."

The dandy's eyebrows arched even higher, but after a few ticks,
he began removing his vest.

Living with a surgeon, Anna had seen nearly every inhabitant
of Mechan unclothed for some reason or another, but this felt different. She ought to avert her eyes, but something—fear, or curiosity, maybe—kept her gaze fixed on his hands as they undid the
buttons of his shirt. As he pulled down the fabric to reveal several
inches of skin, she caught the flash of silver screws at the base of his
throat, and all consideration of propriety fled her mind.

When he'd finished, Anna simply stared. The design mim-
icked her own, an identical steel panel covering the working parts.
She reached to touch the metal but pulled her fingers back at the
last second. "Do you mind if I . . ." She held up her wrench.

Nathaniel nodded. "Go ahead."

Anna's hands moved in a flash, as though activated by his
assent. She removed the small screws, twisting and pulling metal
with her tools, until the panel popped off.

Anna stopped breathing.

Beneath the panel, a familiar machine ticked. Silver sheets
fanned out like flower petals, interwoven with scarred flesh; the
marks of metal from long ago still bloomed angry-red on his skin.
She knew this device inside and out, every nook and cranny. She

was not simply acquainted with it: Anna's relationship to that TICCER was intimate.

It was the same as hers.

Whoever had installed it knew Thatcher's original design, or it *was* Thatcher and he'd lied to her. Both options unsettled her.

"What sort of maintenance do you do?" Anna bent to get a closer look at the intricate machinery.

"Er—none." Nathaniel shrugged, the movement throwing Anna's concentration. "I actually don't even know how it works . . . or exactly what it does."

Anna fiddled with her screwdriver, poking and prodding at the metal as she spoke. "It's a regulator, so it keeps your heartbeat steady. It can't go over one hundred and eighty beats per minute, and obviously if it goes too slowly, that's a problem, too. Using the clock's natural rhythm, it keeps your heartbeat within a normal range."

The TICCER stuttered.

Nathaniel coughed, and it returned to a normal pace.

"Or at least it's supposed to." Anna frowned, peering closer at the machinery. "Does that happen often?"

"Pardon?" Nathaniel asked between coughs.

Anna ran a hand through her hair, pushing the red flyaways out of her face. "What sort of symptoms do you experience?" She shook her head; she was beginning to sound like Thatcher. "Do you often cough or have chest pain?"

"N—yes." Nathaniel cocked his head. "Now that you mention it. But it's only a little cough."

"It most certainly isn't." Anna searched inside her shirt pocket for the L-shaped wrench she used on her own TICCER. Though she'd filled her satchel with every tool she could possibly need for her clients, she kept one close to her heart, just in case. Fitted to her own TICCER, no one else had ever needed it.

Until now.

Thatcher had given it to her on her twelfth birthday. Not exactly the sort of gift one typically gave a young girl. But even at twelve, Anna had wanted to be just like her grandfather, saving people's lives. After Roman's surgery—after she'd failed him—that dream slipped away. It was not an easy lesson to learn at twelve, that surgeons lost more patients than they saved. But a mechanic—a mechanic didn't cut; a mechanic didn't hurt.

To twelve-year-old Anna, that little wrench had signified Thatcher's blessing, his way of giving his approval of her new path. He'd siphoned away that support as the years wore on, but that little wrench still belonged to her—the key to her own tech.

And now it was the key to Nathaniel's.

"Hold still. This might pinch." Anna inserted the wrench, waited a tick, and twisted.

"Oh." A single note escaped Nathaniel's lips, and his gaze locked on to hers. He reached up to his chest, fingers dancing an erratic jig, before his eyes rolled back in his head and he collapsed to the floor.

CHAPTER NINE

Hatred was an unproductive emotion. It did nothing but fester and ferment if left too long. Still, as Eliza made her way back to her apartment, hatred for her betrothed weighed her down, making her steps slow and beleaguered. She wanted nothing more than to shed her layers, peel back her skirts one by one until every shred of lacey armor was gone and with it the anger nestling against her chest.

But she had a job to do for the Queen.

Settling herself at the black enamel vanity, Eliza removed the letter from her dress pocket. She'd known this would be her fate, of course. Three years ago, still fresh from the wounds of her trial, the Queen had given her a title . . . and then she'd given her a fiancé. With the diligence she owed her new position, Eliza had penned letters to Nathaniel Fremont once a month since her betrothal. She'd channeled every ounce of grace and patience into her work on the Tower, leaving nothing behind for letters but her raw, authentic self.

But she couldn't share that girl with Nathaniel. He could not know her, heartbroken and heart-weary as she'd been then—truly, as she was now. Those lesions had never healed, held together only by the patch she sewed over herself each day, woven from determination and resilience. The girl she'd put on paper was only a fraction of herself, a sliver plucked from her open wound and made real through her words. Nathaniel did not know the girl who would someday be his wife. And neither did she know the boy who would someday be her husband. She didn't care to. Husbands were for other people, people who had time for emotions like love and hate.

Eliza shuddered, blinking away the image of herself standing beside a man, dressed in white with flowers in her hair and contrived bliss in her eyes. She'd never spent overlong hours on the idea, never allowed her mind to wander far from the task at hand, but when she'd imagined it—the future, a marriage, a romance—it had never been a *man* at her side.

Once, it had been Marla. She'd been a small, wild thing—a girl Eliza couldn't forget, but could never have, either. She'd made Eliza want to work faster, try harder, be better. She'd made fighting almost as much fun as winning. But in the end, when it had come down to a life with Marla or a life beside the Queen, Eliza had chosen the Queen.

We are made or unmade by our choices, the Queen had taught her. And so Eliza had become her Eyes, dealing in lies instead of love.

It had been years since Eliza last looked into Marla's mutinous green eyes and made promises she couldn't keep. She could barely remember the feel of her skin, the touch of her lips. But still, eyes as green as the planet below haunted her, a love lost to ambition, a love lost to the stars.

But that girl was the past. This boy was the future.

With a flick of her finger, Eliza snapped open the envelope and unfolded the letter. Undisciplined penmanship spilled across the page. Eliza set her jaw and resigned herself to read.

Dear Eliza,

It is such a pleasure to hear from you again. Your last letter could not have arrived at a better time. I find myself lost, as of late, immersed in the murky waters of an ocean I don't understand. My father has so many lines, it's almost impossible not to cross one accidentally now and again. I want to do the right thing, but every time I try, I find the lines have shifted and I no longer know where I stand. I tell myself it's all right as long as it's not on purpose, as long as it's not malicious, as long as I'm sorry.

Everything here is so twisted and complicated——the exact opposite of your life——and I'm sorry you'll have to leave one day to be a part of this mess of a world. I am, truly, sorry for that.

I can't seem to find it in me to be sorry about much else these days.

Wishing you well,
Nathaniel Fremont

Eliza traced his signature with her fingertip. Nathaniel Fremont was not her enemy. He was only a boy with a father he couldn't understand and feelings he couldn't process. They had that in common, at least.

Maybe he *was* just as unsure about their impending nuptials as she. Uncertainty she could work with. She could mold it into anything she wanted—a sword, a sickness, a salve.

Nathaniel was an idealist, and ignorant—not to mention a little awkward—yet he was determined to please his father and certain he never could.

Most of all, he was alone, with one parent in the ground and the other too high up to reach, though it didn't stop him from trying. Eliza was the only one who saw him—and he had no idea the girl he wrote to wasn't even real.

Eliza sighed and refolded the letter, setting it aside. The Eliza she'd crafted in her mind for this boy was everything his fiancée ought to be, but if she was to act the part convincingly, she would need to understand the girl he knew. She would need to become her, make her a person, not just a mask.

Nathaniel Fremont was a person, too, and though she would never love him, the least she could do was try not to hate him.

CHAPTER TEN

When Nathaniel came to, he didn't know where he was or how he'd gotten there.

"Nice to have you back among the living."

A face swam above him. Red hair and freckles moved in and out of focus, and for a moment he couldn't place the girl peering down at him. Then it all came rushing back: He could remember leaving the Settlement and finding Anna, but he couldn't remember how he'd ended up on the floor. Had she attacked him? No—that didn't make sense. He was the intruder here, the one lying to get information.

Nathaniel sat up, blinking his eyes against a dull headache. "What happened?"

Anna offered her arm and he took it, letting her drag him back to his feet.

"I'm not sure." She held his forearm, as if she was afraid he might fall again.

"That's reassuring," he muttered.

Anna pursed her lips. "You haven't wound your TICCER in a while, I'd assume. If you've never done any maintenance, it's a wonder it still works."

Nathaniel rubbed his chest, remembering a hot flash of pain but feeling none at all now. He felt the whisper of her tools and fingers against his skin. A blush crept into his cheeks as he realized his shirt was open, his chest exposed.

He shouldn't have let her know so much. Maybe he shouldn't have come here at all. But he had and he did, and somehow a weight had been lifted now that someone else had seen his innermost secret, the one thing he was never allowed to share.

"So I'll need to do maintenance? What does that mean?" He could hear her perfectly but had trouble registering her words. Perhaps he'd hit his head on the way down.

"I— Why don't you sit?" She guided him by the elbow toward a dusty bench against the wall.

His skin rippled with gooseflesh where her cold fingers touched him, her pulse beating out of time with his own. Was hers faster or slower? He tried to focus, to feel her rhythm, but it unsteadied him. He wished she would let go.

Anna took a deep breath, sucking air through her teeth. "This is more complicated and more curious than I'm comfortable admitting." She let go of his arm, but her shoulder pressed into his. "I'm not sure where to start."

Nathaniel searched her face for a clue but found nothing except freckles and a brow knit in concentration. She sat so close, eyes boring into his. He was struck by the sudden impression that he was supposed to enjoy it, that another boy in his position would. Instead, he was filled with the same sense of expectation, the churning of his stomach that came with Eliza's letters. This was the kind of moment people meant when they said he'd meet someone someday, when they said he'd understand when he was older.

But Nathaniel *was* older, and age had not brought with it the sweeping desire to fall in love or kiss or sit shoulder to shoulder with someone he'd just met.

Nathaniel scooted away a fraction of an inch. "Why don't you start with the simplest part and work from there?" A smile crept onto his lips as he parroted her words. "Begin at the beginning."

"None of this is simple." Anna chewed her bottom lip. "A TICCER is a complicated bit of machinery, and the type you have isn't supposed to run on its own. It needs to be wound regularly, and the panels should have been expanded as you got older. Your heart's quite literally outgrown your TICCER, which is why you don't make any sort of logical sense." She ran her hands through her hair, linking her fingers behind her head.

Nathaniel leaned forward, elbows on his knees. Though he'd come with the foulest of intentions, he found his interest genuine. The Technician had failed to show, but this girl knew about machinery. Perhaps she could shed light where his father couldn't—or wouldn't.

"None of this makes any sense." He let his fingers brush the steel resting in his skin. He'd spent so many years avoiding it, pretending it wasn't real. It was easier that way—better, even. "No one talks about tech in the Settlement."

"Dandies," Anna scoffed.

"Pardon?" Nathaniel could tell she'd meant it as an insult by the pink blush spreading across her cheeks at his question.

"I shouldn't call you that. You aren't one of them." She said the last word the same way she'd said *dandies*. "It's what we call the Commissioner's followers, enemies of tech who don't truly understand what they oppose. They tend to dress, well, like you— elevated. But you're different, right?"

Nathaniel leaned back. Her accusation stung. He wasn't different; he was his father's son. Only she didn't know that—she *couldn't* know that, not if he wanted to meet the fabled Technician. "Some tech is worth opposing, though, isn't it?" He shivered, knowing the answer. Without tech, he wouldn't be alive, but without tech, his mother might not be dead. How could this thing that had brought him such loss also give him life?

Anna laughed, harsh like china breaking. "How can you even ask that? You have metal in your chest keeping you alive, just like me. And you think the Tower and the Commissioner are right to condemn *us* when they don't abide by the same laws?"

"Tech Decree Twenty-Six gives the Commissioner the freedom to use tech when necessary," Nathaniel said. "The law doesn't apply—and the Tower doesn't fall under the same set of laws. As long as it doesn't interfere with Earth Adjacent, they're free to use tech as they will."

"And you see nothing wrong with that?" Anna's eyes grew wide as she scrutinized him.

Nathaniel recoiled at her piercing stare but still managed to say with some level of dignity, "It makes sense. If the Commissioner wants to fight the Tarnished, he must employ the same technologies—level the playing field, as such."

Anna laughed hollowly. "The field has never been level. It doesn't matter if we have the same tools when he has all the power, and always will. You make it sound like some kind of war where both sides have an equal chance."

"Isn't it?" Nathaniel asked before he could stop himself. He ought to have known better than to encourage her—he'd never take any of her propaganda seriously, anyway.

Anna sighed and crossed her arms. "The Commissioner's fighting for the utter destruction of our kind. He wants to wipe us off the map, kill us in our homes, tear us from our hearts. If the Commissioner wins, it means total devastation."

"And if you win?"

"We don't win, Nathaniel." Anna shook her head, lowering her voice to barely a whisper. "We survive."

Nathaniel sat in the wake of Anna's words, letting them wash up and over him like waves. His father had made it seem so clear. The Tarnished were the enemy; they deserved the full force of the Settlement's hostility. But Anna didn't feel like the enemy. She felt like a person, like a teacher, maybe even like a friend. She wasn't trying to destroy the careful peace his father had given the Settlement. She was only trying to live.

That was the power of the Tarnished, though. Nathaniel's father had warned him time and again of their dangerous logic. He couldn't let Anna sway him, he couldn't let her *change* him.

"Some of the laws make sense," Nathaniel said quietly, grasping for the truths he knew.

"That so?" Anna leaned back, her eyes narrowing.

"The Commissioner might be harsh toward tech users, but there's a reason for that." Nathaniel sat straighter. "Tech is dangerous! We destroyed Former Earth with technology."

"And yet we terraformed Earth Adjacent with that same tech."

Nathaniel swallowed, unable to meet Anna's eye. "At least now we have a second chance to do it right."

"You think the Commissioner's right to ban all tech—even if it's helping people, regardless of the lives that might be lost." Anna threw her hands in the air. "What is a planet worth if we aren't alive to live on it?"

"We didn't see the value of our planet all those years ago, and look what happened. So no, I don't think the Commissioner's entirely wrong. Tech is dangerous—its *potential* is dangerous." As the words poured from his lips, Nathaniel wasn't sure he believed them. He'd heard them all his life; they were his mantra, his truth. But now that he'd seen inside his own heart—literally—the threat didn't seem so urgent. "Maybe not all tech," he murmured at last, a whisper he'd never repeat.

"Not *all* tech?" Anna asked incredulously. "So what tech is acceptable? Should I deny an armless boy a prosthetic arm? What about my client who can't walk without a metal leg? Or you? Whose request should I deny? The Settlement won't help you, with or without tech, so where do I draw the line? Or is that privilege reserved only for the wealthy?"

Nathaniel swallowed with difficulty. When she put it like that, he couldn't contest the failings of their society. Though he'd seldom left the manor, he'd never seen anyone with only one arm or leg. Did he simply not see it because he'd been trained to ignore it, or was it hidden away just like him? In what other ways might his eyes have failed him?

He shoved the thought away. His father would not neglect his people. When it had mattered, his father had used tech to save Nathaniel's life. A warm bubble formed in his stomach; the Commissioner had cared about his son so much that Nathaniel's life had been worth going against his own beliefs.

Swallowing his emotions, Nathaniel set his jaw. "Pre-industrial tech is allowed." The words were ghosts of his father's.

Anna laughed again, more like a cackle. "It isn't nearly so simple as that. Do you know what just so happens to be pre-industrial? Clocks." She flicked her chest, sending a metal ping through the air, her own TICCER adding to the debate. "But the Commissioner isn't so fond of pre-industrial tech when you use it for post-industrial science. The minute we combine blood and steel, he no longer cares if that metal's pre-industrial or not. The use of tech on the human body is the highest form of depravity to him. Doesn't matter if it saves lives, it's *wicked*."

Nathaniel's eyebrows crashed together. He'd never thought of it that way.

"We need these to survive, and we're not the only ones. There are more just like you and me, but you won't find any of them sitting on the Commissioner's council. Those at the top will always get what they need, legal or no, and the rest of us will be left to suffer."

"Those at the top," Nathaniel parroted, barely aware he'd spoken at all. She meant him, though of course she couldn't possibly know his identity. She'd no idea how wrong she was. And how right. For wasn't it exactly as she'd said? He'd been given a TICCER, despite the law, and he'd never see the inside of a jail cell. He'd gotten exactly what he needed with no consequences.

Anna pressed her hand against her heart. "When your life is on the line, it's hard to care what a self-important man like the Commissioner thinks of your methods. He calls us Tarnished, as if we're somehow less than—as if it's an insult, not an illness." She prodded Nathaniel's chest, finger colliding with metal. "You shouldn't be alive right now. You shouldn't even exist."

Nathaniel stopped moving. Was it a threat or a warning? "What do you mean by that?"

Anna let her hands fall, turning to look at him. Her eyes, a blue so faint they were almost gray, pinned him with an impervious stare. "You're a medical miracle, and I don't believe in those. You should be dead—you *could* be dead any second."

Nathaniel bit his lip. Never in all his fantasies of how the day might go had this possibility crossed his mind. He'd hoped it would be a simple matter of capturing the Technician—no talk of tech and his own mortality. "What should I do, then?"

Anna said something into her hands that Nathaniel didn't quite catch, but then she looked up and said, "Meet me again in a week."

"Same time, same place?"

Anna shook her head violently. "No, no. Wouldn't want anyone to catch us if you were followed." She held out her palm. "Give it here."

"Wh-what?" Nathaniel's hand flew to his chest, unsure what of his she wanted but entirely certain he didn't want to give it.

"The locket."

Nathaniel fished the locket out from his pants pocket. It wasn't much of a keepsake, but something about the way it spun as he held the chain sent both cold and warmth through his veins.

With fingers that flashed in precise movements, Anna opened the locket. She handed the crumpled note with her instructions back to him before removing a fresh slip of paper from her pocket. She scribbled a few words with a pen and stuffed it inside before returning the locket.

"Another riddle?" Nathaniel asked, twisting the gear with his thumb.

Anna grabbed his hand, prying his fingers away from the locket. "No, no. Don't open it yet."

"I don't suppose you could just tell me what it all means?"

Anna retrieved a wrench from her pack and replaced the metal panel over the clock in his chest. "Not a chance," she said with the smallest of smiles.

Nathaniel's breath hitched. He'd come so far, yet accomplished so little. "And the Technician—will I actually be receiving his services next time?" He tried to sound nonchalant, like it hardly mattered.

Anna only smiled. "The Technician's interest is not easily caught."

The return trip to the Settlement proved an easier walk. His lungs didn't burn with each cresting hill, and he found he'd fatigued only a little when he reached the gates.

No Orbitals milled about now amid whom he could travel back inside, and the officers at the gate stared out at the field, as if anticipating an intruder.

With a sigh, Nathaniel hid behind one the boulders sprawled out between himself and the gate. Perhaps if he waited long enough, he could slip past unnoticed during a guard change. The cover of night would be upon them soon and he could use the darkness to sneak inside.

Fishing the locket out, Nathaniel's mind chased itself in circles. He unfolded the paper inside, fingers shaking.

The Technician thanks you for your patience.

Patient didn't seem the right word to describe his manner during their meeting, but perhaps from her perspective it made sense.

She'd been rather confusing. He had more questions now than ever. He flipped the paper over.

For further maintenance, see a consultant when the moon smiles to the east and the porridge cools at the heart of the Settlement.

Of course she'd changed the pattern. Nathaniel grinned. Anna was many things, but predictable was not one of them.

A commotion near the gate drew Nathaniel's attention, and he stepped out from behind the boulder to get a better look.

A carriage had stopped just inside the Settlement, maroon and gray. He had left the Settlement to bring his father the one thing he wanted most, but his father would see only a disobedient son who'd disappointed him yet again.

As the Commissioner descended from his carriage, the officers surrounding the gate bowed as one. The Commissioner turned toward the Settlement gate, his gaze finding Nathaniel.

Pocketing the locket and the riddle inside, Nathaniel took a deep breath—noting how the air filled his lungs so effortlessly now—and made for the entrance. There was no point putting off their confrontation.

"Get in," the Commissioner said in lieu of a greeting, snatching the garish hat from Nathaniel's head and handing it to one of the officers with a grimace.

Nathaniel didn't need telling twice. He mounted the steps up to the carriage, watching his muddy shoes, rather than the faces around him. He knew what fate awaited him the moment the carriage door closed, and he didn't want to see whether the officers knew it, too.

To Nathaniel's surprise, the Commissioner remained silent for the duration of their ride back to the manor. Truth be told, Nathaniel would have preferred the alternative. He could bear his father's anger, even at its worst, far better than the agony of waiting. The longer the Commissioner said nothing, the more Nathaniel's imagination explored the many ways in which he'd disappointed him—all equally legitimate, equally heinous. How could he have thought this would make his father happy?

But even though he'd broken all his father's rules to do it, Nathaniel had still achieved so much. Maybe he hadn't caught the Technician yet, but he'd come so close—closer than his father's officers had, at any rate. Surely his father would see that he was only trying to help—that he did not mean his actions in the spirit of rebellion.

When the Commissioner finally spoke, it was in a voice so quiet Nathaniel could barely hear him.

"I have no adequate words to describe the disloyalty—the dis-honor—of your actions today." He hissed the words through his teeth. "I thought we understood one another, but once again I hear from my officers you've disobeyed me, leaving the Settlement on your own. I have either underestimated your disregard for rules or overestimated your ability to comprehend them."

Nathaniel kept his lips tightly pressed together. No good would come from interrupting his father.

"Which is it, Nathaniel? Are you a delinquent or an imbecile?"

Nathaniel stayed silent, determined to say nothing that would upset his father more. As he tightened his grip on his leg, metal returned his touch. The locket, so small that it barely made an impression on his hand, gave him hope. Even more, it gave him courage.

"Neither," Nathaniel whispered.

The Commissioner snarled. "Then tell me, what business that is neither idiotic nor disobedient were you engaged in today?"

Nathaniel looked up, finally catching his father's eye. He wished he hadn't. The cold brown stare that met his made Nathaniel's insides shrivel. He squeezed the locket in his pocket as though it held the key to his bravery.

"I just— I wanted to do something for you, Father." Nathaniel found it easier to keep his head up if he let his vision slip out of focus. "I know being Commissioner takes its toll. I thought if I could help carry that burden you might see—I might show you— that I can take on more responsibilities."

"More responsibilities?" The Commissioner's voice turned sharp, but at least he wasn't whispering anymore. "You think you deserve my trust after all this? That's twice in the past month you've disobeyed my rules."

Thrice, if he counted sneaking into the officers' bunker, but Nathaniel wasn't about to admit a third offense. "I'm sorry, Father. I just thought if I—"

"If you what? What could you possibly have been doing outside the Settlement's walls that would impress me?"

The carriage stopped, making the silence that followed even more permeable. Nathaniel's breathing and his heartbeat—*ticks*— were too loud, too strong.

"I was tracking the Technician," Nathaniel said in a small voice.

Silence built between them like an invisible wall, and Nathaniel braced for impact.

But then the Commissioner laughed—he *laughed*!

"The Technician, you say?" His shoulders shook. "My son, you must stop wasting your time on such things. You're embarrassing yourself." He shot Nathaniel a piercing look, all humor gone from his eyes. "And you embarrass me. You must give up this silly notion of catching the Technician. You'll get yourself killed trying."

Nathaniel didn't think it silly, though it was certainly not the time to admit it. The Technician brought only terror to the Settlement—circumnavigating every hole in the Commissioner's laws until they barely applied to him at all. The man was both ghost and goblin, wreaking havoc and ruin through his deeds, but even more so through his ideas, his whispers. If Anna spoke the truth, there were more like her—like Nathaniel. The Tarnished and their movement had not died with his father's rise to power, but remained a very real presence in the Settlement.

The Commissioner sighed, surveying Nathaniel. "If you promise me no more of this recklessness, and truly show me that you mean it, perhaps we can revisit the idea of responsibility." He pushed open the carriage door. "Not one of the men in my army could find the Technician. Whatever made you think you could succeed where they did not?" He shook his head as he began to walk away. "The man who brings me the Technician will be the very best among us, you mark my words. Leave it to the experts, Nathaniel."

The Commissioner left Nathaniel in the carriage with only his shame for company. But his father was right. Nathaniel wasn't a soldier; he was the Commissioner's son. Disloyal and dishonorable he might be, but he was also determined. He would become an expert, and he would show the Commissioner that he—Nathaniel, the frail boy who'd failed him over and over again—was truly the very best among them.

CHAPTER ELEVEN

Anna's mind wound in circles. She didn't usually let anything distract her. She was focused—like she was red-haired or tall. But something about Nathaniel had left her thoughts scattered. When she returned to Mechan, she bypassed the front door and looped around the back, eager to avoid Thatcher at all costs. They'd not spoken since their fight, and Anna had no intention of breaking the record. She'd check on Roman, then slip quietly back to her workshop.

"Roman," she whispered as she cracked open the door.

The little boy's eyes flew open, a smile winging its way onto his face. "Anna!"

Anna's chest swelled to hear his voice had returned to a normal tone, no longer scratchy the way it had been that first day. "How's my brave boy feeling?"

"Pirate! I'm a brave pirate!" Roman hit the blanket atop him with his hand.

"Of course you are. The bravest!" Anna leaned in to ruffle his hair. She tried not to do it too often, but it was just so fluffy, and standing, he was the perfect height for her to rest her hand. "Is the great Pirate Roman up for a little adventure?"

Roman quirked his lips, seeming to consider for a moment. "Will there be plundering?"

"We can't be sure of any plunder, but I can promise a surprise." She held out her hand. "What do you say?"

Roman placed his hand in hers and let her help him to his feet. The trek across Thatcher's lawn to the workshop didn't take as long as she'd expected. Children certainly recovered quickly, she would give them that. Still, Roman leaned against her as they walked, though Anna couldn't tell if he needed her support or if he just liked being close to her.

When Anna approached the door of her faded blue workshop, Roman squealed with glee. "Are we going inside? Will you let me hammer something?"

Anna didn't like to think of what Roman might accomplish with a hammer, so she maneuvered around the question. "I had something a tad more exciting in mind." She pushed open the door, letting Roman half stumble, half skip past her. "How would you like to see your birthday present early?"

Roman's sky-blue eyes popped in his head. "Show me! Show me!"

Anna raised an eyebrow at him, doing her best impression of Ruby's cross expression.

"Please, Auntie Anna. Please show me the present." Roman's lower lip quivered.

Anna beckoned. "This way."

She led Roman between her two workbenches. He tried to climb up, but she had to stop him. It wouldn't be worth all the smiles in the world if he ripped his stitches so soon after surgery. From inside a wooden box, Anna removed a small metal arm. She'd built the framework over the course of several years, creating a dozen prototypes before she'd gotten the right design. This one would be the final product once she finished it—*if* she finished it.

"This is going to be for you." Anna lowered the arm to Roman's eye level.

Roman frowned, staring at the intricate metalwork. "What am I going to do with it?"

"Wear it, silly! See, it will fit here and here." She pointed to the connecting points on the metal cuff and then at his shoulder. "Then you'll be able to do everything with two arms—like sailing your mighty pirate ship!"

"Running." Roman still didn't smile. "Pirates are just stories and games—I want to be a runner like my papa when I'm grown so I can protect you and Mama."

Anna found it suddenly difficult to swallow.

"Won't it be heavy?" Roman asked.

"I used the lightest metal I could, but you'll need to work hard and eat your vegetables so you can grow up to be strong enough to use it."

Fear flickered in his large blue eyes. "Will it hurt?" Roman asked, holding his shoulder.

Anna didn't lie to Roman—she'd made that promise to herself a long time ago. "Yes."

Only then did a grin cross Roman's face. "Cool!" He reached to touch the metal but drew back. "Can I touch it?"

"Of course. Thank you for asking." Anna's chest swelled with pride. What a thoughtful child he'd grown into.

Roman fiddled with the joints in each finger, giggling and gasping as he discovered the full capabilities of the limb.

"You'll be able to do all that once you're big enough to use it, just like your other arm."

Roman cocked his head. "Do I need it?"

Anna had never considered that before. Whenever she made a limb for a client, they'd asked her to. They'd come to her, requested her services. But Roman had never asked for anything but her love—and occasionally something to hammer. Surely someday Roman would need a second arm if he became a runner like Dalton. But as she pondered it, the word *need* felt less and less appropriate.

"I think you get to decide that," Anna said finally. Maybe they weren't the right words, but they were the words she had. "I don't have anything you can hammer, but how would you like to take this apart?" She held up a silver pocket watch and a screwdriver, which Roman took gleefully.

After returning Roman to his recovery room (a room he'd be able to vacate soon, if his energy during their excursion was anything to go by), Anna found her grandfather waiting for her. Thatcher had placed himself between her and the exit, blocking her escape.

"You left the village." Thatcher nodded to the mud caked on her boots.

Anna's breath hitched. She didn't want to explain herself. She shouldn't have to.

"You have to stop. It's too dangerous."

"I can handle myself." Anna's voice rumbled.

Thatcher shook his head, locking the wheels of his chair. "I mean, it's too dangerous for the entire village. What do you suppose will happen if you're followed or captured?"

Anna gritted her teeth. "I won't be."

"You don't know what the Commissioner is like." Thatcher's words came as a whisper, but they still echoed through the house.

"And you do?"

"I do." Thatcher let out a long sigh. "I know the pain of the Commissioner's cruelty firsthand. If he sets his mind to it, he can learn anything from anyone. Believe me, you aren't prepared for his particular brand of torture."

"I won't be told what I can and cannot do. I won't stop helping my clients."

"You have to. For the preservation of Mechan, you have to stop." Again, Thatcher's whisper caught her like a spider's web, holding her there.

"Why do you care so much about Mechan? It's just a town—that's not the same as human lives."

"It's not just a town." Thatcher sighed heavily. "Mechan is freedom. You've never known anything other than this life. You have lived outside a world ruled by misunderstanding and walls. I suppose it's only natural that you don't see it the same way." He unlocked his chair and turned so he faced the window. "We have something here worth protecting."

Anna's stomach clenched. She was worth protecting; her clients were worth protecting. Why couldn't Thatcher see that?

"What would you have me do? Let my clients fend for themselves?" For the second time that day, Anna was struck by the absurdity of defending her right to save lives. Though Nathaniel and Thatcher argued for two separate sides, they essentially wanted the same thing: preservation at the cost of human life. "What of my new client? He has a TICCER, you know. How is he supposed to live without my help? His original surgeon can't help him, and there are no other mechanics." But she couldn't be sure if that was even true.

"He has a TICCER," Thatcher echoed, placing his face in his palms and shaking his head. "How has he survived without maintenance?"

Anna eyed him. There was no way Thatcher knew Nathaniel hadn't had any maintenance, not unless . . .

"You're the other mechanic, aren't you?" She took a step toward him. "His TICCER—it's like mine. You installed it. You installed it, and then you abandoned him."

"I didn't think he'd live." Thatcher buried his face farther into his arms, pulling at his graying hair. "I never expected— I did the right thing. I helped him when he needed me, and I protected my own. His family could have protected him if they'd wanted to."

Anna's jaw dropped. "How old was he when you gave him a TICCER? A year, maybe two? You thought by letting a baby die, you were saving your precious way of life? You thought Mechan was more important than his life?"

Thatcher snapped his head up to reveal red rings around his eyes but dry cheeks. "I thought *your* life was more important than his."

"*My* life?" Anna's arms prickled, and she curled them around her middle, gripping at her sides as if she could pull his choice from within herself, tear it from the past, and hold it up to the light to see for herself.

"Weighing the value of human life is a delicate business, Deirdre-Anne. I do not pretend to be an expert. I did only what my conscience allowed and I cannot regret that." Thatcher paused. "Stay away from the boy."

"I won't leave him to die!"

Thatcher sighed, his eyes boring into hers with a sadness she couldn't account for. "Your pride is as much poison as it is elixir. You are not untouchable, nor are you invincible."

Anna's legs regained feeling as her blood rushed with anger, but before she could reply, Thatcher spun his chair, turning to face her.

"You don't know who he is, do you?"

Anna's stomach dropped as she shook her head.

Thatcher sighed, reaching for the kettle. Anna should have known he would need tea for such a weighty conversation. Once it had been brewed and poured, Thatcher gestured for her to sit opposite him at the kitchen table before speaking.

"You were too young to remember, but before we built Mechan, we lived in the Settlement. It wasn't ideal, but it was home." He threaded his fingers through the mug handle, gripping it tight. "I ran a clinic without fear of persecution, living strictly by the law, helping where I could. Not all my patients lived—and some still haunt me to this day. But everything changed when Commissioner Fremont took office."

Anna sat rigid in her chair. Thatcher had seldom spoken of his life in the Settlement, never lingering on the details of a time before her parents' deaths. She'd asked, of course, but his answers had never satisfied her curiosity, the pain in his eyes telling her far more than his words ever did.

"With the new Commissioner came new laws, new ways to prevent me from treating my patients. And suddenly, children were getting sick with Tarnish. They needed a doctor—in many cases, a surgeon. Sometimes I could help, but as you know well, more often than not I couldn't."

Anna swallowed. The lives lost on Thatcher's table hung heavy on her shoulders, too.

"You come from a long line of rebels, Deirdre-Anne. Your mother had a passion for justice, and your father a defiant streak not unlike your own." Thatcher shook his head, eyes closed. "I never thought I'd find myself here, but they knew all along it was a battle we couldn't win. We were too few, too sick, and the Commissioner too powerful. Your parents didn't stand a chance."

"The Commissioner killed them?" Anna asked, remembering the brief explanation he'd supplied in her childhood.

"I thought so." Thatcher opened his eyes again, new energy in his voice. "When they failed to come home night after night, I thought all was lost. I mourned then—for my child and the grand-child I barely knew."

Thatcher's hand encircled her own, and though Anna's first instinct was to pull away, the tremor in his voice stopped her.

"When they issued the warrant for my arrest, I had no lack of options. Neighbors promised to shield me, and former patients offered to help me escape the city. But I had no reason to flee. If the Commissioner wanted my head, I'd make sure he looked me in the eye before taking it." He inhaled deeply, eyeing Anna as though he was considering her worth. "What you must under-stand is that I had always known too much about tech. The Commissioner—and those who came before him—already knew who I was."

Anna pulled her hand away. Though Thatcher might indulge in sentimentality, she couldn't find the energy to spend emotions on his regrets. "What did the Commissioner want?"

Thatcher chuckled. "He wanted my help, of all things. His son, barely older than you were, was ill—in desperate need of a doctor—and your parents knew exactly who to call."

"The warrant was only a trick?"

"It worked, and lucky it did. The Commissioner's son was destined for an early death. He bore all the signs of heart disease—of Tarnish. I'd never treated it with any lasting success before, and with the technology allowed, I could do very little."

Anna's jaw dropped as the pieces began to fall into place.

"I built that boy a TICCER—out of an old clock they had on hand—in exchange for your life. You're alive because he's alive, but I—" He took in a sharp breath. "I never expected him to live this long. After we left the Settlement and you developed a similar condition, and I saw the many faults of my design, I was sure: Without my help, that boy should have died years ago. But it seems you, of all people, found him."

"Do you mean—"

"Your new client is the Commissioner's son."

Anna's blood ran cold. How could she have been so naive? And yet, how could she have known? Settlement politics interested her only when they concerned her, and since the Commissioner's laws applied only to those who cared, she hadn't paid any attention to the succession—she hadn't even been aware that the Commissioner had an heir.

"You knew all along," Anna growled. But she couldn't be angry with Thatcher, not when she'd spent all her anger on Nathaniel, though her anger at him was misdirected, too. He'd done nothing suspect. Perhaps he truly was just a young man with metal he didn't understand. Maybe it didn't matter who his father was. "Why didn't you tell me sooner?"

Thatcher raised his eyebrows. "I'm telling you now."

"But I could have— If I'd known—"

"Are you telling me, Deirdre-Anne, that if you'd known, you'd have stayed away?" He sipped at his tea. "I don't believe for a moment you would have let this mystery go. I know I certainly haven't."

Anna, who had risen halfway out of her seat, paused, hand gripping the edge of the table. "What mystery?"

Thatcher tilted his head, raised an eyebrow, and said simply, "Him."

Any other time, any other day, Anna might have pressed him, might have made him say it, but the truth stared her in the face like a reflection. She'd been so wrapped up in trying to understand why he shared her exact tech, she'd failed to see the bigger picture.

"He's the only one," she whispered. Out of all her patients from the Settlement, she'd never come across one with a TICCER until Nathaniel. She'd never given it much thought—perhaps children with Tarnish simply died in the Settlement. Without the proper care, it made sense.

But what if it wasn't a matter of high mortality, but a lack of patients altogether?

"Why do only those of us in Mechan need TICCERs?" Anna asked, all accusation gone from her tone.

Thatcher lowered his gaze. "I don't know."

Anna opened her mouth to argue—he always knew. Thatcher had never before admitted defeat, so why now? But it didn't matter. Nathaniel was the key.

Thatcher swirled the remaining liquid in his mug. "All I know is that before I left the Settlement, Tarnish had just begun to spread. I only installed the one TICCER—the technology didn't even exist until I made it for that boy—and now it's the most common surgery I perform." He sighed heavily. "The Commissioner's son is the only boy from the Settlement ever to cross my operating table, and the Settlement has seen no significant drop in its population. The facts are thus: We are still sick, and they are not."

Anna sank back into her chair, thoughts swimming wildly in her mind. "The Commissioner's son," she whispered, putting her head in her hands. "But he seemed so genuine, like he truly wanted my help!"

"Deirdre-Anne, just because someone is not who you expect doesn't mean they are the opposite."

Anna narrowed her eyes. How could Nathaniel be anything but the enemy? He was the child of a cruel and discriminatory leader, but he was also like her, one of Thatcher's patients. She couldn't imagine what he must have endured living with a father who legislated against his very nature. She should have seen it in his eyes or in his tech—maybe in his words. But Thatcher, who had known Nathaniel only as an infant and had felt the wrath of the Commissioner firsthand, looked past Nathaniel's position to recognize his humanity.

Anna looked up, catching Thatcher's gaze. "I thought you didn't want me meeting him again."

Thatcher nodded solemnly. "He is more danger to you than you are help to him." He quirked his lips. "But you might yet help someone. Mechan still needs you. We're getting sicker by the day—Roman is proof of that—but perhaps if you focus your training, you can save us all. You're treating symptoms by patching him up. Think like a physician instead. Visualize the entire problem and diagnose; do not simply apply the bandage."

But Anna wasn't a physician; she was a mechanic. She knew how to fix things with her hands, how to break something and rebuild it better. She didn't do what Thatcher did. She didn't know how to diagnose, how to unravel truths.

But the mystery burned bright against the insides of her mind, keeping her awake long into the night, looking for answers where she hadn't known there was even a question.

CHAPTER TWELVE

When Nathaniel ventured down to the dining room for breakfast the following morning, the Commissioner sat at one end of the long table, politely chewing a scone.

Nathaniel took a surprisingly painless breath before sitting opposite him.

"I highly recommend the marmalade."

"I like them plain."

"Trust me," said the Commissioner, a hard look on his face. He slid a dish across the table. It landed beside Nathaniel's plate, a dollop of jam oozing between the dishes.

He took the offered dish and applied a conservative amount to his breakfast.

The Commissioner allowed his son to eat in peace for exactly five minutes before he pushed away his own plate. "Come along now, Nathaniel."

Nathaniel glanced up from his half-eaten biscuit, feeling some of the undesired jam making its way down his chin. "Where?"

"Since it appears you lack the discipline to structure your own learning, I will lend you some of mine. I will not allow you to continue in this ruinous fashion." He sighed, waiting for Nathaniel to stand. "You were right about one thing, however: It's time you were given more responsibilities. Beginning today, you will attend my council meetings with me."

Nathaniel winced as his father's words cut through him like blades. He couldn't disagree. He *had* lacked discipline as of late. The stack of unread tomes on his desk proved that much, as did his muddy boots, set aside for the servants to clean. Still, he'd gotten what he wanted, hadn't he? His father had invited him into the weekly council meeting. It was a step forward.

So why did it feel like he'd been pushed backward?

As Nathaniel followed his father toward the council chambers, he tried to banish the feeling of self-pity, but it was embedded in him like the metal around his heart. A leader wouldn't feel sorry for himself. His father would never feel sorry for himself.

The room awaiting him on the other side of the doors was wide and expansive—more like a theater than the sort of meeting hall he had imagined. Chairs fanned out in rows from a large wooden table at the center of the room. The reddish wood was carved with leaves and reaching, spiraling vines, reflective of Earth Adjacent's mission to preserve the natural world. The walls, too, were painted with a mural of nature. Large trees towered overhead, stretching toward a cloudless sky. The whole room gave the illusion that they were outside.

"Sit." The Commissioner indicated a chair to his left.

Nathaniel did as he'd been told and laced his fingers together to wait for the rest of the councilors to arrive. A flood of men and women he mostly knew by sight began trickling in, filling the seats on all sides so that curious eyes met his wherever he looked.

"Order." The Commissioner's word halted the chatter that filled the room to its rafters. "As you've no doubt noticed, my son, Nathaniel, is joining us today. He will do so as a matter of practice in the future. As he is shadowing me for the sake of his education, you may carry on as though he is not present. He will be a silent observer of our proceedings."

Nathaniel flushed and dropped his gaze. Perhaps it was for the best; no one would want to hear what he had to say. *Anna did*, said the voice in his head, but Nathaniel had always been too afraid to listen to anyone but his father. Still, in recent days, Nathaniel had listened to Anna, too. Perhaps he was not so cowardly after all.

Perhaps someday he could even be brave.

"Councilor Ming, if you please." The Commissioner sat.

A short man Nathaniel recognized promptly bounded from his seat to press a small button at the center table. A hologram flickered into life and a woman appeared, her image an icy shade of blue. Queen Elizabeth swept the room with a veiled gaze. Even though the Queen was his family, Nathaniel had never met her. He was glad of it—if her hologram sent chills down his spine, he shuddered to think what she might be like in person.

The Commissioner and the councilors stood and bowed to her; Nathaniel followed suit.

"Begin." Her voice carried, lacking the peppery quality of the aged Councilor Ming's.

"First on the agenda is a petition with"—the Commissioner paused to glance down at his paper—"one hundred and fifty signatures." He handed the paper to Councilor Ming.

The councilor bent over the paper and began to read: "'We the people of the Planetary Settlement petition the high office of the Commissioner and his wise council to consider revising Tech

Decree Twenty-Eight, which bans all uses of technology on the human body. We ask for an addendum defining the scope of this law and its impact on medical technology.'"

"Do we even need to discuss this?" The Commissioner glanced around at the councilors, soliciting obedience with his eyes.

"This is the third such petition we've received in a month," said a bearded councilor at the end of the hall.

The councilor beside Nathaniel shook her head. "You'd think they would tire of being told no."

Nathaniel's mind raced. He would have liked to discuss it, if only to understand the full scope of the petition first, but the assembled councilors either did not share Nathaniel's curiosity or did not dare raise opposition to the Commissioner.

"There is no room for movement on this government's stance on tech. I move to have this petition dismissed." The Commissioner looked to the councilors for agreement.

"You're not even going to consider it?" Nathaniel asked, the words escaping his lips before he could rein them in.

The Commissioner eyed him darkly. Nathaniel stared at the table, not daring to look up.

"What was that? Speak up." The Queen's voice boomed through the hall, commanding a power even the Commissioner could not. It was a marvel Nathaniel was related to either of them, his own voice so small.

The Commissioner grabbed the back of Nathaniel's shirt, pulling him into a standing position. "Speak up for the Queen," he snarled.

Nathaniel, still unable to look at his father, cleared his throat. "I— It's only . . . If you've received this petition three times, might that speak to a larger disquiet among the populace?"

Councilor Ming nodded, and others exchanged thoughtful glances among themselves.

Emboldened by their reaction, he continued. "Furthermore, our definition of technology as referred to by these laws is wildly insufficient. It does no one any good to govern on such broad and ill-defined parameters. It seems to me these petitioners seek only to clarify that definition." The words he spoke were his own, but Anna's voice reverberated in his head. He hadn't meant to echo her, though he was surprised at how softly her sentiments landed on his tongue.

The Queen finally broke the silence that followed. "Well said. Well said, indeed." Her veiled face rotated slightly toward the Commissioner. "Oliver, you do not give the boy enough credit. He has found a weakness in your laws where others have not—or at least *he* has the integrity to voice his concerns."

At these words, the councilors exchanged nervous glances. A few murmured noncommittally.

The Commissioner set his jaw, closing his eyes for a moment. "I will not entertain these petitions without first ensuring the safety of the Settlement."

Nathaniel cocked his head, remembering Anna's words. The Tarnished posed no threat to the Settlement if what she'd said was true. She and her fellow tech users simply wanted to be left alone. Why, then, did the Commissioner act as though the Settlement was in constant peril?

The Queen did not appear fazed by the Commissioner's fear-mongering, and she continued as though he'd not spoken. "Who here agrees that we must clarify these definitions before responding to such petitions?"

Slamming his fist down on the desk, the Commissioner turned

an ashy white and barked, "There will be no petitions while the Technician roams free!"

Stunned silence permeated the room for a moment before the Queen shook her veiled head. "Commissioner, it would behoove you to remember you are not the only one in this room with the power to make decisions."

"You dare give orders in *my* council room?" the Commissioner growled.

"I'll *dare* as I please, Commissioner." The Queen jostled her shoulders as if laughing silently. "But I was referring, of course, to your council. Now, revisiting the language in Tech Decree Twenty-Eight to clarify the Settlement's definition of tech—call for a vote."

The Commissioner didn't move.

After a few beats of stillness, Councilor Ming cleared his throat. "All those in favor?"

Every hand in the room shot up in approval, with the notable exception of the Commissioner's.

"Well, you have your survey," said the Queen, gesturing to the many hands in the air. "I would remind you, Commissioner, to interrogate how your doctrine of rigidity serves our greater cause. I admire your commitment to preservation, if not your methods, but we must first seek to build. For without a planetary home that welcomes us all, what is truly worth preserving?"

"Your Majesty." The Commissioner bowed, grinding his teeth.

The Queen's image disappeared. But where the Queen's face had been, the Commissioner's appeared as he crossed the room. A small, spiteful smile tugged the edges of his lips, warning of the punishment yet to come for Nathaniel's insolence.

Nathaniel should never have opened his mouth.

CHAPTER THIRTEEN

A summons from the Queen could come at any time. Eliza had learned this early in her career as the Queen's Eyes, once roused from slumber in the middle of the night by a pinging on her wall com. But nothing—not even her beauty rest—was more important than the Queen's time.

Today, the Queen's com arrived in the middle of an arduous afternoon tea with Lady Beatrix and her cohorts. Eliza secured herself a place in the outer ring where she could lounge and read old scannings of Judith Butler and Sappho from her wrist tab, undetected by the other courtiers. She'd only just looked up from her reading to discover Lord Farley eyeing her from across the room, a combination of terror and fury on his face.

After their last encounter, Eliza didn't fancy entertaining the lord, so when her wrist tab pinged with the Queen's message, she was glad to excuse herself.

When Eliza arrived, the Queen's door slid open and the Queen beckoned her forward.

"Eliza, dear. Do sit down," the Queen said. "I believe I interrupted your tea with Lady Beatrix, but fear not. I've made alternate arrangements." She gestured to a deep blue teapot on her desk.

Eliza sat opposite her, and though she'd had her fill of tea and sandwiches already, she accepted the Queen's offer.

"We need to discuss the details of your mission," the Queen said.

Pleasantries never did last long with the Queen.

"I've just finished quite a revealing discussion with the Commissioner and his council," she continued, lacing her fingers together on her desk. "It certainly reaffirmed my decision to send you—and now is the opportune moment for your entrance. I believe the Commissioner and his government are primed for infiltration, especially of your subtle variety."

Eliza nodded slowly. She'd known her marriage to Nathaniel would be a front for something, but the Queen had yet to relay what.

"The government is fractured. They follow the Commissioner, of course, as law dictates they must, but his councilors are easily swayed by pretty words." The Queen laughed. "The body politic is at a crossroads, indeed."

"And I'm to destabilize it?" Eliza asked.

"Destabilize it? Stars, no! Nothing quite so radical." The Queen dismissed the idea with a wave of her hand. "No, my son—the Commissioner—has a secret, and I need you to discover it for me."

Eliza's breath caught. Finding secrets was her specialty, though it hadn't always been. Three years ago, Eliza and her classmates had each been given a slip of paper on which to pen a secret. Then the Queen had instructed them to protect it at all costs. Only those whose secrets went undiscovered but who also revealed a classmate's secret would advance to the next round of the Queen's game. It forced them to be guarded but also to strike. It taught Eliza balance.

So, too, had it taught her trust.

"What kind of secret?" Eliza asked in barely a whisper.

The Queen readjusted her veil but did not answer, just as Eliza knew she wouldn't. It was not in the Queen's nature to instruct with precision. It left room for interpretation, room for Eliza to find more than what the Queen intended. It made Eliza better at her job.

Three years ago, it had almost been Eliza's downfall. The secret she'd committed to ink, perhaps foolishly, had been true. *I'd like to kiss Marla*, she'd written. It was a secret, after all, and no one was ever supposed to see it. Eliza was the best, and she was going to win—not even Marla and her pretty green eyes could stop her.

Only, of course they *could*. Eliza had been young. She'd been driven and focused, but still young, and Marla was far better at the Queen's game of secrets than Eliza had anticipated. Eliza's run should have been over when Marla's pot of tea had her sleeping soundly at the other girl's table. When Eliza woke, her secret was neatly folded next to the saucer.

Eliza didn't know what to make of it. Marla could have culled the competition then. Eliza *was* the biggest threat—though Marla would not know to what extent for weeks to come—and ending it then would have been the smart move. But Marla always followed her heart, not her head, and Eliza found she loved her for it. Instead, Marla lied, uncovering another girl's secret instead of Eliza's, and the pair of them advanced to the next round.

The following night, Eliza found a different slip of paper beneath her pillow: *I am simply infatuated with Eliza.*

Marla had not broken the rules; she'd circumnavigated them. The Queen had left them room to interpret, and they'd filled the space with the true joy of a first love.

Now Eliza would fill it with false love for a boy she'd never want. She would spin herself a lie so strong, not even Nathaniel Fremont would know the difference, and just as Marla had helped her achieve her dreams then, she'd ally herself once more to find this secret, too.

"So Nathaniel Fremont is not my target?" Eliza asked finally, landing on a safer question.

"He's a troublesome boy, from what I've observed," the Queen replied.

"You've met him, then?" But as she said the words, she was reminded that Nathaniel Fremont was not simply a boy to the Queen; he was her grandson. He'd been born to such privilege, while Eliza still had to work for only a fraction of what he'd achieved by circumstance. She'd prove herself ten times over, out-match him in every test of espionage, and still he would be the Queen's in a way Eliza never could be.

"Not in the flesh." The Queen shook her head, indicating the holocom on her desk. "He was present at today's council meeting. I daresay, he's reckless and rebellious, but brighter than his father thinks. He should be an easy mark, but be wary. Start by gaining his confidence."

"And what next?"

"First, the boy." The Queen pushed away from the desk. "The rest will follow."

"You can trust me," Eliza whispered, not meaning to say the words aloud.

"I keep this secret to protect you, Eliza. The fewer who know, the safer everyone will be." The Queen sighed and gripped the edge of her veil with gloved fingers. "Some secrets are like a blade, their vengeance swift and concentrated. Others are like a pestilence, spreading without prejudice, and I fear not everyone it touches will deserve the affliction."

Eliza shuddered involuntarily. "Yes, Your Majesty."

"You'll have a fair amount of time, never fear." The Queen stood, her imperious shadow falling across Eliza. "The Commissioner won't act against me just yet. He can't afford to use what he knows publicly until he catches some outlaw—the Technician." Her veil swayed dramatically as if she rolled her entire head, not just her eyes. "The Commissioner's warped sense of power may be a boon for once."

"The Technician?" Eliza had never heard the name before, but of course she paid little attention to planetary events. She made a mental note to research the outlaw later.

The Queen gestured for Eliza to rise and led her toward the door. "Remember: If he catches the Technician, your time is up."

Eliza took her leave, feeling no more informed than she'd been upon arriving, but she knew the Queen's words would steep in her mind like tea until the proper time, dormant until awakened as if by magic.

Secrets had always served her well. Secrets were warm, tucked beneath her ribs like muscle, wrapped around her arms like cloth. But this one was different. This secret had turned against her, a cold blade pressed upon her skin. It would not do to fight it, not when she was so close to achieving everything she wanted. Instead, she would wrap her fingers around this secret and draw it close— make it her own.

CHAPTER FOURTEEN

Anna didn't like asking for help. Perhaps she'd learned the habit from living with Thatcher, whose assistance always came with a healthy dose of lecture. But Anna could not do *this* alone.

If every case of Tarnish occurred in Mechan—apart from Nathaniel, of course—then there had to be a reason. After some careful thought, it seemed clear enough to Anna: Someone must be poisoning Mechan.

And as far as Anna was concerned, it had to be the Commissioner. Poisoning the town certainly wasn't outside the scope of the Commissioner's brand of evil, never mind that he didn't know where Mechan was. Anna would work out that flaw in her theory later. First, Anna needed to put aside her pride, and her habits, for she needed more than medicine and machinery. If a poison had caused Tarnish, she'd need alchemy to combat it.

Anna knew only one alchemist, and she was dead. Ruby's mother, lost to the Commissioner's men some ten years ago, had been a light in a harsh world during Anna's childhood. Most of her memories involved the woman with a skip in her step and a spin in her skirts. Her death had been a blow, but to Ruby most of all— another untimely death in her family.

Anna knocked three times on the green painted door of Ruby's house.

"Anna?" Ruby asked, opening the door and letting Anna inside. "What are you doing here so early? Roman's still sleeping; you'll have to wait if you want to take him on a walk."

Anna shook her head. Though she'd promised to take Roman on a walk every day now that he'd returned to his mother's house (and his stamina and distance were increasing at an impressive rate), her reasons for visiting were entirely selfish. "I'm not here for Roman."

Ruby pursed her lips. "Truth be told, I wish you wouldn't take him on so many outings." She held up a hand at Anna's protest. "I know he needs the exercise, but he's developing such an adventurous streak. I worry he'll wander off one day."

Anna laughed. The thought of Roman—needy, loving Roman—running off was almost too absurd to consider. "I'll try not to be such a horrid influence on him."

Ruby didn't smile with her. "Since we're on the subject, for days he's talked of nothing but some metal arm you made him."

"Oh! Does he like it?" Anna took hold of the new conversation thread gladly, but Ruby's disapproval still didn't sit well with her. "I've been working on it for months."

"He does." Ruby crossed her arms. "I don't."

"I—" Anna flinched.

"He's a seven-year-old child, Anna. What did you think you were doing, showing him that arm?"

Anna took a step back, nearly colliding with the closed door. "I *thought* it was a kind gesture. He needed cheering, and it seemed to lift his spirits well enough."

Ruby's expression darkened. "Do you know what he asked me last night? He asked if he was *broken*."

Anna opened her mouth to speak, but Ruby cut her off.

"I've worked tirelessly to make sure that boy feels loved—to ensure he knows that he is enough exactly the way he is." She crossed her arms. "How do you justify telling him that he is less than he ought to be?"

"I didn't! I would never . . ."

But she had. Not in so many words, exactly, but she remembered the odd confusion on Roman's face when she'd shown him the arm. Even he had seen her gift for what it really was.

"I'm sorry."

Ruby nodded once. "Good." She gestured to a pair of brown armchairs. "Now sit down and speak your piece. Why have you come to call so early?"

"I need your help."

Ruby moved to the kitchen and poured two mugs of tea. "With what?"

Half-truths had no place between Anna and Ruby, and Thatcher's words rang through Anna's mind so loudly, she was sure Ruby could hear them, too: *Visualize the entire problem and diagnose; do not simply apply the bandage.*

Anna sucked in a deep breath. "I want to find a cure."

Ruby offered Anna her choice of chipped mugs and sat beside her. "You what?"

"I spend so much time treating heart disease with tech. But I have no inkling of what causes the damage in the first place. I think if I can diagnose the problem, then I can find a solution, not just a patch like the TICCER. A real cure."

Ruby sipped her tea, a cautious smile tugging at her lips. "Thatcher got to you."

"What makes you say that?" Anna hated the defensive tremor in her voice.

"You don't say things like *diagnose*. That's a Thatcher word, if ever I heard one."

Anna grimaced. Her eyes darted to the bottles of salves and tonics on the kitchen counter. "I'm not an alchemist, either, which is why I need your help."

"No!" Ruby set her mug down forcefully, tea sloshing over the side. "No, no, no."

"You don't even know what I'm going—"

"Not a chance! I make tonics. That's it. I'm not an alchemist. I'm not my mother." Ruby leaned back in her chair, her eyes frantic.

"And I'm not asking you to be! If you would just hear me out—"

"I swear, Anna, if you think for even a second . . . You saw what happened to my mother."

"Alchemy didn't kill your mother."

Ruby's eyes were daggers. "You treat the law like a machine you can take apart and reassemble to fit the life you want to live, Anna. It's dangerous, and it's deadly."

"What law? It's not like we live in the Settlement."

Ruby stood, backing away toward the kitchen. "I was only a little older than Roman is now when my mother died. Maybe you can't understand what that's like, but I won't make Roman an orphan—not again."

"I *do* understand. My parents are dead, too, remember?"

Ruby's hands shook. "You still have Thatcher. I have no one."

Anna's stomach clenched. Thatcher had raised her, taught her, but never loved her. Anna was not generous enough anymore to call that family. She'd been alone a long time.

It was easier that way.

Anna lowered her voice. "Think about the good we could do, Ruby. Think about all the people we could help—all the *children* we could save."

"Don't bring children into it. I can't . . . Don't make me choose." She pressed a hand against her stomach. The unborn child she carried couldn't yet breathe or scream, but someday its heart would beat an arrhythmic beat, and Thatcher would have to crack open its chest to put metal inside.

Anna crossed the room to join Ruby at the kitchen counter, the whisper of an idea forming on her tongue. "What if you didn't have to actually perform the alchemy?"

"I don't see how that—"

"You could teach me. That way you wouldn't be putting yourself in any danger." Anna grinned, rather pleased with herself for such an ingenious plan, but Ruby shook her head.

"Alchemy isn't something you can learn in a day." She rubbed the sides of her face, pulling brown skin tight over her cheekbones. "It isn't as simple as tossing ingredients together and hoping. It isn't like learning to cook. You have to understand the elements and the breakdown of . . ." She let out a long sigh. "Listen, Anna, I know you mean well, but alchemy isn't just some trade. It's something my mother and I shared—until it got her arrested and killed. I'm not ready to revisit it."

"But—"

"I won't argue about this." Ruby stalked away, disappearing behind her bedroom door, leaving Anna with little more than hampered spirits and a mug of lukewarm tea.

Anna made her way back home, trying to imagine what it must be like for Ruby. Ruby's mother had died, but that wasn't exactly the alchemy's fault. It certainly didn't justify Ruby turning away from this opportunity. How she could let one accident keep her from helping, Anna couldn't understand.

Except . . . she could.

Anna felt the same way about surgery. It took only one mistake—one careless stroke with a scalpel—to turn a completely salvageable arm into a residuum. And Ruby was right: Anna couldn't fix that mistake with a metal arm. Roman wasn't a machine to be fixed. He was a happy, human boy.

When Anna returned to her workshop, a mess of metal greeted her on the other side. Usually, her workshop was comfortable. But now every gear and cog reminded her that anything she could do with steel would never be enough—would never mend the world.

Hours later, when a knock sounded at the door, Anna considered pretending she wasn't in. She bore Thatcher's condescension with difficulty on the best of days, and Anna had not yet overcome Ruby's blow to her plans that morning.

But when Anna answered the door, it wasn't Thatcher. Instead, Ruby stood awkwardly outside, eyes shifting to look at anything but Anna. She carried a large clothbound book.

"I thought it over," Ruby began. "I'm not going to do any alchemy. But, well . . . here." She let the book slide onto the worktable, a layer of dust ballooning out from its pages. "Mother always used this when she worked. It's not the same as a real teacher, but perhaps it will serve your purposes."

Anna traced her finger down the book's spine. The cloth cover, made gray by all its years, looked as though it had once been blue. She flipped through the pages to see mostly handwritten entries and diagrams, presumably by Ruby's mother.

"Thank you," Anna breathed.

"You're welcome," Ruby said mechanically, turning to leave.

"I'm sorry." Anna lifted her hand from the book, suddenly feeling like an intruder in a relationship she didn't understand. She should never have insisted Ruby compromise her emotions—Ruby, who had already given up so much.

Ruby paused, her hand on the door handle. "Start with a blood sample," she said. "If there's something to be found, it will be in the blood."

CHAPTER FIFTEEN

Nathaniel left the council hall in a hurry, eager to avoid his father at all costs. He needed to do something right—and fast. After his abysmal performance in front of his father's advisors and the Queen, proving himself was no longer a simple fancy, but a necessity. He needed to catch the Technician once and for all.

The locket lay on Nathaniel's desk where he'd left it, the shiny metal catching rays of sunlight. The intricate craftsmanship struck him. What a pity his father's greatest enemy had made it.

Nathaniel withdrew the slip of paper, tracing Anna's spiraling purple letters with his pinkie.

The heart of the Settlement.

That had to be the city center. But Nathaniel knew before the thought finished crossing his mind that he was wrong. The Technician had yet to be quite so obvious with his clues. Why start now? No, Nathaniel would have to look past the easy answer for the true solution to this riddle.

Pulling the map of the island from his desk, Nathaniel ran his fingers over the page. Smooth paper did not do the terrain justice, the ache in his muscles from his excursion reminding him of the rolling hills and rocky coast. The map beneath his fingers barely even scraped the surface. The Settlement, centered in the middle of the page, spilled out in arcs with the market closest to the gate and the Commissioner's manor and its grounds farthest away. Each quarter had been drawn with precision, a careful hand that knew the weight of its pen.

Past the Settlement gates, however, it seemed detail had been sacrificed for artistry. The farmlands were marked, of course, but from there the island became a suggestion rather than a statement.

It was like the map's author didn't know what was outside the city's walls, or simply didn't care.

Or both.

Nathaniel had been just as ignorant only days ago, but now his hands itched to fill in the rest of the map, to see and know and care what else their world had to offer.

And there had to be something else, something his father didn't want him to know. Anna had implied as much, and now that she and the Technician had drawn him out from beneath his father's protective roof, he wasn't sure he wanted to go back to a place of not knowing, not caring . . . Not sure if he even could.

But this riddle didn't lead him toward the unknown, toward exploration. Rather, it pushed him back. The heart of the Settlement had to be inside its walls.

Returning to the map, Nathaniel stuck his finger on the very center of the Settlement. It wasn't the answer, of course, but it seemed an appropriate starting point. He could, at the very least, mark it off his list of possibilities. From there, he traced the streets with his left hand, and followed the beat of his own heart with his right. It had been the key to the first riddle, after all.

If the Settlement was a body, where would its heart be? Not the center, that was for sure. But the upper left quadrant of the city yielded no obvious meeting place, either. He squinted at the small markings for houses. Was this where the Technician lived?

No, that was absurd. Nathaniel leaned back in his chair, lip caught between his teeth. He was thinking too linearly. Last time, he'd literally needed to flip his thinking upside down to understand.

Nathaniel turned the map over.

It was a blessing no one could see him. His father would laugh in his face, tell him an upside-down map was worthless and inaccurate. Nathaniel truly was an embarrassment, if this was the best he could do. He couldn't let his father be right about him—worthless, indeed.

But not everyone thought him worthless. The Queen, much to his father's chagrin, had praised him, hadn't she? And Anna wouldn't laugh at him, at least not for this. Anna wouldn't call him—or his upside-down map—worthless. Because a map flipped over was still a map, just read from a different perspective.

A grin spread across Nathaniel's face, and he let his eyes fall back to the page. He just needed a new perspective.

Inverted, the Settlement looked a stranger, with its streets weaving in unfamiliar patterns. The manor left a lump along the side of the Settlement where one didn't belong, and on the opposite side, the city's clock tower mirrored it, a growth on the otherwise circular city.

Nathaniel sighed and closed the book. He was getting nowhere.

He crossed the room, stretching his legs. If only he understood the Technician's thinking better, but that wasn't possible. Nathaniel only knew Anna, not the outlaw. He'd only been studying the case for a few days. No one could expect him to crack the code of the Settlement's most wanted criminal that quickly.

His father certainly wouldn't expect it.

But Nathaniel was determined to confound expectations. If he couldn't outdo his father's own men, then . . . well, then Nathaniel would not deserve his father's recognition. Snatching the Technician file he'd lifted from the officers' bunker, Nathaniel settled against the window. He leafed through the pages, but the other riddles bore little significance to the one he held between his fingers.

The Technician thanks you for your patience.

That had to be some kind of joke. Nathaniel didn't think he had any patience left. But as his eyes flicked between the note he held and riddles in the file, his breath caught.

They were the same. The capital *T* leaned forward with a small but precise loop in its tail. The same letter, the same handwriting, graced all four slips of paper—the two from the file, the one from the market, and the one Anna had given him yesterday. She'd penned it with her own hand. She'd written them all.

She was more than just one of many assistants. She had to be an apprentice at the very least.

The Technician thanks you for your patronage.
The Technician thanks you for your patience.

But how could the Technician thank him if they'd never met?

Nathaniel's heart sank with realization. The elusive Technician, too busy to see his customers, had never even been a factor. There had only ever been Nathaniel and Anna. She'd written the riddles, she'd answered his questions, and she'd fixed his faulty, illicit, tarnished heart.

Anna was the Technician.

He'd had her. And then he'd let her go.

He should have brought her to his father regardless. Even without knowing her true identity, she would have been valuable. The Technician's agent would have been an excellent arrest. Perhaps an officer or the Commissioner himself would have been able to prove she was the outlaw as well.

His father's words rang in his ears: *Leave it to the experts, Nathaniel.*

Nathaniel tried to swallow, but his throat scratched and scraped against the motion. It didn't matter that he was not a soldier or an expert. *He* had an appointment with the Technician, not his father. *He* had the power.

But the riddle in his palm wasn't going to solve itself, and he was running out of time. In a few days, Anna would go to the heart of the Settlement, wherever that was, and Nathaniel had to be there to meet her.

He pressed his nose against the windowpane, staring out at the city.

"Where are you?" he whispered into the glass.

In the distance, the clock tower chimed three times in reply.

Clearing the fog from the window, Nathaniel gaped. The tower, with its iconic celestial clock face, stood resolute against a blue sky, the waterwheel below spitting water as though it mocked him.

The heart of the Settlement.

Could his heart be the key to the riddle twice in a row? His chest pounded back an answer. Still, it was not only an echo of his own heart's machinery; the waterwheel, turning to the rhythm of the clock above, pumped water to every corner of the Settlement, flowing through the city like blood through veins.

Experts be damned. Nathaniel would catch the Technician.

When Nathaniel finally decided to leave his room, stomach growling, pride forgotten, he found an envelope on the hallway floor bearing the seal of the Commissioner.

His cheeks flushed. Were things so strained between them that his father couldn't knock, couldn't ask to speak with him? Nathaniel wasn't sure he didn't prefer it this way. Another confrontation with his father could only cause more pain.

Breaking the seal with his finger, Nathaniel unfolded the note.

Nathaniel,
I have gone to the Tower on business and will return within a
week. While I am away, Councilor Ming will serve as interim
Commissioner. Perhaps you will learn from him what I am unable
to teach you.

Commissioner Oliver Fremont

Nathaniel read the note twice. To the untrained eye, it was not accusatory—it wasn't even unpleasant. It was merely a father informing a son of the status quo, or perhaps a leader informing his heir, his words lacking familial intimacy. The Commissioner had even signed his full title, not "your father." And yet, only a father's expectations could cause the ache between Nathaniel's ribs.

A tingling began in Nathaniel's extremities, then traveled to his core. He would be alone for a week without a chaperone. He would try once again to capture the Technician, this time armed with knowledge. With his father gone, there would be no one but himself to berate him if he failed.

Only this time he wouldn't fail.

CHAPTER SIXTEEN

The morning of Anna's meeting with Nathaniel came faster than she'd anticipated, the days between blurring in her memory. So when she departed Mechan, Anna had not yet made up her mind about the Commissioner's son.

She reminded herself that he was a noble, tied to people she never wanted to meet. Thatcher was probably right: She should stay away. Still, Anna couldn't shake the feeling that Nathaniel's identity transcended his father's. When she'd met him at the abandoned cottage, he'd been real, and human, and curious—not a servant of the Settlement. Thatcher had once believed him worth saving, and this fact, oddly enough, rooted itself in her core. Maybe he was worth saving, and maybe he wasn't.

With Ruby's book, syringes and vials for a blood sample, and a choice selection of wrenches in her satchel, Anna took the path through the center of town, sunlight sprinkling across the waves. The silence so early in the morning instilled a certainty in Anna's steps she couldn't replicate in her mind.

As Anna reached the top of the ridge, she cast her gaze down at the town below, still sleeping under a lavender sky. Thatcher wouldn't know for hours that she'd left Mechan, and she did not relish his lecture upon her return. Anna didn't have time to worry over Thatcher's feelings, though. She needed to reach her chosen meeting place before the sun rose fully in the sky, before the gate watch changed from the exhausted guards who would think her just a shadow in their sleep-stained eyes.

Cold wind ripped through her layers, slowing her progress, but she pushed on toward the old clock tower. It rose up from the Settlement's outer wall, the waterwheel like a massive crimson planet hanging against the sunrise, the clock face a solitary moon in orbit.

Turning away to let the wind beat against her back for a moment, Anna pulled her coat tighter across her chest. She squinted into the distance, searching the path behind her, but she saw no one, only tall blades of grass swaying in the wind. It made no sense that someone would be following her when she headed *toward* the Settlement, and yet she couldn't shake the feeling someone was watching her.

Whipping around without warning, Anna narrowed her vision at the grassy expanse behind her. A flash of white disappeared into the grass, and Anna's throat constricted. She'd been right after all; she should have trusted her instincts.

Anna withdrew the heftiest wrench from her satchel, ready to strike, but she found no malcontent lurking in her wake. Crouched in the tall grass, head bent low to hide his distinctive light hair behind the green blades, was Roman.

Anna let her arm fall to her side, releasing the tension from her muscles with difficulty. "Roman! What do you think you're doing?"

Roman looked up, a sheepish grin on his face. "I wanted to come with you. Mama said she was worried about you and—and you were courting danger!" He said the last part triumphantly, like he was proud to have remembered his mother's words.

Anna sighed and knelt beside him, cold dew wetting the knees of her trousers. "Your mother worries too much. I'll be just fine."

"Mama says lying is wrong." Roman pouted and crossed his arms.

"Your mother says a lot of things, doesn't she?" Anna smiled and patted Roman's fluffy hair. "She'll be worried sick if she wakes to find you've run off."

Roman's pout fell away, replaced by a ponderous expression.

"You shouldn't be anywhere near the Settlement. You're still healing from your surgery and it isn't a good idea to stray too far from Thatcher. He's supposed to help if you start to feel any pain. If you're here with me and your chest starts to hurt, he can't help you." She put the wrench back in her satchel and pointed to his chest. "Let me examine your incision."

"It won't hurt, promise! I'm brave, remember?" Roman frowned, but he let her open the top of his shirt.

"I'm sure you're quite courageous, but your mother's not wrong. It isn't safe where I'm going." She prodded the skin around the incision lightly. Red irritation bloomed beneath her fingers. He needed to be in his bed, at home with his mother, but they were quite beyond that. The walk home would be too much for him to handle, and she didn't have the proper tools with her if his incision split.

Glancing at the clock tower, Anna saw it was nearly time. She couldn't be late for her appointment, but neither could she send Roman home on his own. "I think it's best you stay put."

Roman shook his head. "I can protect you from the dandy folk, Auntie Anna! They don't scare me."

Something twisted in Anna's chest, his bravery cutting through her like a scalpel. It had been a long time since Anna lived without fear, without worry. She couldn't remember the last time she'd spent a day in complete safety, secure in her own town, in her own home, in her own skin. And yet she'd presented herself as fearless, an example for Roman to follow. He'd no idea of the danger inside those walls, no idea of the unease beneath her mask.

"Well, they scare *me*." She rose back up to her full height and reached for Roman's hand. "And I won't be able to focus on my work today if I don't know that you're completely safe."

Anna wanted desperately to send him home, to have Thatcher look after him instead of her, but Roman's angry incision worried her. He needed rest, not a long trek back to Mechan. "I need you to do something for me." She pointed to the line of trees a few yards away. "I want you to hide in those trees there and be a lookout, just like the pirate who watches from the—uh—the top of the ship."

Roman tilted his head to look up at her. "The crow's nest?"

Anna nodded. "I need someone to keep an eye on those guards."

Roman's face split into a smile. "What do I do if they follow you? Should I fetch my sword and do battle?"

"Stars, no!" Anna gripped his shoulder tight. "I want you to think like a runner, all right? Runners don't stay to fight alone— their job is to warn us of danger. If anything happens, I want you to go back to Mechan by yourself and tell your mother."

Roman nodded his assent.

"Good. Now, do you have any questions?"

"Yes." Roman scratched his head thoughtfully. "Who is Danger, and why does Mama think you're courting them?"

············*

Once Anna was sure Roman would stay put in the tree line, she returned to the clock tower, climbing up the far side, out of the guards' lines of sight. With Roman nearby, she didn't dare approach the gate, even with her passport. The rope ladder she'd placed behind the vines and overgrowth had weakened, worn down by the spray from the waterwheel, but it did its job. In seconds she made it to the top and over the side without incident. A quick glance at the clock told her she was right on time.

She pulled herself up onto the side of the tower and crawled through the stone archway just below the number six. As she disentangled herself from the rope, wood creaked beneath her feet. She much preferred her metals, sleek and relatively silent. It was this flaw in her meeting place, perhaps, that alerted the approaching officers to her presence.

Two uniformed men mounted the stairs with speed and vigor, eyes glued to Anna.

She whipped around, ready to fling herself back down the rope ladder, but as she turned, she nearly crashed into something—someone.

Nathaniel.

A cold, collected dandy, eyes hard like steel, jaw set, stood before her instead of the nervous, inquisitive boy she'd met. Where had he come from? If Anna hadn't been distracted by Roman before, she would have arrived first. She would have had the upper hand. She would have escaped easily.

Nathaniel smiled and snapped cuffs over her hands as she tried to push him away.

"So good of you to arrive promptly, Lady Technician," Nathaniel said. Though his gaze was stony, his voice wobbled.

So he knew her secret. She knew his, too.

She bared her teeth. "I should have expected nothing less deceitful from the Commissioner's son." Testing the cuffs around her wrists, Anna found herself quite stuck. The Commissioner might not approve of tech, but his smiths certainly knew their way around metal.

Nathaniel smiled again, and her heart sank. If Anna hadn't known better, she might have thought it good-natured. But he wasn't good. He was the enemy.

She'd been wrong about him, and she would have to live—or die—with it. Her heart plummeted as the reality of her predicament sank in. She'd been beaten at her own game, but it wasn't over. He'd taken her this round, but she'd win the match.

Nathaniel waved to the officers, and they took each of her elbows in their iron grip.

"And to think," he said as they led her away, "I thought this introduction might be awkward and uncomfortable."

But Anna found nothing about her current predicament nearly as awkward and uncomfortable as explaining it all to Thatcher would be.

If she ever got the chance to tell him.

CHAPTER SEVENTEEN

Nathaniel had always wondered how it would feel to win. The rush of adrenaline as he'd snapped the handcuffs around the Technician's wrists consumed him, pulsing through his blood. He wanted to savor it. It tasted of triumph, of victory.

But as Nathaniel led the restrained Technician down the stairs of the crimson clock tower, watching her descend with heavy footfalls, something else ran through him. Her gaze was sharp but resigned—the blade of a straight razor turned harmless only by the will of he who controlled it. And Nathaniel controlled her now.

So why did she stare at him? No one dared look at his father like that.

"What?" he asked, throwing the word at her with the same velocity as one of his father's punches.

Anna's eyes narrowed, but she said nothing.

"Surely you must have expected something like this would happen eventually," Nathaniel continued as he and the officers marched her along the cobblestone streets. "You're a criminal, and criminals always get caught."

Again, Anna glared at him, but this time she spoke, voice quiet but steady. "Only if there's someone to catch them. You don't have to do this, Nathaniel. You could still let me go."

Nathaniel's eyebrows rose. "Let you go? Why would I want to do that? Today I caught the most dangerous outlaw in the Settlement. Today I'm a hero." He clenched his jaw, unsure if his father would agree.

"Just because the law isn't on my side, it doesn't mean I'm evil." The intensity of Anna's gaze wavered as they crossed over from the public streets onto the private grounds of the manor.

Nathaniel sniffed. Not the Tech Decrees again. Her ideas about tech and his father's legislature had gotten him in enough trouble already. He didn't need to hear more of her nonsense. "Laws exist for a reason. My father isn't a bad man just because you don't like them."

"That's debatable," Anna scoffed. "But I'd say he's a bad man for lots of other reasons, like what he's done to you."

Nathaniel froze on the threshold, hand poised to open the door to the manor. She knew nothing about his relationship with his father. What right did she have to judge his family? His father had disciplined Nathaniel, certainly, but his lectures were not uncalled for, and Nathaniel felt he'd deserved every one of his father's blows, every lash of his father's belt and tongue.

So why did her words dig so deep?

"Leave us here." Nathaniel dismissed the officers with a poor imitation of his father's authority. Though the officers obeyed him without question, he knew it wouldn't last. When his father returned, any semblance of power he might have wielded in the Commissioner's absence would be gone. Taking hold of Anna's handcuffs, he led her through the door. He would endure her jabs, but he didn't want others to hear them, too.

Once they were inside, Nathaniel turned his eyes on his captive. "Whatever you think you know—"

"I don't think. I *know*."

Nathaniel felt himself shrinking against the solid assurance of Anna's tone—the Technician's tone. It was time he started thinking of her as the Technician, the criminal mastermind his father wanted above all else, not Anna, the young girl who'd taken pity on him and his condition. But it was harder to separate the two than he'd expected. It was not impossible, after all, for her to be both kind and fundamentally wrong, just as it was not impossible for his father to be unkind but righteous.

"Don't try to distract me with your lies. It won't work, Technician." Nathaniel tugged on the handcuffs, but he could not bring himself to pull hard enough to cause pain.

"I don't make a habit of lying," she growled, but with a look from Nathaniel, her face softened. "I'm not sorry I didn't tell you who I was. You can't possibly expect that while holding me captive."

Nathaniel turned around, bringing her forward and across the foyer. "No, but I don't make a habit of listening to liars."

"I find that hard to believe." She stopped fighting the handcuffs. "Tell me, do you not know or do you simply not care that your father is the reason you need a TICCER?"

Nathaniel bit his lip. "You can't blame him for saving his only son. Tech may not be legal, and it may not be safe, but it has kept me alive."

"If you think your father's only crime against you was putting tech in your chest, then you're missing the bigger picture."

"What bigger picture?" Nathaniel asked before he could stop himself.

"You're not asking the right questions," Anna said, fixing him with ocean eyes—chaotic, like waves in a storm. "It isn't why he gave you a TICCER that matters; it's why he needed to at all."

Nathaniel's chest constricted in protest. It mattered. His father had put Nathaniel first. It proved his father cared, even if he'd only done it once.

"Why do you think you're the only one in the entire Settlement with the same tech as all of us living outside it?" Anna pressed on. "You don't think it's just chance, do you?"

Nathaniel came to a stop outside the door to his father's study. That was exactly what he'd thought. He'd been born with a rare heart condition, one the medical treatments of Earth Adjacent could not fix. His father, in a striking act of love, had cast aside his biases against tech in order to save him.

"I do." Removing the key from the crack above the door, Nathaniel unlocked the study, sending Anna stumbling inside. "I really, truly do."

But he didn't.

Nathaniel's hands shook as he locked the door on her, his captive, his gift to his father. That's what she was—an offering to the man he admired, proof of his commitment and capability. She was the key to his father's respect.

But she was also the key to his past, questions left unasked and unanswered through all the years.

His father would not have let such obvious trickery sway him. His father would have killed her already. But his father hadn't caught the Technician; Nathaniel had.

CHAPTER EIGHTEEN

Eliza's bags were packed. With what, she couldn't be sure. Aside from the three overdresses she owned, and of course the blade she used far less than she would have liked, Eliza had little in the way of possessions and certainly not enough to fill so many cases. The rest of her apartment had been scrubbed bare, erasing her years of habitation. Someone else would live there soon—a lord's daughter, or a newly minted couple.

Or the Queen's new set of Eyes.

Eliza's stomach twisted. The Queen would lift up some new girl, some new nobody, and give her Eliza's home, Eliza's job, Eliza's life. The Queen would not feel the loss for even a moment, while Eliza would be left alone. She'd risen so high, only to be sent down further than she'd started. To become a Planetary after all this, to be denied the recognition she deserved—well, it only meant she'd have to scramble and scrape her way back to the top.

She'd earn her crown, never mind the Queen didn't wear one. When Eliza sat on the throne, she wanted everyone who'd ever looked at her with pity or disgust to remember her face, remember how she'd gotten there.

Running a hand over her hair, pulled into coiffure, Eliza tried to imagine finding metal, the weight of cold silver against her brow. She imagined herself ruling the Tower, all eyes on her.

Eliza was used to watching, not being watched, but in her new position on Earth Adjacent, fiancée to the Commissioner's son, she would be a public figure, at the center of society. She would have to find a way to get used to it.

Eyeing a circular box atop the cluster of trunks and bags by the door, Eliza crossed the room and flipped up the lid. A delicate, wide-brimmed tea hat rested inside, confectionary pink with crimson roses clustered on one side.

It wasn't a crown, but it would do for now.

Before she could pin it in place, a knock sounded and the door to her apartment swung open. No one entered her room without permission—or key card for that matter—but a gentleman she didn't recognize stood in the doorway, a sharp jaw and salt-and-pepper hair that had once been a dusty brown.

"Pardon me," he said, clearing his throat.

Eliza dropped the hat.

The man bent to pick it up. "I'm looking for Eliza—is that you?"

She took the hat and pinned it in place, eyeing him shrewdly. "You're the courier? You can take these, I suppose." She pointed to the bags, but the man only stared. "You *are* here to take me to the ship, yes?"

The man blinked once, twice, thrice, then lifted one of her bags. "Right this way."

Eliza paused at the door and took one last look at the room. She would leave behind absolutely nothing, yet it felt like everything. Eliza always knew how to make an entrance, but leaving . . . Leaving was an entirely different art.

Eliza turned, pushing down the swell in her throat and the pain beneath her ribs. She would move, one foot in front of the other, until there was nowhere to go, nowhere to climb.

"So, Earth Adjacent," the man said, waiting for her to catch up. "Are you looking forward to your visit?"

Eliza's head snapped up. "My visit?" More like banishment. "I don't imagine the Queen would have ordered quite so many bags packed if it were only a visit."

The man smiled slightly, readjusting her bag in his arms. "Quite right—the Queen certainly knows how to communicate her intent."

Eliza choked back a response, unsure if she intended to laugh or to chastise. Surely even a Planetary knew better than to speak in such a manner about their Queen.

"I do hope you'll enjoy yourself and not think of our planet as a chore." He slowed his pace as they approached the upper ring. "Once you're on the surface, I suspect you'll see things differently."

Who was this man to predict her thoughts and opinions? Eliza halted, casting her gaze over him once more. He wore a crisp suit, clean and recently pressed. He stood tall, as though pride, not bones, held him together. And he spoke clearly, patiently.

"You're not the courier, are you?"

"Eliza!" The Queen's voice carried across the hall. She walked toward them, steps smooth and even as though she were floating. "I see you've met your new host."

Eliza's eyes found the man-who-was-not-the-courier's. Her stomach dropped.

"Commissioner, how kind of you to avoid me." The Queen wrapped her gloved hand around the man's arm, drumming her fingers against his sleeve. "I'm afraid it won't do, but I appreciate the gesture all the same."

"Commissioner." Eliza let the word pass through her lips, not a greeting, not an accusation, just a word. To her, it still had no meaning—not yet.

The Commissioner bowed his head ever so slightly, a frown weaving its way across his lips. "Please, Mother, you'll make me seem inhospitable to my future daughter-in-law." He unhooked his arm from hers. "Allow me to escort Miss Eliza aboard, then I'll join you for an early tea."

Though Eliza couldn't see the Queen's face, she could imagine the sort of expression that might rest behind her veil just from the set of the Queen's shoulders—off-kilter, holding tension on the left. Eliza did not envy the wrath the Commissioner would face once behind closed doors.

Tension practically sang through the air between them, making Eliza both wish to disappear and to watch their exchange continue. The things she might learn—the weaknesses she might discover—could be vital in her quest to outdo him, to become the favored child, shared blood or not.

"Very well," the Queen said, releasing him and stepping back.

"After you." The Commissioner gestured toward a slate-gray door ahead of them.

Eliza waited a beat, knowing she would not earn an invitation. This was it. This was the doorway to her new life, her new task. Ahead was an expanse of stars, a world she didn't know, and a boy she didn't love. Behind her was the Queen—silent.

Eliza took a step. And then another, and another. Still, the Queen said nothing. Eliza turned to look over her shoulder, holding her breath.

"She'll never say it," the Commissioner murmured so only she could hear.

Breath failed her, lungs shattering into a million shards. But she couldn't fall apart now. This would be Eliza's last chance to show her quality before she descended to Earth. She would stand tall; she would stand strong. Beside the Queen's natural son, she would not break.

Eliza would see the Queen again someday, and she'd ensure the Queen knew how truly loyal she could be.

CHAPTER NINETEEN

Anna had walked into a trap she'd seen clear as day. She'd jumped into it readily like a bird from its perch, except a bird could fly, and Anna could only hope the ground below her would be soft. Optimism had infected her worse than any disease. Where had her cynicism gone, her mistrust, her caution? Anyone might have seen Nathaniel for what he was—Thatcher certainly had—but Anna had overlooked it, forgiven it, all for the small hope that he genuinely needed her help.

Was she truly so desperate to be needed?

Anna put her face in her hands, the question in her mind more abrasive than the metal cuffs that bound her. Scrunching her nose, she glared at the steel. If only she could remove them, she might be able to find a way out of this mess.

Nathaniel had taken her bag full of useful tools, even remembering to take the small Allen wrench she kept in her shirt pocket, but perhaps she could find a suitable lockpick inside her prison, which looked to be more of an office than a jail cell. Books lined the walls from floor to ceiling, and a solitary desk stood in the middle of the room, littered with papers and ink.

Anna stepped away from the door and into the room, scouring her vision for anything thin and pointy—a sewing needle or hatpin would do nicely, but as she reached the desk, it was clear she'd find nothing of the sort. On a black plate, letters etched in gold, were the words *Commissioner Oliver Fremont*.

Of all the offices Nathaniel might have locked her in, it was the Commissioner's. All things considered, it was much smaller than she would have thought. The Commissioner, while conservative in his politics, seemed the sort for extravagance, judging by the enormous chandelier in the entrance hall. So why did the Commissioner hide in a windowless prison of dark wood and dusty books?

Anna wouldn't die in a place like this. With any luck, she wouldn't die at all.

With a flick of her fingers, she opened the top drawer of the desk. Sorting through its contents took longer than she'd expected with her maneuverability limited by the handcuffs. Not since she had accidentally slammed her thumb with a hammer when she was eleven had she struggled so much with the simple task of holding things.

The first drawer held mostly paper—a few letters and hastily scribbled notes Anna didn't bother with. Nothing there would help with her current predicament. The second drawer held mostly writing utensils. Perhaps a stylus would do the trick, but before she could reach inside to sort through the pens, she caught sight of a circular metal device. She'd never seen any tech like it before.

While removing it from the drawer, Anna noticed a flashing red light. Her curious fingers flitted across the metal toward it. Did it flash in a discernable pattern, spelling out a code? A dial with four slots rested just below it, spelling nonsense. Her mind buzzed with the desire to unravel the mystery—but no, she didn't have time for diversions. Nathaniel could be back at any moment with his father. She needed to get out of this office.

She needed to return to Roman.

Horror gripped her insides at the thought of Roman alone. How long would he stand outside the Settlement, waiting for her return? Certainly he'd go home if she didn't come back soon, but with his incision so irritated, would he make it back in one piece? Worse still was the possibility that he wouldn't return home at all—that he'd come looking for her.

She was the one who was supposed to protect him.

Anna flipped the device over. If she could loosen one of the screws holding it together, she might be able to use it to pry the handcuffs off her wrists. She dug a thumbnail into the screw head and went to work. She'd torn through two fingernails and rubbed her wrists raw by the time she loosened the screw, but it was enough to free her of her confines. Flexing her wrists, Anna exhaled heavily. She'd done it. Now to take on the door.

But curiosity overtook her, and she snatched up the device. The second screw took half as long to loosen, and soon she was pulling the bottom off the device to reveal a complex web of circuitry the likes of which Anna had never seen before.

She leaned closer, mapping the tech with her mind. If the Commissioner was so against steam power and mechanical limbs, what was he doing with tech like this? It wasn't just post-industrial; it looked post-post-industrial. It looked like the kind of tech that had taken down Former Earth, the kind the Commissioner supposedly feared above all else.

Anna's stomach twisted, coiling and curving back and forth like the circuitry. A voice in her head told her to put it down, leave it where she'd found it, and never look back, but the voice sounded an awful lot like Thatcher. Only a few hours ago, that alone would have been enough to spur her on. Her grandfather's orders irked her nearly as much as the Commissioner's Tech Decrees as of late. But Thatcher had been right about Nathaniel, and Anna had been wrong.

Anna wouldn't be wrong again. She set the device back inside the Commissioner's drawer. She could let this mystery go unsolved . . . for now.

First Anna needed to escape this office, leave the Settlement, and bring Roman home—if she could get to him in time.

CHAPTER TWENTY

Patience had never been one of Nathaniel's strengths. His father would return soon, and Nathaniel wanted to be sure the first thing he heard was that his son had captured the Technician. But as the hours wore on and Nathaniel tired from pacing, he began to wonder if his father would come home at all. Perhaps he already had.

What if his father returned to his study without Nathaniel? What would he do with the girl inside? He probably wouldn't even know she was the Technician. More important, he wouldn't know that it was Nathaniel, not his officers, who'd caught her.

Nathaniel couldn't just stand and wait in the foyer any longer. Casting a furtive glance back at the front door, which remained stubbornly shut, he made his way back through the halls. Likely, she would be hungry by now. He could bring her a slice of bread— there would be no harm in some kindness.

With a plate of bread in hand, Nathaniel exited the kitchen. He dallied over whether to add jam to the plate, but he reminded himself that Anna was a prisoner, not a guest. He needn't offer her hospitality. As he walked, however, Nathaniel's breathing turned shallow, unsure if he should risk facing her again.

She was smart, she was savvy, and she was something else he couldn't define. It was in the way she stood taller than him but looked at him like an equal. She was hard like metal, and also soft like warm rain. She escaped his understanding—he could see her branches and leaves, but miles of twisted roots lay beneath her surface.

Whatever her nature, she was *definitely* dangerous. The danger came not from her fists, but her words. She wielded Nathaniel's own uncertainty against him with uncanny skill; she'd already sown the seeds of doubt in his mind. He would have to steel himself against her words.

But when he rounded the corner and the study came into view, all thoughts of courtesy fled his mind. The door was open, a set of shiny handcuffs hanging from the handle.

The plate slipped from Nathaniel's hand and clattered to the ground. Ceramic shattered at his feet, spreading sharp splinters every which way, but Nathaniel didn't have time to clean them up.

She'd escaped through some trickery. Had he forgotten to lock the door? No, he distinctly remembered turning the key in the lock.

He should have stayed to guard the door.

Snatching the handcuffs from the handle, Nathaniel sped off. She couldn't have gone far with him standing guard over the main entrance. He could still catch her. He could still fix this.

Nathaniel tore through the halls and past the stairs. Wrenching the front door open, he caught sight of red hair as it disappeared behind a hedge. Two officers flanked the garden's only exit. He had her cornered. But just as a smile stretched onto his lips, she reappeared just above the hedge.

She was climbing the fence.

Nathaniel cursed and sped back the way he'd come. He knew that climbing would only set him farther behind. His upper body strength was laughable. If she got the better of him because he couldn't climb a blasted fence, Nathaniel resolved to dedicate himself to a physical regimen in addition to his academics.

He set off after the outlaw. Running had always landed Nathaniel in trouble before—not with his father, but with his heart. He hoped now that Anna had fixed it, it would help him catch her. The officers at the gate gave him odd looks but did not impede his progress. One of them called after him, but Nathaniel couldn't hear his words, only wind and determination sounded against his ears.

Nathaniel made his way toward the Settlement exit. He'd lost track of Anna as soon as they'd entered the busier streets near the market district, but even if she hid somewhere inside the Settlement, she'd have to pass through the exit eventually. He didn't care how long it took; he would sit by the gate all night if he had to. The Technician wouldn't evade him again.

But as he approached the gate, dodging through the crowd and knocking into more than one disgruntled shopper, Nathaniel saw a flash of coppery hair in the street before him. His pulse quickened and he pushed past a family blocking his view.

He caught sight of her speaking to one of the officers, handing him a slip of paper from her pocket.

"Stop!" Nathaniel yelled, but the wind drowned out his words.

The officer gestured for her to pass, and Nathaniel's stomach dropped. For a moment, time seemed to stand still as Anna crossed over from the Settlement into her own, lawless world.

With a shout, Nathaniel launched himself toward her. He barreled down the street, his feet pounding against the stone.

"Sir!" One of the officers held out a hand to stop him. "A government-issued passport is required to——"

"Isn't that the young Master Fremont?" Nathaniel heard the second officer say as he reached them, but he tore right past without slowing. He wasn't about to let something like paperwork stand in his way.

Nathaniel caught up to Anna just before the tree line outside the gates. He had no weapon, no upper hand—he had only his speed and a set of handcuffs. He could do only one thing.

He tackled her.

The seconds that followed, as the grassy earth slowed his momentum with almighty force, were a flurry of fists and legs. The world spun as Nathaniel sat up, but Anna had already regained her footing, poised to run again.

Nathaniel, kneeling in the grass, grabbed her foot. She kicked him hard, her boot colliding with his face. Nathaniel brought his arm down on her outstretched leg. She fell back to the ground.

Scrambling toward her, Nathaniel readied the handcuffs, but she righted herself and lifted her fists, landing a blow to the side of his head.

"Get away from me!" she yelled, scooping up a handful of mud and throwing it at him.

Nathaniel dodged inexpertly. He wiped the splatter off his arm and clicked the handcuffs against each other.

"Not a chance." Nathaniel took a step toward her. "I'm sorry, but I can't let you walk away."

Anna glared, widening her stance. "I'm not sorry at all."

She intended to fight him.

Nathaniel eyed her warily. She wasn't particularly muscled, but she was taller. She'd probably been in fights before—she'd probably *won* fights before.

With little more than an arm's length between them, they squared off, sizing up each other. Nathaniel was not a fighter; even with a weapon, he'd be hard-pressed to swing a sword or fire a gun. It simply wasn't in his nature.

Nathaniel was more adept at taking punches than giving them.

His father would laugh if he could see him now.

But before Nathaniel could make his move, a form hurtled across the grass toward them, small but loud.

A boy, no more than seven or eight years old, approached with an expression as fierce as a feral tomcat protecting its catch. The boy snarled, eyes wildly flickering over Nathaniel's face and arms.

"You stay away from my Anna!" he shouted, raising his fist. "She hasn't done anything to you!"

Nathaniel clenched his jaw. She represented everything wrong in the world—the symbol of chaos in the Settlement, and disorder, distraction, disgust. But the boy was right.

Anna had done nothing to Nathaniel—nothing at all but show him he wasn't alone.

CHAPTER TWENTY-ONE

Anna could hardly count her lucky stars. She'd walked into a trap. And she'd walked right back out. But nothing was this easy— something *had* to go wrong.

And wrong it went.

Roman, small but sure, stood between her and Nathaniel. He should have run back to Mechan and warned the others. A rescue should have come from the runners—trained scouts who knew when to fight and when to flee, when to cut their losses— not from a seven-year-old child. But Roman didn't understand any of that. He knew only that Anna needed help, and just like his father and like the pirates in the stories she told him, he would never back down from a fight. But Roman wasn't part of this. She couldn't let Roman suffer for her mistakes.

"I can take care of myself, Roman. You run along." Anna tried to keep her tone as level as possible. He couldn't know how afraid she was. She needed him to believe her words, even if she didn't. "I'll be fine. You go get your mother."

Roman glanced over his shoulder, fixing Anna with a look reminiscent of an irritated Ruby. "No! I'm here to protect you."

"Get out of the way." Nathaniel took a step toward Roman.

Every instinct in Anna's body told her to run, but she couldn't very well leave Roman there. What would she tell Ruby?

"Roman, go!" She stepped forward to move in front of him. "You can't help me with this." The hurt in Roman's eyes was almost as heartbreaking as what she was about to do, but she couldn't let his feelings change her mind.

"Move!" Nathaniel barked, swinging his arm in an exaggerated gesture.

Roman stumbled to the side, ducking out of the way of Nathaniel's arm, though he swept several feet over Roman's head.

"I-I'll go with you," Anna said hurriedly. "Leave him out of it and I'll come quietly." She held her hands before her, waiting for the cuffs.

"No, Anna!" Roman grabbed for her arm but missed.

"How do I know this isn't a trick?" Nathaniel asked, eyeing her with suspicion.

Anna rolled her eyes. She couldn't help herself. "You're the one who tricked me, remember? Deception seems to run in your veins, not mine."

"What is that supposed to mean?" Nathaniel snapped.

"You dandies are all liars. I may be a criminal, but at least I care about people, about the truth."

"I do care!"

"Your father doesn't." Anna crossed her arms.

"Of course he does." Nathaniel shook his head.

"Does he?" She tapped the metal plate of her TICCER, regaining her confidence at the doubt in his voice. She might not be able to escape her circumstances, but she could still sow the seeds of doubt.

Nathaniel's gaze snapped up. "I don't know what you're playing at—"

"I'm not playing." Anna raised her arms above her head in surrender. "Let him go, and I'll be your prisoner."

Anna glanced quickly at Roman. Why wasn't he gone yet? She'd told him to run twice, but he was either defiant or terrible at following directions. She would have words with his mother later.

Only she wouldn't.

There weren't many people she'd miss once the Commissioner had done his worst. There weren't many who'd miss her, either. Thatcher would grieve but only the exact appropriate amount. Perhaps he'd even be glad to be rid of her—she would no longer be a threat to Mechan, her exploits over, their secrets safe.

But Ruby—Ruby had been her true family, part sister, part mother. Anna would be sad to leave such a friend behind.

Nathaniel clenched his jaw before nodding. "All right." He stepped forward, cuffs in hand.

Anna stretched out her hands, hoping she'd made the right choice. She'd do her best to turn him to her side, to make him see the truth about his father. And if that didn't work, well . . . she'd escaped once before; she could do it again.

But as Nathaniel flipped open the cuffs and reached for Anna's outstretched hands, Roman stepped between them and took hold of Nathaniel's wrist.

"No!" Roman cried. "Stay back!"

"Out of my way!" Nathaniel tried to brush him aside, but Roman came at him stronger, swinging his fist. Nathaniel took a deep breath and shoved the boy to the side.

Roman stumbled back but returned with as much determination as before. "Leave Anna alone!"

"Enough!" Anna jumped forward, trying to get between them. But it was too late.

Nathaniel's elbow connected with Roman's chest, eliciting a tinny clunk. Rubbing his arm where he'd hit Roman, concern and confusion laced his gaze.

Roman's eyes widened as his hand snaked up to rest against his chest—his TICCER.

Anna's heart stopped—or it would have, if not for the machine keeping it pounding heavily, painfully, inside her body. Roman's eyes flicked to hers and his mouth formed the beginnings of a word he never spoke.

His body crumpled, falling like it was no longer made of the boy who loved to run and play, the boy who dreamt of becoming a pirate—or a runner—one day. He looked like a doll or a scarecrow, playing at life, not living it.

Anna lunged to the ground beside Roman, reaching for his wrist to find a pulse. But when her hand connected with his, she could feel it already fading. Red blossomed across the boy's chest.

Anna tore his shirt open and tried to wipe away the blood, to see the damage underneath. She could still save him, if she did everything right. But as she examined his chest, a memory flashed before her eyes of the same boy lying beneath her scalpel, sedated, vulnerable. He'd had no idea she was about to cut into his skin, too deep—too *wrong*. What if she couldn't sew him back together again this time? What if she tried but failed anyway?

"I-I only meant to push him out of the way." Nathaniel's voice wavered.

But even a push was enough to rupture the stitches of a post-op patient. Anna had seen the redness around the incision that morning, the irritated skin. Roman should never have walked so far; she should never have allowed it. She should have taken him home the moment she saw him following her, but instead she'd played along with his game, more concerned with her mission than with his health.

There was no difference between the blood on her hands now and the blood in her memory. Thatcher had saved Roman's life then, but there was no Thatcher in the field to save him now.

Anna would have to do it.

Red pooled against her skin and iron burned her nostrils. She saw the infant arm in her hand, barely recognizable as what it had once been, blood pouring, spurting, spraying across her vision.

She shook her head to clear it. Right now she needed to be a doctor. She needed to be Thatcher.

Roman's skin was ripped in two along his incision. The stitches had not just spontaneously burst; they'd been worn down, weakened. His hike chasing her that morning had been the true culprit, Nathaniel's elbow only the catalyst.

She had to get him back to Mechan. Thatcher could help, surely—but no, she knew better. Mechan was nearly an hour away. Roman couldn't wait that long for a medical technique that didn't exist. If only it was a problem with his TICCER. Metal, she could mend.

As Anna formulated the beginnings of a plan, Roman's fingers curled against Anna's, his blue eyes wide and urgent. His mouth opened, as if to speak, but all that came out was a stuttering, staggering breath, blood pooling in his mouth. Roman's chest rose and fell one last time. There was so much blood—*too much* blood. He couldn't lose any more. She would have to clear the airway.

But it didn't matter. It was over. He was already gone.

"I didn't mean to hurt him." Nathaniel spoke as if from far away, his words muddled and distant. "Let me help—what can I do?"

It took several ticks before Anna realized he'd said anything. She couldn't hear, couldn't breathe, couldn't think. She wrapped her tongue around words of blame, of anger, of sorrow, but they rose and died before ever passing her lips. Anna sat back on her heels, hot tears scorching her skin. There were no words worth saying, no words that could adequately represent the way her chest ached, the way her blood boiled. There were no words for emotions, only facts.

"You can't do anything."

Nathaniel rushed to her side, one knee on the ground beside her. "No, please let me help. I can fetch a doctor, or—"

"He's dead."

"No. He can't be— He was just— I didn't mean to—"

"He's *dead*." The words didn't feel real on her lips—like lies. Only Anna did not lie to Roman, and she wouldn't lie to herself, either.

Nathaniel froze. "I-I didn't mean to— I'm not a killer."

"You are now." Anna tried to yell, but it came out a croak. She couldn't look at him. "I might become one, too, if you're still here in five seconds."

Nathaniel rose to his feet. "Please don't— I can get someone to help. Let me do something."

"You've done enough. Go home."

He didn't move.

Anna clenched her fist around the grass and tugged, uprooting it as she yelled, "Go!"

Nathaniel's shadow slowly retreated, but she would not look away from Roman's body. Leaning forward, she removed the

TICCER, unhooking the device. Tears fell from her cheeks onto the metal, cleaning away the blood one drop at a time.

But the clock never stopped ticking, unaware that the boy it served was no more.

Tick.

Tick.

Tick.

CHAPTER TWENTY-TWO

Nathaniel wished the boy didn't have a name. It would be easier if he were no one. It would be easier if he were still alive.

Roman.

Nathaniel could still feel the metal against his arm, hard where the boy's chest ought to have been soft.

He'd killed someone.

But hadn't he intended to cause harm all along? He'd been willing to let Anna suffer so that his father would see him in a new light. But his father would never see him—not really, not in the way that Anna had back when she'd fixed his heart. He should have left things there. He'd learned far more from her that day than he had in eighteen years with his father. And how had he repaid her? By capturing her and then killing her friend—a child who had a name.

A child who had a family.

A lump formed in his throat, massive and suffocating. Anna would have to tell Roman's parents, whoever they were. He'd left her there in that field with a dead body and a burden far larger than the weight of Nathaniel's pride.

Nathaniel strayed off the main road, lodging himself in the shadows between two dwellings. There, he let his emotions run free. Tears cascaded down his cheeks, falling hot against his palms and knees, wetting the cloth of his trousers in tiny pinpricks, not unlike one of Former Earth's paintings of ladies with umbrellas. Only Nathaniel's pointillism was not a colorful scene of aristocrats enjoying a Sunday by the river; his was distilled in death and soaked in sorrow.

When Nathaniel eventually regained his feet, darkness encroached on the city. Cold whipped through his clothes as images of the dying boy raced through his mind. Nathaniel might have stayed in the alley for hours more, but his stomach had begun rumbling, and a stray dog had come wandering past more than once, whining incessantly, as though Nathaniel was in his spot.

It was a good spot, hidden and protected from the outside world. What Nathaniel would not give to curl up on the hard ground and forget the day had ever happened.

But Nathaniel could never forget. Forgetting was a privilege for boys without clockwork hearts. In another life, Nathaniel could have been the boy he'd killed—Roman. The metal in Nathaniel's chest dragged him down in a way it never had before. It had always seemed an accessory, something he wore like a glove. Now it was more like skin, but someone else's, silver and foreign, sewn into him like patchwork.

When he returned to the manor, Nathaniel decided he would go straight to bed. He did not have the energy to eat or think. He needed the comfort of pillows against his skin and dreams against his memories, softening the whispers of hard metal against his elbow, stifling the sound of Anna's sobs as he'd retreated, erasing the smell of blood from his nostrils.

The manor, however, wasn't empty when Nathaniel entered, tracking a generous amount of mud inside.

"There you are!" his father barked.

Nathaniel couldn't summon the energy to flinch.

The Commissioner glared at Nathaniel, looking him up and down. "Out again, I see. Don't tell me." He held up a hand. "You were chasing the damn Technician again, weren't you? I thought I told you to let it alone."

Nathaniel could barely hear him, his father's voice muffled by an invisible barrier between them.

That morning, Nathaniel had cared only about catching the Technician. She had given him a reason to get out of bed, to act instead of wait. Now he wished he'd never met her that day in the market. If he'd never met her, he'd never have hurt Roman.

"You're right," Nathaniel mumbled. "I'm sorry. I'm done chasing the Technician." And he found it was the truth.

There were things worse than letting a criminal go free, even if catching her would buy his father's pride, even if catching her would prove Nathaniel's worth.

Nothing was worth the life of an innocent boy.

He turned toward the stairs.

"Where do you think you're going?" Nathaniel's father grabbed his arm, yanking him back to face him.

Nathaniel's arm hurt—but not in a way he could feel, just in a way that he knew it hurt, like he'd read it in a book. It had become something more than an arm the minute it hit Roman's body, muscle made weapon. But he could not divorce himself from his limb, no matter how painful the memory of its actions—*his* actions.

"I need to clean up," Nathaniel mumbled.

The Commissioner sneered. "You gave up that right when you walked out the door. You made the choice to muddy your boots and—have you been sorting through rubbish bins? You smell like the back end of a— Never mind." He sighed, loosening his grip on Nathaniel's arm. "We have an important guest. It's time you met."

Nathaniel's stomach dropped. The Commissioner was dressed for company, his silk cravat tucked into a double-breasted vest with silver buttons. He even wore a coat and tails. Whoever his father intended to introduce, Nathaniel was not fit to meet them.

The door to the sitting room opened. "I thought I heard voices, Commissioner. Is Nathaniel home now? Oh!"

Nathaniel laid eyes on her the same moment she saw him. She was positively lovely, with ash-blond hair and dark eyes. Her lips, arranged in a pout, matched her dress and hat—an overwhelming pink.

"Eliza." Nathaniel whispered her name, but the acoustics of the high-ceilinged foyer carried the word around and around until it encircled him, ensnared him.

"*Miss* Eliza." The Commissioner bowed. "May I present my disheveled son, Nathaniel?"

Nathaniel must have looked a wreck, not the upstanding Commissioner's son she'd been expecting. He crossed his arms self-consciously, but it did nothing to hide the mud splatter on his legs or his sweaty face.

Though his father had pointed out his most obvious fault already, Eliza showed no discomfort. To the contrary, her smile spread to her eyes, and she swept across the room to take Nathaniel's arm as if they were old friends.

They *were* old friends, Nathaniel reminded himself. Their letters, at least, suggested that.

So close to him, surely Eliza would smell whatever his father had refrained from describing, but to her credit, she did not show it.

"I'm so very pleased to meet you," she said in a fluttery voice, then frowned. "No, that isn't right. It seems ever so wrong that we have not met, and yet I feel I know you completely. Don't you agree?"

Nathaniel only nodded.

"Let us adjourn to the sitting room." Nathaniel's father motioned for them to follow, leading their party into the next room.

"It's such a difference, being planetside," Eliza said as she steered him toward the door, her arm steadier and firmer than he'd expected. "The Tower is so cramped. We don't have enough space for homes like this." She gestured around them at the high arching walls. "You may not believe it, but I lived in a one-room apartment on the Tower."

Nathaniel had never stopped to consider that life on the Tower might be anything but better in every aspect. He supposed Earth Adjacent had the one benefit of simply being larger.

"Do sit down, Eliza." The Commissioner motioned toward the center of the room. "Can I get you a refreshment?"

"Please." She settled on the loveseat, leaving room for Nathaniel to sit beside her—the farthest end from the Commissioner.

Nathaniel sat gratefully, pressing himself against the armrest so as not to sit too close to Eliza. It would not do for him to dirty her fine clothes. Despite his efforts, he still found layers of her skirt beneath him, as it was too large to contain on one end of the seat.

"Miss Eliza was just telling me all about her schooling on the Tower," the Commissioner said. "She could be a great help to you with your own studies."

"Oh, I doubt Nathaniel needs my help. He has always been the picture of intellect in his letters." Eliza rested her hand on Nathaniel's, just barely touching his skin.

He wished she wouldn't. He did not deserve to be touched, marred by dirt and filth and the kind of blood no one could see.

"You'd be surprised," the Commissioner muttered into his drink.

Eliza flushed, pressing her fingers harder against Nathaniel's knuckles. "I do apologize." Her words carried more force now, leaving behind the airy lightness from before. "I feel somewhat uneasy. I don't know how to treat you, Nathaniel. We know so much about each other, and yet it is as if we know nothing at all."

Before Nathaniel could devise a reply, the Commissioner spoke again. "Perhaps once Nathaniel has had a chance to tidy himself, he can oblige you with a tour of our gardens and you may become better acquainted." The Commissioner handed her a crystal glass filled with a pink beverage to match her ensemble.

On another day, Nathaniel might have flushed at his father's insult, but he could not find it in himself to feel embarrassment, not even in front of Eliza. He couldn't feel anything at all.

Eliza fixed Nathaniel with a winning smile, full lips parted just so. "I do hope so! I've only ever seen replicas of real flowers before." She pointed to the silk roses adorning her hat, made from deep crimson cloth, red like the real thing, red like so many things.

Like Anna's hair. Like Roman's blood.

Nathaniel let go of her hand and stood abruptly. "I'll take my leave now." Stepping around the furniture carefully, so as not to accidentally tread on Eliza's skirts, he made his way toward the door. "As my father said, I must tidy myself. Do excuse me."

He did not wait for his father's permission. Nathaniel bolted from the room, and not a moment too soon. Bile threatened his throat, and he removed his cravat to cover his mouth just in time. He heaved, his whole body shaking, sweat streaming from every pore.

When Nathaniel calmed himself, he pulled the cravat from his mouth. It was dotted with bile and saliva, but Nathaniel barely saw it. He could have sworn it had been sky-blue silk when he donned it that morning, but now in his hands it was red.

CHAPTER TWENTY-THREE

Eliza couldn't remember the last time she'd laughed in earnest. She'd given foolish nobles a chuckle for a favor, a giggle for their confidence, but she was hard-pressed to think of a time in the last five years she'd laughed for herself.

Now, seated on the Commissioner's sofa, watching her mud-covered fiancé run from her like a scared child, Eliza laughed, full and unrestrained. The Queen had been without substantial companionship for too long, warping her sense of humor. This engagement was her idea of a joke; there was no other explanation.

Only the Queen did not joke.

"Another drink?" the Commissioner asked, pointing to the nearly empty crystal glass in her hand.

"Thank you." Eliza handed it back, having poured its contents into the potted plant only moments ago. She knew better than to drink from a strange glass, though the temptation of alcohol weighed heavily as reality settled down around her. Nathaniel, no more than a child with mud on his shoes, was her future. She'd gone from the Queen's right hand to the would-be wife of a boy who could never be her equal. Would that he was a girl, she could bear the wildness. She might even find she liked it.

Now more than ever, Eliza felt Marla's absence acutely. Once, they'd promised when they visited Earth Adjacent, they'd go together. Hand in hand, step-by-step, they'd explore the planet. But Marla had always been better at keeping promises than Eliza. Marla had been better at so many things. She'd simply been *better*.

Eliza gripped the sofa cushion beneath her, nails biting into fabric. It did not serve her to compare Marla to Nathaniel. Yet she'd left Marla out of duty, and now she would marry Nathaniel for the same obligation. Everything always came back to the Queen.

The Commissioner busied himself with her drink, giving Eliza time to compose herself, so when he turned back, she'd arranged her face in a pleasant display of apathy.

"A few business items before we indulge," Eliza said, setting the offered beverage on the coffee table. Better to establish the power dynamic before the Commissioner had a chance to assert himself, and with Nathaniel out of the room, she'd no need to play demure.

The Commissioner leaned against the armchair opposite her with a sigh but did not protest.

"I'm sure you're in no hurry to see your son and I wed; after all I've only just arrived and there's so much planning to be done for a wedding as momentous as ours." She paused, remembering the Queen's lessons on oration and on the power of silence. Here, she would allow the Commissioner's mind to fill in the blank she left with the possibility for splendor, the opportunity to show off.

"Certainly, it will take some time to arrange the event," the Commissioner agreed, his voice strained as though coming from far away.

Now that she'd reminded him what was to be gained by their union, she would dangle a morsel before him to keep him satisfied until Eliza could complete her mission. "Still, it would be a shame to wait until the wedding to celebrate. After all, I've not yet met any of the planetary lords."

"Councilors." The Commissioner cleared his throat. "I have councilors, not lords."

"All the same." Eliza waved her hand, brushing off his correction. "If I'm to be Nathaniel's wife someday, I ought to know the Settlement's elite. What say you to an engagement party?" If all went as planned, there'd be no wedding at all, but Eliza needed to make connections, and what better way to get to know the Commissioner's trusted advisors than to charm them the way she had the Tower's aristocrats?

The Commissioner considered, eyeing her with narrowed focus. "Perhaps you're right. It would be best to present you sooner rather than later. The Settlement could use a bright spot of news, and you'll certainly light up that old ballroom."

Eliza kept her gaze relaxed, her smile loose, but inside her mind churned. The Commissioner had taken the bait so easily. She'd expected him to push back. Judging by the state of his foyer— the dusty chandelier he clearly never used, and the poorly lit entrance—the Commissioner did not often entertain. Perhaps the Settlement was in need of a morale boost after all, or perhaps he'd something to hide, using her arrival as the perfect distraction.

No matter; whether he knew it or not, he'd given her far more than she'd asked for.

"Shall we plan for a week, or is that too soon?" Eliza pouted her lower lip just so.

"My staff is perfectly capable of—"

"Oh! I didn't intend to insult your staff, Commissioner." The lie spilled forth, practiced and unassuming. She cast her gaze down and to the left, waiting. In a moment, his pride would get the better of him and . . .

"Four days," the Commissioner snapped.

Eliza leaned back, letting her eyes fall upon the Commissioner's face. "Impressive! I look forward to enjoying an evening of celebration with my betrothed and the Settlement."

"He's a handful," the Commissioner said, settling himself back in his armchair, legs crossed, elbow propped on his knee. "Truth be told, it's a relief to pass this burden on to you."

Eliza's stomach clenched. "I'm sure he's not so bad," she said, the defense slipping from her lips before she could stop it. She was, in fact, not sure. Only moments before, she'd thought him and their entire arrangement a chore. Nothing had changed. Nothing *would* change.

Now it was the Commissioner's turn to laugh, a hollow, unforgiving laugh. "I assure you, he is." He leaned forward, eyes boring into hers. "I know it must seem an imposition, leaving your home to come live here, to marry my disappointment of a son."

Eliza blanched. She'd read Nathaniel's letters, felt his loneliness acutely, but she'd thought it an exaggeration, the kind of adolescent fancy she never allowed herself. But the Commissioner had truly called his own son a disappointment, the disdain on his lips enough to shock even Eliza.

"I won't lie to you. My son is insubordinate, inept, and frankly an idiot."

Eliza's heart beat a bruise against her chest to the cadence of his words. It was not her job to stop this abuse. Eliza did not deal in the business of right and wrong, only in necessity. She did not *need* to protect Nathaniel from this. But even in the face of his absurd appearance—perhaps because of it—Eliza could not bring herself to ignore the Commissioner's words. She imagined herself rising from her seat and hurling her glass at the man's head. She would leave the room and find Nathaniel, tell him he was none of those things, though she knew not how true her words would be. She would wrap him in her arms, even endeavor not to care if he got mud on her dress. She would retire her blade to become his shield.

"My hope is you might find a way to reach him. Though I have failed to impress upon him the weight of his position, someone like you might have a chance to mold him." The Commissioner eyed her. "He *can* be broken. And he *can* be fixed."

Eliza fought the urge to turn her fantasy into a reality. She'd heard those words before, an accusation, a weapon. But she'd never needed fixing, and neither did Nathaniel.

Though Eliza longed to impale the Commissioner on the sharp heel of her shoe, she needed to maintain the appearance of neutrality. She pushed down every violent impulse she had, and instead said, "We understand each other, Commissioner. Your son is young and impressionable."

The Commissioner nodded. "So you'll attempt to . . . influence him?"

Eliza stood. "I hope I can provide him direction." She would remain vague about what direction that might be.

If Nathaniel was a rusty blade, unpracticed and unfocused, she'd teach him to be sharp, then guide him straight through his father's heart to take his place. The Queen needed something from the Commissioner, and if this one would not bend, she'd make sure the next one would.

CHAPTER TWENTY-FOUR

Anna had known many people to die during her lifetime—an occupational hazard of being a surgeon, or so Thatcher would say. In Anna's experience, death came faster to those who least deserved it, lost to illness, to surgery, or to the Commissioner's soldiers.

But Anna had never lost anyone she loved before.

She'd loved the boy who lay dead in the grass. He was her family, and she'd never told him. Now he would never know.

He knew, said a voice in her head. But that didn't make it better, didn't change his fate. Roman had been everything she couldn't be: honest, brave, and full of affection. Anna thought when she died, she'd have no regrets. But she'd assumed she would go well before anyone else. She hadn't expected to live long enough to bury anyone, least of all Roman.

Running her bloodstained hands through Roman's hair, feeling its bounce for the last time, Anna wiped her tears with her wrist, leaving behind a streak of red on her skin.

She had to move. She had to bring him home.

Anna slid her hands beneath his body and lifted with all the strength she had left. She didn't remember him being so heavy. She didn't remember him being so small.

One step at a time, she forced herself toward Mechan. The Settlement gates were just out of sight, and it wasn't safe. Any minute Nathaniel might return with a dozen officers to arrest her.

Let them come. She didn't care. She'd fight them tooth and nail until they put a rusty bullet in her head. Then, at least, Roman wouldn't be alone.

But someone had to tell Ruby. It had been only months since Ruby's husband was shot. A merciful death, they'd called it when they told her in the yard of her little cottage. Runners weren't usually so lucky, more often held for questioning and hanged in the square. To be shot outside the gates where other runners could still collect his body and personal effects—well, that was a downright blessing.

Anna couldn't let the runners tell Ruby her son was dead, too. She couldn't save Roman's arm all those years ago, and she couldn't save his life there in the field, but she could carry him home to his mother where he belonged, each step a penance for wrongs she could never make right.

When she arrived outside Mechan, two runners, Kate and Theo, met her on the path.

They spoke words she did not hear, gesturing wildly, conversing with frantic eyes.

A storm raged all around her—bodies moved in a frenzy, but she stood at the center where nothing moved, nothing mattered.

Kate tried to pry Roman's body from her arms and Anna returned to the present, sound rushing at her from every direction.

"No," she said, the word quiet on her lips, her arms tight around the boy who turned colder with every second. She couldn't let go.

And then the world stood still, and Kate and Theo fell silent, turning their heads slowly away.

Ruby stood in the center of the path, mouth open as though waiting on a word that wouldn't come. Her arms hung at her sides, and the worry lines in her forehead were as deep as Anna had ever seen them.

She locked eyes with Anna for a breathless moment before her gaze drifted down to the boy in her arms. Anna could only imagine what a sight she was, covered in mud and Roman's blood. She must have looked a nightmare, one Ruby had imagined before.

Slowly—ever so slowly—Ruby took a hesitant step forward, her hand reaching with the ghost of a wish, before she collapsed, knees hitting the dusty ground. Her hands recoiled to her neck and chest, shaking and scratching like the scream on her face was stuck silent in her throat.

"Someone fetch Thatcher," Theo said.

Anna blinked, unsticking her eyes from Ruby for a moment to look at Roman's face. Even in death, he looked joyous, his lips upturned in a smile.

"It's too late." The words came out a whisper, but everyone could hear her; the square was so very silent. "He's already gone."

Theo turned to Anna, something akin to kindness or pity in his eyes—Anna could no longer tell the difference between the two.

"No, for her." He pointed to Ruby as she clawed against the fabric at her throat, trying desperately to breathe.

When Kate returned with Thatcher, pushing his chair with considerable force, Ruby was gasping for air, eyes darting and hands shaking as she tried to undo the collar of her shirt.

"Get her inside," Thatcher said, waving at his house behind him.

The runners got Ruby to her feet and half walked, half carried her to the door.

Anna sucked in a long breath as Ruby disappeared, but then Thatcher turned his eyes on her. His gaze swept over her blood-stained clothes and he sighed, all the muscles in his face falling.

"Come." It was neither an order nor a plea but a suggestion.

Anna had no argument left inside her, only the emptiness that came after tears and the fullness that came before pain.

When they, too, were inside, Thatcher ushered her into the operating room and gestured for her to place Roman's body on the table.

She wanted to explain that he could do nothing—that no surgery could save Roman now. But she just stood in the doorway, holding on to a boy who had already let go.

"I need to clean him up." Thatcher's voice wavered, though his hands were steady. "Ruby will want to see him when she's calm again, and she can't see him like this."

Anna looked down at Roman. The blood had dried now, a dark stain against the white shirt he'd worn.

With more effort than it had taken to lift him, Anna relaxed her arms. Her joints stuck like rusty gears, unaccustomed to moving, stuttering with every inch she gave. Disentangling herself from Roman, Anna stepped back from the table, blood cascading down her front. A considerable amount had pooled between them, kept from spilling over by the pressure of her grip.

"I can handle it from here." Thatcher lifted a pair of scissors and began to cut the soiled fabric away from Roman's body. "You go clean up."

Anna shook her head, hand still wrapped around Roman's, cold and tiny. "I don't want him to be alone," she croaked.

Thatcher's jaw relaxed, and he set down the scissors. Wheeling himself back and around the table, he reached up to put his hand over hers. "My dear," he murmured, "he's already alone."

Anna splashed her face and arms with cold water, though she couldn't tell the difference. It was as if she'd left every nerve, every part of her that could feel anything back in the field by the Settlement. It was just as well. Anna didn't deserve to wallow, not with Ruby a room away. Grief would have to wait.

The pit in Anna's stomach began to fill with something else, something more powerful. Nathaniel's surprised face burned in her memory, feeding the fire within.

She wanted to find him and hurt him. She wanted to make him feel the way she felt—the way Ruby felt. He didn't deserve to walk away.

But he had.

And so had she.

Anna had moved all her belongings out to her workshop, so she had no other clothes. She scrubbed the blood away as best she could with shaking hands, but a dark stain still ran from her collar to her waist. Even if she could change her clothes, she could not change Roman's death. It would sit against her skin far longer than the blood.

When she returned to the kitchen, Ruby sat near the hearth with a mug of tea in front of her. She no longer shook, and judging by the even rise and fall of her shoulders, her breathing had returned to normal.

Anna knew she ought to say something—anything—but words froze on her tongue. Ruby's eyes bored into hers, her silence volumes louder than any word, filling all the hollow places in Anna's chest with a prickling sensation, neither pleasant nor painful.

"You can see him now," Thatcher said from the doorway to the operating room, hands folded in his lap, chin down.

Ruby's gaze fell. "Not yet," she whispered.

"Of course." Thatcher wheeled into the room, taking his place at the foot of the table. "Take whatever time you need."

Ruby nodded slowly and raised her hand, fingers straining for her mug against an invisible tether that kept her arms close to her body. "What happened?"

Thatcher fixed worried eyes on Anna, giving a little shake of his head to indicate she should stay silent.

She didn't need to be told—Anna didn't think she could speak even if she tried.

But Ruby wouldn't allow it. "I want to know," she said. "I *need* to know." She set her mug down on the table, sloshing hot water over the side and onto the floor.

Anna watched the water's progress as it soaked into the wood flooring. In a few minutes, the wet spot would be gone, evaporated into air. If only blood disappeared so easily.

"Anna?"

Ruby's voice, speaking Anna's name like her last hope, her last remaining lifeline, sent shivers down Anna's spine. She'd wanted something actionable to do—like stab something, or break something. Explaining to Ruby how her son had died was actionable. This, she could do.

"He f-followed me," Anna began. The words felt odd, like they were a different language. But she couldn't break. She couldn't show the pain in her heart, because Ruby's was so much greater. She had to hold firm. She had to be strong.

With a deep breath, Anna launched into the explanation.

Ruby stared at a fixed spot on the table long after Anna had finished speaking, letting the final words of her story hang in the air like cobwebs.

Anna longed to wipe them away, but the facts remained that Roman was dead, killed by the Commissioner's son, killed by a faulty heart, killed by circumstance and chance.

"You should have sent him home," Ruby said finally. "He's a child, not a runner."

Anna nodded. She knew this. She'd thought this. But it did Ruby no good if Anna didn't let her say it aloud.

"He shouldn't have been wandering around with his incision still healing. I should have kept him inside." Ruby buried her face in her hands.

Thatcher let out a noise that sounded like a grunt and a whistle at the same time. "Walking was good for him. It wasn't exercise that killed him, most likely."

Ruby shook her head. "He should never have been there in the first place. Anna, you should have sent him home."

"I tried," Anna said quietly, remembering the boy's heartwarming pledge to protect her. He had been so sure that he was invincible against the world. But it was Roman who'd needed protecting, and Anna should have been the one to look out for him. "I just— I thought there would be no harm in waiting, and sending him to walk home on his own seemed too risky. If I'd known my meeting would go so poorly, I would never have gone in the first place."

"*Poorly* is one hell of an understatement," Thatcher muttered.

Anna leaned forward onto the back of her empty chair. She picked at a sliver of wood, chipping away at the roughly carved dowel. "I didn't mean for him to get mixed up in my work."

"Well, he did!" Ruby snapped, voice high and harsh.

Anna nodded again but stopped quickly. A headache inched across her eyes, sending pinpricks into the bridge of her nose. "If I'd thought it would be dangerous, I wouldn't have let him stay."

Thatcher shook his head. "This is my fault. I should never have let you leave Mechan."

Anna narrowed her eyes. They'd been over this before, and she would have never taken orders from him anyway—still wouldn't, even after all that had happened.

"I thought after I warned you about him, you would see reason, but I suppose even the Commissioner's son is fair game for you and your business." Thatcher slammed his palm into the armrest on his chair, sadness—more than anger—flashing through his eyes.

"You knew?" Ruby's head shot up. "You knew it was the Commissioner's son you were meeting?"

"Yes, but—"

"Then you knew it was dangerous! You knew and you went anyway." She ran her hands over her face and hair. "I thought this was all just chance—unavoidable chance. But you knew."

Anna bit her tongue. She *had* known. There was no denying it. She'd hoped Nathaniel would be genuine, she'd hoped he would be curious, she'd hoped he would not be his father's son. But she'd been wrong to hope. Hope had been a worse poison than all the Commissioner's combined.

Ruby stood up and stalked past Anna without looking at her. "You *knew*," she whispered, pausing at the door to the operating room. "I need to see my son now. I need to see someone who loves—loved—the people around him."

As Ruby disappeared into the operating room, Anna wished more than anything she could go with her, but Anna was not welcome. She was not as good as Roman, not as true. Was Ruby right about her—that she didn't love the people around her? Anna didn't have an answer.

Maybe that was her answer.

"Deirdre-Anne," Thatcher said, clearing away Ruby's mug. "Do something about the blood on your shirt."

The words settled into Anna's pores, digging deep into her skin. She could do nothing about Ruby's pain, but she could do something about the red stain down her front.

She could do something about the blood.

She could spill some more.

CHAPTER TWENTY-FIVE

Once Nathaniel had bathed and dressed more appropriately to entertain their guest, he spent several minutes standing in front of his bedroom door staring at the brass doorknob. He'd waited a long time to finally meet Eliza. It had always seemed a far-off future, unlikely and full of what-ifs.

Now that day had finally come, and Nathaniel couldn't muster any enthusiasm. Even though he was clean now, he still felt stained from the inside out, tainted by things he could not undo.

Eliza met him at the bottom of the stairs, wearing a smile as large as her hat.

Nathaniel wished he could smile back.

"I thought we might take a walk outside," she said, her words like honey in his ears.

Nathaniel nodded gratefully, offering his arm. "Will you be cold?" he asked, thinking of the sun long gone from the sky. It had just chimed nine o'clock.

Eliza paused at the door, hand poised to turn the handle. "I hadn't thought of that. You have weather variations here."

"Of course we do. What did you expect?"

"We have temperature regulation on the Tower. It doesn't get cold." She opened the door and a gust of wind rushed through them, jostling Eliza's perfectly curled hair. She laughed as it pushed her hat askew. "We don't have wind, either."

Taking Nathaniel's hand, Eliza pulled him onto the dark garden path with a stronger grip than he'd expected. Once they were obscured by a long row of hedges, Eliza dropped his hand and slowed to a leisurely stroll.

"Nathaniel," she began, "I know we aren't all that well acquainted, but I thought"—she hesitated—"I thought you would have been more . . . forthcoming about your father."

Nathaniel's head snapped up. "What about him?" He could still see her face by the light of the moon—smiling to the east.

Eliza's eyes narrowed in scrutiny.

"The way you wrote about him, I didn't realize—" She took his arm again, her skin brushing against the thin cloth of his sleeve. "He was cruel back there to treat you with such contempt."

The storm in his stomach returned in full force. His father wasn't cruel; he only did what was necessary, what was best for Nathaniel.

"I've done some things of late to displease my father," Nathaniel said, though it seemed an understatement somehow. He had done things, but they were not the same things that grated at Nathaniel now. His father cared so much about appearances and order, but how could those things matter when a boy—an innocent child—was dead? "I fear I will never live up to his expectations."

Eliza fixed him with a quizzical look. "Do you *want* to live up to his expectations?"

The words struck him forcefully. His father's approval had always been the goal, but maybe it wasn't worth chasing. The Technician certainly hadn't been.

Maybe he was not fit to be Commissioner, to fill his father's shoes. If he was unwilling to do whatever it took—regardless of consequence, regardless of tragedy—then perhaps he was too weak to be Commissioner.

But he didn't need to be just like his father, cold and calculated. He could be different. His father would balk at such musings, but Nathaniel couldn't help but hold a little tighter to the part of himself that didn't care. It wasn't a new feeling but a very old one he'd buried long ago. Now it awoke as if from a deep sleep, bringing with it the radical concept that Nathaniel was worth more than his father's opinion of him.

Maybe Nathaniel could simply be himself.

"I don't know," Nathaniel said, surprised to hear his own honesty. "Sometimes I think it's the only thing that matters, and sometimes I think there's so much more to care about, but I just—"

"He's your father. I understand." Eliza plucked a rose from its stem, brushing her thumb lightly across the thorns as though testing them. "Family can feel like forever, like it's sewn into your skin."

A chill that had nothing to do with the night air prickled across Nathaniel's neck and arms. She was right. No matter his feelings, he was bound to his father forever.

"Is it like that for you?" Nathaniel asked, eyes fixed on Eliza's fingers as they tore rose petals from the stem, a delicate dismantling of nature. "I mean—is your family like that, too?"

Eliza paused, frowning at the flower in her hands. "Family can mean a lot of things. For you, it is your father—he gave you life in a traditional sense. For me, it's the Queen and her court. They gave me life, too, in a way."

Nathaniel wondered for a moment if Eliza was the Queen without her veil. To Nathaniel, she was only a blue specter, more pixel than person. He considered asking, but no matter how he spun it, the question was rude. Instead, he asked, "What is she like, the Queen?"

"You don't know? I presumed because of your father—"

Nathaniel shook his head. "I've spoken only a dozen words to her. Truth be told, even though she's my grandmother, I don't think I know any more about her than your average citizen of Earth Adjacent. She's just a figure in the sky to most of us—not even really *our* Queen."

Eliza let the flower fall, red petals staining the grassy earth, scattered and splintered in a most dignified death.

"I'm going to tell you something, Nathaniel. Something I don't often tell people. Try not to be alarmed—in fact, try not to react at all." Eliza's voice returned to a heavier register. "There's no telling who might be watching."

Nathaniel kept his face as still as he could. "You think someone is watching us?"

Eliza squeezed his arm gently. "You are the Commissioner's son, heir to the most powerful seat of government on this planet, and I'm your fiancée. There are many who would benefit from keeping tabs on the two of us."

Nathaniel swallowed, suddenly aware of all his limbs, where he placed them, how he held them. "What is it?"

"I'm not only your fiancée like your father thinks. I'm also the Queen's Eyes—her agent."

Nathaniel couldn't wrap his tongue around a reply. He didn't know what she meant, or how it related to him, only that it seemed important.

"You are allowed to breathe, Nathaniel." Eliza squeezed his arm. "Go on, lead me through the gardens as you would normally."

Nathaniel did not have a *normally* when it came to walking the gardens. Still, he made his way through the hedges toward a plot of moonflowers, petals open to the night air.

Eliza bent to smell their aroma and smiled. "It's important that you understand I'm not simply a noble from the Tower chosen at random to be your bride. I am, as I said, an extension of the Queen herself—her spy."

Nathaniel's stomach turned. He should have been more careful with his words. Why had he been so honest? Of course Eliza would bring his words right back to his father. Of course she could not be trusted.

"The Queen has yet to make my purpose here clear, but I can guess it will have something to do with your father." She took his arm again and pointed toward a bush with yellow flowers, an excited gleam in her eye that did not reflect the tenor of their conversation. "I tell you this, Nathaniel, because I want to make one thing clear."

What would Eliza report back to the Queen about that night? Would she tell the Queen about Nathaniel's entrance, covered in mud, or about the way his father cut him down? Nathaniel was unsure which he preferred. "And what is that?"

"I trust you."

Nathaniel hadn't expected that. He did not deserve her trust—he didn't deserve anyone's trust. He'd wasted Anna's already.

"You trust me?"

"I do." Eliza buried her nose in the honey-colored flowers. "In my line of work, secrets are a kind of currency. You can buy almost anything with a secret. I've just given you one of mine, and it's up to you how you spend it."

"Spend it? What do you mean?" Nathaniel's head spun in circles, as if deprived of oxygen.

"Your father is a dangerous and difficult man. Give him my secret, and you might gain an inch, earn a fraction of his respect." She shrugged, moving on to the next flower bush. "Or you can keep it and prove you are worthy of my trust."

Nathaniel's throat constricted. He'd not even thought to tell his father. Maybe his instincts were changing.

A small flame of hope flickered to life in his stomach. "I won't betray you."

"Good." She straightened once more and continued on their promenade. "I told you this, Nathaniel, because I believe honesty is the key to any lasting relationship, and I do so hope that we can be friends through all this."

Nathaniel frowned. "Friends." It sounded absurd even as he said the word. He'd never truly had a friend before. His father certainly couldn't be counted as one, and Anna—she might have become one if he hadn't ruined everything.

"Yes, friends." Eliza brushed his cheek with her fingertip. "Friends help each other, and I'd like your help. I don't need it, I should clarify—I'll get what I want one way or another. But it will be much easier and more enjoyable, I'd imagine, with you in my corner."

"Wh-what do you want help with?"

"I don't know yet, exactly, but when I do, I want to make sure I'm the one holding all the cards."

"And I'm one of them?"

Eliza smiled, her eyes alight like stars. "No, you're a person, not a card." She took his hand in hers, lacing their fingers together. "I just hope you'll help me hold them."

Nathaniel pulled his hand away, the feel of skin on skin so foreign. She was his fiancée, and he knew they'd have to breach the topic eventually, but not now, not yet. He couldn't tell her how he felt when he himself didn't fully understand it. He couldn't tell her he wanted her near but not too close. He couldn't tell her he wanted to know her, like her—but not love her.

Instead, Nathaniel took a deep breath and said, "How do I know I can trust you?"

"You don't, same as me. The best either of us can do is take the leap and hope it pays off, in the end." She extended her hand again, an offering.

Nathaniel shook it.

"What do you think you're doing?" Eliza raised an eyebrow. "You're supposed bow and kiss it. What sort of society were you raised in?"

Nathaniel cracked a smile—a real one—but before he could decide whether or not he wanted to oblige her, Eliza ripped her hand from his, turning at the sound of rustling leaves.

"Who's there?" she called into the darkness, eyes narrowed at the path behind him.

Nathaniel followed the line of her gaze, eyes landing on a dark form hidden within the shadows of the hedges.

The newcomer stepped forward, and moonlight illuminated copper hair and loose clothes, splattered with blood. Anna fixed him with a wild stare for a moment, taking the breath from his lungs, before she let her eyes drop to his center.

She lunged, and Nathaniel didn't see the knife in her hand until it was too late.

CHAPTER TWENTY-SIX

Anna liked the weight of the knife in her hand. She was used to wrenches and screwdrivers, not weapons, but this one suited her well enough. She swung the blade high, ready to stab Nathaniel's face, his chest, his throat, his heart. But a hand caught hers, yanking her back and away from him.

Anna whipped around. A girl in pink, perfect and poised, with an outrageous floral hat, restrained her. Anna snarled. She didn't care if the pink lady interfered. As long as Anna got her revenge, she didn't care what came after. That thought alone had driven her from Thatcher's kitchen, through the Settlement, and over the garden wall.

Now Nathaniel stood before her, looking shaken but clean. Anna was dirty and bloody and angry; how dare he be anything other than the same? He didn't deserve to be clean. He deserved her knife in his chest, and she deserved her revenge.

But *revenge* was just a fancy word for murder.

Could she even do it? Could she lift the blade and plunge it into living flesh? Could she kill someone?

Yes.

She could do it for Roman—for Roman, who would never have wanted her to kill. But Roman couldn't tell her to stop. He would never tell her anything again.

Anna lunged, hitting Nathaniel with her forearm, and again, the petite pink girl fought her in Nathaniel's stead. The girl grabbed hold of Anna's shirt, ripping it down the back and jerking her away from Nathaniel.

"Give me that," the girl snarled, plucking the knife from Anna's fingers before Anna could think to lash out. "You're going to hurt someone, Red."

"That's the idea." Anna swung her fist and reached for the knife, but the girl pointed it toward her, nicking the skin along Anna's fingertips. Pain blossomed at her extremities and she recoiled. Now her own blood stained her clothes, too, a crimson badge.

A growl erupted from Anna's throat as animalistic rage surged through her body. She didn't need a knife to hurt someone. But before she could lay a hand on Nathaniel, the other girl grabbed Anna by the hair and kicked at her knees. Anna tripped and staggered back, but before she could recover, the girl put her in a headlock, Anna's own knife pressed against her neck.

"Now," the girl said, "why did you attack us?"

Anna didn't move. She wanted to, but she knew the second she breathed too deeply, shifted too much, the knife would become acquainted with her veins.

"Not you," Anna said, voice strangled. "Him."

Though the girl stood considerably shorter, with Anna held at such an awkward angle, she was able to speak directly into her ear. "That man is the Commissioner's heir. Are you sure you want to admit to treason?" Her words brushed Anna's neck, a blistering wind, too warm, too close.

Nathaniel rose to his feet, approaching with a hand raised. "Eliza, I don't think—"

The girl, Eliza, tightened her hold on Anna, her touch searing an invisible brand into Anna's skin. "This ruffian just tried to kill you." She glanced at Anna with a critical eye. "Is that blood?"

"It will be if you don't let me at him." Anna ground her teeth, practically choking on the floral scent of her captor, the fragrance clouding her mind. If Eliza would only let her go, she'd be able to think straight again.

Nathaniel sighed, leaning back against the garden wall. "Anna, please."

Eliza's grip loosened on Anna, but the knife still pressed against her flesh at a dangerous angle. She glanced from Anna to Nathaniel and back again. "You know each other?"

"She's the Technician." Nathaniel sank into a seated position on the ledge of the garden bed.

"The what?" Eliza asked.

"My father's most wanted criminal. She's responsible for practically the entire illegal tech market. I had her in custody, but then—"

"Actually, I don't care." Eliza's hold on Anna's throat tightened.

"He killed a child!" Anna spat, and Eliza's fingers scraped against her skin.

Nathaniel put his head in his hands. "He's really dead, then."

"Do you think I'd be here if he wasn't?" Anna struggled against Eliza—if she could only reach Nathaniel, this would all be over.

"You saw him die. You killed him. Did you think he'd somehow miraculously survive?"

Nathaniel shook his head. "I know what I did."

"What did you do?" Eliza asked Nathaniel. Then, turning to Anna, she raised her eyebrow, the small mole just above it bouncing into her hairline. "What did he do?"

Nathaniel curled in on himself, burying his face in the fabric of his sleeves. "I'm sorry. I'm so sorry." He repeated it over and over until it became a barely audible mumble.

Anna wished she could curl into a ball like that, hide from the world, hide from her feelings.

"All right." Eliza sighed. "One of you had better explain all this, or I flay the girl."

Anna's breath caught as Eliza's eyes narrowed. Though the other girl made a show of tightening her hold on Anna, it didn't feel threatening. She was bluffing, and only Anna, who could feel Eliza's rapid heartbeat against her shoulder, knew the truth. But the realization struck Anna with more fear than relief; the girl who dressed like a flower—smelled like one, too—had a plan, while Anna's dissolved into nothing the longer she stood trapped in the garden.

Nathaniel's head snapped up, revealing puffy eyes. "She doesn't deserve to die."

Eliza frowned. "No one deserves to die." She slid around Anna to face her, but she kept the knife up and at the ready. "Don't try to run. I may be small, but I'm faster and fiercer than you by leagues." She fixed Anna with sharp eyes, almost black in the night. "I won't play the peace weaver without information. What happened, and what do you want?"

Anna could run, and maybe Eliza would catch her, but in those skirts—nearly as wide as Eliza was tall—Anna wasn't so sure. But Anna did not want to run. She could still fight, even if she couldn't win.

"He has to pay for what he did." Anna felt the words fall flat even as she said them. "I want him to bleed as much as Roman did." She locked eyes with Nathaniel, watching as any remaining resistance flitted from his gaze.

"Maybe I deserve that," Nathaniel murmured.

Eliza shot him a cutting look. "No one is dying tonight."

"Why not? I want to kill him and he wants to let me." Anna reached for the knife, but Eliza caught her hand. Her touch sent gooseflesh up Anna's arms.

"What do you want?" Eliza repeated, taking a step closer, dark, endless eyes boring into Anna's.

Anna flinched. Her stare made Anna's stomach writhe. Breathing was harder with Eliza's eyes on her. She pushed the discomfort away and moved forward until they were only inches apart, until she could see every sharp angle and every soft curve of the girl's flawless face. "I told you. I want him dead."

"No, you don't. Tell me what you really want."

"I did!" But the word *want* echoed in Anna's ears, a harsh beat of an invisible drum asking her over and over.

What *did* she want?

She wanted Nathaniel to pay for what he'd done to Roman. She wanted Thatcher and Ruby to forgive her. She wanted Eliza to stop asking, stop touching, stop looking. And she wanted to stay there, never moving, never choosing, poised in the moment before falling.

Eliza's lip curled. "If you'd really wanted him dead, you would have tried to kill me, too, when I let go. If you truly wanted a dead body, you'd have one—maybe even two." She flipped the knife expertly in her other hand and lowered it so it no longer pointed at Anna. "You might want him dead, but I don't think you want to kill him."

Anna shrank beneath her words. Eliza had read her like a book, unraveled her like cloth. No one had ever spent so long analyzing her movements, her actions, her intent.

Coming here to the Settlement, let alone the Commissioner's manor, might have been the most foolish thing she'd ever done, risking her life, and risking Mechan for a shot at revenge. If she didn't kill Nathaniel now, how would she justify it?

"Think, Red," Eliza said. "If you kill him, he dies—ceases to exist, to feel. He cannot know the pain he put you through, and he can't ever make up for it." Eliza's eyes glanced to the knife in her hand. "So if what you truly want is revenge, then take the knife and we'll see how you fair. My guess is I'll have you in a headlock again in seconds, and unlike you, I don't hesitate when I want to take a life." A smirk flashed across her lips as though she was imagining it, savoring it. "But if what you want is justice, you'll tell me what happened, and you'll see what an excellent ally I can be."

"Excuse me if I find it difficult to trust you with my own knife pointed at me," Anna growled.

Eliza smiled, turning her hand to direct the blade toward herself. "Trust is forged not by the direction of the blade but by the wielder's choice not to use it." She offered Anna the hilt.

Anna's eyes bounced from Eliza's face to the knife to Nathaniel. It was a test. Eliza spun words not unlike Thatcher, with a preference for proverb. The blade was just a blade, and Anna's power now lay in this choice to put her trust in the noble girl, rather than her weapon.

She shook her head, refusing the knife. "Justice." Anna tried the word on her tongue, but she couldn't tell if she liked it. She'd wanted blood, she'd wanted death—but Eliza was right. Revenge lasted only a moment, and then it would be over. If she killed Nathaniel, she wouldn't live to enjoy it. And on the off chance that she wasn't immediately killed by an officer or Eliza herself, she'd almost certainly live to regret it. "What kind of justice are you offering?"

Eliza smiled. "That depends entirely on you."

Openness wasn't a trait Anna had ever prided herself on, preferring the comfort of secrets, but they didn't feel like secrets anymore. They wouldn't keep her safe now. They were only walls, protecting her from a different foe.

So Anna told her everything: the locket, the betrayal, the boy now dead and buried. Eliza didn't look at Anna with kindness or with hatred as she spoke but with eyes that listened.

When Anna finished, Eliza leaned back against the hedge. "It seems we have an enemy in common," she said at last. "The Commissioner has caused you a great deal of pain, and he stands in my way, too. Nathaniel may have hurt you, but I don't think he's your real enemy—the Commissioner is the reason he went after you in the first place."

Nathaniel averted his eyes, and Anna's stomach twisted with something distressingly akin to pity. In a way, the Commissioner had pulled all their strings.

"If he's poisoning his people," Eliza continued, "and we can present enough evidence to that effect, we may very well be able to remove him from power—and the longer he's in power, the worse it will be for both of us."

Anna had fantasized about rushing the Settlement with a thousand soldiers, or creating some type of explosive made up of all the tech the Commissioner hated, but she had never thought of a legal approach to her problem. She'd never had any avenue to pursue one. But with two allies on the inside, she might actually succeed. Maybe then she could return to Mechan, if not with pride and triumph, then at least with welcome arms awaiting her.

Anna hadn't thought she'd walk away from this encounter, never expected to live long enough to make the next move, a realization that struck her with a force to rival Eliza's fists. "You want to help me overthrow the Commissioner?" Anna asked, well aware she spoke treason.

"No." Eliza shook her head, a smirk rising from her lips in a way that made Anna's stomach crawl, curl, clench. "I want *you* to help *us* overthrow the Commissioner."

CHAPTER TWENTY-SEVEN

Any ruined evening could be salvaged with a knife fight.

Eliza had thought her visit to Earth Adjacent might be dull—infiltration rarely required use of a blade—but thus far, it had exceeded expectations.

"How do you propose we do that, exactly?" Anna asked, lowering her voice. "Overthrow the Commissioner, I mean."

Eliza frowned, flipping the girl's blade back and forth between her hands. It looked to be of the kitchen variety, sporting remnants of piecrust, but still sufficiently sharp. It hardly measured up to Eliza's weaponry, but it would do its job well enough—not unlike the disheveled girl before her.

Anna was, in a word, a disaster. From her too-red head to her too-worn shoes, nothing about her was remotely decent—not even for something as undignified as a coup—but with a bit of polishing, Eliza could make use of her.

Tucking the knife into her bodice, Eliza pushed herself away from the hedge. "Let's begin by finding you a change of clothes."

"What's wrong with—" Anna paused, glancing at her blood-stained clothes. "Right."

"Nathaniel?" Eliza nudged his shoulder.

"Yes. What?" He startled with each word, as though the sound of his own voice frightened him.

"Care to lead the way inside? We can't very well do all our plotting in the garden." Eliza gestured up at the manor, the windows now dark.

He complied, albeit slowly. Clearly, he'd experienced something of a shock, the ramifications of which Eliza would tend to eventually. For now, she needed to get Anna out of sight and into a clean shirt.

From the moment Eliza laid eyes on their attacker, she knew she wanted to tame her. Another operative might have simply eliminated the threat. But for better or worse, Eliza had decided to let Anna live.

The eyes are the window to the soul, fragile like glass, the Queen had often said. *Toss the right stone, and you may well break through.* She spoke of interrogation, of course, but the same principle applied now. Though Anna's blade had been sharp, something in her face had softened Eliza. Behind the rage, there had been pain in Anna's eyes—the kind of pain that came with loss. Eliza knew that pain, and so she'd made a choice based on instinct rather than tactics.

It was the choice Marla would have made.

Mercy was never a weapon in Marla's hands, but Eliza learned to wield it from her just the same. Marla would have made a terrible set of Eyes for the Queen, too kind and honest to deal in secrets, to deliver death. Still, she'd made Eliza what she was—and paid dearly for it.

"Not the salon," Eliza hissed as Nathaniel led them on toward the sitting room they'd occupied earlier. "Somewhere less conspicuous, like your bedroom."

"M-my room?" Nathaniel withered before her.

Eliza huffed. "We don't have time for modesty. Look at her!" She gestured to Anna's unseemly appearance. "She's positively repellant!"

"I'm standing right here."

But Anna made no further argument, following as Nathaniel ushered them into his bedroom.

It was a smaller room than Eliza expected—larger than her apartment on the Tower but smaller than her guest room in the manor. There was an oak bedframe with a canopy in one corner, and a matching desk opposite littered with papers. Aside from the wardrobe, wedged between the wall and the foot of the bed, the room was empty. Where were his things?

He had no things. He had no *one*.

All the loneliness inked into Nathaniel's letters rushed at her like a shooting star, and it was all Eliza could do not to let it show. Instead, she crossed to the wardrobe, hiding her face as she rummaged through the drawers for a suitable change of clothes for Anna.

Eliza had thought *she'd* been alone all this time, friendless and estranged by the nobles on the Tower. But that was nothing to the isolation and abuse suffered in this room.

Gathering herself, Eliza turned and handed Anna a clean button-up and a pair of trousers. Hardly an ensemble for polite company, but it would do for now.

Anna made a face as she snatched them, her glare piercing Eliza with far more precision than she'd had with a knife. A dangerous storm churned in her blue eyes, something alarming yet oddly familiar lurking below the surface.

Eliza forgot, for a moment, they were Anna's eyes. A calm face framed with sleek black locks unfurled across her vision, and there she was, as real as she'd ever been: Marla.

It had been three years—quieter, emptier, lonelier years than ever Eliza could have imagined. How she'd missed those green eyes, those perfect dimples, that generous smile. What she wouldn't give to have them all back. But Eliza had chosen the Queen's service; she'd chosen a life alone. She had no room in her heart for regret.

"Stars! Would you turn around? I promise I'll change—you don't have to watch me."

Eliza jumped, and Anna's angry freckles reappeared. Marla was gone.

"Right." Eliza turned on her heel and marched to the other side of the room, leaning over Nathaniel's desk. She let her cheeks redden, embarrassment a luxury she did not often indulge. How could she have lost control like that? How had she let such an odd daydream distract her? Anna and Marla were nothing alike. To begin, Anna's eyes were blue, and Marla's were green. Anna was fierce, and Marla was calm. Anna was rebellious, and Marla was mannered. Anna was impulsive, and Marla was cautious.

Most of all, Anna was alive, and Marla was dead.

And yet, even as Eliza's mind enumerated their differences, she found the parallel running through them both, guiding them from their cores. Marla had always been composed, and yet she acted on emotion, letting her heart guide her choices.

Anna did the same. It had been anger that drove her to attack. It was compassion—though Eliza had needed to guide her to it—that had stopped her hand. And it was love for her family and her home that kept Anna there.

Anna had convictions, and now Eliza understood her. This, she could use. She had a new weapon for her armory.

Two, if she counted the knife.

CHAPTER TWENTY-EIGHT

Nathaniel never thought he'd commit treason, but a lot had changed overnight.

As Anna and Eliza discussed something—Nathaniel wasn't listening—he watched their easy exchange. Anna gestured as she spoke, and Eliza leaned toward her, hands planted on either corner of the desk. Their initial meeting had been so very fraught, and as best he could tell, their sudden acquaintanceship continued in the same vein, with each of them flinging insults, venom in their smiles. But as contentious as they were, it seemed to stem from a mutual, if begrudging, respect.

Nathaniel had never been respected like that.

"Nathaniel?" Eliza snapped her fingers in front of his face. "Are you all right?"

"What?" Nathaniel straightened, pushing away from the bedpost.

"You weren't listening." Eliza sighed, exchanging a look with Anna.

"I'm all right with whatever plan you decide is best." Even if he disagreed, he wouldn't say so. It wasn't his place. He was a killer; his opinion wasn't worth sharing.

"You're not," Eliza said. "It bothers you."

It *did* bother him. There were laws he'd bend and laws he'd break, but actively working to overthrow his father was a far stretch.

Still, the memory of blood spilled haunted him in ways his father's words never had. Before, he'd thought if only he could become the perfect son, he could earn his father's love, but Nathaniel could no longer aspire to be his father's definition of perfect. He would instead rebuild himself on the foundation of his mistakes, his faults aplenty, born in defiance of the man who shaped him.

Anna crossed her arms. "Maybe it's best if we don't involve him. He's too close to the Commissioner and—"

"It doesn't matter." Nathaniel couldn't let them do this without him—if only so he wasn't alone with his thoughts. "I'll go along with this regardless. I owe you that."

Anna shook her head and sat in the desk chair, scooting it around to face him. "I don't want you doing this because you owe me."

Nathaniel drew back, knocking into Eliza. He'd forgotten she stood beside him. "I thought that was the deal." His eyes flitted between the two girls. "You won't kill me, I won't turn you in, and we work together to . . . to . . ."

"Overthrow your father." Anna fixed him with a hard look.

Nathaniel gulped. "Yes. Then my debt will be paid." Anna had made her feelings on the Commissioner clear long before she'd known who Nathaniel was, her words still ringing in his ears. Anna saw his father only as a tyrannical leader working against her interests, and Nathaniel was beginning to agree. He *needed* to agree.

Anna leaned back in her chair, crossing her legs. The trousers he'd lent her fit surprisingly well, but they were too short, riding up over her boots. She looked only slightly more civilized than she had the night before, hair a tangled mess and circles beneath her eyes, but at least she was no longer covered in blood.

"It isn't about debt," she said. "You can't just do what I say and expect me to forgive you. I'd rather have your help because you believe what we're doing is right than because you feel beholden. Doing me a favor just because you feel you owe me won't earn my forgiveness."

"I want to help. I want to believe in this. It's just that . . ." Nathaniel chewed his lip. "He's my father."

Eliza placed a hand on his shoulder and squeezed. "Your father is a frightening man. I understand defying him may be difficult."

Nathaniel hugged his middle. "I suppose I just don't see why—"

"Your father is a bad man. He does bad things." Anna threw her hands in the air.

Nathaniel stared at his shoes. "I've done bad things, too."

"Yes. You have," Anna spat.

Eliza looked from Anna to Nathaniel, worry etched into her brow. "Nathaniel, you killed one boy, and it was an accident. Your guilt is proof that you can do better."

Nathaniel buried his face in his hands. They didn't understand— they *couldn't*. Removing his father from power, whether it was right or not, left only Nathaniel to fill the vacancy, and Nathaniel wasn't sure he'd be any better as Commissioner than his father.

Moreover, Nathaniel wasn't sure he wanted to find out.

Anna spoke low, almost gently. "I don't forgive you, but I can't pretend you're worse than the Commissioner."

"At least he hasn't killed anyone." Nathaniel's words came out muffled.

Anna let out a harsh sigh. "You still don't get it."

Nathaniel looked up, catching sight of her reddened cheeks and narrowed eyes before Eliza stepped between them.

"Murder comes in many shapes, Nathaniel," Eliza said. "You don't always have to look someone in the eye and watch them die to be their killer."

"What do you mean?" he asked.

"Your father's been killing my friends for years." Anna ran her hands across the back of her neck, pulling at the skin. "You killed my friend—and I hate you for it, don't get me wrong—but the Commissioner's killed dozens, if not hundreds."

"So you're saying I'm the lesser evil?"

"No!"

"Yes."

Eliza and Anna spoke simultaneously, each shooting the other a look that spoke volumes more than their words, even as they broke out into an argument Nathaniel couldn't follow.

Nathaniel shook his head to clear it. If only he could be alone, even for a minute, he'd be able to think this through. "What's the plan? What's our next step?"

They paused, falling silent, eyes locked in battle. Then Eliza lowered her gaze and tilted her chin in surrender.

"We begin at the beginning," Anna said in barely more than a whisper. "We start with our hearts."

Eliza's face pinched. "Your what?"

Anna didn't take her eyes off Nathaniel, speaking only to him as if no one else, not even Eliza, mattered. "I think—I know—he has a vendetta against my grandfather. You see, you're only alive because my grandfather gave you that TICCER."

Nathaniel's hand flitted up to his chest. It bewildered him to think it had been Anna's grandfather, not just because the whole mess was so interconnected, but because he had never imagined Anna as the type of person who had family.

Of course she had family. Everyone had family.

"I suppose your father must just hate him because he ruined his perfect, tech-less family. I don't really understand it, but I don't need to," Anna said.

Nathaniel shook his head. "My father is difficult to understand, but I don't think he hates your grandfather. This thing saved my life. I'd wager he's more angry with me for needing it in the first place."

"All I know is that every single person born in my village needs a TICCER, and you're the only person inside the Settlement to ever get one."

Nathaniel paused, letting her words surround him. "What does that mean?"

"What does *any* of this mean?" Eliza grumbled, crossing her arms.

Anna ignored her and reached to touch her own TICCER. "I'm not sure, but I intend to find out."

"My father . . ." Nathaniel unfocused his eyes for a moment, Anna's freckles becoming a blur in his vision. "I'm not saying I agree with you, but if he really did poison your village, then what about me? Why do I—"

"Someone is poisoning all of us," Anna said. "Likely, that same person poisoned you."

"But why would my father poison me?" Nathaniel regretted the question the moment it left his lips. He could think of half a dozen reasons his father might want him dead—but no, his father had *saved* him. He'd put aside his prejudice against tech in order to keep him alive. Anna's story didn't track, not with what Nathaniel knew of his father, anyway. But it would do no good to argue now. He'd already committed to following her, no matter where she led. It would be his penance, his punishment.

"What do we do to prove it?" he asked instead.

Anna's lips turned up in a smile. "Nathaniel, it seems I'll need your blood after all."

CHAPTER TWENTY-NINE

Anna let herself enjoy the look of horror on Nathaniel's face for exactly five seconds before saving him.

"I just need a blood sample to run some tests. I'm not going to hurt you." Well, not much. She could make no promises when it came to her needle and his arm. She might find it difficult to locate a vein. She might make it difficult on purpose.

"If you two are quite certain you aren't going to kill each other, I'll take my leave," Eliza said.

Anna jumped. She'd almost forgotten the noble girl in the corner. She'd been quiet for so long, letting Anna take charge with Nathaniel.

"If you're going to ignore my questions, I may as well go freshen up. And I'd advise you both to do the same." Her eyes lingered on Anna's hair.

Anna reached up to touch her braid, sprouting wild curls from last night's activity. The other girl's eyes on her made Anna squirm, as though she was a specimen in a jar, kept only for observation.

"Of course," Nathaniel said. "You've traveled a long way and it's nearly dawn—you must be tired."

Eliza dropped her eyes in deference before heading for the door, but she paused with her fingers on the handle. "Do try not to kill him while I'm gone, Red. You're quite enough mess all on your own without adding his body into the mix."

Before Anna could muster up a retort, Eliza's outrageous hat disappeared around the corner.

"Who does she think she is?" Anna wrinkled her forehead, staring at the place Eliza had just been. "Seriously, she's your . . ." Anna waited for Nathaniel to jump in.

"What?" Nathaniel's head snapped up.

"Cousin? Friend? Surprisingly animated hat rack?"

"Oh. She's my fiancée." His voice wobbled.

"Oh." A fire lit in her cheeks. Determined to hide the reaction, Anna bent her head, unlatching her satchel and searching aimlessly inside it. She hadn't thought of Nathaniel as the kind of boy with a fiancée. All this time, she'd felt inexplicably drawn to him, as though wires wrapped around each of their hearts, as though magnets pulled them together. But it wasn't the kind of attraction that burned deep in her stomach or fluttered high in her throat. It was the kind that burrowed just beneath her skin, a constant pressure on her spine. It wasn't romantic; it wasn't desire. It was the unrelenting sameness, a kinship ticking a steady rhythm through both their veins.

And to think Eliza would be his bride. Anna had felt drawn to her, too, but in an entirely different way. She didn't have time to think about Eliza. She needed to forget her insipid blond curls and her perfectly arched brows, banish the floral aroma—the stench—she'd left behind, dismiss the thrill of Eliza's fingers—no, the knife—against her skin.

Nathaniel took a step forward, tilting his head to catch her eye. "We've been betrothed since we were fifteen, but I only just met her for the first time yesterday."

"Betrothed?" Anna tried not to choke on the word, unsure why it gave her tongue such trouble. But Nathaniel still looked at her like he thought she'd lost a cog, so she scoffed and added, "What a fancy word."

Nathaniel frowned. "It's a political marriage."

"Doesn't sound like much of a marriage," Anna muttered, surprised to find her words more hopeful than hateful. "My satchel— do you still have it?" Anna cast her gaze around the room for the bag he'd taken from her at the clock tower.

Nathaniel blushed but fished her bag out of a drawer and set it on the desk.

Anna rummaged inside for a syringe, glad to shift the conversation back to medicine. "Roll up your sleeve."

Nathaniel leaned away. "Why?"

"I need to draw your blood." She waved the syringe in front of him. "For my tests."

Nathaniel stared at the needle, eyes wide and unblinking.

"Don't be nervous."

"Right, because I can just turn that on and off."

Anna bit her lip. "I know how unnerving medical procedures can be. My grandfather is a surgeon, so I'm used to it, but I remember when I was young and everything he did terrified me. But once I'd asked him to explain, it was easier."

Nathaniel's gaze flickered up to hers, and for a moment Anna's world stopped. Reflected in his eyes was Roman's facade of strength, masking his fear.

"Would you?" Nathaniel asked, voice small. "Explain, I mean."

Anna pulled the chair back, gesturing for him to sit. "It's fairly simple. I'll have to locate a vein in your arm." She pointed to her inner elbow. "I'll clean the area, to avoid infection, and then—"

"I didn't mean— I don't want the details." Nathaniel grimaced. "Would you just explain why? What are you going to use my blood for, exactly?"

"Oh." Anna frowned. Of course he'd asked that question—anyone would. It just happened to be the one question she wasn't prepared to answer with any kind of certainty. "I want to test your blood sample and compare it to mine."

Nathaniel nodded, piecing it all together. "You think there will be a similar component in our blood that can explain all this."

"That's my hypothesis," she said. "Once I understand the anomaly, I can isolate it. Maybe then I can figure out exactly what's causing Tarnish." *And maybe even find a cure.* She didn't dare give voice to those words. If she could do it, she wasn't sure it would help her or Nathaniel—their hearts already too affected by the poison—and if she couldn't, well, she couldn't bear disappointing anyone else, even Nathaniel.

Anna affixed the needle to a small glass vial. "I need better light." In Thatcher's operating room, lighting was one thing they never went without, even at night, but with the sun's rays barely cresting the horizon outside, the flickering light from the candle on the desk would make for difficult work. "Come closer to the window. I can't see a thing in the dark, and I don't want to accidentally stab you."

"I thought that's exactly what you wanted," Nathaniel said.

For a tense moment, Anna held her breath. Killing him had seemed the thing to do the night before, but Eliza had been right. Nathaniel's death would have only ruined her, drained her until she was empty. More death wouldn't bring her peace, and Nathaniel was more use to her alive than dead.

But then Nathaniel laughed as though he'd actually made a joke, and Anna forced a smile, trying to mask her relief.

"All right. I'm ready." Nathaniel rolled up his shirtsleeve to expose his arm.

Anna pressed her thumb against his inner elbow, and he flinched.

"I'm sorry. Are my hands cold?" Anna curled her fingers, trying to warm them.

"No, it's just— Is it going to hurt?"

For a moment, the boy before her wasn't Nathaniel. He was Roman, asking to play a game, asking to be a part of something Anna had no business including him in. She blinked, and he was the dandy again. Sitting, Nathaniel was considerably shorter, smaller, more childlike, but he was still Nathaniel, asking his physician the question all first-time patients asked.

"I'll do mine first. You can watch and see for yourself." She rolled up her own sleeve so that she matched Nathaniel. "Can I have your cravat?"

Nathaniel undid the scarf at his neck, handing it to her with a question in his eyes.

She'd never had to draw her own blood before. She wished she was back in Mechan where she had her own tools, her own workshop. Instead, she would have to make do with whatever provisions Nathaniel could help her find.

"Do you have any alcohol? Whiskey, maybe?"

Nathaniel's forehead creased. "We might have some scotch in the other room, but I'd prefer you didn't drink before sticking me with a needle."

Chuckling, Anna tied the cravat around her upper arm. "No, not for drinking. It's to clean the area and prevent infection." She thought of her grandfather's insistence that every tool and surface in his operating room be sanitized. It would do them no good to discover the secret behind their condition only to die from infection.

"Oh, of course." Nathaniel ducked out, the door clicking behind him.

Anna was alone. The feeling caught her like a gust of wind, knocking her back. Her breath came in waves, overtaking her from above and pulling at her from below. She'd left home without so much as a goodbye, and now she was here, in the bedroom of the Commissioner's son. If Thatcher and Ruby could see Anna now—not that they'd spare a thought for her anyway. To them, she was irresponsible, unfeeling . . . a killer.

To them, she was dead.

Yesterday, Anna had rushed at Nathaniel in the garden, ready to die for revenge. Now she held a syringe in her hand, preparing to take the first step toward saving them all.

The sun's tendrils reached for the desk, illuminating scraps of paper, bottles of ink, and a silver locket, gears interlocking across its face. It seemed years had passed since she'd first met Nathaniel at the market, but as her fingers closed around Mechan steel, she could almost feel his clockwork pulse ticking against her skin.

What wouldn't she give to turn back time, to go back to outlaw and nobleman, not yet foes and not yet allies?

But she couldn't. There was nothing she could do to unravel their meeting, to take back her trust, to bring back a boy who should never have died. All she could do was take this step forward, and another, and another, until she was running full force. This time, she wouldn't run from the law—she'd run toward it, fists raised. She'd take the Commissioner apart piece by piece until she had what she came for: an answer, a cure, the right to be alive.

The door swung open, and Nathaniel returned, scotch in tow.

"Don't think anyone's touched this in years, but it should be fine." He poured the amber liquid into a crystal glass and handed it to Anna.

Anna released the locket, letting it fall back to the desk with a clunk.

Nathaniel stared at it for a moment, as if he, too, had been taken back to their first meeting. A solitary *tick* fell between.

"Well then," Nathaniel said. "I'm ready, if you are."

Anna's chest tightened. She wasn't the only one who'd left something of herself behind. Before tonight, Nathaniel had been a nobleman—heir to the state. He'd had a future, a plan, a destiny, and she'd taken it from him, not with her knife like she'd intended, but with her inquiries, her theories.

Nathaniel might have been hesitant to be party to their plotting, but Anna could see in his eyes now he didn't lie. He wanted to know the truth as much as she did, and he would follow the trail to its end, no matter the result.

Anna took the glass, wrapping her fingers around it as if it was Nathaniel's trust, delicate and, somehow, valuable. She swabbed her skin with the alcohol, cringing at the smell before leveling the needle, the morning light now bright enough to see by. Only after she'd located a vein and blood had begun to pool in the vial did she glance up at Nathaniel.

His face had gone ashy white.

"It isn't so bad," Anna said, doing her best to reassure him.

"I think I'll close my eyes." Nathaniel looked away and stuck out his arm. "Don't warn me when you're about to do it. It will be worse if I know it's coming."

Anna removed the needle from her arm and capped the vial. She was so used to blood, it never occurred to her that others might not be. Even in Thatcher's operating room, she'd been shocked to find that some patients fainted at the sight of blood. It struck her that Nathaniel probably had had little to do with doctors in the past. He would not have been able to receive medical care in the Settlement without the risk of exposing his tech. Thatcher may have been his one and only physician all those years ago.

With as much confidence as she could muster, Anna took out a new needle and repeated the procedure on Nathaniel. To his credit, he flinched only twice, but he did not open his eyes again until Anna told him it was safe.

"What now?" he asked, pressing his lavender cravat against the wound to stop the blood.

"I'm not sure." Thatcher usually tested blood for iron levels, but she'd only ever watched him do it. She didn't even know how to test for other things—or even what to test for. But if she told this to Nathaniel, it wouldn't exactly inspire confidence, and she needed to keep them moving forward toward an answer, even if she didn't quite know what the question was. "We'll need a control sample as well from someone unaffected." She set the vials on Nathaniel's desk, returning her tools to her satchel.

Nathaniel gave her a quizzical look. "Good luck getting Eliza to roll up her sleeves for you."

Anna blinked away the image of Eliza, not Nathaniel, standing before her, looking up at her with vulnerable eyes. A gentle prickle ran up her spine at the thought of Eliza's delicate skin, so perfect it would almost be a shame to puncture it.

Anna's stomach flipped, but she ignored it. "Perhaps we should wait—let her have her beauty rest." Not that she needed it. Anna rolled her eyes dramatically, as much at the pink girl as at herself, and then glanced at Nathaniel to see if he'd noticed.

But Nathaniel's eyes were trained on the vials she'd abandoned.

Anna followed his gaze, and her breath caught. Dawn trickled over the horizon, sending coils of light across the room, but this was more than just a trick of the light, a mirage of sun and sleepless eyes.

The twin vials sat side by side, but where deep red blood had been before, a soft golden light emanated from the samples inside.

"What is it?" Nathaniel asked in a whisper.

Anna had no answer, no hypothesis, not even a wild guess, but from the depths of her mind crawled the image of a dusty-blue book and a nervous daughter afraid to give away her mother's secrets. Ruby's book was still in her satchel, and a word rose unbidden from Anna's throat like a memory she didn't know she had.

"Alchemy."

CHAPTER THIRTY

Eliza needed a hot bath, a nap, and a change of clothes. After the night she'd had, she richly deserved all three, but she had time for only one.

Throwing open the closet doors to her bedroom, she scanned the dozens of dresses hanging inside for a suitable alternative to her pink traveling dress. One of the Commissioner's servants must have unpacked her things the night prior; the garments hung haphazardly with no discernible organizational pattern. She would have to do it herself later. With so many new dresses, Eliza would need to mentally inventory each, cataloging every possible use for her expansive wardrobe.

Casting her mind to her purpose today, Eliza's hands drifted toward a mauve creation. She could be unassuming in mauve, unthreatening. But why continue to play the part when Nathaniel already knew her for what she was? She didn't need to perpetuate the lie the Queen had built for her. The Queen was far away, in her silver palace in the sky. She would be no help to Eliza here. Still, she wasn't exactly alone.

The decision to bring Nathaniel into the fold had been easy, albeit risky. Seeing how his father treated him, holding him at arm's length, talking about him rather than to him, Eliza's instinct had been to be the opposite. Where the Commissioner was alienating, she would be welcoming. Where the Commissioner excluded him, she would include him. It was her best tactic to gain the boy's trust, which was the only direction the Queen had given her thus far.

Anna, on the other hand, had already proven to be useful, despite her treacherous start. They'd make a solid team, though Eliza might someday regret letting the redhead come at her with a knife and live to tell the tale.

A quiet beeping sound interrupted Eliza's musings. She spun around, searching for the source. From across the room, Eliza was met with a blinking green light—the holocom the Queen had given her. Rushing to answer the call, Eliza keyed in her passcode and stepped back.

A blue hologram appeared—a small replica of the Queen, veil and all, sitting at her desk, a cup of tea in hand.

"Y-Your Majesty!" Eliza sank into a curtsy. She hoped for her own sake the Queen had not been waiting long.

"Finally! You ought to carry the holocom with you. It would be unfortunate if I couldn't contact my one trusted agent planetside."

Eliza's chest warmed. The Queen trusted her—she'd nearly forgotten. This mission was not banishment, not exile. It was important, whatever the Queen had sent her to do.

"Quite right, Your Majesty."

The Queen tilted her head to the left. "Well? Report."

Eliza straightened, suddenly conscious of the sleepless bags beneath her eyes and the chaos of curls escaping her hat. Though she looked a mess, she would endeavor to be professional.

"I've not had a chance to investigate the manor much, Your Majesty. I've been planetside only fourteen hours. I can tell you very little, I expect."

The Queen waved her hand. "Tell it so we can move on."

"Of course." Eliza cleared her throat to stall for time. So much had happened since she'd arrived, and yet none of it seemed relevant. The Commissioner was unpleasant, his son far more complex than she'd expected. She couldn't tell the Queen about the struggle in the garden. That would mean telling her about their plans, and Eliza could not afford for the Queen to know those details yet. The Queen had sent her there to be a spy, not to topple the Commissioner's regime. And it would mean telling her about Anna, and Eliza wasn't ready to put voice to the girl whose ferocity stuck with her, like earth beneath her fingernails.

"The Commissioner is, as you said, stubborn and guarded," Eliza began slowly, weighing her words. "But he's emotional when it comes to his son, frustrated by the boy's disposition. Could be a weakness."

The Queen scoffed. "People can be precious about their children. I can't imagine where he learned that."

Eliza tried not to wince. She would not feel sorry for the Commissioner, no matter how fraught his own childhood might have been. The Queen had not treated him so unjustly, for the Queen was always fair, always measured. Had he been a better son, more loyal, more talented, she would have loved him better.

She would love Eliza better.

But even as she thought it, Eliza felt a pang. Was that not the same logic that had harmed Nathaniel so, his desperation for a father's love, and a father who couldn't give it?

As discomfort settled through her, Eliza changed course. "Your Majesty, if you could give me more direction, perhaps I could use my time here to do your will more effectively."

The Queen laced her fingers together. "You've done well, my dear, but do not make the mistake of thinking this will be a quick mission. You must earn your new family's trust. You must become a fixture, a permanent piece of the decor. You must position yourself so when the time is right, you can infiltrate the Commissioner's offices, and no one will question your right to be there. And if that doesn't yield what I need, you must infiltrate his confidence, earn his trust, and take his secrets."

Eliza nodded slowly, her heart sinking. Had she made a mistake, thinking she should take on the Commissioner? She knew she could do it; he was no different from any other man she'd had the pleasure of ruining, and he would be no more challenging. But the Queen had said it herself—this was not a quick mission. Eliza had thought if she could eliminate the Commissioner, it would speed things along. With the Commissioner dethroned, she could take his power, and with his power, she could take everything else. But what if whatever the Queen wanted wasn't tangible? Eliza was good, but even she could not retrieve an idea from a dead man's head.

"The Commissioner has put us all at risk, Eliza. You know it is my life's work—the work of my mother, and her mother before, to bring everyone planetside, to retire this space station to the stars and embrace our earthly home."

"Of course," Eliza murmured, but a part of her still yearned to return to the steel hallways in the sky.

"We are much closer to that future than you may even realize. At this very moment, the Commissioner is keeping vital information that would help lead us to that eventuality, holding back the secret to finally terraforming this planet fully so that we may all safely descend and live as we once did, hundreds of years ago on Former Earth."

"But why?" Eliza asked, fearing the answer almost as much as she craved it.

"To keep the glory for himself." The Queen sighed, her veil fluttering. "He cares not for the generations of our family who turned this lifeless rock into a lush and vibrant planet, nor the people living on it now."

Eliza's breath caught. "What do you mean, the people living here now?"

The Queen waved her hand dismissively. "Without proper terraforming, the planet has the potential to cause all sorts of health problems in the population."

"Like heart disorders?"

"Certainly. Or other unexplainable illness, birth defects—it's simply unsafe. I cannot responsibly retire the Tower while our planet is so unstable," the Queen continued. "It would be unconscionable to bring my people to Earth Adjacent while the Commissioner still withholds this information."

Eliza's thumb rubbed the skin of her forearm raw as she listened. She'd spent the last several hours focused on problems not her own, finding ways to make Anna's and Nathaniel's goals align with hers. But was it possible they were more connected than she realized? With the context the Queen provided, Anna's story suddenly made more sense, and the Commissioner she'd met and the Commissioner the Queen described overlapped far more convincingly than the murderous monster Anna had made him out to be.

If the Commissioner hadn't poisoned Anna's village, and instead simply neglected to provide them the proper terraforming technology, Eliza could connect his methods to motives with exactly the same result. Anna's people were dying, and it was the Commissioner's fault. She could use this to fuel the fire of Anna's rage while controlling its direction.

The Queen was still talking when Eliza emerged from her thoughts.

"My ancestors knew they would never live to see the day Earth Adjacent became our permanent home, but still they pushed for a better world. The Commissioner thinks if he can outlive me, he can claim this victory for himself, forgetting the women who came before, the women who made this planet—who made *him*. But you, Eliza, you will not betray me as he has. You will protect me and my legacy, will you not?"

"Of course," Eliza said, her body humming with possibility. This was her destiny, her chance to make history. This was how she could earn the Queen's respect, the Queen's love. She'd already begun the preparations, and with Nathaniel's and Anna's cooperation, she would find the Commissioner's secret, she would crush him, and she would take his place as the Queen's heir.

Some of Eliza's mirth must have shown on her face, for the Queen leaned in and said, "Be careful, Eliza. The Commissioner can be a dangerous foe."

"As can I," Eliza murmured as the Queen's image faded away.

Eliza stared at the vanity. For a moment, she'd forgotten they were separated by steel walls and a starry sky. It had felt as it used to, the Queen giving commands and Eliza taking them. The Queen's instructions had made Eliza what she was, *who* she was.

And who was she today? Eliza the spy, hiding in plain sight, waiting and watching? Or Eliza the rebel, taking what she wanted regardless of her orders?

She turned back to the wardrobe, but instead of choosing a gown befitting either, she reached for the pale pink tea dress she'd worn the day the Queen gave her this mission. This Eliza was neither and both, somewhere in between. She was the girl who'd dreamt of belonging, of respect, the girl who'd navigated the world easily, wielding secrets, not keeping them.

Eliza couldn't be that girl again. Too much had changed. But she wore the dress anyway, finding comfort in the familiar cotton folds. She smoothed out the creases and combed her hair back with her fingers. Lastly, almost as an afterthought, she lifted the holocom from the vanity and slipped it into her pocket.

Sharp pain lanced her finger, and she yelped. A bloody pinprick dotted the end of her finger. She knew this pain, she knew this wound. She withdrew the culprit with a careful hand, laying the remains of the rose she'd taken from Lord Farley weeks ago, forgotten in her dress pocket.

The carcass of the flower, petals dry and withered, color faded, was somehow still as lovely as it had been when she'd found it—still as dangerous, too. She twirled the stem between her uninjured fingers, catching golden rays of morning light. How odd that in death, the flower could shine, glittering like the Queen's court, light tracing golden veins through translucent petals.

Eliza blinked, and it was only a dead flower again. The light, or sleeplessness, had tricked her into believing it was more. She discarded it on the vanity where it could do no more harm. But even still, something dragged her back.

Because no matter how she viewed it, vibrant or dull, soft or hard, alive or dead, it was still a flower at its core. Beneath all the lace, she, too, would be unchanged. It had been years since Eliza had gone without a costume, without a mask, and when the time finally came to shed her armor, Eliza didn't know who she'd find underneath.

CHAPTER THIRTY-ONE

Nathaniel hadn't bled very often—sometimes his father would hit him a little too hard, but even then, Nathaniel didn't usually examine his wounds closely.

But blood didn't glow—not naturally, anyway.

No, if his blood was glowing, there was only one explanation. Only Nathaniel didn't believe in magic. He didn't believe in things like true love or mismatched socks, either.

"It's not possible," Anna said as she charged down the hall.

Nathaniel hurried to keep up with her long legs. He was supposed to be leading her to Eliza's room, not the other way around. He should have been in front, looking out for the Commissioner. If he found Anna running around the manor, well, Nathaniel didn't know what he would do.

"It must be the poison." Anna's voice sounded strained, and she slowed as they came to a fork in the hallway.

"To the left," Nathaniel said, nearly jogging now. "So do you think the poison is—" He swallowed, mustering the courage to say the word aloud, but instead of *alchemy* it came out, "Magic?"

Anna didn't reply, her eyes trained on the end of the hallway, arms swinging.

Nathaniel had to reach for the back of her shirt—his shirt, really—and pull to stop her in time. He gestured to the door. "You wanted her blood sample, right?"

She glared at him but reached for the doorknob anyhow, her hand closing around the metal with firm determination. "It's not magic. There's no such thing."

Nathaniel nodded, though her words lacked conviction.

"It's not magic," she repeated before pushing open the door.

"In polite society, we knock." Eliza stood by the vanity, its mirrors reflecting an army of Elizas back at them.

Nathaniel stepped forward instinctually, ready to put himself between them the way Eliza had done for him and Anna the night before, but there was no need.

Neither girl moved to strike the other. Instead, Anna let out a tinny laugh and said, "Polite society sounds dull." She shrugged and set her satchel down on an armchair by the door. "We need your help."

"Well, are you going to enlighten me first?" Eliza asked, eyes trained on Anna. "It would be ever so rude for you to barge into my bedroom, demanding my help, only to deny my curiosity yet again."

Anna's cheeks turned an alarming shade, but she cleared her throat. "Right. Of course."

As she explained their conditions to Eliza, their suspicions and their findings, Anna morphed from hostile outlaw into the same girl who'd taught Nathaniel about his TICCER for the first time, the girl who'd shown him how to see his own worth. Only minutes ago, he'd witnessed the same transformation when he'd been nervous about her taking his blood. He'd expected her to tease and taunt him, but instead she'd shown sympathy, understanding that everything she took for granted, he found new and unnerving.

Which was she, really—enemy or equal?

If he couldn't trust her to be one or the other, he'd have to accept she could be both. Just as tech could be right as well as wrong, and the golden sheen to their blood could be both magic and science. The duality of Anna, of the way she saw the world, spread through him like tree roots, digging deep into the earth and taking hold.

"It's all a bit confusing," Anna said, wrapping up her explanation weakly.

"That's certainly an understatement." Eliza lowered herself onto the edge of the vanity. "How do you plan to use any of this against the Commissioner? Not to be pessimistic, but no one's going to believe anything you say about glowing blood—and even if they did . . ." She trailed off, eyes falling to her knees for a moment. "Glowing blood—you really did say glowing blood, right?"

"Look, if you don't believe us . . ." Anna crossed her arms.

Eliza looked up then, eyes locking with Anna's. "The thing is, I think I do. There's something not quite right about this planet, and I'm not about to dismiss any theory out of hand."

Nathaniel didn't realize he'd taken a step back until he collided with the wall. The urge to leave overcame him, like he was not only unnecessary in this conversation but somehow unwelcome. He'd been given a chance to process with only Anna as his witness; why shouldn't he give Eliza that same courtesy?

Before he could move on the impulse, Anna turned her head, knocking him back again with a look. "My satchel, blue book."

It took Nathaniel a moment to understand it was a request, not a statement, and he scrambled. He didn't have to search long. The satchel was small and the book fairly large.

She took the book from him and tapped the cover. "I'm hoping there will be some answers in here."

Eliza snatched the book from Anna's grasp. "What is it?"

"Hey! Give that back!" Anna grabbed for the book, but Eliza held it out of reach, flipping through the pages. "Typical nobility, thinking you can just take things. Where's your polite society now?" Anna crossed her arms and leaned against the bedframe.

Eliza's brow pinched. "It's only a book." But she handed it back to Anna, who hugged it to her chest like a shield against Eliza's scrutiny. "So? What's the plan?"

Anna released her grip on the book. "We have blood samples from both of us, but we need one more."

For a moment, Nathaniel thought Eliza might refuse. Her gaze was venom, as if the mere thought was enough to put an early end to their partnership. But then she nodded and rolled up her sleeve.

"You know what you're doing?" Eliza asked.

Anna crossed the room to swap the book for her tools. "He's still alive, isn't he?" She prodded Nathaniel's shoulder with her pointer finger. "Go ahead, ask him yourself."

She didn't. Instead, Eliza turned toward Anna as she approached with the sterilized needle in hand.

Nathaniel looked away. Even though it was only a prick of a needle, a brush of a thumb between Anna and Eliza, such movements felt magnified. When it had been his arm in Anna's grasp, everything had been clinical, no more contact than was necessary. But now, Nathaniel didn't need to watch to know this was different.

Glancing down at the book in his lap, Nathaniel thumbed through it. Spiderweb penmanship filled the pages, recipes for ointments and salves. But as he progressed, symbols and letters he didn't comprehend appeared with more frequency. Sentences became equations, equations became diagrams, and diagrams became sentences once more. These were not the simple instructions of a physician as they had been in the early pages, but strings of ideas and questions, more like a diary.

"Aha!"

Nathaniel's head shot up.

Anna leaned against the window, dangling a vial of blood in the sunlight.

"I don't see anything." Eliza stood to join her.

"Exactly!" Anna's triumph seeped through her voice. "You're from the Tower, so you wouldn't have whatever's turned our blood gold. No one's poisoned you." She gave Eliza a pointed look before adding, "Yet."

"Even if there's an anomaly in your blood, poison will be difficult to prove," Eliza said. "It could be anything."

Anna glanced back at Nathaniel. "Anything of use in there?" she asked.

Nathaniel frowned. "I'm not sure." He pointed to the page he'd landed on. "I can't make sense of it, but this bit here seems . . . I'm not sure."

Anna and Eliza closed in on him.

"What is it?" Anna asked.

Nathaniel held up the book for them to see, not trusting himself to put voice to words that weren't his. Just as Anna and Eliza's glances and touches seemed private, so did the words winding across the page:

Too weary of digging, the treasure hunter turns to alchemy. But what good is transmuting lead when the very earth bleeds gold? Sometimes I think in the moments between night and day, so, too, do we all, stars streaming through our gilded veins.

"Well that's nonsense." Anna settled back on her heels.

"Is it poetry?" Eliza asked.

Nathaniel had to swallow a laugh. They were both wrong, and the irony of it filled Nathaniel up. For once, he had the answer. "Come, Anna. Surely you recognize a riddle when you see one?"

Anna snatched the book from him to read the lines again. "It's not a riddle."

Eliza stood on her toes to read over Anna's shoulder. "Maybe not, but we can treat it like one. Let's each take a line and see what we can make of it. A close reading, if you will."

They knelt together, crowded around the page. Nathaniel took the first line, Eliza the second, and Anna the third.

After several minutes of silence, Anna was the first to speak. "If we take the last line literally, that's exactly what we experienced. It was barely dawn when we took our blood sample. Maybe the light has something to do with the poison's visibility. It would explain why I've never noticed before."

Eliza nodded. "Do you still have the blood samples? It's fully morning now. Let's see if there's been a change."

Anna fished in her satchel for the vials, but when she held all three up to the window, Nathaniel couldn't tell the difference between theirs and Eliza's, all three a deep red.

"I think the second line refers to the same phenomenon, only in the flora and fauna of the planet. I noticed it, too, with a flower this morning." Eliza indicated a wilted rose on her vanity. "Perhaps it's naturally occurring, an effect of the planet."

"It isn't natural," Anna growled.

"You don't know that," Eliza shot back.

Anna's eyes sharpened to points. "Don't you dare tell me my entire village is dying because of some kind of luck, some survival of the fittest rubbish. It isn't chance that my people are sick and none of yours are."

Nathaniel cleared his throat.

"Sorry. *One* of yours is."

"No, that's not it." Nathaniel ran a hand through his hair. "It's just— My line, the first line. It's about alchemy."

Alchemy, the impossible science, his mother's killer. Nathaniel's stomach dropped as the word left his lips, emptiness replacing it inside him. Alchemy had always been forbidden to him, and the rest of the Settlement, for that matter. Perhaps Nathaniel was the only person on all of Earth Adjacent who knew the Commissioner's true rationale.

"What of it?" Anna asked, as if daring him to say anything of worth.

Nathaniel swallowed, unsure how to best express himself. If he told her the truth, she'd have one more piece of him. And if he kept it to himself, it would just be another thing he couldn't share. "It's illegal," Nathaniel said at last. "If it's too dangerous for my father's government to control, then—"

"Control," Anna scoffed. "That's all the Commissioner cares about, isn't it?"

"That's what government is for," Eliza said.

"Funny. I thought it was supposed to make people safer."

"Perhaps safer from their own idiocy."

Anna took a step away from Eliza. "Not you, too," she grumbled. "I know you're an Orbital, but I thought you'd understand."

"And why is that?" Eliza's eyes bored into Anna's.

Anna opened her mouth and closed it several times before finally saying, "I don't know. I thought you were different. Clearly I was mistaken."

Nathaniel watched them fling words back and forth, acutely aware that he understood only the surface of what they said. Their eyes told a different story—Eliza's harsh and unrelenting, Anna's uncharacteristically jumpy. Even when Eliza had held Anna at knife-point in the garden, the two had seemed less at odds. Something had changed.

No one had ever looked at Nathaniel that way—and he was glad of it. Still, it left him on the outside looking in on something he wasn't sure he was supposed to see.

"I'd imagine you're mistaken about a great many things, Red."

Nathaniel couldn't listen to them bicker any longer, and the truth bubbled up inside him like a kettle left too long on the fire. "My mother died in an alchemy accident."

Silence fell in the wake of his words, and Anna and Eliza exchanged a look he couldn't read.

"That's terrible," Eliza said softly.

"It is terrible," Nathaniel said. "It happened when I was very young. I don't remember it—I don't remember *her*." He'd already lost her. He couldn't lose them, too.

"I'm so sorry, Nathaniel." Eliza's hand drifted toward his shoulder, but he shifted away.

"We never talk about it. My father treats it like a family secret, a family shame. Like if we never mention it, it's almost as if it never happened. But it did happen. My mother died, and my heart failed, and forgetting doesn't make it any less real."

Anna leaned forward. "But don't you understand? This could help us learn the truth about our hearts."

Nathaniel sighed. "I want to know the truth—I do—but not if it means risking our lives."

"We've already risked our lives, Nathaniel," Eliza said. "If the Commissioner finds out about any of this, do you really think he'll let us go unpunished?"

Anna nodded her agreement. "I've been risking my life for three years as the Technician. This isn't anything new."

Nathaniel's throat went dry. The closest he'd ever come to risking his life was when he'd left the Settlement the first time, but even then, it was an abstract danger of the unknown world, not the wrath of an angry ruler that threatened them now. Anna and Eliza were practiced at risk, cohorts of danger. But Nathaniel couldn't let them do this. He couldn't let them die.

"I don't want to put either of you in harm's way," he said quietly.

Anna threw the book down on the vanity. "That isn't your decision to make." Her eyes gripped his with a fierce stare. "You owe me, remember? You don't get to change your mind."

Though Nathaniel feared Anna's rage, it was nothing to the threat of alchemy. "I thought you said you didn't want me to help you simply because I felt beholden."

Anna's eyes bulged with restrained emotion. "Your father is already dangerous. Alchemy doesn't increase the risk."

Nathaniel couldn't see past the imagined scene in his head: a woman, his mother, lying dead on the floor, a trickle of colorful liquid on her chin. He knew it wasn't real—he'd not been old enough when she died to remember her body, or even her face. He knew she had dark hair, a small chin, and maybe long limbs. She was an equation, a sum of the parts of himself Nathaniel couldn't place in his father's reflection.

He couldn't save her, but Nathaniel could still keep Anna and Eliza safe—he *should* keep them safe. It was all he had left.

"I hate to agree with Red here, but she's right." Eliza's voice was gentle, as if she knew he was a gaping wound, raw and exposed. "If we have any chance at all of discovering the truth, it won't be without risk. And if we have any chance at all, we should do it now."

"Do what?" Anna and Nathaniel said in unison.

"Do what all rebellions must."

"Attack?" Anna asked, a hopeful glint in her eye.

Nathaniel rather thought *fail* was the more apt word, though he refrained from saying so.

"Certainly not! We have no weapons." Eliza rested her hand atop Anna's as though stopping a motion she'd not yet made. "Not blades—information. All good rebellions rely on good intelligence, and we have none at all."

"I don't need intelligence to ram a knife through the Commissioner's throat," Anna grumbled.

"In good time," Eliza said. "But first, I propose we infiltrate the Commissioner's office and see what we can find. If you're correct and the Commissioner is poisoning your village, there will be evidence somewhere, and his office is as good a place as any to start."

Anna frowned. "I had no trouble getting out. Shouldn't be too difficult to get in, right, Nathaniel?"

Nathaniel's cheeks burned with embarrassment. Anna's escape, though perhaps for the best, still hung shamefully around his shoulders. "My father wasn't home then. It won't be so easy now he's back." Nathaniel met her determined blue eyes. There would be no dissuading either of them. He would simply have to wait and watch, hope and help. "He spends almost all his time in his study, so we'll need a good distraction to lure him out."

"So it's settled?" Eliza asked. "You're all right with this, Nathaniel?"

"I suppose I have to be." Nathaniel bit his lip. "I want to be."

Eliza nodded. "I'm not choosy about how we bring him down, as long as it's legal."

Anna opened her mouth as if to argue, but Eliza cut her off.

"If that doesn't work, you can try it your way. Does that appease our little revolutionary?"

Though *little* was hardly the right word for Anna, neither of them argued.

Eliza clapped her hands and exclaimed, "Good!"

"What about the distraction? How are we going to lure my father away from his work?"

"Oh, I've got just the thing." Eliza smiled, a glint in her eye. "I don't suppose either of you knows how to dance?"

CHAPTER THIRTY-TWO

"A dance? You want to waste time on a silly party?" Anna asked.

"Not just any party—our engagement party." Eliza closed the alchemy book, sending a plume of dust into the air.

Anna had forgotten about their supposed engagement. It had seemed such a triviality, before. A *political marriage*, Nathaniel had called it. A party to celebrate would solidify it as real. Not that it mattered. Anna had no vested interest in the marital status of her coconspirators.

"The Commissioner and I already arranged it. As Nathaniel's father, he'll have to participate as the host. He can't hide in his office, and most of the manor staff will be tied up welcoming me to Earth Adjacent. Everyone will be too busy congratulating me on my impending nuptials to pay any attention to you two." Eliza ran her thumb across Nathaniel's forehead, brushing aside his dark curls. "It's a perfect distraction."

Anna's chest tightened as she watched Eliza's fingers. Before when she'd taken Eliza's blood, they'd seen only each other. Anna had held Eliza's arm in her grasp, skin on skin, their pulses thundering as if racing one another toward some unknown finish line. Something about the noble girl intoxicated Anna, more noxious than any poison. It was her aura, her aroma, her audacity to look into Anna, not just at her.

"What about Nathaniel?" Anna asked, her words coming out a fraction higher than usual. "Won't people miss him if he disappears from his own engagement party?"

Eliza dropped her hand from Nathaniel's face and frowned. "Please," she scoffed. "No one will be paying him any attention once I arrive. Mark my words, every eye in that ballroom will be mine."

"You sure think a lot of yourself."

Eliza shrugged. "Nobles are shallow, and I'm stunning. I don't need to be a scientist to understand that equation. Besides, you haven't seen the dress I plan to wear." Her eyes narrowed as her gaze swept over Anna. "Now, what to do with you?"

Anna pushed away her first thought, that Eliza could do anything she wanted with her, and instead asked, "What do you mean?"

"The Commissioner can't find you lurking about dressed like that."

Anna glanced down at her clothes, borrowed from Nathaniel. The fit was poor, but at least they were clean. "What's wrong with how I'm dressed?"

Eliza raised her eyebrows. "Well, the implications are rather salacious—when you wear someone else's clothes, there's a certain assumption of intimacy." She eyed Anna's collar, tapping her finger against her own bare skin, miming unbuttoning an invisible shirt.

Anna's heart thundered in her ears. "What would you suggest? I can't very well wear my own. They're covered in blood, if you recall."

"Never mind what you're wearing," Nathaniel said. "The Commissioner can't find you at all. We'll need a believable disguise for you."

"The Commissioner doesn't know what I look like, does he?" She eyed Nathaniel. "Unless you've told him who I am, I don't see why he'd be suspicious."

Eliza pursed her lips. "One does not need to know you're an infamous outlaw to know you don't belong here." She ran a finger through her own hair, staring pointedly at Anna's, braid tangled and matted.

"We'll need to hide you more effectively," Nathaniel said.

"If I might make a suggestion?" Eliza crossed the room and circled Anna like a vulture. "Aristocrats have excellent eyes for abnormalities, but they are unlikely to look too closely at their scenery. You might blend in if we were to dress you like one of the servants." She tugged at Anna's collar.

"I'm *not* a servant," Anna shot back, brushing Eliza's hand away, absorbing the shock of contact as best she could.

"Eliza isn't wrong. Even I don't notice the staff." Nathaniel shook his head.

"The Commissioner, if my read on him is correct, won't be so aware. Once dressed in uniform, I wager you'll become practically invisible to him." Eliza swept a hand in front of Anna's face, as if erasing her completely. "Now we must decide where to hide you."

"I won't be your lady's maid, if that's what you're thinking," Anna fumed.

"I doubt you'd know the first thing about ladies." Eliza turned up her nose. It was as much an accusation as a challenge.

Anna's cheeks burned a warning. She wanted to smack the self-important look off Eliza's face. She wanted to feel Eliza's smooth skin against her palm again. She wanted somewhere to put the concoction of anger and attraction coiling together in her chest.

"You've no idea how much I know," she said instead. If they were alone, she'd show her exactly what she knew.

As if Eliza could see inside Anna's mind, she whispered, "I'd like to see you prove it."

"It's not a terrible idea," said Nathaniel, his voice shattering the tension. "If you pose as Eliza's lady-in-waiting, you'll be under her employ, not my father's, and you won't have to actually do any servant work. Stay here, and we'll fetch you a uniform."

Anna didn't need more convincing, her breath still short, her cheeks still warm. "Fine, but I won't be treated like I'm lower class."

"You aren't *lower* class," Eliza said as Nathaniel led her toward the door. "I'd be surprised if you had any class at all."

Anna was still fuming when she closed the door after Nathaniel and Eliza left. Eliza's words stung in ways Anna didn't know possible. The girl was pure, aristocratic toxin—everything Anna despised about nobility and Orbitals. She even smelled like the false flowers she wore.

How dare she call Anna classless? How dare she have an opinion on Anna at all?

But though her words were vile, Eliza wasn't wrong. Anna belonged to neither high society nor low. She was not of society in the first place. The Technician bowed to no law, carried no class. She did not care what a lady of Nathaniel's world thought of her. Because Anna's world, broken as it was, mattered more, and she'd be damned if she couldn't find a way to fix it. Ruby and Thatcher hung heavy on her mind, their despair, their disappointment. If she could just earn them back, it wouldn't matter what Eliza thought of her.

Still, Eliza's comments buried themselves in Anna's skin like splinters. And her eyes—*her eyes*! They were daggers, and yet Anna did not bleed. She wanted to shut Eliza away so she couldn't see her, and at the same time, Anna wanted to stare at her for hours on end, memorizing Eliza's face so she could take it with her everywhere she went.

It was a foolish fancy. Eliza had made it clear she detested everything about Anna, from her frizzy hair to her lack of propriety. And so Anna would detest her right back. She would detest her perfect curls and her rosy cheeks, and especially her high manner.

Anna resolved to care less about the Orbital, and also to wash and detangle her hair.

And then there was Nathaniel, whose convictions were as murky as ocean waves. His stance on their rebellion had changed so often that Anna didn't know whether or not this new uncertainty would stick. She might wake to discover he had recommitted to acting against his father. Or perhaps half a dozen officers would haul her from her sleep to be executed.

He was the worst kind of unpredictable: loyal to everyone except himself. He wanted to please his unappeasable father, protect his dead mother, and earn Anna's forgiveness all at once. She ought to put him out of his misery, but how could she forgive him when she couldn't forgive herself? Roman's death was not hers to forgive. It was hers to carry, and she wasn't ready to bear the weight alone.

Even so, pity rose from the depths of her chest. Not for the first time, Anna was struck by a sameness hanging between them, as if one was an echo of the other. Anna had been too young to remember her parents' deaths, but loss was no stranger to her. Mechan quaked with tragedy nearly every day, so common she'd stopped feeling the tremors. But Nathaniel, who'd known privilege and safety all his life, still endured the loss of his mother as though it had been yesterday. It held him back, coiled around his wrists like chains, while Roman's death, which had truly been just yesterday, propelled her forward.

Their grief was different. And it was the same.

Anna let her hand trail over the alchemy book, dust finding its way beneath her fingernails. She'd been so sure she'd find answers inside, but instead more questions found their way to the surface. The cure she wanted was still out of reach, an idea, a possibility, intangible and delicate.

She had to do right by Roman. She had to do right by Ruby. In this, she had no allies, only Ruby's mother to guide her from the past. She could count on neither Nathaniel nor Eliza to help her.

She would save Mechan the only way she knew how.

Alone.

Eliza returned an hour later with good news and a maid uniform.

"Three days till the ball," she said, tossing the maroon-and-gray garment at Anna.

"That's soon." Anna scowled at the colors she'd spent her whole life hating. Too many lives had been taken by maroon and gray.

"Not as soon as I'd like."

"I would have thought you'd want more time to prepare. Don't you have decorating to do or something?"

Eliza leaned toward the vanity, dabbing at a dark smudge beneath her eye. "The Commissioner has a staff for that. I'm more concerned three days will be too many to keep you out of trouble."

"So now I'm the impatient one?"

Eliza eyed her, making Anna's skin prickle. "No, you're right. Three days is too few to properly prepare you for a public display."

Anna sighed. She didn't have the energy to quarrel with someone so adept at verbal sparring. "I'll brush my hair, if that's what you mean, but with any luck, no one will be looking at me anyway." She held up the uniform. "I'll be invisible, remember?"

Eliza stared at the garment for one tick, two ticks, three ticks, before plucking it from Anna's hand and throwing it on the vanity. "No, that simply won't do."

"Well, unless you want me attending your party in nothing but my underthings, I'm afraid we're out of options."

Eliza looked as though she might be considering it, but then she stormed across the room and flung open her wardrobe, revealing an array of gowns in every color. "Oh, we have options," she said, before pulling dress after dress from inside.

Anna took a step back. "No, no—I'm supposed to be your lady-in-waiting. I can't wear any of those."

Eliza paused, a deep blue frock in her hands. "Do you know what a lady-in-waiting is?"

Anna blinked. She thought she did. Was this just another opportunity for Eliza to lord her superiority over her?

"I used to be one," Eliza said quietly, sinking back onto the bed. "I used to be a lot of things before I was me."

Anna peered down at her, catching the slightest tremble of Eliza's lip.

"I'm not a noble," she whispered. "I've seen how they treat anyone who's not, and I don't— I shouldn't act like them in an effort to be one. It's unhelpful, and it's unkind."

At first, Anna thought she'd misheard her. "Are you all right?" The Eliza before her was softer, like she'd been blurred at the edges.

Eliza shrugged. "It's not your fault you're unrefined."

There was the Eliza that Anna had come to know. It was as close to an apology she was likely to get, so instead of a retort, she asked, "Exactly what *is* a lady-in-waiting, then?"

Eliza's voice returned to its usual level. "A lady-in-waiting is not a servant. Behind closed doors, she is a confidant, a comfort, perhaps even a friend. But to the public eye, she's a reflection of her mistress."

"I'm not calling you mistress," Anna huffed, crossing her arms.

"Of course not." Eliza frowned.

"And I'm not going to wait on you."

"Wouldn't dream of asking you to." The corner of Eliza's lip twitched. "But you'll wear the dress?"

Anna narrowed her eyes, the ghost of her itchy market costume brushing against her skin.

Eliza tilted her head down to look up at her through thick eyelashes. "Please?"

"Fine," Anna grumbled. "Which one of these monstrosities do you want me to wear?"

Eliza's lips turned up in a smile, setting Anna's heart alight. "Nothing too dark—it's a soirée, after all, and nothing bright. We don't want to draw too much attention to you, and your hair's already practically a beacon."

Anna tugged on her braid.

"Something pleasant and pastel, perhaps?" Eliza laid out three gowns on the bed—a light pink dress made of lace, a green abomination of layered sheer fabric, and pale blue frock with a gray silk sash. "You choose."

Anna held her breath. She preferred her borrowed trousers to any of the gowns Eliza had shown her, but at least Eliza was giving her a choice.

"The blue one."

"Good." Eliza picked up the dress and held it up to Anna's side. "It'll be a little short, but it'll cover your heart, at least—can't have anyone spotting your tech. Plus, it will match your eyes."

Anna stared at her boots.

"Go ahead, try it on!" Eliza shoved it toward her. "I won't look, I promise."

Anna couldn't decide if it would be more tolerable for Eliza to see her in a dress or completely bare. At least with the latter, she would still look like herself.

"All right, I think I've got it," Anna said once she'd fastened the sash around her waist with shaking hands.

Eliza turned around, hands wound together in a knot of fingers. She took one look at Anna before bursting into laughter.

Anna's heart sank. She'd known it must look as ridiculous as her usual Celestial Market costume, but she'd not thought herself laughable. She never should have agreed to wear it in the first place. Anna grabbed for the lace around her neck and tugged.

"No! Don't!" Eliza threw out a hand, but it was too late.

Fabric split beneath Anna's fingers as she struggled, a small hole blooming on the cloth across her chest. Every inch of her skin reddened. "See? I should wear the uniform instead. I'll just take this off."

"Don't you dare!" Eliza bounded to her side and tugged her in front of the vanity to see her reflection. "You've got your head through one of the armholes, see?" She pointed to the frills around Anna's neck.

"So it's not supposed to look like this?" Anna asked, relieved.

"Let me help." Eliza pulled the sleeve over Anna's head.

Anna did not breathe as Eliza laced up the back of the dress, her fingertips grazing every inch of Anna's spine. Slowly, skin slid across skin as though Eliza was not only dressing her but painting a masterpiece on the small of Anna's back. Eliza penned the finishing touch—a gentle brush of her thumb against the base of Anna's neck—before letting out a long breath.

"That's better," Eliza said.

"It doesn't matter. I ruined the dress."

"You ruined nothing at all." From a drawer in the vanity, Eliza whipped a needle and thread. "Nothing I can't mend, anyway. Now hold still."

Anna tried to keep her heart rate under control as Eliza's fingers danced across the fabric, pulling and tugging it into place. But then Eliza stopped, her pinkie pressed against Anna's shoulder, eyes fixed to the tear in the dress—to her chest.

Anna tipped her head down, their faces only inches apart. She held her breath, waiting, watching, wanting.

"I'm sorry, I didn't mean to—" Eliza pulled back her hand.

Anna looked down. The tear in the dress, only an inch or two long, revealed scars and steel—the top of her TICCER exposed.

Eliza hadn't seen a TICCER before. Neither had most people, for that matter. But the TICCER was simply part of Anna, as constant as every freckle on her skin.

"It's all right. I can stitch skin well enough. I'm sure I can sew up fabric." Anna reached for the needle.

But Eliza did not hand it over. Instead, her free hand tangled with Anna's sleeve, fingers brushing against fingers. "I've had a hundred questions all day, but now I can only think to ask . . . is it cold?"

Anna couldn't think. Not with Eliza's face so close, with their hands barely touching. So she stopped trying to make sense of the other girl. Instead, she grabbed Eliza's hand and guided it to the laceration in her dress, laying her fingers flat against metal.

Eliza didn't pull away this time, eyes falling somewhere between her hand and Anna's chin. They stayed like that for a moment. One tick, two ticks, three ticks . . . Then, without a word, Eliza lifted her fingers and replaced them with her needle, weaving back and forth to sew her dress back up.

"There we are." Eliza let her hands fall away. "Now you look every part the lady-in-waiting."

The dress made Anna feel false, like a doll in a costume, but Eliza's eyes on her made her feel real. It didn't matter what she wore, as long as it made Eliza look at her—touch her—like that.

Swallowing, Anna pulled on her braid. "What about my hair? Should I put it up like yours?"

"No. Leave it in a braid."

Anna raised an eyebrow. "It's not too unrefined?"

Eliza took the braid from her, running her fingers over the uneven plait, and said, "I like you a little unrefined."

CHAPTER THIRTY-THREE

Eliza was not accustomed to being caught, and yet three times she'd allowed Anna to see her staring. No, staring wasn't the right word. Eliza did not stare; she observed. Not that Anna would know the difference.

"What?" Anna asked sharply.

Eliza startled. "I— Nothing. What?"

"You keep staring at me."

"I do not!" Eliza averted her gaze, turning in her chair back toward the vanity. She had more self-control than anyone she knew, so why couldn't she summon it?

Their eyes met in the vanity mirror.

"If you're so offended by my appearance, you don't have to look at me."

Eliza's chest tightened. "I—"

"Seriously, read a book or something. It'll do you good." She held up the alchemy book. "Hell, *pretend* to read a book."

"I read plenty, I'll have you know."

Anna wasn't wrong. Some light reading might be beneficial, but Eliza had something a little heavier in mind. After she'd left Nathaniel by the stairs—with him ascending to his room and her returning to Anna with the uniform—a hollow feeling had pooled in her stomach. She'd dismissed it as sleep deprivation or hunger, but she'd taken a nap and eaten some cake and still the feeling persisted.

Eliza was a player short. There was no denying it. The uncertainty she'd expected to find at any moment in Anna instead had surfaced in the waver of Nathaniel's gaze, in the tremor of his voice. She'd hoped the promise of her protection against his father, though unspoken, would be enough to keep him by her side, but it wasn't the key to controlling Nathaniel.

The game had changed, but Eliza hadn't. She was still the Queen's Eyes, the most skilled strategist on the Tower. She couldn't let something as simple as unpredictability best her. Nathaniel was her target, and though she'd misunderstood the root of his particular weakness, she could still learn more about it.

And then she could exploit it.

She'd listened as his soul reached out to connect—to her, to Anna, to his father. Nathaniel had lost so much so young, but the pain behind his eyes was fresh. Eliza, too, had lost someone—she knew how acutely those pangs could hit, even years later. Marla still haunted her every day, and she knew no matter how it ebbed, no matter how she healed, Marla's death would lurk under her skin until Eliza joined her.

But that was the thing about loss: Death could rip love from life, but those memories stayed behind, burning a hole through the heart. And Nathaniel hadn't lost his father—he'd never truly had one; he'd lost a mother, a woman he didn't know, a woman he clearly loved.

Eliza couldn't bring back the dead, but she could do the next best thing. She flung open the vanity drawer, withdrawing her holocom.

"What is that?" Anna asked, a wave of wrinkles distorting her freckled skin.

Eliza sighed, turning back to face her. "Just because it doesn't have pages doesn't make my reading material any less valuable."

Anna set down her book and crossed the room. "No, I really mean—what is that?"

"It's a holocom."

"How illuminating," Anna deadpanned.

"Everyone on the Tower has one, or something like it." Eliza set it down on the vanity and pulled up the command panel. "They're all synced to a general library of information full of important documents, literature, logs from Former Earth. Really, you can access anything, as long as it was written somewhere and uploaded to the cloud."

Anna's fingers shook as she reached for the device, her eyes wide and hungry.

Scooting the holocom to the side, Eliza placed herself between it and Anna. "Why the sudden interest? Isn't your book enough for you?"

Anna didn't take her eyes off the holocom, speaking in barely more than a whisper. "I want to know how it works. Ever since I saw one in the Commissioner's office—"

"You saw the Commissioner's holocom?" Eliza asked, her voice sharper than she'd intended.

"Yes, when Nathaniel locked me in his office." Anna finally tore her eyes from the holocom, meeting Eliza's. "Is it such a surprise he'd have one? He's from the Tower, isn't he?"

Eliza stood up, gripping the edge of the vanity hard. "Of course—I can't believe I didn't think of it before," she murmured.

It was no surprise, indeed. The Commissioner would need to communicate with the Queen the same as Eliza, but it was the device's other uses that would serve Eliza best.

Finding the Commissioner's secrets had seemed a tedious process only moments ago. She'd assumed, as had the Queen, it would be a matter of assimilating and ingratiating herself to her host. But that method would take months, if not longer. Eliza did not care to spend that kind of time on a man who did not deserve it, and maybe she wouldn't have to.

"Didn't think of what before?" Anna asked, following Eliza's progress with her eyes as Eliza paced back and forth.

Eliza ran her fingers through her hair, destabilizing the careful curls she'd spent hours fixing. "The holocom—the holocom's the key."

"Excellent. That definitely clears things up." Anna rolled her eyes. "If you're not going to explain it to me, the least you can do is keep your cryptic mutterings to yourself."

Eliza forced herself to sit, tucking one foot behind the other, composing herself to stall for time. She couldn't tell Anna of the Queen's mission. Though the girl had proved trustworthy thus far, Eliza still had not forgotten that Anna had tried to stab her only yesterday. She would need to reframe this in terms Anna could understand—in terms Eliza *wanted* Anna to understand.

"We need the Commissioner's holocom."

"Why? We have yours."

Eliza sighed, shaking her head. For a tech expert, Anna certainly knew nothing about the sort of tech Eliza was used to. "Every holocom is different. The Commissioner's may have information we can use."

"Like what?" Anna leaned her head against the vanity, her braid swinging forward to be reflected in the mirror, twice as offensive—twice as intriguing.

"His search history, for a start." Eliza chuckled. "I'm more interested in what he might have uploaded to his personal database, to be honest. Holocoms are notorious for holding personal documents you don't want anyone to see." She shifted, remembering the secrets she'd kept on her own wrist tab back on the Tower before becoming the Queen's Eyes—before she knew better than to commit her secrets to the written word.

"And you think he'll have something incriminating in his personal documents?"

Eliza nodded, remembering what the Queen had said about the planet's terraforming, about the health problems. "If there's evidence of him tampering with your town, I'd wager that's where we'll find it."

Anna grinned. "Then I guess I'll have to steal it."

"Not so fast." Eliza held up her hand. "The Commissioner will notice if his holocom goes missing, especially if he has sensitive documents on it. We can't simply take it. You'll need to search its contents during the party. I'll keep him occupied while you and Nathaniel break into his office and learn what you can."

Anna raised her eyebrows. "Are you sure Nathaniel should be the one to come with me? Maybe it would be better if you—"

Eliza pursed her lips. "As much as it pains me to miss the fun, Nathaniel will serve you better. He knows the manor, and he knows his father far better than he'd like to admit, I imagine."

"I don't need him to show me where the office is," Anna grumbled.

"But you do need him to guess the passcode." Eliza lifted her own holocom and indicated the dial on the side.

"And if he can't guess it?"

"Well, then he'll have you. Who better to dissect the Commissioner's holocom than the fabled Technician?" When Eliza had met Anna in the garden, it had been difficult to see past her bloodied clothes and wild eyes—not to mention her poor form. Truly, the girl had no talent for knife fighting. But she did have a talent for technology, and that was something Eliza could respect.

Anna's cheeks reddened, clashing spectacularly with her hair, but her eyes glinted mischievously. "I do love taking things apart."

Eliza could relate, as she dismantled the precarious stability of the Commissioner's rule. She'd take the Settlement apart piece by piece, discarding the parts she didn't want. She only hoped when it was all over she'd be able to put it back together again.

CHAPTER THIRTY-FOUR

Nathaniel was not prepared for friendship. He'd gone all his life without, but somehow he'd found himself with two, if not friends, allies. But now Nathaniel needed to be alone—he needed to be asleep.

Nathaniel found no rest behind closed eyes. He deserved neither Eliza's gentleness nor Anna's forgiveness, and yet he wanted both so desperately—*too* desperately. Treason he could stomach, but alchemy kept him awake, sending his mind spinning and whirring like the metal cogs of Anna's locket.

Dragging himself from his bed, Nathaniel crossed to the desk as if in a trance. He was so very tired, but his fingers itched with unspent energy. He needed to hold the locket in his hands, remind himself of the weight of their mission. He'd failed so much—so many people.

But mostly he'd failed Anna. They were a matched set, an outlaw and her hunter, both marked by metal and loss. They were two sides of a coin, a reflection in a spoon—almost touching, always chasing, never quite on the same page.

He wouldn't fail her again.

But when Nathaniel opened the desk drawer, his hand found only parchment and ink bottles, no cold metal. The locket was gone.

Before panic could crawl through his chest, there was a knock at the door. Nathaniel slammed the drawer shut and answered. Eliza had changed into a lacy, pale pink dress that matched the cakes she carried. "I thought I might join you for tea."

Nathaniel took a cake and invited her inside, glad to see she'd come alone. He needed the respite. The otherness he'd felt before as Anna and Eliza looked at one another still stretched over him like a net he'd not learned to move properly beneath.

"Where's Anna?" he asked, leading Eliza to the small coffee table in the corner.

"When I left her, she was nose deep in that alchemy book of hers. She won't notice my absence until I return, I expect." Eliza sat, curling her legs beneath her on the armchair.

Nathaniel doubted it but wasn't sure how to articulate the magnetism he felt between them whenever the two were in the room, or how it bypassed him entirely.

"I'll admit, I thought it best we speak alone," Eliza continued.

Nathaniel's stomach churned as he settled himself across from her. With a tray of cakes and Eliza's own honeyed smile, her presence seemed ominous rather than comforting. Sweet things always spoiled eventually.

"Wh-why's that?" Hands shaking, Nathaniel tried to take a bite, depositing icing on his nose instead.

"I want to show you something, and I didn't think this needed an audience." Eliza pulled a holocom from her pocket.

"Did you steal that from my father?" Nathaniel asked before he could stop himself.

Eliza narrowed her eyes. "No, this is my holocom. I use it to communicate with the Queen."

"Oh, right." Nathaniel had almost forgotten Eliza's purpose in coming to Earth Adjacent. She was always so deliberate in her choices, it seemed an impossibility that someone else was responsible for making them. But she answered to the Queen, acting on behalf of the crown, not herself. She had perfected the art of loyalty in a way he never could. "You're not going to call the Queen, are you?"

Eliza set the holocom on the coffee table between them and pressed a button on the side. "It does a lot more than that. Holocoms are communicators, recording devices, databases—both shared and personal. This is my link to the Tower's database. I can look up anything, any word, any place . . . any person." She let the last word hang in the air.

Nathaniel swallowed with difficulty, though he'd not managed to consume any cake yet. "Like who?" He wondered if she'd searched his name. He hoped she hadn't.

Eliza's finger spun a dial on the side of the device, and the blue image focused on a single name:

Isla Fremont, née Perl.

Nathaniel half placed, half dropped the cake back onto his plate as he leaned forward.

"You mentioned your mother earlier, and I didn't know whether or not you'd want to see her record. I know facts can't heal your wounds, but it's a start."

Nathaniel stared at his mother's name for a long time. It was as if the world had frozen around him, encasing him in a bubble where anything was possible—where his mother wasn't dead, where his mother could be brought back to life through data and code. The letters in her name danced across his fingertips as he reached for them, but then his hand passed through the image and the world came crashing back.

"Wh-what did you find?" Nathaniel's voice came out hoarse and distant.

Eliza pressed another button on the holocom and the text vanished, replaced by an image of a woman not much older than Nathaniel. The woman had a soft face, devoid of the rigidity Nathaniel shared with his father, but he could see himself in her broad forehead, her crinkled eyes, her wavy hair.

"There's more in here than I thought there would be." Eliza hit another button and the image disappeared. "She was born on the Tower, an only child like you." She pulled up more text. "Showed an early proclivity for the sciences before she moved planetside, where they were banned. Most of the records here are from the minutes of her father's council meetings—he was Earth Adjacent's first Commissioner. Seems she had no trouble standing up to power."

Nathaniel's chest tightened. There was one difference between them, at least. Would his mother be disappointed in him because he couldn't do the same, or because he'd never truly tried?

Eliza stopped scrolling. "This is the interesting part."

Nathaniel thought it had all been interesting, but he sat forward to listen just the same.

"Nineteen years ago, your parents were married, and eighteen years ago, your grandfather died."

"I know." Nathaniel might not have been particularly diligent in his studies, but this part of his family history could hardly be missed. "And my father became Commissioner."

"No, he didn't." Eliza gave a thin, sad smile. "Your mother did."

Nathaniel straightened. Nowhere in all his readings and lessons had he been taught that. Even the tech decrees went straight from Commissioner Perl to Commissioner Fremont, although now that he thought about it, his mother could have been Commissioner Fremont as easily as his father. None of the documentation ever included a first name.

"There's only a brief mention of it in a memo here." Eliza pointed to a paragraph in the middle of the displayed text.

It is with pride and confidence that the council writes to inform Your Majesty of the ascension of Isla Fremont to the status of Commissioner of Earth Adjacent. She wishes to continue her predecessor's work to build a positive and productive relationship with the Tower and is supported by the full council.

"She's referenced here as Isla Fremont, but from here on out, she's *Commissioner* Fremont."

Nathaniel ran his fingers through his hair with one hand, reaching with the other for the holocom controls to read on. "That makes for confusing record keeping, doesn't it?"

"That was my thought as well," Eliza agreed. "It makes it tricky to differentiate between your mother's actions as Commissioner and your father's."

"Well, isn't everything dated? Everything before my mother's death is her, and everything after is my father . . ." Nathaniel trailed off, letting the text come to a halt.

"When did your mother die, Nathaniel?"

"I'm not sure—I was only a few years old." He spoke slowly, as if each word was a puzzle piece falling into place. "Wait. Shouldn't there be another memo to the Queen when my father became Commissioner? That would tell us when she died."

"That's just it—there is no second memo." Eliza moved his hand so she could key in a different search term. *Oliver Fremont* flashed in blue letters across the top, followed by the year he became Commissioner: 2874.

"Eighteen years ago," Nathaniel whispered. "This doesn't make sense."

Eliza sighed and leaned back in her chair. "Someone doesn't want us to know what happened to your mother. Someone wants us to forget she ever existed in the first place."

Nathaniel shuddered. He didn't need Eliza to tell him who. Only one person had the kind of power needed to erase someone from history.

"Why would he do this? Why keep me—all of us—in the dark about her? What good does it do to forget?"

"What good *does* it do?" Eliza raised a brow. "That wasn't rhetorical. What does your father have to gain from minimizing her life and covering up her death?"

"Nothing!" It came out louder than Nathaniel had intended, and he found himself suddenly on his feet. His insides writhed, as though something was attempting to claw its way out of him. "Absolutely nothing at all! There's no point—there's never been any point."

"Hasn't there?" Eliza asked, calm as ever.

Nathaniel fell back into the chair, his limbs too heavy to hold him. "No," he whispered. "But I don't see how this benefits him unless . . ."

Eliza inclined her head. "Unless?"

Their eyes met, and Nathaniel knew instantly where she'd led him, where he'd followed, where his father's treachery had been all along, waiting to be found.

"Unless he killed my mother." He wished he'd screamed the words, wished he'd stood up and tipped the table over. He would feel better, if he could wreck something, but Nathaniel had no rage to spend. Instead, he let his head sink, palms pressing against his eyes.

His father was a murderer. If he'd killed his own wife, there was no telling what he'd be willing to do to Nathaniel. He'd thought he could have his father's love if only he was smart enough, strong enough, good enough. But that love had never been attainable. Moreover, Nathaniel did not want it—not anymore. Every inch of him felt contaminated, as though the very skin he wore had been tarnished—not by illness but by murder, his father's crimes a sin coursing through his blood.

"Don't tell Anna," Nathaniel whispered.

Eliza cocked her head. "Why not?"

Nathaniel wasn't sure he had an answer, only an instinct. "I don't want her to know where I come from; I don't want her to know I carry this death, too."

"Do you think this will change her opinion of you?" Eliza asked. "It won't. We both know you are not your father."

Nathaniel nodded slowly. Anna reacted first and thought later, preferring to attack a problem rather than dissect it. But Nathaniel couldn't do that. He couldn't simply throw all his rage at his father and hope catharsis would come. He needed to sit with this; he needed to decide how it would change him—how it would change everything.

"Anna will want to use this to turn me against my father, and I *am* against him, don't misunderstand. I want to be angry—I do—but not until I'm ready. I don't want her to decide how I'm supposed to feel about this."

Eliza nodded slowly. "Is that . . . how we made you feel? Like you don't get to decide?"

A bubble in Nathaniel's chest burst, releasing the weight he carried. His feelings had always been a tangle. His father stifled them, Anna riled them, but Eliza somehow understood them.

"I'm scared," Nathaniel said finally. "I'm afraid of what we might become if we continue down this path."

"Some wicked paths are worth walking if the destination sets you free. Your father's hurt you in ways I can't fathom. Don't ever question whether you deserve to live without that fear."

But it wasn't only about their rebellion. It was about how Anna and Eliza looked at each other in a way Nathaniel couldn't, how they shared an unspoken connection Nathaniel didn't want. It was about more than right and wrong, anger and revenge. It was about the love Nathaniel didn't feel—about the love maybe they did.

"That's not what I meant." Nathaniel shook his head to clear it. "I don't want us to become my parents, fighting over a title." Nathaniel gestured to the holocom text.

He did not want to be the boy he'd been in the service of his father, taking what he wanted without thought for others, and he feared he'd be no different in service of himself. But more than anything, he feared marriage would swallow him up. He would disappear just like his mother, eclipsed by the ambitions of those around him.

"We won't," Eliza said. "We can do better. We are not doomed to become them."

They *could* do better, but only if they were honest with each other. Nathaniel liked Eliza well enough, but he didn't want her. He liked that she defended him from his father. He liked that she spoke to him like an ally, not a soldier. Most of all, he liked that

Eliza did not look at him with the same intensity with which she looked at Anna.

"I don't want to marry you." Nathaniel bit his lip, but he'd waded in this far already, he might as well make the dive. "You're a lovely girl, and I know I'm supposed to feel lucky to be with you, but I don't want you to be disappointed. I don't want you to expect more than I can give."

Eliza pinched her brow. "More than you can give?"

Nathaniel covered his face in his hands. She was going to make him spell it out for her. "I don't feel the way I should feel about you, I know, and I—"

"Stars, Nathaniel! You feel how you feel—there is no *should* about it." She climbed from her chair and crossed to kneel beside him, prying his fingers from his face so she could look him in the eye. "Did you think I would be angry with you? It's not any more your fault that you're not attracted to me as it is mine for not being attracted to you."

The glass walls he'd built around this feeling shattered. "You—you knew I wasn't attracted to you?"

Eliza smiled. "Of course. I've known since we met."

"And you're not upset?"

"Are you?" Eliza asked.

Nathaniel paused to consider. "No. No, I'm not. I think maybe I was—upset with myself, I mean. I wanted to be what you expected, but I didn't know how."

"Rest assured, you are nothing like what I expected." Eliza quirked her lips in a smile. "Thank the stars, you're so much more."

Nathaniel exhaled slowly, unsure if he could trust the compliment.

"Is there someone else?" Eliza asked. "Someone from your childhood, perhaps? Anna?"

"Anna?" Nathaniel almost laughed.

"I understand your disinterest in me, after all, I'm the girl chosen for you by your father. I wouldn't want me, either, if I was you. But Anna is a rebellion with pretty eyes, and if I were you—well, I don't have to be you to want her." She laughed. "So that begs the question—if not me, and not her . . . then who?"

Nathaniel resented the question. It implied there had to be an answer.

Leaning forward, Eliza fixed him with an inquisitive stare. "Do we, perhaps, have more in common than I first thought?"

Nathaniel matched her gaze, searching for the meaning beneath. He knew he was meant to understand her on some imperceptible level, but he didn't. They were nothing alike. Eliza was a refined lady, his father seemed to adore her, and she knew exactly what she wanted. And she didn't want him—at least there was that.

But what she wanted was Anna.

Something in Nathaniel's mind slid into place. "I don't— I'm not attracted to men, either. I'm not attracted to anyone. I never have been, and I don't think I ever will be." He'd never said those words aloud, and now that he had, they felt silly and small, like none of it mattered—like *he* didn't matter.

"Oh!" Eliza inclined her head. "I see."

"So. Not so similar after all."

Eliza stood up and perched herself on the arm of his chair, looking down at him with soft eyes. "We do not have to use the same words or share the same definitions to be similar, to understand one another."

Nathaniel suddenly found it difficult to swallow. "I don't know if there's even a word for it."

Eliza chewed her lip. "I don't want to presume—there are myriad ways to understand yourself, and as many words to describe it. You could be asexual, if you don't experience sexual attraction. Or, if you don't experience romantic attraction, you might be aromantic."

"Could I be both?"

Eliza smiled. "You can be both, or neither, or different levels of each. The truly beautiful part is you have the rest of your life to decide—and if you never know or change your mind, that's all right."

"How do you know all this?" Nathaniel felt small in the wake of her vocabulary. Were these words he ought to know? Had her education on the Tower somehow prepared her to understand something he'd spent his whole life experiencing but never truly grasping?

"I've done quite a bit of reading on the subject. There's not much else to do on the Tower, you know, besides attend parties with the same insipid group of nobles day in and day out." She rolled her eyes. "As the Queen's Eyes, I have special access to all sorts of documents written by the scholars of Former Earth. Luckily, they had quite a lot to say on the matter. There are entire volumes dedicated to different types of attraction, whole digital archives." She gestured to the holocom, a smile on her face. "Maybe it's silly, but having the vocabulary to describe what I felt made me feel less alone, made me feel like I wasn't the only one."

Nathaniel swallowed, trying the words she'd given him in his mind—he wasn't yet ready to give them voice.

Asexual. Aromantic.

"Of course," Eliza continued, a look of concern on her face, "language is limiting. Not all feelings can be described in a single word, and sometimes words aren't enough. When I finally found a definition, it freed me. It's all right if it's not the same for you."

"When did you know? About yourself, I mean?" Nathaniel gripped his knees, too nervous to do anything else.

"I don't know, exactly," Eliza said, eyes drifting. "It wasn't so much a thing to know about myself as a thing to know about everyone else. I knew when the girls around me didn't like other girls the way I did, and when boys didn't understand why I wouldn't step out with them."

Nathaniel wrinkled his nose. "How awful." He tried to imagine how it must feel for Eliza, to be seen so contrary to how she saw herself. But he didn't have to stretch his imagination far. He, too, had been treated the same, expectations placed on his shoulders for a romantic future he never wanted.

"It was awful at times, yes. Still is, on occasion." She gave him a pointed look.

"Oh, Eliza!" Nathaniel ran a hand through his hair. "I'm sorry. This must be painful for you, too. I didn't even think—this engagement—"

Eliza waved his concern away. "It isn't your fault. When I became the Queen's Eyes, I knew what I'd signed on for. My life stopped being my own the moment I entered her service. But even though she owns my actions, she doesn't own my feelings. She might choose whom I marry, but no one can choose whom I love."

"What is love like?"

He shivered, wondering when last he'd been loved. It was a different kind of love, the kind his mother might have felt for him, not the kind Eliza might feel for Anna. He knew the barbed love he still felt in some twisted, tainted way for his father, like the stump of a tree whose roots still wrapped firmly around his heart. Eliza and Anna, too, though he'd known them for only a short time, grew beside him as small sprouts, barely peeking out of the earth. He knew a kind of love. It was painful, but it was real.

"Romantic love, I mean," he clarified.

Eliza took a breath, but then she paused on the cusp of words before exhaling. "That's a complicated question, and it's different for everyone, and different *with* everyone. No two loves are exactly the same, just like stars in the sky."

"You've been in love more than once?"

"No. Just once." Eliza cast her eyes to the side as though searching for something. "She was wondrous and brave, and I let her go. I traded our love for power and status, so maybe it wasn't really love after all."

For the first time since he'd met her, Eliza wasn't in motion, charging toward a finish line he couldn't see. For this moment, she was still, as if she'd left her body behind to be somewhere else.

"Do you regret it?" Nathaniel asked without thinking. "I'm sorry—that was rude."

"No, it's all right. I don't give much credence to regret. I can't go back and change what's done. All I can do is take what I learned and do better next time. So yes, yes I regret it. And I'll do better next time."

"So . . . Anna?"

Eliza's eyes came back to life, and her cheeks reddened. "What about her?"

"I think you two make a good match." Nathaniel raised his eyebrows.

"I don't know yet," Eliza said, but she couldn't hold back a smile. "That's part of the fun of it—it could be something, or perhaps we'll never find out. Either way, it's valuable time, and worth every second, even if it has to end eventually."

"I'm sorry," Nathaniel said, his face falling. His hand found hers, no longer so averse to her touch now the lines had been drawn. "If our engagement is the reason it has to end, I—"

"Don't be silly!" Eliza cut him off. "We're only engaged. We have plenty of time to call off the wedding. But we ought to wait at least until we've tasted a few sample cakes," she said with a wink. "Don't you agree?"

CHAPTER THIRTY-FIVE

Anna had never felt this way before—short of breath, a tight knot in her stomach, and ever so warm.

Truly, her dress was too tight.

It didn't help that Eliza's gaze followed her everywhere around the grand ballroom. Not that she minded, exactly, but she wished Eliza would touch her with more than just her eyes. It was beginning to aggravate, all the flitting glances, the catching one another looking at the other, the endless eye contact as each wordlessly dared the other to break first.

But Anna wouldn't break first. She'd learned her lesson at the ripe age of thirteen when she'd kissed Billy Harmon behind the storehouse. It hadn't mattered that he'd kissed her back. All anyone talked about for the next three weeks were Anna's lips, and she had no intention of repeating the experience. She'd spent more than enough time resenting Billy Harmon; she didn't want to resent Eliza, too.

Of course, she might resent her anyway if she had to stay in this ballroom for much longer. She had a job to do, and standing around trying to avoid dancing with strangers certainly wasn't it. If only she could catch Nathaniel's eye to signal him to slip away, but as the focus of the night's festivities, he'd been difficult to separate from well-wishers.

"Enjoying yourself?" Eliza's voice set Anna's ears aflame.

"Not in the slightest."

Anna turned, and it was all she could do not to gape. From across the room, Eliza had certainly been eye-catching, her dress a glittering starscape on deep purple silk. But now Anna could see crystals had been sewn into the fabric in a mesmerizing floral pattern. It was the kind of extravagance Anna usually detested, but she hated herself even more for wanting to run her finger along the path of crystals winding across Eliza's bodice.

"You look like a princess," Anna breathed, not meaning to speak at all.

"Thank you. And you look . . ." Eliza's eyes traveled the length of Anna's form. "Presentable."

Anna narrowed her eyes. "I don't need to be presentable—I need to be investigating, breaking and entering, ransacking this place for the answers we need," she growled. "I don't understand why you and Nathaniel couldn't just serve as the distraction."

"And what will you say when an officer or rogue party guest catches you wandering the halls on your own? No one will believe a pretty thing like you just ventured off to explore without an escort." Eliza sighed, reaching forward.

For a split second, Anna thought she was about to touch her and braced for impact, still not fully recovered from the last time Eliza had been this close. But Eliza bypassed her entirely, plucking a frosted pink square from the table next to Anna's elbow.

"Besides, it would be a shame to go through all the trouble of lacing you into that dress only for no one to see it."

Anna's cheeks turned a shade to match the dessert in Eliza's gloved hand. "You aren't worried about the implications? It is your dress, after all." If wearing Nathaniel's clothes would provoke gossip, what would the courtiers say if they knew she wore their hostess's dress?

Eliza paused with the confection inches from her lips. "Worried? No."

Anna's throat constricted. Of course Eliza wasn't worried— why would she be? A lady's maid wearing her mistress's dress wouldn't cause a scandal. It was probably expected. Anna—the real outlaw mechanic or the fictitious lady's maid—could not afford such luxuries. Besides, it was preposterous to think a girl like Eliza and a girl like Anna . . .

But a twinkle glinted in Eliza's eye, not unlike the crystals on her dress. "I find it rather delights me," she said, reaching for another cake. This time, she paused with her pinkie pressed against Anna's forearm. "A pity my dance card's all filled up. I so would love to shock our guests tonight by taking you for a spin around the dance floor."

Anna didn't have time to tell Eliza that she didn't know how to dance before they were interrupted.

"Eliza, my dear. I do hope you're enjoying yourself." An older gentleman approached, giving Eliza a short bow.

Eliza turned to welcome the newcomer. "I can see you spared no expense."

"Nothing but the best for my future daughter-in-law."

Anna's stomach dropped out from under her. It was the Commissioner. She had never seen him in person, but she'd know his face anywhere. Sharp nose, high cheekbones, and dimpled chin: He was Nathaniel's double, with salt-and-pepper hair and a crease in his forehead. Except for the eyes, which shone like polished steel.

Of all the times and all the places for Anna to finally come face-to-face with her enemy, she'd never expected to be wearing such a ludicrous outfit.

A uniformed officer approached, and Anna took in a sharp breath. Perhaps he'd come to fetch the Commissioner. He would lure him away to some other corner of the ballroom, and Anna would be left alone to breathe like a normal person again. Yes, everything would go as planned.

But after the officer bowed, he didn't address the Commissioner. "My lady, I do believe you promised me this dance." He held out his hand to Eliza.

To Anna's horror, Eliza took it. "Of course. Lead the way!"

And with that, she left Anna alone to face the Commissioner.

The Commissioner watched them go, a cold smile sewn onto his face, before catching Anna's eye. "It's all quite good, you know," the Commissioner said, gesturing at the colorful confections beside her. "We don't skimp on the refreshments, no matter how inane the occasion."

Anna nodded and picked up a cream puff, if only to give her hands something to do. Left to her own devices, she feared she might strangle him in front of all his guests. She'd certainly have stabbed him, if not for the absence of readily available cutlery.

The Commissioner leaned against the wall beside her, searching her with sharp eyes. His gaze lingered on her left shoulder— where her TICCER lay beneath the surface. Though the acoustics in the ballroom sent the orchestral music soaring around the room, all Anna could hear was the loud ticking of her heart. Could the Commissioner hear it, too? Could he sense the steel?

Without meaning to, Anna's free hand rose to cover her heart, as if she could shield it from view, and her finger snagged on the freshly sewn tear. The Commissioner couldn't see her TICCER after all—he was not some all-knowing mind reader, only a snob.

"I apologize for my rudeness, but have we met before?" he asked finally. "I've been laughably out of touch with society these past few months, and I fear I've missed a whole new crop of young ladies coming out this season. Do I know your family?"

Anna choked on her own tongue. The Commissioner did, indeed, know her family—or at least he'd known them at one point or another. Thatcher had once saved Nathaniel's life, and as thanks, the Commissioner had murdered Anna's mother and father. Could he see her grandfather reflected in her freckled nose and cloudy eyes the way she saw Nathaniel, filtered through cruelty and confidence?

"No, I don't think so," Anna squeaked.

"That's a relief. I haven't had time for the usual rounds of social calls. I've been so tied up with this and that—especially this outbreak of tech in the city." He reached for another cream puff, not bothering to excuse his reach, blocking Anna in.

"Outbreak?" Anna repeated, more to herself than to the Commissioner. Certainly, she'd made inroads over the last few years, managing to smuggle tech into every corner of the Settlement, and she knew it irked the Commissioner enough to put out a warrant for her arrest, but to hear the Commissioner speak about it himself—well, the part of her that wanted to run would have to contend with the part of her that wanted to bask in her success.

"That damn Technician got a jump on me this year, but I'll find him, mark my words," the Commissioner said. "Old man can't evade me forever. We've both been at this too long, but I'll catch him, in the end. Or outlive him." He laughed, cold and hard. "Soon, very soon."

Anna tried to keep her face placid, but behind her painfully taut forehead, her mind churned. The Commissioner didn't suspect her after all; he thought her an old man, and it didn't take a genius to guess why. The Commissioner didn't know her, but he knew her grandfather.

"What did you say your name was, again?" the Commissioner asked.

Anna shoved the whole cream puff into her mouth.

"What a fast song!" Eliza sashayed toward them, waving her dance card in the air. "It's the Viennese waltz, and I believe you're quite promised to me, Commissioner!"

"Rightly so." The Commissioner bowed, then turned to Anna. "Do excuse me."

"Anna, go to my fiancé and make sure he finds me in time for the quickstep. It's in twelve songs." As Eliza led the Commissioner away, Anna heard her explain under her breath, "My lady-in-waiting—still breaking her in somewhat, but she'll do for now."

Twelve songs wouldn't last long. Anna guessed they had less than an hour to break into the Commissioner's study and find whatever they were looking for. That didn't leave much time, and Anna wasted none of it, rudely extricating Nathaniel from the ballroom, much to his well-wishers' disappointment.

"Go! Go!" Anna urged him on under her breath.

"I'm going!" he shot back, slipping through the door before she could push him out.

Anna waited a few ticks before following.

"Lead on," she whispered. "Eliza's bought us some time, but not much. If you can get me into the office quickly, we'll have about half an hour."

It took them longer than Anna would have liked to reach the Commissioner's office, their progress slowed by Nathaniel's insistence they look as natural as possible. He, like Eliza, thought others would be less suspicious if it appeared he was giving her a tour of some sort. They passed several guests in the halls, yet none of them paid them any mind, though Anna was loathe to give Nathaniel credit.

Once the office door clicked shut behind them, Nathaniel said, "All right, the holocom should be in his desk, right?"

Anna paused on the threshold. The last time she'd been in this office, she'd been under arrest, and Nathaniel had been the one to put her there. She couldn't help but wish Eliza had accompanied her, not Nathaniel.

Crossing the room, Anna tugged open the drawer.

There was nothing inside. She stared at the empty drawer for a moment before looking back up at Nathaniel. "It's not here."

Nathaniel joined her. "Are you sure this is where you found it?"

"Yes, there was a pile of pens and such, too. Where did he put it all?" Anna glanced around, but her own words gave her pause. She could excuse the holocom's absence easily enough, but the Commissioner had moved the entire contents of his drawer.

"He uses it frequently to communicate with the Queen. Could be he's carrying the holocom with him."

Anna's heart sank. There would be no separating the Commissioner from the holocom in that case. They were back to square one with nothing to go on, minutes wasted searching for something they wouldn't find. Dropping into the Commissioner's chair, Anna looked up at the ceiling, following the wooden beams with her eyes. There had to be something in this office she could use, some hint or some clue to help them bring this man down.

Think like a physician instead. Visualize the entire problem and diagnose; do not simply apply the bandage.

Thatcher's words echoed in her mind, an untimely reminder of her failures. She couldn't fix this problem with a scalpel and gauze. She couldn't split open the world and expect to patch it back together without consequence.

When she'd been locked in here before, something about the room had felt off. That same wrongness chorused through her as she spun in the chair, surveying the Commissioner's bookshelves. They were neat—too neat—with titles like *The Creation of Earths: A Terraforming History*, *The People's Planet*, and *Earth Adjacent: A World Away*. Nothing pointed to illicit activity. In fact, it was everything an official's study ought to be, clean and stark—and way too small.

"Visualize the entire problem," Anna muttered. "Big picture, Anna." She closed her eyes, mapping everything she'd seen. *Books, empty drawer, clean desk, wooden ceiling beams.*

Anna's eyes flew open.

There, on the ceiling, was her missing link: Wooden beams— pine, maybe—ran in even lines, except for the center beam. It looked nearly identical to the others, except where the ceiling met the wall. The middle beam ended several feet before the edge to make room for the door to swing open.

Standing, Anna crossed to the door and pulled it open, watching its progress through the space. Yes, the shorter beam was not a purely aesthetic choice.

"What are you doing?" Nathaniel pushed the door shut again.

"I'm visualizing the problem."

"So you said. What does that mean?"

"There's something not right about this room. Things that should be here aren't."

"The holocom?" Nathaniel asked. "I'm not sure that's particularly significant."

"Not just the holocom." Stepping back to the other wall, Anna ran her hand along the bookshelves, peering at the space between the books and the wall. "Where are his documents, his records? He's the Commissioner of Earth Adjacent—he must have paperwork."

"Maybe he keeps them somewhere else?"

"Why keep an office with nothing in it?"

Nathaniel cleared his throat. "I-I suppose it might be for appearances."

"Exactly." Anna stuck her hand between the bookshelves, feeling for what she couldn't see. "The only reason to have a fake office is to divert attention from the real one." Her hand hit cold metal. "This is no mere bookshelf."

"What?" Nathaniel's brows collided.

Grinning, Anna felt the hinges beneath her fingers. "It's a door."

CHAPTER THIRTY-SIX

Anna made quick work of the door, all things considered. Nathaniel watched in awe as she dismantled the hinges one-handed with only a wrench and no light to see by. If he could be half as skilled at anything as she was at taking things apart, he'd count himself lucky.

"Finished!" Anna held out a hand full of metal parts.

Nathaniel took them, feeling the smooth metal with his fingers. To think such small parts made up such a large secret.

"Help me move it?"

Nathaniel deposited the parts on his father's desk before moving to the other side of the bookshelf. "If this is really a door, shouldn't we have been able to just open it?"

Anna paused, her face contorted in a pained expression.

Nathaniel stared at her. "Don't tell me you didn't think of that."

Anna shrugged. "No, I . . . I . . . did not, in fact, think of that." She bit her lip. "I'm sure this was faster than figuring out the secret contraption that opens it, though." Anna sighed, her shoulders drooping. "Don't tell Eliza?"

His laugh died on its way to his throat, coming out as a cough instead.

Anna, fueled by fire and a thirst for vengeance, still had space inside her to be nervous about a girl. After his conversation with Eliza, Nathaniel was inclined to find it endearing rather than frightening. Somehow, knowing it was all right to be on the outside—to be himself, as different as it might be—made his discomfort at their affection less acute.

And yet, her phrasing struck him through the middle. *Don't tell Eliza.* He'd given the same directive to Eliza about Anna only days ago. So much was unspoken among the three of them, whether it was only embarrassment or family secrets long hidden. Hadn't Nathaniel decided to trust them that night in the garden? Hadn't they, in turn, shown they trusted him?

Swallowing the words he couldn't say, Nathaniel helped her move the bookshelf, creating a gap large enough for them both to slip through.

The room beyond was nothing like the one they'd just left. It was cramped, nearly half the size yet twice as full. Two desks sat in the middle of the room, both covered in loose papers and scrolls. Rather than books crowding the shelves, the walls were lined with equipment not unlike the tools and vials Anna carried in her satchel.

This wasn't only the Commissioner's office; it was his laboratory.

Nathaniel's stomach dropped out from under him as the room morphed before his eyes. His mother had stood here once, too, unaware she would die by the alchemical solutions she brewed. If Anna was right, if the Commissioner truly had poisoned her village, had his mother lent a hand with the poison? Or had she learned of his plot and suffered for it?

Anna inhaled sharply beside him as she, too, caught sight of the alchemy instruments. For a moment, they both stood there, eyes glued to the far wall. Then, as though compelled by the same force, they crossed the room together.

"You were right," Nathaniel whispered, fingers trailing over the glass vials, small tubes filled with various liquids, some clear, some cloudy, others completely opaque. Each had a small label attached, combinations of numbers and letters Nathaniel didn't understand.

Anna bent to examine the lower shelves, reaching to pluck a vial from its stand. "Look at this." She held it up for him to see. Liquid gold swirled inside, shimmery and thick.

"Do you think that's it—the poison?" Nathaniel shrank back involuntarily.

Anna pointed to the label: *Au-A* was penned in faded writing.

"Au is the symbol for gold, so if my alchemy book is anything to go on, I'd say there's a good chance this is our culprit." She turned the vial in her hand to read the label herself. "I'm not sure what the second *A* is for. Your father must have some notes. Maybe there's a legend somewhere." She gestured to the heaps of paper on each desk and slipped the vial into her pocket.

Nathaniel didn't need to be told twice. He began sifting through documents as Anna inventoried the contents of the drawers.

"He must have notes somewhere." Anna gestured to the shelves around them. "Any scientist worth their weight keeps records of some kind. It's irresponsible not to."

"Or clever. No one can stumble across incriminating evidence if you don't keep any."

"Mistrustful old man!" Anna spat. "Who's going to come wandering across all this anyway?"

"Maybe this lack of documentation actually tells us what we need to know," Nathaniel said slowly, thinking of his mother. "Absence can speak just as loudly sometimes. It shows he knows what he's doing is wrong."

"You know, that isn't half-stupid. You might be onto something."

"Although, there is one place we haven't looked." Nathaniel pulled the holocom from beneath a pile of agriculture reports.

Anna grabbed it, a smile on her lips. "Not half-stupid at all!" She flipped it over and tugged a small wrench from her satchel.

"What are you doing?" Nathaniel asked, snatching the holocom back.

"What do you think? I need to see what's on it."

"And you need to take it apart for that?"

"Well, yes. How else do you propose we see your father's secret documents?"

Nathaniel pointed to the dial on the side. "The normal way. You can't just take everything apart. What do you think my father would think if he came back to his office to find it in pieces?"

Anna bit her lip, looking put out. "Fine. So we guess the passcode."

Nathaniel nodded, fiddling with the dial. "Four digits." He turned it in his hands, peering at the buttons along the side. It was identical to Eliza's in every way. Had his mother's past been only four digits away his entire life?

Anna sighed. "Okay. What's his birthday? No, wait—when did he become Commissioner?"

Nathaniel spun the dials on the side all the way through the options. "It's letters only, no numbers."

"Try N-A-T-E."

Nathaniel winced, unsure if it would be more painful to discover his father hadn't used his name as his passcode or if he had. "No one calls me Nate."

Anna took the holocom from him. She tried G-O-L-D; then Nathaniel tried T-E-C-H.

"Really? Tech?" Anna snatched the holocom from him. "That would be like naming your cat Cat, if you were famous for hating cats."

"Well, let's see you come up with something better."

"He's *your* father. If anyone can guess the code, it's you."

Staring down at the holocom in his hands, Nathaniel spun the dials. Why did people keep saying that? He didn't know his father at all. He didn't even know what his father liked—besides power—or disliked—besides Nathaniel. The Commissioner was as much a mystery to him as his mother.

If it was Nathaniel's passcode, he knew what he'd choose.

I-S-L-A.

The green light clicked on.

Nathaniel's breath caught. Isla—his mother—was the key. His father, who would never speak her name aloud, who'd erased her from the history books and refused to discuss her with Nathaniel, still used her name as his passcode. After all these years, she lived on only in the mind of a tyrant.

"See? You did it!" Anna patted him on the shoulder gingerly.

"You do know *I'm* not a cat, don't you?"

Anna glared. "I was only trying to— Whatever. It's working now. Let's see what the Commissioner has to hide."

Imitating Eliza's movements, Nathaniel pressed the button on the side, bringing up the control panel. Blue light shot up from the surface of the holocom, forming a command center. A search tool topped a long list of Settlement documents: reports from his various councilors on agriculture, the economy, the census . . . and personal notes.

What would the Commissioner consider *personal*?

"Give me that." Anna snatched the holocom, keying in *Au-A* into the search bar and clicking on the first result.

"'I call it Au-A. Clever, isn't it? Gold Adjacent,'" she read aloud. "Full of himself, isn't he?"

"She," Nathaniel corrected. "My mother was the alchemist, not my father." Nathaniel leaned over Anna's shoulder to read with her.

The compound, if prepared correctly, will suppress the effects of Tarnish and prevent further cases of the disease. As the element cannot be fully combatted by terraforming efforts, a vaccine will have to do instead. —Isla Fremont, 2874

"So it isn't poison after all," Nathaniel whispered.

Anna grunted.

"But what good is transmuting lead when the very earth bleeds gold?"

Anna wrinkled her face. "What are you talking about?"

"The alchemy book—that's what it said. This must be what it meant. *The very earth bleeds gold.* It meant that Tarnish is naturally occurring in the planet, and Gold Adjacent is the cure."

"What difference does it make?" Anna said through tight lips. "So the Commissioner didn't poison us, simply withheld the vaccine. It's the same. People died because of your father."

Nathaniel rooted himself to the floor against the force of her words. He'd thought they'd made so much progress, trusting one another, working together. But in the end, he was still the Commissioner's son, and she would always hold it against him.

"And it's not a cure; it's a vaccine," she added, pointing to the word on the holocom projection. "I don't think Tarnish can be cured—it has already damaged our hearts. Nothing can erase that."

"Then what is this for?" Nathaniel held up the vial, staring at the shimmering liquid. Some part of him had thought maybe, just maybe, he could still become an heir worthy of his father. But if that was the case, his father would have given him the cure years ago.

Anna fixed him with a baffled expression. "For the future, of course. It's too late for us, but not for the next generation." She took the vial from him and shook it. "With this, we can ensure no one's affected by Tarnish again."

A chill went up Nathaniel's spine. The next generation could live without the fear of heart failure, without the taint of metal sewn into flesh. "Why would my father keep this a secret, then? Why not give you the cure? Without Tarnish, you'd have no need for tech, and the Settlement and your village could live in peace."

"There is no peace to be had. Tech isn't only good for TICCERs. There are plenty who use it for other things. Limiting tech hurts those already disenfranchised, and your father knows it. It's a power play—like everything he does."

Nathaniel swallowed a retort. His father was not worth defending.

"Here—another entry." Anna pointed to the holocom.

At first, I thought Tarnish would affect us all on Earth Adjacent, but my research has proven otherwise. While adults are not immune, the malady appears most commonly in children. Children transplanted from the Tower,

*like myself, do not develop Tarnish, regardless of age, and the disease is only
present in those who were born planetside.*

*My experiments have yielded little in terms of pinpointing when Tarnish
takes hold, as it appears to vary from child to child, impacting them anywhere from birth until adolescence. However, as long as Tarnish has not
developed, the vaccine has proven effective in preliminary experiments. I
theorize the vaccine will be most successful when administered to expectant
mothers prior to birth, but more study is necessary to determine how and when
Tarnish enters the bloodstream.*

*As the vaccine appears to have no ill effects on those without Tarnish, I
plan to propose introducing Au-A into the general water supply of the
Settlement. Until I can isolate the direct cause of Tarnish, this is the surest
way to secure a healthy populace and mitigate any further damage from
Tarnish. —Isla Fremont, 2875*

"The water supply," Anna murmured. "All right, she *is* clever.
I'll give her that."

"Was," Nathaniel corrected before he could stop himself.

"Right. Sorry."

Nathaniel bit his cheek. He'd not meant to divert the conversation. "But this explains why no one else in the Settlement has
Tarnish, doesn't it?"

Anna nodded, returning her attention to the holocom. "It
does, but these notes aren't sufficient for replicating the solution. I
need an ingredient list or an alchemical formula to take home." She
scrolled through the search results, selecting the most recent entry
dated from a few months ago.

*I am running out of Au-A—and time. No success replicating the for-
mula. Isla's notes incomplete. I need help. The Queen, not an option for
obvious reasons. I need an alchemist . . . I need the damn Technician.*

Nathaniel froze. So did Anna.

Ever so slowly, Nathaniel tore his eyes from the holocom to look at her, but he couldn't summon words—he couldn't even summon thought.

"Me?" Anna blinked at the holocom. "Why would he need me, except to hang me publicly and laugh?"

Nathaniel flinched. The Commissioner was capable of such cruelty, but looking at the short, hopeless cadence of his father's notes, Nathaniel almost felt sorry for him. He sought the Technician with as much desperation as Nathaniel had, only Nathaniel had wanted her to gain his father's respect while his father wanted her to save the Settlement.

"It's not like I'd help him, anyway, selfish, sniveling snake of a—" She stopped, jaw dropping.

"What is it?"

But Anna didn't respond, her eyes glued to the desk. Nathaniel followed her gaze to a partially obscured piece of paper he recognized as a map of their island. He'd used an almost identical map to find Anna's secret meeting place. How faraway that memory felt, as if it was from a different time entirely, as if he'd been a different person.

"What's wrong?" Nathaniel asked again.

Anna dropped the holocom, letting it fall onto the desk, and pointed to the map with a shaking finger.

Nathaniel leaned in. The Settlement had been drawn in detail, just like the map back in his room. But across from it, beyond the farmlands and uncharted terrain was a hand-drawn star.

Anna lowered her finger ever so slowly to touch the mark. "That's Mechan—that's my home," she whispered.

Her wide eyes met his, sending a chill down his spine.

"H-how did he find it?" But Nathaniel didn't need an answer. A silver chain protruded from beneath the map. He knew what it was before he saw it: a locket.

His locket.

Nathaniel's stomach plummeted. With the revelation of his mother's murder, Nathaniel had forgotten about his missing locket.

He picked it up to find it broken—the front had been torn off its hinges. Underneath, he found a folded piece of paper. The handwriting wasn't the looping purple of Anna's riddles but severe black letters, pointed like blades.

Properties of locket's metal: iron, carbon, and sphalerite zinc. When compared to Settlement steel, percentages differ. Settlement smiths use nickel and molybdenum, not zinc, to create steel alloys, as there is no substantial source of zinc near the Settlement. Scouts report zinc more likely found on the eastern side of the island but found no sign of habitation or mining. Sea salt residue found on exterior of locket. Oceanside town? Southeast ocean ridge blocks coastal access. View obscured. Town below?

"The Commissioner knows," she whispered.

Nathaniel's stomach flipped. If his father knew where her village was, if he'd found them, what was keeping him from tearing it to pieces? What would stop him from taking everything from Anna and destroying her family just like he had his own?

The answer came to Nathaniel as natural as a breath.

He would.

Nathaniel and Anna had been through so much already—he'd taken her captive, she'd escaped, he'd accidentally killed her friend, and she'd turned around and tried to kill him right back. But never had he seen Anna afraid until now. Though he'd no idea how he'd put the hidden door back on its hinges or explain his absence from the ballroom to his father, Nathaniel knew he couldn't ask her to stay.

"Go," he said. "You have to go."

She'd gotten him this far. He'd do the rest alone.

CHAPTER THIRTY-SEVEN

Eliza's feet ached, but her heart soared high above the dance floor. Whirling about a glittering hall, every eye was pointed her direction, every gentleman clamoring for the opportunity to claim her next dance. Back home on the Tower, she would have counted herself lucky to have a dance card half-full.

"Miss Eliza, the next foxtrot, if you please?"

"Miss Eliza, do me the honor of a waltz?"

Eliza had to admit, Earth Adjacent was growing on her. Here on Earth Adjacent, it did not matter that she came from nothing, that she had no family name to flaunt. She was the newest jewel in the Commissioner's court, the most important lady in the Settlement. She was from the *Tower*, and that was enough.

Of course, she couldn't let herself enjoy the night too much. Anna and Nathaniel were hard at work, and it would be a poor repayment of their time if she didn't do her best to help. Turning down several partners in favor of the Commissioner was not Eliza's idea of a grand time, but she would endure his company until Anna and Nathaniel returned. At least he was a competent dancer.

But the quickstep she'd been meant to share with her fiancé came and went with no sign of her cohorts. What was taking so long? She couldn't divert the Commissioner forever. Even he would eventually notice his son's absence.

Rather than dance to yet another fast song, she pled exhaustion and stepped outside the ballroom where the courtiers could not bombard her with invitations. No one who'd paid any attention could blame her for needing a break after fifteen dances in a row. Still, she traipsed away from the entrance, slowly making her way toward the Commissioner's office.

Over an hour had passed since she'd left Anna in her corner of the ballroom. The poor girl was not made for sophisticated society, every essence of her being clashing with the elegance around her. Not a soul on the Tower would consider her a suitable wall decoration, let alone a proper partner. She could practically hear Lord Farley's jarring voice in her head calling her uncivilized.

None of that would matter once Eliza completed her mission. No one would dare question her—or her choice in companionship—once the Queen had publicly declared Eliza her heir. The Commissioner would fall, and Eliza would rise, and she'd bring Anna and Nathaniel up with her.

If only she could find them.

Before Eliza could get far in her search, she heard a gentle pinging sound.

"Not now," she grumbled, ducking into a closet before withdrawing the holocom from her dress pocket. "Your Majesty?"

The Queen stuttered into view, blue and transparent, on the surface of the holocom.

"It's been three days, Eliza," the Queen said.

Eliza nodded. "Yes, Your Majesty."

"Well? What have you found?"

Eliza blinked rapidly. What could she possibly have found in three days given next to no instruction? But Eliza couldn't ask. Yet another lesson she'd learned from the Queen herself.

Cultivate your conversations as though they are works of art for all to see, she'd told her once. *Paint only the strokes of which you're certain, for just like with paint you can never truly take back a poorly chosen word, or a poorly chosen hue. You may cover it up, but the mistake will always be there beneath the surface.*

Eliza would never bring herself to lie to the Queen, but neither could she be free with her words now. She swallowed her frustration and said instead, "I'm actually in the middle of a search operation, Your Majesty. I hope to have something to share with you soon."

"Make it sooner rather than later."

Eliza could not help herself. "Didn't you expect this to be a lengthy operation, Your Majesty? I'm still installing myself here as you directed—"

"Our agenda has changed," the Queen snapped. "I spoke with the Commissioner earlier this evening, and he made his intentions clear. The last obstacle in his governance is about to be made obsolete. Without it, he will cement himself as the leader of Earth Adjacent, relegating me to a mere footnote of history."

Eliza swallowed, the waver in the Queen's voice coiling around Eliza's heart. She knew all too well the Commissioner's track record with powerful women he wanted to erase. If he'd done it to his own wife, he could do it to his mother. And without the Queen, Eliza's chance to climb her way to the top would be over. This would be her summit, and the rest of her journey would be a descent.

"I can't afford to wait for you to infiltrate slowly anymore." The Queen shook her head, veil swinging before her face. "This is no longer an undercover operation. I know how you love your masks and manipulations, but you'll have to give up your pretense and get the job done."

Eliza clenched her fist. It had been at the Queen's insistence that she take on this secret identity in the first place. It had been the Queen who'd kept her in the dark about her mission, and the Queen who'd taught her every trick she had. For her to turn it all on Eliza, to place the frustration she had with the Commissioner on Eliza's shoulders—well, simply put, it was unfair.

But nothing had ever been fair in Eliza's experience. Now would be an odd time for it to start.

"I understand, Your Majesty," Eliza said, enunciating carefully. "What is my mission?"

The Queen let out a long breath, her veil rippling, and said, "The secret to fully terraforming the planet lies somewhere in the Commissioner's manor—the cure for their planetary malady. I don't know where he keeps it. I need you to find it."

"I know—you said before. But what am I looking for? Is it a scribbled set of instructions? A formal document?" Eliza no longer cared if she sounded polite. She would not let herself fail this mission simply because the Queen gave her inadequate instructions. What if there was nothing to find? If the secret was simply in the Commissioner's head, there wasn't much she could do to extract it by force.

For a moment, Eliza thought the Queen would refuse to answer again, but then: "An alchemical formula. Even a sample of the solution will be sufficient. Do this for me, Eliza, and I will reward you beyond measure."

Eliza's chest swelled. "Yes, Your Majesty."

"I need it in twelve hours."

"Twelve hours?" Eliza blanched. Short of torture, she could think of no other way to get the Commissioner to confide in her so quickly.

"Yes," the Queen said. "Bring me that secret by morning—or don't come back at all."

CHAPTER THIRTY-EIGHT

Anna ran. She didn't have the time to walk, and she didn't have the sense to sneak. The Commissioner's halls were as good as any other path back to Mechan, and she would bowl over anyone who stood in her way. He could send his strongest guards after her, and it wouldn't matter. She would run faster, farther, fiercer than them all.

Of all the things Anna had seen over the years, Mechan marked on the Commissioner's map had to be one of the worst. When she'd spotted it, she'd first thought it was a mistake, just an innocuous smudge. But in the short time Anna had known the Commissioner, she'd learned he did nothing by mistake.

Including the star on the map now crumpled in her hand.

The Commissioner knew about Mechan. How long before he sent officers their way to storm the streets, to tear families from the homes they'd thought were safe, to destroy the haven Thatcher built? And for what?

To find the Technician.

No matter how Anna looked at it, this was her fault. After all those years funneling tech into the Settlement, Thatcher's prediction had finally come true—and it was her locket that had led the Commissioner to Mechan. She'd never thought to use a different steel alloy for her lockets, never considered the combination of metals they used in Mechan might be different from the Settlement's. Anna had brought this on them all. If Ruby, or Thatcher, or a single other innocent was killed in the Commissioner's raid, she'd have to carry that burden alone.

But Anna didn't want to be alone anymore.

Racing through the halls, Anna flew past brightly colored blurs—guests or paintings, Anna couldn't tell. Nothing would stop her, nothing would slow her down.

Anna collided with something solid, sending her barreling toward the hard floor.

"Oof!" The impact knocked the air from her lungs.

"Red?" Eliza's voice, low and hollow, sounded from beside her on the floor.

Scrambling to her feet, Anna righted herself. "I have to go," she muttered, and made to take off again in the direction of the exit, but Eliza grabbed her by the arm.

"What's going on? What happened? Are you and Nathaniel all right?"

Eliza had too many questions that Anna didn't have the time, or breath, to answer. Instead, she managed, "Commissioner's office, secret door, alchemy tools, found a map—"

"Alchemy tools?" Eliza's eyes sharpened. "Slow down."

Anna shook her head, gesturing to the map. "I can't—I have to go. My town's in trouble."

Eliza took the map from her, glancing down before her gaze locked on Anna. "Take a breath with me. Come, breathe." She inhaled, and Anna followed suit.

"I can't stay here," Anna said once the air had vacated her lungs. "I have to save my people."

"Of course. But first, tell me what you found."

Anna tried to pull her wrist from Eliza's grasp, but either Eliza's grip was too tight, or Anna's intent too weak. "There's a hidden door in the Commissioner's office—behind the bookcase."

Eliza's eyes widened. "How original."

"He has a whole laboratory inside—vials and samples of all sorts of alchemical solutions." Anna pulled the vial from her dress pocket, letting the golden liquid inside reflect the dim hall light. "We found this—a vaccine for Tarnish."

Eliza released Anna's wrist, fingers closing on the vial instead. "You did it," she whispered.

"Yes, but like I said—I have to leave. Nathaniel can fill you in."

Eliza didn't say anything, staring intently at the vial in both their hands, holding tight.

Nothing the noble did made any sense to Anna, but she didn't have time to puzzle over her now. She needed to get to Mechan— she needed to warn them.

"I need to go," Anna repeated.

Eliza seemed to return to the present. "Yes, of course. Good luck," she said, but still did not let go of the vial.

Anna raised her eyebrows. "Right. I'm just going to take this back with me."

Eliza's lip twitched. "I'm so sorry, Anna. I can't let you do that."

It had to be a misunderstanding. "Yes, you can."

"I wish I could." Eliza smiled sadly. "But I need you to leave this here with me. You see, I need it more than you do."

Anna gaped. "*You* need it? I'm sorry, are your friends and family dying of a mysterious poison? Did you have to watch your best friend's son die in front of you because of it?"

Eliza bit her lip. "I'm not going to argue with you. You can stay here and fight with me over this vial, or you can go to your family and fight for them. Choose your battle, Anna, difficult though it may be."

But it wasn't difficult. Not by any standard. The vial in her hand was a promise of a brighter tomorrow, a chance at a future for Mechan without heart disease, the life Ruby wanted for her unborn child. But a vial for the future meant nothing if Anna couldn't salvage the present.

Three days ago, Anna would have sooner lopped off Eliza's hand than leave without the vaccine. That vial was Anna's chance to earn back her grandfather's trust, her chance to make up for Roman's death. But now none of that seemed so important. Thatcher had been right all along—Mechan was the most important thing.

It wasn't just a place. It wasn't just an idea. It was a family. It was *her* family.

Anna let go, leaving Eliza behind, burying a rage she could embolden tomorrow, a loss she could mourn once she had the time to do anything but run.

Darkness had already fallen by the time Anna reached the Settlement walls. She'd left her satchel behind in Eliza's bedroom. She had no passport, but her fine clothes hardly matched her false identity of a farmer's daughter anyway. With only the wrench, heavy in her pocket, for company, she slipped into the cover of the clock tower, her steps drowned out by the sound of falling water. She fumbled in the dark for the rope ladder she'd hidden among the vines as the clock above ticked a heavy rhythm into the night.

She dropped down, tearing the ladder with her. She would take no chances this time—no one would follow her.

Her shadow fell across the grassy pastures as she ran, reaching for something just out of her grasp. She slowed when she caught sight of the ridge shielding Mechan from view. As a cloud moved to block the moon, she watched her shadow grow and grow to touch the ridge's edge. Then she picked up her feet and chased it.

When she reached Thatcher's house, she paused on the threshold, hand outstretched to turn the handle. This was it—the last moment between before and after. She would walk through that door, an unwelcome intruder in her own home. She would rouse Thatcher from slumber or summon him from surgery to deliver the news.

Would it be like last time? Would she enter her grandfather's house, carrying a warning instead of a body, to be greeted only with disgust and blame? Would Thatcher turn her away?

No. It would be different. She was the messenger once again, but this time at least, she knew where to place the blame. She would not run from what she'd wrought. She would face it, and she would do her best to salvage what she'd lost.

Anna turned the handle, but the door was locked.

No one in Mechan locked their doors at night. The town's golden rule wasn't so much *love thy neighbor* as it was *trust thy neighbor*. Without trust, they were but many frazzled lawbreakers; with it, they were a community.

No one answered the door when she knocked softly. Thatcher made no sounds inside the house, not even his usual snores. Perhaps he only snored when she was home to irritate her. It seemed the sort of thing he would do, but when Anna pounded her fist against the door, she was met only by a gust of wind.

Anna stared out at the rest of the town. She could knock on any door, wake any neighbor to raise the alarm. She didn't need to tell Thatcher.

But she wanted to. Her chest tightened with the realization. She didn't only want to bring her town to safety. She wanted to confront her faults, she wanted to own up to her mistakes, and she wanted Thatcher as her witness.

As though pulled by an invisible force, Anna made her way down the path, across the town square, to a green door she'd walked through a hundred times. Never before had her heart thundered with such ferocity, her skin prickled with such hesitation, her breath dragged with such difficulty, as she lifted her hand to knock.

Ruby answered the door, a blanket wrapped around her shoulders. Her hair fell in tight curls around her tired face, but her eyes were alight, alert. "What's th— Anna?"

For a moment, Anna thought she might be sick. Ruby, who'd done nothing wrong, who'd deserved everything right, stood tall and strong despite everything, while Anna wilted before her. Anna didn't deserve to look her in the eye and ask forgiveness, she didn't deserve to be forgiven.

But that wasn't why she'd come. Anna could live without Ruby's absolution, but she couldn't live without Ruby. A thousand apologies bubbled at the precipice of Anna's throat.

Instead, she said only, "The Commissioner knows we're here. We have to run."

Ruby didn't argue. She set her jaw, slipped on her shoes, and stepped onto the stoop, shutting the door behind her. She caught Anna's gaze and held it. "Tell everyone to get out. Take only what they need. In fifteen minutes, we evacuate to the north." And with that, they parted ways, Ruby taking the eastern half of town, Anna taking the west.

Anna met little resistance as she made her way through the houses, doling out instructions like prescriptions. She might not have been a doctor anymore, not like Thatcher, but she could still save lives.

As she ushered out the last family, following on behind, she scanned the crowd making their way out of town for a familiar wrinkled face, straining her ears for the creak of metal wheels.

"Where's Thatcher?" she breathed, catching up to Ruby.

"Not here." Ruby's face tightened. "He left at dawn."

Anna's stomach took a steep dive. "Where did he go?"

Ruby's lips narrowed, and her eyes found the skyline. "He went looking for you."

CHAPTER THIRTY-NINE

Nathaniel didn't return to the ballroom. He knew he ought to go, cut his losses, and salvage what he could of the night, but something kept him rooted to the spot. This room held more than the key to his heart condition. Nathaniel needed to know the truth about his mother. His mother's death had left behind a hole, and Nathaniel had filled it in with hope—hope that if one parent loved him, it wouldn't matter that the other was dead. Instead, his father's criticism had chipped away at that hope, leaving Nathaniel empty.

Nathaniel let the hinges fall between his fingers, hitting the desk with a harsh clack. He didn't have a mind for metal the way Anna did, and piecing the door back together would only delay a confrontation years in the making.

Nathaniel turned his attention back to the holocom, abandoned where the map had been. Anna had been willing to drop everything she'd worked for, the justice she'd so desperately wanted—so surely deserved—to protect what she loved. Nathaniel's chest constricted. He'd been too young to protect his mother from his father, but he'd been given chance after chance to do the right thing, to protect everyone else.

Instead, he'd only protected himself.

Such thinking wouldn't help him now. He was only dissecting his past mistakes rather than making new ones. Because that's what awaited him—more mistakes. He could not avoid them.

That's what Anna would tell him were she still by his side. She would tell him no one ever did anything great without first doing it wrong. In response, Eliza would cock her head and fix Anna with a mirthful stare, proclaiming such a proverb nonsense. Anna would roll her eyes and say something about perfection being a useless aspiration. And Eliza would let her sit in her accusation for exactly one moment longer than Anna's comfort allowed before putting an end to the discussion with something like, *There are no mistakes, only choices and what you do with them.*

Nathaniel hadn't had a choice when his mother died, but he had a choice now.

He'd choose to finish Anna's work. He'd find out what else his father was hiding and bring it before the council. He'd abolish his father's regulations on tech and knock down the Settlement's walls. He wouldn't let his father make anyone else with mechanical hearts—or limbs, or lives—somehow against the law. He would put an end to his father's tenure, even if it meant taking on the mantle himself.

He'd do it for his mother. He'd do it for Anna—and Roman. He'd do it for himself.

Returning to the holocom's main display, Nathaniel selected the label *Personal Notes*. If there was anything worth finding, it would be there. But when the first document loaded, it wasn't scientific notes full of numbers and formulas. It was a scanned copy of an old letter, written by hand. Pointed and heavy, though not as severe as it was now, Nathaniel recognized his father's handwriting immediately.

Dear Miss Perl,

It was a pleasure to make your acquaintance this evening. I particularly enjoyed your joke about the pudding.

As you know, my mission to your planet is diplomatic, on behalf of the Queen, so I will likely meet with your father again. I do so hope you will be in attendance, as his heir, but also as a familiar face. It is so much less agonizing to sit through so much dullness when I know there's a chance to hear your voice—which is both lovely and so insightful on matters of state.

> *Wishing you well, and hopeful we will*
> *continue to encounter each other,*
> *Oliver Fremont*

Nathaniel's breath hitched. This was, undoubtedly, the first letter his father had ever sent his mother. He'd never considered a time before they'd met, but to see they'd exchanged letters, not unlike Nathaniel and Eliza had, Nathaniel suddenly felt small. They'd had a life before him, a life before his father changed. Nathaniel scrolled farther down and selected another.

My dearest Oliver,

As your time here draws closer to an end, I can't help but think in what-ifs.

What if you were not beholden to the Tower?

What if the Queen didn't need you by her side?

What if Earth Adjacent needed you more?

I know it is unfair of me to think such things. You are your own person, and you must choose for yourself. I know the Tower is your home and the Queen your family. It would be wrong for me to ask you to stay.

And still, I ask, because it would be just as wrong for me not to.

What if you stayed?

What if Earth Adjacent was your home?

What if I became your family?

I know you are not one for subtlety, and so I will be plain. What if, my dearest, you did not go back, and, instead, what if you married me?

Yours,

Isla

Nathaniel felt like his mouth was stuck shut, jaw clenched, tongue dry. Eliza had shown him only facts, names and dates and events. But this was intimate and personal.

He opened the last record in the file.

Isla,

I left the samples you asked for in the cabinet where it's dark. I hope their brief exposure to sunlight doesn't ruin them. There's a surprise in there for you as well.

I love you.

Oliver

Nathaniel let out a long, slow breath. This was the last letter his parents had exchanged. It hardly felt like a letter at all— more like a note you'd leave before going out. It was casual, concise—routine. Before his mother had died, they'd had a life, all three of them. His mother was the Commissioner, but she was also a scientist, and she'd loved his father enough to marry him. They'd had no mandate, like Nathaniel and Eliza. They'd chosen this life.

And then his father had chosen her death.

Nathaniel nearly retched. *There's a surprise for you in there as well.* Had that been the poison? Had he left her some treat, laced with death? She probably trusted him; she probably never saw it coming.

I love you. His father's last written words to his mother had been such a blatant lie.

"Nathaniel?"

Nathaniel looked up, eyes aching and watery, to see his father ducking behind the hidden doorway.

Nathaniel fought the urge to run, but it was replaced by a stronger desire to launch himself at his father. However, no matter how badly Nathaniel wanted to hurt him, he couldn't bring himself to raise his fists. Roman's death, only a few days ago, still haunted him, and if he struck another human being, Nathaniel feared it would shatter him.

That would make them the same, and Nathaniel didn't want to be his father. Not anymore.

The Commissioner's gaze swept over the scene, taking in the holocom in Nathaniel's hand.

Nathaniel set it down, closing the files. "I-I only—"

"What are you doing?" his father growled.

"I only wanted t-to get away from the party. The crowd, and all the dancing . . ."

His father crossed the room to the desk, standing opposite Nathaniel. He glanced down and picked up one of the hinges from the table. "And so you thought you'd hide from your fiancée in *my* office? And these, what, fell off in your hand?"

Nathaniel swallowed slowly. "I didn't do it." It was a half-truth, but talking to a liar, even a half-truth felt generous.

His father raised an eyebrow. "And who might have snuck into my office to dismantle the hinges on my bookcase door, leaving it open for you to find?"

"You wouldn't believe me if I told you," Nathaniel muttered.

"Don't tell me—it was the Technician, wasn't it? Is that the lie you've concocted in that minuscule brain of yours?"

"What? No— I—"

"Don't bother, Nathaniel. It's too late. I captured the Technician already. There is no more outlaw for you to chase, no more bounty to be won."

Nathaniel's stomach sank. So Anna hadn't made it out after all. If his father had caught her already, she'd not had time to warn her village. They'd all be in danger if his father was left unchecked.

So Nathaniel would have to check him.

His father shook his head dismissively. "Come. I'll deal with your treachery later. We have things to discuss, and I don't want you knocking anything over in here."

"No." The word slipped out before Nathaniel could catch it— but he didn't want to. He couldn't afford to let his father walk away from this room. He had to keep him here talking. He needed him to admit his sins, confess his crimes. He couldn't let him commit more.

"What did you say?" his father snapped.

"No," Nathaniel repeated himself, more loudly this time. "You can't keep this from me. This place isn't yours to keep."

His father slammed his palms down on the desk, leaning over it. "Do not disobey me!"

Nathaniel's instinct was to shrink away, to nod and take the blow he knew was coming, but somewhere inside him burned a small, Anna-shaped flame, urging him to fight back, urging him to stay strong. It was easy for her to stand against his father—she was on the outside looking in. Nathaniel had been inside for so long, never truly seeing, never allowing himself to react. But now he was on the outside, too. The Commissioner had treated Nathaniel's mother with as much love as he showed Nathaniel. If one relationship was so clearly manipulative, why had it taken him so long to see his own with his father the same way?

"I'm not one of your officers." Nathaniel clenched his fists. "I don't take orders."

The Commissioner ground his teeth. "I am your father. I am your commander. I am your law! I did not raise you to be this way."

"You didn't raise me at all." Nathaniel's fingernails sliced into his palms, but he could feel no pain, only anger. "You pushed me down. You brought me into a world that didn't want me, and instead of fighting for me, you hid me away. You made my heart a secret when you should have made it legal!"

The Commissioner's eyes narrowed, and he grabbed Nathaniel by the collar. "How dare you! I broke the law *for* you. I summoned my greatest enemy—swallowing pride and principle—to save *you*. My love is what kept you alive, and this is how you repay me?"

"How regrettable that your love couldn't do the same for my mother." Nathaniel ground his teeth together, raising his eyes to meet his father's. "Tell me, did you feel anything at all when she died?"

Nathaniel didn't see the punch coming—only felt the impact. He would have staggered back if not for the Commissioner holding him. Pain spread out across his face, his nose almost certainly broken.

"Do not talk to me about things you don't understand."

Nathaniel squinted against the pain but still managed to speak. "You're the one who doesn't understand. You aren't supposed to kill the ones you love."

When the Commissioner's second punch came, Nathaniel was ready for it, but that didn't matter. His vision went splotchy as his head snapped back, and the last thing he saw before he blacked out was the Commissioner's bulging, deep-set eyes.

CHAPTER FORTY

Eliza watched Anna go, chest tight, grip tighter. The vial in her hand represented everything she'd worked for—a bright future, gilded and charmed at the side of the Queen. Deep down, she'd known it would come to this, one way or another. Anna and Nathaniel had been convenient allies, and had the Queen kept to the original plan, Eliza might have followed through on her promise to get Anna her justice and teach Nathaniel to be confident. She might have won her prize with them beside her.

Instead, she acted alone, with only her secrets by her side. But such was the way of a spy. Knowledge was power, not allies, and just as the Queen held more than Eliza, Eliza had held more than Anna and Nathaniel. She'd always planned to use it to her advantage. To pretend otherwise would be dishonest.

Still, she'd thought Anna would at least hesitate. She'd expected to see pain, to see heartbreak or at least the smallest sign of regret in those gray-blue eyes. But instead she'd seen only the fierce determination that drew her to Anna in the first place.

Eliza hadn't hesitated, either. The Queen's instructions were all that mattered, and a little flirtation couldn't stand up to a lifetime of service—of loyalty. Love certainly hadn't been enough three years ago when Marla had asked Eliza to run with her. Eliza thought it would be easier to let go than last time. Last time, Eliza had been younger, she'd loved deeper, and she'd lost more, all in service of the Queen—no, all in service of herself. Had she cared less about becoming the Queen's Eyes . . . No, it did not bear rehashing. She'd chosen this life. She would make no room for regret.

So why did her breaths come in short bursts, her lungs too small for air? Eliza forced herself to breathe, just as she'd coached Anna earlier.

Holding tight to the vial in one hand and the wrinkled map in the other, Eliza slipped back through the halls. Her mission was over. All that was left was to tell the Queen she was coming home.

Home.

She'd return to the Tower, to the glamour, to the society. Once again, Eliza would be among lords and ladies of status. They were the company she deserved, and yet, she realized with a pang, not the company she wanted. She'd been gone less than a week, but somehow Earth Adjacent felt more familiar than all the halls in the Queen's sky.

Eliza shook herself. It was foolish to think such things. Once she returned, she'd be greeted with the greatest reward of all. It would not matter where she lived or whose company she kept. The Queen would finally see her for what she was: the best.

Before Eliza could escape through the front doors, however, the Commissioner approached looking ruffled. Eliza had kept tabs on him for most of the night. He must have slipped out while she was speaking with the Queen.

Hurriedly shoving the vial and map into her pockets, Eliza straightened and plastered a smile to her face, ready to be the charming future daughter-in-law once more—for the last time—but the Commissioner didn't stop to acknowledge her, charging into the ballroom, fists clenched, shoulders back.

Something was off. Eliza cast her gaze about for Nathaniel. Surely with Anna gone he'd be back by now. Had his father apprehended him?

Nathaniel wasn't her responsibility anymore. She didn't have time to dawdle at all, but something in the Commissioner's tight features turned her feet toward the ballroom. Through the open double doors, she watched him cross the room straight through the dance floor and step onto the stage. The musicians' waltz came to a screechy halt, and the Commissioner turned to face the now rapt audience.

"Apologies for interrupting your evening," he began, his voice hard and direct. "I have an important announcement that simply cannot wait, and I believe you'll all join me in agreement once you hear it."

Eliza ought to use this distraction to escape, duck out while everyone's eyes were on the Commissioner, but she couldn't tear herself from the scene.

The Commissioner cleared his throat, an eerie smile spreading out across his face. "This evening, my officers informed me they apprehended and arrested the Technician. The criminal is in custody, awaiting the council's judgment."

The room burst into whispers and applause. The Commissioner bowed, his smile spreading as he continued to speak.

Eliza didn't hear what came next, her ears ringing. *The Technician.* The Commissioner had caught her.

He'd caught Anna.

Eliza's stomach turned once, and then it turned again, rolling and writhing as though someone had scrambled the gravity controls. She'd seen Anna only moments ago—off to save her village. Now she wouldn't get the chance. Her village would be destroyed, and there was no one left to care. But Eliza cared.

She cared so much, she'd nearly missed the signs. It was in the way Anna's drive pushed her own, the way getting justice for Anna had felt like getting justice for herself, and the way her whole being ached at the thought of Anna locked up and alone. She'd let her chance at love go once before, off into the stars, lost to worlds unknown. This was the same.

And it was different. Anna wasn't gone—not yet, anyway— and Eliza could still choose to stay.

Eliza retreated, slipping out into the cool night air before anyone could stop her. In the low light from the windows, she smoothed out the map in her hand and traced the outline of the Settlement before finding the small star marked near the coast. This was what Anna cared about—her village, her people. She'd never forgive Eliza for rescuing her if she let Anna's family die in the process. Anna didn't need saving, her village did.

Eliza would do what Anna couldn't behind bars, and she would hope when they reunited, it would be enough. Hearts were delicate things, and Eliza could not con her way back into Anna's. She would have to earn it.

Eliza balled her fists and set off into the night, cursing herself for not correcting her path sooner. She should have seen she'd strayed too far long ago—she should have known when she'd let go of Marla, when she'd sacrificed self for status.

Really, she should have known the second Anna had come at her with that knife and Eliza had chosen not to kill her.

Eliza left the Settlement, sneaking up and over the wall with as much grace as she could. Cool wind wrapped her up like a chilly blanket and lifted her hat from her head along with the weight from her shoulders. Behind her was the life of some other girl, some other Eliza—a girl willing to sacrifice freedom for power.

When had Eliza decided the only way to be happy was to be powerful? When had she decided the only way to be powerful was to be merciless?

Setting the holocom down on the edge of the wall, Eliza stared into her own eyes reflected in the steel. The Queen thought she knew her, heart and soul, she thought she owned her. But even queens could be wrong, and even queens could be beaten.

Eliza could be happy, and she could be powerful.

She stepped forward, passing over the holocom, and over the edge. She would leave the Queen behind, she would not turn back, and she would choose to be free.

Eliza landed softly in the grassy field outside the Settlement, looking out on a dark abyss of trees. Finding Anna's village would be harder in the dark, but she had the map to guide her. She'd found smaller things with less to go on before. But when Eliza reached the point on the map, there was nothing but a cliff and a vicious sea below. Wind whipped through her, sending shivers up her spine. She wrapped her arms around herself and crouched behind a massive rock, slim and pointed like a finger—a choice hand gesture for the moment, indeed.

As she leaned against it, however, Eliza saw the flash of metal in the moonlight. She bent lower, flattening herself against the muddy ground to see.

It was a handle, steel and sturdy, attached to the side of the cliff face. As she pushed herself out farther, she tried not to look down. It was a far drop to earth—one she wouldn't survive if she toppled over the edge. Heights had never been a particular love of hers. Thank the stars it was too dark to see the bottom.

Eliza reached as far as she dared and her fingers connected with cold metal. The crank turned under her touch. Pushing and pulling, a platform rose up from the darkness, an elevator of sorts. She braced herself against the cliff's edge, gathering her strength of will, and let herself drop.

The platform held steady. Straightening, Eliza examined the mechanism. It was a pulley system—simple but effective—running along a groove in the side of the cliff, invisible to anyone who didn't already know it was there. Eliza located the right rope and released it through controlled fingers, letting the platform descend.

When she reached the bottom, dozens of small houses stretched out along the dirt path with colorful doors and planters full of herbs. The town was as mismatched and wild as Anna.

A smile rose to Eliza's lips, and she let it spread out across her face, unfettered, uncontrolled. No one could see here in the dark, but even so, she didn't care. There was no reason to hide this feeling from anyone.

Stepping out onto the dirt path, Eliza surveyed the town. Where ought she to start? She didn't know anyone here, didn't know where Anna's family lived. Before she could decide, Eliza heard the muffled sound of voices and saw two shadows approaching.

Acting on instinct, Eliza leapt behind a large bush near the side of the closest house, squeezing her enormous dress into the space between. Then she exhaled. This was silly. She didn't need to hide from anyone. She was here to help, not hurt.

"Nothing on my end. You?" one of the newcomers said, voice a quiet soprano.

"Nope. Town's as empty as we left it," said the other. "You think this was a drill? Seems if it was a real threat we'd have seen some action by now."

"Theo! Don't say that!"

"Come on, Kate. Let's head back to camp."

Taking her cue, Eliza stepped out from behind her bush. Though mud and brambles stuck to the front of her dress, she knew she must be quite the sight, dressed in crystals under a bright moon. But that was all right by her. Eliza didn't need to pass herself off as the scenery; she needed to stand out.

"Tonight's your lucky night, then." Eliza raised her hands to show she wasn't armed—never mind the knife in her pocket, or the one in her boot, or the one in her bodice. "My name is Eliza. I've just come from the Settlement. You're all in quite a lot of danger."

Kate and Theo exchanged a quick glance before they pounced.

Eliza didn't fight back as they pinned her to the ground, or as they tied her wrists and ankles with coarse rope and slipped a cloth over her face. But she didn't need her eyes for this mission. She needed only her voice and a set of ears that would listen.

CHAPTER FORTY-ONE

Anna had been nine when the runners had come back one afternoon with panic in their eyes and a warning on their tongues. She'd been ferried out of town along with everyone else, but she'd had no one to cling to. Thatcher had been too busy doing his part as de facto leader of Mechan to keep track of a child, and besides, Anna had been too willful to let him corral her. Even back then, she'd walked apart from the group, as though she'd had something to prove by standing alone.

Anna was alone now, too, but she'd nothing to prove by isolating herself. She understood now that she was stronger with Mechan, just as she'd been stronger with Nathaniel and Eliza, before Eliza had turned on her. She'd expected it to be Nathaniel—that would have been bearable, predictable—but Eliza's betrayal hurt worse, cut deeper.

She'd misplaced her trust, or perhaps Eliza had misused it.

Anna's eyes wandered to Ruby, watching as the other girl checked on each family, asking if they needed anything, despite the fact she'd nothing to give.

Anna had misused Ruby's trust, too. Ruby had placed Roman under Anna's care, and now Roman was gone. There was nothing

Anna could do to make Ruby hurt less, just as there'd been nothing Nathaniel could have done to lessen Anna's pain. She wouldn't burden Ruby with her presence.

But Ruby didn't seem to want to be left alone. Once she'd made the rounds, she returned to Anna's side. "We buried him yesterday, by the sea," she said finally, her voice a foreign, quiet thing. "I wanted to wait for you to come back, but the body . . . Thatcher said it wouldn't keep."

"I'm sorry," Anna blurted. It was the only thing to say. It was the only thing she felt. There was nothing in that moment other than her guilt and Ruby's pain. "I-I shouldn't have— There are so many things I wish I could undo." Anna shook her head. "No, I know that doesn't help. I should have been more careful."

"Yes, you should have," Ruby said, rocking on her heels.

"I'm so sorry, Ruby. I never meant for anything to happen to him. I'm sorry."

"I believe you—I believe you're sorry for what happened to Roman. But that isn't why you should be sorry." Her tone wasn't laced with anger like it had been back in Thatcher's kitchen when everything had been so raw. Instead, it was tight with unshed tears.

"I know. It's more than that. Thatcher was right all along. I put you in danger. My business isn't safe, and I didn't think—I didn't *want* to think—about how it might affect everyone else. It was one thing when it was just me in danger, but I put the entire town at risk." Anna swallowed with difficulty. "You're safe now. I should probably leave."

Ruby narrowed her eyes. "Still, you don't understand." She sighed and settled on the ground, looking up at the stars. "Get some rest. Perhaps it'll be clearer in the morning."

But Anna couldn't sleep. This was her fault. All of it. She'd tried, she'd apologized. She knew that Roman's death was still fresh for Ruby—it was still fresh for Anna, too—but she'd thought, or perhaps just hoped, Ruby would find a way to forgive her.

Anna rolled over and met Ruby's eyes. Ruby should have been asleep. She was grieving, and she was pregnant. She needed to take care of herself, but maybe Ruby hurt too much to think of her own needs.

With a pang, Anna realized she was the one who usually took care of Ruby. When Ruby's mother and father died, Anna had sat by Ruby's side while the rest of the town worried about what to do with orphan Ruby. And when Dalton died, others had let her cry on their shoulders while Anna had kept Roman occupied. Anna wasn't any good with words or feelings, but she'd still been there, helping.

"I left." Anna felt the words fly from her lips like a startled honeybee.

Ruby sat up. "You left."

Anna rose, too. "But you were so angry, and you said things—I thought it was better this way. I thought it would be easier for you to grieve and heal if I wasn't here."

"You ran!" Ruby turned her gaze on Anna now, eyes glistening with tears. "It's what you do. When things get too hard, you run. You did it with surgery, you did it with Thatcher. But I never thought you'd run from me."

"I'm so sorry, Ruby." Anna reached a hand toward her, but Ruby knocked it away.

"I thought you died!" She spoke her words like a whip. "But you only disappeared for a few days doing . . . whatever it is you do. Did you take one second to think about who you left behind?"

"Of course I did—I thought about you, and Roman." But they weren't all she'd thought about. Should she have spent her days away deep in her guilt, letting it tear her apart from the inside? It was what she deserved, more than likely, but instead she'd entertained fantasies of vengeance and justice—and fantasies of other things, private things.

Anna lowered her voice. "You said I didn't love the people around me. I was afraid you were right, and I was angry. I was so angry." She shook her head. "I needed to do something—I needed to blame someone else."

Ruby stopped crying. She locked eyes with Anna, searching her face. "I shouldn't have said that," she whispered. "I was angry, too, but that doesn't— I shouldn't have said that you don't love people. I know you loved Roman."

"And you, too," Anna said. "I'm just not very good at showing it. No one ever really taught me."

"I never thought— I was so busy building my own family, I forgot to hold on to the family I already had. And now you're all I have left." She looked up, eyes still watery with tears. "You were my best friend, and somehow I lost you. I failed you, and I didn't see it. I'm sorry."

Whatever composure Anna had been clinging to came undone. Tears overflowed, racing down her cheeks as though she'd been holding them back for far too long. She had so much to cry for, it seemed: Roman, who'd died in Anna's quest—for what? Information? Revenge? She didn't even know what she'd been searching for.

Anna had hurt Ruby in a way she couldn't truly feel. She'd been too young when her parents died, and Roman still didn't seem like hers to grieve over, not in the same way he was Ruby's. And Thatcher—Anna didn't know she meant enough to him to hurt her grandfather, but he'd left, risking his life to look for her. Maybe there was still something there worth salvaging.

Anna gathered her arms to wrap them around herself, but before she could, Ruby was holding her. They stayed like that for a long time, sitting together, crying together—just *being* together—before either of them spoke.

"I shouldn't have run," Anna finally managed.

"But you came back." Ruby sniffed. "Where did you go, anyway?"

Anna sat on her heels, glancing down at her borrowed dress, the fine fabric ruined by the elements. "The Commissioner's manor."

Ruby's jaw dropped. "You—you what?"

Anna tucked her chin, unsure of how much to tell Ruby. All this—everything she'd done so far—had been unbelievably reckless. Once again, Anna had thought only of herself and her own goals. But no, that wasn't it. She had thought of Ruby, and Ruby's unborn child. So much of what she'd done had been for them.

"I went looking for a cure—or maybe just revenge. Maybe it was foolish. It doesn't really matter." She swallowed back a sob, acutely aware that the pang she felt was for more than just the vaccine she'd left behind, but for the girl she'd lost. Eliza meant far less to her than all Mechan, but she didn't mean nothing.

"Are you two awake?"

Anna nearly jumped out of her skin. She'd forgotten there was anyone but her and Ruby.

Ruby stood up, dragging Anna with her. "What is it?" she asked.

Anna turned to see a tall boy only a few years older than her—Theo, one of the runners. He looked tired, shoulders hunched, brow furrowed.

"Kate and I did a sweep of the village."

Ruby nodded. "And?"

"We found a scout. We've got her detained up the river a bit, and I wasn't sure exactly who— It's just she's a bit— I don't think—"

Ruby inclined her head. "Spit it out, Theo."

"She's saying she knows Anna." Theo jabbed a finger at Anna, his eyebrows knitted together like finely woven cloth. "She's saying Anna's in trouble, but obviously Anna's here, so I don't know exactly—"

Anna stepped forward. "This scout you found—is she blond? Well dressed? Annoyingly high-mannered?"

Theo nodded.

"Take me to her," Anna said, glad the darkness hid the nervous shake of her hands.

"You're not worried it's some kind of deception?" Ruby murmured, grabbing Anna's arm.

"Worried? No." Anna shook her head. "I'm absolutely certain it is."

Eliza looked like a diminished version of herself, hair disheveled, dress torn and muddied, her hands and feet bound with rope. She looked almost defeated, but Anna knew better. Rope and a single guard were not enough to keep Eliza subdued. The runners finding her was no accident. Eliza didn't do anything she didn't want to, and when she looked up at their approach, her eyes lit up, a cross between fire and release.

"Anna!" Eliza tried to step forward but wobbled, falling to her knees instead.

"Did you follow me?"

Eliza shook her head, eyes wide and clear. "The map."

"Right." Anna's breaths came too shallow, too fast. Eliza wasn't supposed to be here. Anna had put her in a convenient pocket of her mind, to be sewn up, never to emerge again. "Why are you here? I thought you'd be back on the Tower by now."

Still, Eliza's gaze didn't waver. "And I thought you were in danger." Her hands strained at her ropes as if she meant to reach for Anna.

Anna recoiled. It didn't matter that every cell in her body wanted to lean into Eliza's touch. She couldn't let whatever attraction she had to Eliza get in the way of protecting Mechan.

Ruby stepped between them. "Who is this, Anna? Do you know her?"

"I thought I did." Anna narrowed her eyes. She couldn't explain the depth of Eliza's betrayal, the sharp ache between her ribs that pulsed with every breath. She didn't want Ruby or the runners to know—and she didn't want Eliza to know. Finally, she said, "She's the Commissioner's future daughter-in-law."

Something like pain flickered across Eliza's eyes—or perhaps it was only a reflection of the lightening sky.

"What do we do with her?" Ruby bent toward Anna, speaking quietly. "We can't let her go back, but I don't know if I have it in me to—"

"You're not going to kill me," Eliza said, her voice carrying over the sound of the river splashing against the rocks.

"How can you be so sure?" Anna growled, but even she knew it sounded unconvincing.

"Because if you kill me, you'll never know how sorry I am." Eliza's words sounded strained, as though she'd never apologized before and meant it. "I cannot begin to apologize for what I did—it was unconscionable."

"Yeah. It wasn't great." But as Anna's eyes met Eliza's, the sting of her betrayal lessened. She clenched her jaw. This was a trick of biology, a manipulation Eliza planned to use against her. Anna couldn't trust anything she said.

"I want to give this back," Eliza said, indicating her pocket with her bound hands. "It should be yours. I never should have taken it—I never should have equated my ambition with your village's future."

Anna eyed her skeptically but motioned for the runners to untie her.

"Are you sure?" Ruby asked

"Just her hands," Anna said. "Don't want her getting any ideas."

Once freed, Eliza stretched her fingers, then withdrew the small vile of golden liquid from her pocket. "This is yours."

Anna took it, trying not to react to the shock of Eliza's fingers brushing against her own.

Silence settled, taking the shape of the space between them. A small part of her wanted to step forward, demolish it with her body, and take back the ground they'd lost. But there was no returning to the time before Eliza had taken away her hope. Even though she'd given it back now, it didn't undo the hollow feeling in her chest when she thought about Eliza's hands on her waist, on her spine, on the place above her heart where skin met steel.

"What is it?" Ruby asked.

Anna raised the vial for Ruby to see. This was what she'd been fighting for. Golden liquid swirled against the glass, a shining promise for the future of Mechan, for Ruby's unborn child.

"It's the vaccine," Anna murmured.

"The Queen wanted me to retrieve it for her, but you need it far more than she does." Eliza sighed. "Power makes fools of us all. I'm sorry."

"Thank you," Ruby said, turning to Eliza. "You don't know what this will mean for us, how this will change our lives."

Anna's chest tightened. What thanks was needed? Eliza had done nothing more than the decent thing to do, giving back what she'd stolen. But it had been so long since an outsider had treated Mechan with decency.

Anna opened her mouth to echo Ruby, but instead she said, "So you took this from me because the Queen told you to?" Her words came out more accusatory than she'd meant them.

"I didn't truly realize until the moment you showed me the vial that we were looking for the same thing, just calling it by different names." Eliza shook her head, blond curls falling from their pins.

"So why didn't you just let me have it?"

Eliza squeezed her eyes shut. "I thought I was doing the right thing. I thought the Queen wanted what was best for the planet— and she does—but she wants it on her own terms. Waiting for it to be convenient for her would only lose more lives, and I've already lost too many people because I was waiting for things to change. I wasn't about to let you be one of them."

Anna felt cracks forming in the shell she'd built around herself, but she couldn't let it shatter.

"How do I know I can trust you?" Anna asked, the answer forming on her tongue as quickly as the question. "I don't."

"You don't." Eliza nodded. "But you should anyway."

"Why's that?"

"Because I'm not lying." Eliza let out a heavy breath. "I made the wrong choice. It may have taken you being captured to turn me around, but now I'm trying to make the right choice—"

"Wait." Ruby stepped forward, eyes skipping from Eliza to Anna. "She'd been captured?"

"I thought so, at least. The Commissioner announced it this evening. He said he caught the Technician, but if Anna's safe, then—"

"Then who did the Commissioner arrest?" Anna asked, but the answer burned a hole through her stomach. The Commissioner had as much as told her who he thought the Technician was. *Old man*, he'd said.

If the Commissioner thought he had the Technician, there was only one person it could be. Thatcher, who had scolded and schooled her, had now surrendered himself to save her. But Anna would not stand by and watch the Commissioner destroy Thatcher for what she'd done.

Crossing the space, Anna took Theo's knife and split the rope at Eliza's feet.

"Thank you," Eliza breathed.

"Are you sure?" Ruby asked.

Anna nodded and fixed Eliza with what she hoped was an intimidating stare.

"What do you want me to do?" Eliza asked, their faces so close together, Anna could feel Eliza's breath against her jaw.

"Why, Eliza, I thought you'd never ask." She gritted her teeth, clenched her fists, and said, "I want you to help me overthrow the Commissioner."

CHAPTER FORTY-TWO

When Nathaniel woke, his head hurt and something hard pressed against the side of his face. Either his bed had become much less comfortable than he remembered, or he'd fallen out of it again. Opening his eyes, light swept over him in blurry waves. He wasn't in his bedroom.

He sat up quickly, blinking the room into focus, and memory flooded back to him in bright bursts. His father yelling at him, hitting him, and then darkness.

It wasn't dark anymore. Sunlight filtered in from a window above him, metal bars casting shadows across the floor. He was in a jail cell.

"Rest well?"

Nathaniel jumped, raising his hands to shield himself from a blow that never came. The voice was smoother than his father's, not clipped and precise, the words gentler. Nathaniel lowered his hands. Across from him an older man with broad shoulders and graying hair with a suggestion of crimson sat on the floor.

"Wh-who are you?" Nathaniel meant to say something less rude, but his thoughts still swam through a fog, weighed down by the pulsing ache in his temple.

The man laughed—a gentle sound, with something heavy lying just below the surface. "No one important—the Commissioner's latest catch, I suppose." His lips turned up in a lopsided smile—a familiar smile.

Nathaniel narrowed his eyes. "The Commissioner's latest catch?" Something snagged in his mind just out of reach. His father said he'd caught—"The Technician!" Nathaniel staggered to his feet, tripping over nothing but air. "Where's Anna? I have to find her—get her out."

"Anna's not here."

Nathaniel crossed the cell in four steps and rattled the door. It was locked, of course. Casting his gaze up and down the hallway, Nathaniel found they were in the previously empty cell in the officers' bunker. "Of course she is. I have to get her out so she can . . ." His memory clinked into place like a teacup finding its saucer.

"And there we are," the man said, turning to look up at him with storm clouds in his eyes.

"Anna's not here." Nathaniel's mind raced to catch up to him. "But you're not the Technician."

"Oh, but I am today. No need to ask who you are, of course. I never forget a patient."

Nathaniel released the bars as the fog lifted. "You're her grandfather."

Anna's grandfather inclined his head.

"So she's safe. My father didn't catch her, and she's on her way home now?"

"I'd assume so."

Nathaniel sank to the floor, metal bars pressed against his back. That was one weight off his mind. His father still needed to be stopped, one way or another, but at least Anna was safe, at least he did not have to carry her ghost, too.

"So what did you do?" the man asked. "I can't imagine the Commissioner throws his son in prison for nothing."

The rest of the previous night filtered back into Nathaniel's consciousness. He'd stood up to his father. He'd confronted him about his mother, about his heart, about his right to decide his own place in all this.

"My father wanted me to be someone I'm not. I finally told him no."

Anna's grandfather chortled. "I bet Oliver loved that."

Nathaniel fingered the bruise forming on the side of his head and winced. "*Loved* might be a strong word. Should have kept my mouth shut."

Anna's grandfather pursed his lips. "Very little is ever gained through silence. If you have something to say and the means to say it, you should."

Nathaniel was inclined to agree, but he *had* said something, and all he'd gotten for it was a lump on his head and a jail cell. "All due respect, Mr. Thatcher, you don't know my father like I do."

"Just Thatcher is fine," he said. "Your father killed my son. I think we're beyond honorifics."

Nathaniel's stomach dove. "My father's killed a lot of people. I'm sorry one of them was your son." He hadn't known Anna's parents were dead—or perhaps he'd simply forgotten. "He killed my mother, too, and he'll kill more if he gets the chance."

"Best not give him one, then." Thatcher fixed Nathaniel with Anna's stare, expectant and resolved, waiting for Nathaniel to do the right thing as though it was a foregone conclusion, not a question.

But Nathaniel was truly spent. He'd done the impossible and been beaten for it. At least Anna was free. "What can I do against him? He's the Commissioner—I'm just his Tarnished son."

"Yes, you are." Thatcher sat up straighter. "You are his son, and you are Tarnished. One does not diminish the other."

"I didn't mean— I'm not— I don't think I'm strong enough." Nathaniel hugged his knees to his chest.

"Strength comes in many forms. Your father's is his voice— sometimes his fists. Mine is patience; Anna's is passion."

Nathaniel laughed hollowly. "What's mine?"

"Your heart."

Nathaniel looked up, hand sneaking up to the metal place beneath his shirt. "My heart?"

"You stood up to your father, your own family, because you disagreed. Not everyone would do that."

"It took me eighteen years." Despite the shame in his words, pride bloomed in his cheeks.

"A short time, all things considered. Now, how about we get you out of this cell so you can get back to stopping your father from committing worse carnage?"

Nathaniel set his teeth but nodded.

"Good. Now give me your cuff links."

"My what?"

"Your cuff links, son. I do believe I can fashion them into a lock-pick of sorts." He nodded to the silver stars at Nathaniel's wrists. "Your father was smart enough to take my tools, but I don't think he considered what you might bring to the table."

Nathaniel grinned. If he'd had any doubt in his mind, this proved Thatcher was truly Anna's relation. Removing the cuff links, Nathaniel said, "How—how do you know I'll do the right thing? I mean, you said my strength was my heart, but what if you're wrong? What if my heart isn't any good?"

Thatcher took the cuff links, eyeing them closely. "I've seen your heart, young man—held it in my own two hands—and let me tell you, it was as golden as the sun." He propped himself up against the metal bars, reaching for the lock with one hand and wielding the cuff links with the other. "Not exactly what you want, medically speaking, of course."

"A lot has happened since then," Nathaniel said, thinking of Roman. Did Thatcher know the boy? Did he know Nathaniel was responsible for his death?

"Tarnish eats muscle, not morals."

Nathaniel sighed. "I guess all that doesn't really matter."

Thatcher paused, turning to face him. "It matters. It matters what happened to your heart—but not in the way you think. It matters because this disease has hurt you. It matters because others use it to excuse their bigotry. It matters because this is who you are—but it is not *all* you are. It does not make you weak, nor does it make you strong. You make yourself one or the other through the choices you make."

Nathaniel shrank under the weight of Thatcher's words. If they were true, it meant Nathaniel would be responsible for himself alone. There was no one he could blame if he didn't try, if he sat by and let his father decimate Anna's village. He knew the facts now, and no one could make this decision but him. "I should choose to be strong . . . I should *want* to be strong. But won't that make me exactly like my father, chasing power for power's sake?"

"Power is not the same as strength." Thatcher dropped the cuff links into Nathaniel's palm. "Some days strength is control, and some days strength is release. Perhaps today, strength is understanding that being like your father isn't inherently bad, and that two men may be alike and still make different choices."

Nathaniel stood up, scratching his wrists. "Come with me," he said. "We can face him together."

Thatcher laughed—somewhere between a cackle and cough. "No, thank you. I've had my fair share of your father for a lifetime. My strength today is in surrender. Letting your father believe I'm his most wanted criminal means saving the one life I've always fought to protect. If Anna lives because of this sacrifice, well—I can live with that, or rather, die with that."

"But isn't that giving up?"

"Not all winning moves are offense. For me, surrender means victory. I get what I want, even if the Commissioner gets what he wants, too." He eyed the door. "Besides, they took my wheelchair, and no offense, young man, but I don't trust those spindly arms of yours to carry me."

"I'll come back for you," Nathaniel said, hoping it was true.

Thatcher surveyed him, as if searching for the cracks in his words. "I'll wait."

Nathaniel paused at the cell door, now open thanks to Thatcher's quick hands. "I'll try not to disappoint you."

"What I think matters very little, Nathaniel," he said with a hint of a smile. "Instead—try not to disappoint yourself."

For the first time in Nathaniel's life, he was certain. He would not back down this time. He had a plan, and he would see it through.

Dipping into a side room, Nathaniel donned an officer's uniform. Though the hallway outside the cell was empty, his father would not be so foolish as to leave them without a guard. Nathaniel he might underestimate, but the Technician was too valuable a prisoner to leave unguarded for long.

Nathaniel squeezed his limbs into uniform once again. Before it had felt overwhelming, like the clothes wore him, a maroon-and-gray prison—his father's in every way. Today, the heavy boots made him feel stronger, the high collar made him feel taller. He was the heir to his father's manor, city, and legacy. These colors belonged to him, too.

Taking care to give his father's officers and servants a wide berth, Nathaniel wound his way back to the manor. He didn't have time for a run-in with anyone, but when he reached the outer sanctum of his father's offices, he wasn't alone. Anna and Eliza skulked inside, bent together in whispered conversation. Nathaniel couldn't decide which looked less like herself—Anna in her fine dress, or Eliza in her muddied one.

"Do you have a plan?" Eliza was saying as Anna pulled at the metal hinges securing the bookcase to the wall.

"Never needed one before. Don't intend to start now," Anna said through a clenched jaw.

"Wait!" Nathaniel called, crossing the room at a jog.

Before he could continue, Anna leapt toward him, bringing her heavy wrench down on his head.

Nathaniel fell back, crashing into his father's desk as stars shot across his vision. "Hey! Ow!"

"Nathaniel!" Eliza swept toward them, pulling Anna back.

"Nathaniel?" Anna asked incredulously, but then her eyes met his and her jaw dropped.

Nathaniel blinked against the pain. "I'm glad you're all right," he said, struggling to his feet.

Anna stared at him, brow furrowed. "Did you hit your head?"

Nathaniel blinked, pointing to the wrench at their feet. "You hit me."

"He did—look." Eliza smoothed his hair down, pointing to his skull where his wound from his father's blow still smarted.

"Ow!" Nathaniel swatted her hand away. "I'll be fine. What about your village?"

"Evacuated," Anna said, retrieving her wrench. She cringed, as though the words were painful. "Are you sure you're all right—"

Nathaniel waved her off. "There's no time. Now listen to me. We have to stop my father. He's gone too far, and we must put an end to his abuse of power."

Anna and Eliza blinked at him.

"Good to see you've caught up, then," Anna said.

"We have to do this carefully." Nathaniel gestured toward the bookcase. "He's a powerful man and he won't be brought down easily."

Eliza nodded. "Remember to breathe. No sense rushing this with so much on the line."

"With so much on the line, I can't afford to take things slow." Anna pushed past them both and gave the bookcase an almighty shove, sending it—books and all—crashing to the floor.

"Where is he?" Anna yelled, thundering through the archway. "Where is my grandfather?"

Nathaniel put his face in his hands. This was going to go just swimmingly.

The Commissioner was waiting for them behind his desk, eyes narrowed, back straight. "Your grandfather?" His eyes widened. "You were that small, freckly thing."

"I swear, if you say you knew me in diapers, I'll shove this wrench right through you just so"—she gave the wrench in her hand a little twirl—"you'll need diapers for the rest of *your* life— short though it may be."

"Anna, wait," Nathaniel said, throwing his arm between them. But before he could tell her Thatcher was fine, the Commissioner had pinned Anna against the desk, wrestling for the wrench in her hand. They were a tangle of fingers and elbows and knees.

When he'd told Thatcher he would fight his father, Nathaniel hadn't expected it to be so literal. He grabbed the back of his father's dress coat, splitting the fabric down the center seam before his father caught him in the stomach with an elbow. He redoubled his efforts, scratching his father's neck. His father stomped on his foot. Nathaniel swiped, meeting nothing but air.

"If you could all stop fighting for a moment," Eliza said, her voice distant. "Oh, for heaven's sake."

Before he knew it, Nathaniel was on the ground, Eliza's face looming over him. "We can't get a confession if you beat him to a pulp," she hissed, before tearing Anna and the Commissioner apart, the first by her hair, the second by his throat.

A confession. Of course! They didn't need to fight the Commissioner; they needed to get him to talk.

"Really, what a terribly pathetic excuse for fighting." Eliza shook her head and pulled a dagger from her skirt pocket. "My turn." She turned the knife on the Commissioner, whose pupils dilated at the sight of the steel eye on the end of the hilt.

"Of course," he muttered. "You're the Eyes of the Queen. I should never have brought you here."

Eliza sneered. "As if you ever had a choice."

Nathaniel exchanged a look with Anna, whose fury burned red against her cheeks. The melee had been personal for her, a culmination of the rage she'd been brewing for years. Nathaniel was beginning to understand what that felt like.

The Commissioner lifted his hands above his head, eyes on the dagger. "What does my mother want this time?"

"Who can truly tell with her?" Eliza shrugged. "I'm much more interested in what you want—and why."

Eliza seemed to have everything under control. She held the knife, and Nathaniel had seen her wield it. His father didn't stand a chance, and yet Nathaniel's heart raced. Had it really been as simple as giving Eliza a blade and hoping for the element of surprise?

Eliza gestured toward the chair behind the desk. "Why don't you sit? This may take a while."

The Commissioner did as he was told, muttering under his breath, "Blasted Eyes."

Eliza slapped the side of the blade against her open palm, beating a rhythm into the silence as she surveyed the Commissioner. "You are a conundrum," she said after a moment.

"I'd take that as a compliment if I didn't know better," the Commissioner growled.

"Don't proclaim to know what I haven't yet decided." Eliza pursed her lips. "Now, where to begin unraveling you?"

"He's already unraveled," Anna muttered. "Everyone knows that."

Nathaniel was about to agree, but a thought stopped his tongue. Not everyone knew. He did, they did—perhaps even some of the

Settlement's citizens did—but the council didn't. They were the ones who mattered. No one but the full council could depose a sitting Commissioner, and his father had spun an elaborate lie to keep his power. Nathaniel needed to show them the truth.

"Let us begin with your contradictions," Eliza said, pacing along the side of the desk. "Why does tech offend you so greatly? Why make technology illegal but use it to save your son's life?"

Nathaniel stood carefully, eyes sweeping over the desk. What good was a confession unless the council could hear it? Nathaniel's gaze landed on metal. The holocom. Eliza had told him the holocom could do more than call the Queen. It could store information—and record it. He would catch the Commissioner's words and replay them for all to hear.

"Why ban the advancement of science but build an alchemy lab in your . . . Please tell me you don't think of this as your lair?" She waved the dagger at their surroundings.

The Commissioner cleared his throat but said nothing.

"I'll get you to talk one way or another."

Nathaniel needed to turn on the holocom first. He could slip beside Eliza, casually lean over and grab it—but no, that was too obvious. He needed a distraction.

Nathaniel crossed the room and lunged toward his father with as much ferocity as he could. "Why did you kill my mother?" Nathaniel waved his arm wildly. With the other, he slipped the holocom from the desk and into his pocket.

The Commissioner's eyes connected with Nathaniel's, soft and sad, a stark contrast to the violent storm he'd seen there last.

"I didn't."

"You're lying!" Nathaniel balled his fist, dialing in the passcode with his other hand. Wherever this was headed, the council would hear every word.

"I would never hurt her—I never *did*," his father said, dropping his gaze. "Everything I've done, I've done for her. Since I-I found her body, I've done nothing but try to honor her, honor what she would have wanted."

Nathaniel's heart thundered in his chest. The floor had been ripped out from under him when he'd discovered his father's treachery. Now, faced with yet another explanation, he tumbled through miles of empty space searching for ground to stand on.

"Then why the secrecy?" Eliza asked, eyes narrowed. "You took her title without a proper hearing, without due course. There's no record of you assuming the Commissioner's duties, and yet here you are."

"The Queen's doing. She wanted me in power, but the council never would have allowed it. My wife died under dubious circumstances, and we couldn't have them investigate." He shuddered. "The Queen arranged for a brand-new council and cemented me as their leader without a confirmation hearing. I simply became Commissioner Fremont, as if there had been no change."

Nathaniel fought the urge to shiver. This was not the answer he'd expected. If his father hadn't seized power out of greed, was he truly the monster Nathaniel thought him to be, or was there something worse waiting in the wings?

"What do you mean, dubious circumstances?" Eliza asked. "If you didn't kill her, who did?"

The Commissioner shook his head. "You misunderstand—my wife wasn't murdered."

Anna stepped forward, withdrawing the vaccine from her pocket, the golden liquid catching the light. "It was Tarnish, wasn't it?"

The Commissioner nodded. "She wanted to make the world," he said, choking on the words. "That's what she told me the first time we met. The first cases of Tarnish had only just been discovered in the first generation of planetary children, and she thought she could find a cure. Infants were dying, and she wanted to save them." He shook his head, pressing his palms against his eyes. "We never expected our own son to fall ill."

Nathaniel tensed. He'd never heard this story from his father's own lips. He'd woven his own narrative, imagining the desperation that forced his father to let tech save his only son. If Nathaniel had asked, his father would only have lied to him. But his father did not appear to be lying now, absorbed in a web of memory and melancholy.

"I'll admit, it demoralized me, but it only spurred your mother on. She spent so much time pouring over alchemy bottles, studying compounds, and testing theories. I always knew she'd succeed eventually, but alchemy is dangerous, and the chemicals she worked with even more so. The compound she found running through the very core of the planet was unstable and toxic." He shrugged, letting his hands fall from his face, eyes finding his son's. "By the time she'd invented a vaccine, it was too late. She was too far gone, Earth Adjacent's natural poisons tearing her apart from the inside."

Nathaniel surveyed his father, searching for some tell. His father had painted him a world filled with truths as compelling as lies, and Nathaniel didn't know how to tell the difference anymore.

"Say her name," Nathaniel said finally, voice shaking.

"What?" the Commissioner asked.

"Say her name. You always call her your wife or my mother. You never say her name. Say it, and then maybe I'll believe you."

The Commissioner looked at his feet, and Nathaniel thought he might refuse, but then he gripped the edge of the desk, and opened his mouth.

"Isla."

Her name rolled over him like warm blanket, like a missing puzzle piece, like a single note of a melancholy song.

"I didn't realize how long it's been—I almost forgot what her name sounds like." His father's voice hitched as he said her name again. "Isla."

This time, her name drove through him, a word made steel, each syllable a stab to the gut.

"Why keep her work a secret?" Anna asked. "Why let Mechan suffer? If you had the ability to save us, why didn't you?" She slammed her fist on the desk. "Why hunt us like prey, why tear us apart and leave us to stitch ourselves back together?" Tears speckled the corners of her eyes. "Why let us die, when you could have let us live?"

The Commissioner gripped the arms of his chair with white knuckles, his lips pressed together into a thin line. "Because—"

"Because of me." A smooth, familiar voice sounded through the room.

The Queen had come to call at last.

CHAPTER FORTY-THREE

Anna had never before seen the woman standing in the archway, but she knew immediately who she must be. Of medium build with wide, imposing skirts, she was Eliza's shadow, menacing and majestic. Black velvet sleeves caught the light like scales, and a whisper of a veil fell past her chin.

"Your Majesty," Eliza breathed, her words so quiet Anna thought she must be the only one to hear them.

"That's what you were going to say, is it not, Commissioner?" The Queen's words languished like a wilted flower. "You were about to blame your cruel and unnecessary practices on me. How rude."

The Commissioner, who had shrunk beneath Eliza's scrutiny, became even smaller, if possible. He gripped the arms of his chair, white-knuckled and wide-eyed.

Eliza said she wanted to unravel him. Well, now he was a tangle of loose thread, a nervous boy in the body of a man. Anna saw a familiar flicker of despair in his eyes, a twitch in his lip—just like Nathaniel. But Nathaniel had found a way to stand where the Commissioner still sat.

Anna nearly felt sorry for him.

Nearly.

"Y-you forced my hand," the Commissioner stammered, but then he looked up, meeting the Queen's gaze. "I can't let you take credit for work you didn't do."

"Let's not spin delusions, Commissioner. Neither of us *deserves* the credit." She laughed.

Anna traced the invisible pathways between the Commissioner and the Queen. Before, it had been simple: three against one. Now with the Queen added to the mix, Anna couldn't be sure of anyone. She didn't understand the lines connecting them all.

The Queen turned her covered face toward Eliza, crossing her arms, her fingers wrapping around her elbows. "And here you are, my wayward pupil. Your time has quite run out. Do you have the cure or not?"

Eliza didn't move. Anna couldn't be sure she was even breathing. The only sign that she was alive was her hand still firmly gripping her knife.

Anna couldn't rely on Eliza to corral the players in the room anymore. She had only herself. If she wanted to know the truth, she'd have to ask for it.

Stepping forward, Anna balled her fists. "What do you want with the cure?"

The Queen turned her head a fraction, as if she'd only just noticed Anna's presence. "I want to save the human race. Isn't that a worthy goal?"

Anna swallowed. The Queen's words were too sweet to be true. If the Commissioner was to be believed, his wife had wanted to save the world, and so, too, had he. It hadn't stopped him from hunting her people like prey. Wanting to do the right thing wasn't enough to be righteous, and Anna was running low on trust.

"He won't let you?" Anna jabbed her thumb back at the Commissioner, who stood.

"Wait just a minute," the Commissioner spat. "Saving the human race is all well and good, but I won't let you trample over my—"

"Trample? Truly, Commissioner, you must try harder if you wish to retain the high ground."

"You think yourself righteous because you sit above us on your throne among the stars." The Commissioner stepped out from behind his desk, squaring his shoulders. "But you're nothing more than a thief, stealing glory from those who've earned it."

Anna crossed her arms. "If this is just about pride—"

"A girl like you wouldn't understand the intricacies of politics," the Queen snapped, inclining her head ever so slightly, as if to measure Anna's worth.

"I'm guessing you haven't met many girls like me."

The Queen adjusted her shoulders but didn't respond. Instead, she turned to Eliza. "Come now, Eliza. The cure. I don't have time for this nonsense."

Still Eliza didn't respond.

Anna didn't have time for nonsense, either. One way or another, she would get the answers she wanted. She would get her cure, she would get her grandfather, and she would get out. But with the Queen and the Commissioner in her way, she'd have to think like Eliza; she'd have to devise a plan.

Anna held up the golden liquid for the Queen to see. "This cure? It's the last vial, you know." She bent down, placing it beneath the toe of her boot. "Now, how about you clarify—unless you'd rather not explain to a girl like me." She made as if to lower her foot onto the vial, hoping her gamble would pay off.

The Queen didn't move. "You won't."

Anna shrugged. "It's a simple trade. Give me answers, I don't crush this vial. Give me answers I like, maybe I'll give it to you, and you won't even have to fight me for it."

The Queen settled back on her heels. "Who are you?"

Anna let a small smile creep across her lips. "The Technician—maybe you've heard of me?"

The Commissioner's gaze snapped to her. "The what?"

Anna couldn't help herself. She grinned. "You heard me."

"But that's impossible! I captured the Technician!"

Nathaniel coughed. "I think you've got the wrong outlaw."

"But she's so young!" The Commissioner's brow wrinkled in frustration.

"Really." Anna sighed, glancing from the Commissioner to the Queen. "If you continue to underestimate me, you'll regret it."

"Very well." The Queen nodded. "The Commissioner wants to hold that cure over your heads. As long as he controls the cure, he controls the Tarnished. If you submit to him and his laws, your future generations can benefit from better health than you. But, of course, you and your people will still be considered criminals. The cure won't save you from the law." She laughed coolly. "Generous, my son."

The Commissioner made a sound of protest, but whether he disagreed with her assessment or her calling him her son, Anna couldn't tell, nor did she care.

Anna clutched her TICCER through her clothes. The cure wasn't really a cure. Her heart condition, no matter its cause, was irreversible. To conform to the Commissioner's laws, they'd have to lose their tech, and for most of them, that meant a quick death. Without her TICCER, Anna's heart wouldn't beat properly. It wouldn't matter if Ruby's child could be born without a heart condition if the rest of them had to die for it.

Anna would never risk all Mechan just so one person could have a chance to live without tech. Life with a TICCER was still a life, and life outside the law was still better than death inside it.

"Not a chance," Anna growled, shooting the Commissioner a glare. But the man who'd terrorized her village, who'd haunted her by night, who'd hunted her by day, looked almost defeated rather than deadly.

"Good girl," the Queen said, taking a step forward. "Now for my offer—if you give me the cure, I won't withhold it. I want the entire planet to be safe, for those who live on it, and those on my Tower who hope to finally join you."

It sounded too good to be true. "Why would you do that?" Anna asked, but still she withdrew the vial from beneath her boot, ready to hand it over.

"Because," the Queen said, voice airy as though she floated rather than walked toward Anna, "I am a magnanimous queen, I am a righteous queen, and I am the queen who will bring about the next planetary age."

As the Queen's fingers reached for the vial in Anna's hand, Anna felt the urge to give it to her, the Queen's vision for the future acknowledging, if not aligning with, Anna's. Better a queen who would do right by her people than a commissioner who would wrong them—no matter how egocentric her reasons.

"But you didn't," Nathaniel said, stepping between them.

Anna snatched the vial back toward her chest.

"You didn't bring about the planetary age." Nathaniel's voice gained stability, but his eyes darted from the Queen to his father.

"You didn't discover the vaccine—my mother did. If anyone deserves credit, it's her."

The Queen laughed. "Your mother was only a scientist with no brain for politics or leadership. She didn't deserve anything except the death she got."

"Do not speak ill of the dead," the Commissioner growled, eyes alight with fury. "Apologize to my son."

Anna's throat constricted. Here was a man demanding recompense—not for himself, but for his son, whose every day he'd haunted with abuse. The contradiction twisted inside her, her hatred for the Commissioner warring with her agreement with his words. Nathaniel deserved an apology, but more than that, he deserved to be truly loved.

"Careful, Commissioner, or I'll send you the same way as your wife." The Queen turned to Nathaniel. "I am sorry, you know, that neither of your parents had enough sense to stay out of my way. Your mother, at least, died without a struggle—poison goes down easily."

The Commissioner lunged, letting out an animalistic sound.

"No!" Nathaniel grabbed for the Queen but missed.

The Commissioner recoiled, falling back over his feet toward the ground, hand clutching his throat.

Anna didn't see the knife until it was too late.

"A pity." The Queen shook her head, wiping the blade on her skirt, a large star adorning its hilt. "I thought my own son would meet death with more dignity."

Anna's stomach rolled as she inhaled, the air metallic and sharp with the telltale scent of freshly spilled blood.

CHAPTER FORTY-FOUR

The Queen spoke, and Eliza's world changed. She was no longer the rebel spy who'd corralled her allies into a coup; she was a child again, the Queen's pupil working for the smallest scrap of approval. She'd spent so much of her life with the Queen at the center. It was foolish to think one little rebellion could break such a strong orbit.

When Anna launched herself at the Queen, Eliza had no choice but to move. The Queen was in danger, and it was Eliza's duty to protect her. The Queen came first, before country, before self. But Eliza paused as memory overtook instinct. She'd left the Queen's service, promised to do better, to earn Anna's trust. She ought to be rushing to help Anna, but her body betrayed her, itching to fight the hands that assaulted her Queen.

Instead, Eliza stalled halfway between steps.

"How dare you!" Anna cried. "You made him an orphan! You pretend to have a conscience, pretend to care about my people, but you don't care about anyone, do you?"

The Queen gasped for air, managing to rasp, "Are you going to kill me, then?"

If Anna hesitated, the Queen would turn the tables on her. The Queen was older now than she had been when she'd trained

Eliza, but she was still a formidable opponent, and against Anna's inexperience, she would surely win.

Anna let go, and Eliza's heart sank.

"I'm not a killer." She took a step back, and another.

The Queen laughed, a coiled, weak thing. "Anyone can be a killer if you teach them how." And she turned her veiled face on Eliza.

Eliza shuddered under her eyeless gaze. This wasn't about Anna or the Commissioner; it had all been about Eliza. She had refused an order—and no one refused the Queen. Every Eyes before her had died in the Queen's service. Would Eliza be the first to die by her hand?

"Eliza, take the vial from her."

Eliza made it halfway across the room before she processed the Queen's words. She glanced at Anna, whose eyes grew wide. Her hands were balled at her sides, her legs shaking beneath her.

She clearly thought Eliza was going to attack her.

Eliza *was* going to attack her.

The Queen's words drummed a militant beat through Eliza's veins, instructing her limbs without her consent. She'd been acting on orders so long, she'd forgotten how to act on her own. It was easier to listen than to think, easier to do as she was told.

The Queen had forced her hand once before, and now Eliza would let her do it again.

Anna raised her fists, her lips a thin line. Determination radiated from Anna's eyes, solid and secure in her position, her soul hardened stone.

"Give me the vial," Eliza whispered, the words forming half a question, half an answer.

"Don't do this," Anna growled. "Not again."

She meant Eliza's betrayal, when she'd taken the vial from her by force. She couldn't know about Marla—it wasn't possible.

Not again.

Anna's words drilled a hole through Eliza's heart, and suddenly it was three years ago and the Queen was ordering her to kill Marla, not Anna.

It was the final test. In the end, Eliza and Marla were the last ones standing in the Queen's competition. They'd reached the end together, but they couldn't both win. One would become the Queen's Eyes, and the other would die.

The Queen had given her the order, but it was Eliza who'd chosen to break her promise to run away with Marla, Eliza who'd shut the door between them, and Eliza who'd detonated Marla's ship as it flew toward freedom.

Eliza had chosen her Queen over her heart.

We are made or unmade by our choices.

"Do it, Eliza," the Queen hissed.

Eliza moved with precision, hitting Anna to demobilize but not to hurt her.

Anna hit back, her fists pounding against Eliza's ribs, her arms, her stomach. The bruises, Eliza could bear, but if she did to Anna what she'd done to Marla, Eliza knew she could never trust herself to love again. Neither medic nor mechanic could heal that wound. She did not deserve to recover from a heart she'd broken herself.

With as much force as she could muster, Eliza rushed Anna toward the wall, slamming her against the racks of alchemy instruments and bottles. Anna shoved back, spilling a vial of dark liquid onto the floor.

"Don't do this," Anna said, eyes pleading.

"I won't," Eliza whispered, her voice so quiet, she wasn't sure even Anna could hear it. Raising her voice, Eliza said, "Give me the vial, or I'll take it from you."

Anna's eyes widened and she thrashed against Eliza. It was exactly the distraction Eliza had been hoping for. As she half-heartedly fought Anna's limbs, she slipped her hand behind Anna's body and snatched another vial from the shelf, then backed away.

"Eliza?" The Queen beckoned, her hand moving through the air with urgency.

"I've got it," Eliza panted, holding up the vial in her hand, careful to obscure its contents with her fingers.

Anna scrambled toward her, eyes wild and desperate, but Eliza brandished her knife. "Don't."

Anna took a step back, gaze jumping from Eliza's eyes to the single eye on the hilt of Eliza's dagger.

"Come, Eliza. It's time for us to return to the Tower." The Queen extended her hand.

Eliza pocketed the vial and reached tentatively, the Queen's voice drawing her in. She wanted to be the Queen's Eyes again; she wanted to be the best.

"Eliza?" Anna's voice shook, a quiet tendril catching her by the heart.

Eliza couldn't afford to look back at her. The eyes, as the Queen always said, were the window to the soul, and Eliza knew if she looked into Anna's, she would crumble.

"Come with me, and all will be well."

But not all would be well. The Queen did not forgive; the Queen did not forget. Eliza could bear whatever punishment the Queen gave her if it meant Anna could live. Anna deserved better than a girl who would always disappoint her. Anna deserved the world she wanted—a world free of heart disease and prejudice, a world where she didn't have to run, where she could stand tall and proud of who she was.

But the Queen wouldn't give it to her.

If only Eliza could see into the Queen's soul, she could truly know if she'd made the right choice. If she looked into the Queen's face and saw light and hope, she would know to go with her, and if all that looked back was a monster—well, Eliza could be a monster, too.

The Queen's fingers were inches away. It would only take a moment before Eliza was back within her grasp, forever bound.

Eliza reached, hand closing around the lace veil. The Queen took a sharp intake of breath, and Eliza pulled.

Beneath her veil, the Queen was both older in the eyes and younger in the face than Eliza had expected. Her hair was the same peppered gray as the Commissioner's, curly and cropped below her ears. She wore no cosmetics, and though the lords and ladies of her court would have all carried loud opinions about her appearance if they'd seen her, Eliza knew it did not matter. She would always find the Queen beautiful beyond comparison.

Because the Queen had been her teacher, her mother, her world.

Eliza held the Queen's gaze. She needed to know who the Queen was at her core, if she was worth fighting or worth fighting *for*. But the eyes told her nothing at all, no story lay in her dark gray irises, no central truth to guide Eliza. She saw no strength; she saw no weakness. She saw nothing at all.

We are made or unmade by our choices.

She would make the Queen choose and see who she made herself to be.

"Give that back!" The Queen snatched for the veil, but Eliza was too quick, holding it out of reach.

"No," Eliza growled.

"Eliza, this is highly unlike you!"

"You don't know what's like me—you don't know *me*. You only know the version of me you wanted, the version of me that suits you." Eliza couldn't seem to stop, though she knew she'd gone too far. "You want me to go back with you, it'll be the real me, the whole me."

"This is ridiculous." The Queen shook her head. "I will not tolerate this kind of behavior. I'll decide what to do with you later. Now give me the vial."

"You want the vial? I stay behind." She had no plan, no scheme. She only wanted to know which the Queen would choose—her legacy, or Eliza. "You want me, you leave it with Anna."

"You do not give me orders! I am your Queen! I trained you, I taught you! Who do you think you are, to disobey me?" the Queen snarled, raising her still bloodied dagger.

Eliza leveled her own, ready. This was no training exercise in the Queen's office; this was life and death, right and wrong, truth and lies.

"You are nothing without me—you *are* me. Eliza—little Elizabeth. You are only what I've made you!"

"We are made or unmade by our choices," Eliza said, spinning the Queen's own words. "And I have chosen. From now on, I make myself."

Eliza didn't wait for the Queen to strike, dropping the veil and lunging forward with her blade.

The Queen blocked her attack, eyes darting from Eliza's blade to her eyes.

Eliza ducked just in time, the Queen's dagger searing through the space where her face had been.

"Choose," Eliza said. "Me or the vial."

"I do not choose!" the Queen screamed as she brought her knife down, eyes wide and wild.

Eliza dodged again, evading her blows with more ease than was natural. Was the Queen doing it on purpose to lull her into a false sense of security? Two could play at that game.

Eliza sliced forward with her dagger, staring pointedly at the Queen's shoulder. She let her grip falter, hesitated a step. It worked. The Queen caught her wrist in a tight hold, bending her arm backward in a painful twist. Her gaze narrowed on Eliza's center, and her blade found Eliza's chest.

A hot searing burn pierced through flesh and muscle. Eliza stumbled back, looking down at the silver hilt protruding from purple velvet. She inhaled, and sharp pain erupted across her chest.

The Queen had drawn first blood, but the fight wasn't over. She'd disarmed the Queen, and that was worth all the pain in the world.

"Still, so sloppy with your tells. You've learned nothing," the Queen spat.

"Don't forget yours." Eliza suppressed a grin. I didn't matter if Eliza hadn't improved. Where Eliza was weak, the Queen was weaker. Without her veil, the Queen's eyes told Eliza all she needed to know, every move she intended to make.

The Queen's jaw dropped. "How dare you!"

Eliza didn't have time for the Queen's pride. The Queen stretched out to reclaim the dagger in Eliza's chest. Eliza ducked under the Queen's arm and came up with her own under her chin, pinning the Queen against the wall.

"You are my Eyes—*my* Eyes," the Queen croaked.

"You have no eyes," Eliza replied, and she plunged the knife deep into skin and bone, carving out whatever was left of the Queen's soul.

CHAPTER FORTY-FIVE

The world froze while Nathaniel's father fell. His face was slack, his eyes wide, a crimson streak across his throat. It seemed to take years for Nathaniel to reach him, knees crashing into the hard ground beside him.

"Father!" Nathaniel reached for his head, cushioning it against the floor. "Father, say something. Can you hear me?"

Nathaniel's father didn't move.

In the distance, Nathaniel could hear yelling—was it Anna? He didn't care. His father lay bleeding, and though he'd made Nathaniel bleed and bruise on occasion, this was different.

His father was many things to many people—an adversary to Eliza, a nuisance to the Queen, a tormentor to Anna. He'd ruined lives; he'd saved Nathaniel's. He'd been a role model to Nathaniel, and at the same time, he'd been an abuser. He was father, and he was foe; Nathaniel wasn't ready to accept that was all his father could be.

There was so much blood. Nathaniel scrambled to stop the wound, but his fingers slipped across skin until his hands were stained red. His father had not blinked in minutes, and as Nathaniel dropped his gaze to his father's chest, he saw it did not rise or fall. The wound was too deep, the damage too much.

If his father died, Nathaniel would never have the chance to confront him about the things that truly mattered, or the chance to change his mind. He wasn't ready for his father to die.

But death didn't care if Nathaniel was ready. Death had come, and it wore a veil.

Nathaniel would make the Queen pay for what she'd taken, but as he turned, his breath left his body. When he'd rushed to his father's side, he'd left Anna and Eliza to face the Queen.

Now the Queen had no face.

"Wh-what did you do?" he breathed, rising up on his knees.

Anna blinked at him and then turned to Eliza, as if to echo the question.

Eliza stared down at the corpse at her feet. Blood pooled around the Queen's body, rapidly spreading out beneath her. She looked as though she'd met a thousand blades, but Eliza held only one.

Nathaniel tasted bile in his mouth. There was so much blood— so much death. He held tighter to his father's body.

Eliza stared down at her hand, her arm and chest covered in blood splatter, a silver knife protruding from her chest. "I didn't want her to hurt you," Eliza whispered, her eyes wide, her breaths shallow, and then she, too, fell to the floor.

Anna rushed to her side. "Eliza!"

"The vaccine," Eliza croaked, pointing to Anna's pocket, a smile playing on her lips before her eyes fluttered shut.

Anna bent over Eliza's body, examining the knife embedded in her chest. "Not good," she muttered.

"Is she all right?" Nathaniel asked.

"She's been stabbed. Of course she's not all right!"

Nathaniel looked down at the body beside him, still and lifeless. There was nothing he could do for his father—nothing except be the kind of man he'd always wanted him to be, the kind of heir to carry on his legacy. But the Fremont legacy was as much his father's as Nathaniel's to shape.

Nathaniel let go of his father's body and stood on shaking legs. "What can I do?" he asked, crossing the room to assist Anna.

"Nothing," Anna snapped, sitting back on her heels. "Get my satchel—no, there's nothing useful in there." She shook her head, hands shaking. "I can't visualize the injury like this. I can't see what the knife's hit—we could be dealing with a severed artery, or a punctured heart. I need my grandfather's tools, but Mechan is too far and I—"

"What if I can get you something better?"

Anna fixed him with a humorless stare, as though she might add him to the list of the dead if he didn't follow through.

"Your grandfather—I can fetch him. He's a doctor, right? He can help."

Anna stared at him for a long moment. "What are you waiting for? Go!"

Nathaniel didn't need telling twice. He took off, sprinting from the office and back toward the officers' bunker. He didn't have time to let his thoughts linger on the father he'd lost, or the father he'd never truly had. The Commissioner was dead, but Eliza could still be saved.

When he arrived back at the holding cell, Thatcher sat against the wall, eyes closed. "Mr. Thatcher!" Nathaniel cried, forgetting the man had waived the honorific. "Please wake up. I need your help."

"Don't wake an old man from his nap—hasn't anyone taught you manners?" Thatcher blinked rapidly, squinting at him through the bars. "Stars! What happened to you?"

Nathaniel looked down. His father's blood covered his arms and knees, a stain to carry with him forever, his father's weight added to Roman's across his shoulders. "Never mind this." He gestured to his appearance. "Anna needs your help."

Thatcher sat straighter. "Is that her blood? Is Anna—"

"No, she's fine. This is my— The Commissioner's."

Thatcher eyed him, a long, searching stare. "So you stopped him."

Nathaniel didn't know if he could truly take credit for the Commissioner's downfall—didn't know if he *wanted* to. Now wasn't the time to argue semantics, though, so he nodded.

"Then you did what you set out to do. You should be proud. You saved many lives today."

"There's one more life that needs saving, if you'll help. Anna's doing her best, but she needs you."

"She doesn't need me." Thatcher frowned but gestured for Nathaniel to help him. "Take me to her—and try not to drop me."

Nathaniel carefully eased the man into his arms, but compared to the lives Nathaniel was used to carrying, Thatcher's body weighed nothing at all.

When they returned to the Commissioner's office, Thatcher took charge of the scene.

"We'll need good light—move her here onto the desk."

Nathaniel positioned himself at Eliza's head, helping Anna move her from the floor.

"Careful not to jostle her. Keep her level so the knife doesn't move."

Nathaniel reached for the hilt—sleek steel with a vine-patterned pommel. To think such a small blade had taken down a giant like his father.

"Don't touch it!" Anna pushed him out of the way. "We can't remove the knife until we know what it hit."

Nathaniel stepped back as Anna and Thatcher carefully cut away Eliza's dress, exposing the wound. They volleyed words Nathaniel didn't understand, falling into an easy rhythm as Anna moved around the office, fetching tools from the Commissioner's shelves, Thatcher barking orders.

Eliza lay in an ambiguous state of consciousness, her lashes fluttering, her limbs twitching. He'd never seen her so vulnerable and exposed. She'd always been the one in control; now her life lay in their hands.

Looking down at his own, Nathaniel saw his father's blood dried and flaking from his skin. He'd been powerless to save his father, and now again he could do nothing to help Eliza. If she died, he would have done nothing to stop it, and if she lived—well, she'd be furious he let Anna and Thatcher ruin her dress.

Nathaniel backed out of the room. Anna and Thatcher would not miss him, and he couldn't stand just watching while they worked—not with two dead bodies on the floor. He needed to wash the blood from his hands.

Back in his bedroom, Nathaniel drew himself a bath, but as he removed his bloodstained clothes, something heavy dropped from his pocket. The holocom. It was still recording.

It seemed like ages ago he'd snuck it into his pocket, hoping to record his father's confession. It had worked, in a sense, but the confessions he'd caught hadn't been so much incriminating as enlightening. His father hadn't murdered Nathaniel's mother, and he hadn't poisoned Anna's village. Instead, he'd admitted to a deep, painful love for Isla Fremont—risking everything to ensure she got credit for the vaccine. Nathaniel couldn't fault him for that.

And the Queen—Nathaniel had once thought kindly of his grandmother. She'd stood up for him in his father's council meeting, and though she always seemed intimidating, he'd never thought her cruel.

It didn't matter. They were both dead.

Nathaniel climbed into the bathtub, letting warm water wash over his tired body. He scrubbed and scraped the blood away, rinsing the remains of their deaths down the drain. Then he picked up the holocom and deleted the recording. It was a tactic worthy of his father—showing the council how much worse his father had been in the hopes of making himself look better. He wanted to be Commissioner, but he didn't want it like that. He wanted to earn it on his own.

CHAPTER FORTY-SIX

Anna had forgotten how it felt to cut into skin. She'd swung her fists more than a few times in the last day, but pressing the blade of a scalpel against flesh was different.

Flesh was fragile.

But Eliza wasn't. She was strong and solid beneath Anna's fingers, life beating through her like a drum. It would take more than a blade to bring her down, more than a queen. Still, Anna's heart thundered a nervous rhythm.

Together, she and Thatcher prepared the makeshift operating table, gathering the tools they had, hoping they wouldn't need the ones they didn't. As they worked, sterilizing blades, preparing gauze, he talked through the steps of the operation. This was how it always worked; Thatcher explained, and then Thatcher cut.

But Anna didn't want him to.

Eliza was more than some villager from Mechan being fitted for a TICCER. Eliza meant something to Anna, even if she couldn't articulate what.

Responsibility had finally caught up with her, or maybe she'd slowed down to meet it. Either way, Anna wouldn't let someone else take the blame for what she'd done or what she'd yet to do. All the years she'd spent running from her guilt over Roman's surgery were years she spent running from Roman himself. She wouldn't let herself do the same to Eliza.

Eliza had stood between Anna and death. She'd fought the Queen for her; she'd *killed* the Queen for her. She'd chosen Anna.

And now Anna would choose her back. Eliza was hers to save, even if she wasn't hers in any other way.

"Let me." The words were barely a whisper, but in the quiet, they sounded like a shout.

Thatcher eyed her with overcast eyes. "Are you certain, Deirdre-Anne?"

"It's Anna," she said.

"Anna." Thatcher nodded and handed her the scalpel.

She pressed the blade to Eliza's skin and made the first cut.

When the surgery was over, they moved Eliza back to her room to recover, but Anna couldn't bring herself to visit. She'd walked past Eliza's door a dozen times but couldn't go inside. Eliza would wake soon, confused and in pain. Anna wasn't ready to face her. Too many things were changing at once, and when she confronted her feelings for Eliza, one way or another, their relationship would change, too.

Thatcher returned to Mechan to add the vaccine to their well as soon as Nathaniel recovered his wheelchair. Tarnish had already done its damage, and it wouldn't save most of the citizens of Mechan. Still, lives would change.

If the serum worked, Ruby might very well get her wish: Thatcher would never see her child on his operating table. At least not for a TICCER. It would never make up for Roman—nothing ever could. That place in their hearts, in their home, would be forever empty. But in this one small way, Anna had succeeded.

"Ah, there you are!" Eliza said, leaning against her doorframe. "When you didn't come to see me, I thought maybe— But you're all right."

Anna stepped back. When had Eliza opened her door?

Eliza had changed into a lavender silk robe, and her hair was back under control—though Anna noted she hadn't put it back into its carefully curled style, letting it fall loose across her shoulders. She looked somehow small without some type of hat perched on her head.

"I'm fine, I was just—" Anna let her words fall flat. She'd been doing nothing at all, for once in her life. "How are you feeling?"

Eliza beckoned Anna inside. "As well as can be expected. I've killed before, of course, but I imagine the Queen will haunt me for a long time to come."

Anna nodded, taking a hesitant step into the room. "It's hard to lose the ones we love."

"Yes, of course. You're right." She shook her head as though to clear it, returning to Anna with a smile too bright for the occasion. "I'll be all right."

"What about your chest? Are you in pain?" It was easier to be the doctor checking on her patient than the nervous girl with confusing feelings she carried inside her skin.

"I was stabbed, you know."

Anna cracked a grin. "I do know. I saw it happen."

"Nathaniel stopped by earlier. He said you patched me up?" Eliza's fingers brushed against her chest, wincing at her own touch.

"Let me have a look—make sure it's healing all right." Anna pulled a chair across the room as Eliza disrobed and sat on the edge of her bed.

"Well? What's the verdict? Will I have a scar?"

"Probably." Anna reached for Eliza's shoulder, removing the bandage so she could see the wound properly. "But don't worry—I like scars."

"Do you, now?" Eliza's lips quirked into a sly smile.

Anna blushed. It had been only days since they'd first met. How Anna's opinion of her had changed in that time. The pretentious noble, too good for Anna—too good for anyone—was gone. In her place was the girl who'd fought a queen to save Anna, who'd fought *herself* to save Anna.

Dropping her hands, she tried to calm her rapidly beating heart. Eliza was just another patient. Touching her was nothing to be nervous about.

"I didn't realize you were a surgeon, too. I thought with a name like the Technician you'd be more involved with tech." Eliza leaned back against her pillows.

Anna held back a denial. She was so used to saying she wasn't a surgeon, but it wasn't exactly true anymore. The word had embodied an entire identity she couldn't claim, an identity that belonged to Thatcher and Thatcher alone. But now it seemed less of a burden. *Surgeon* was no longer a commitment she had to make but a role she could choose to play—or not.

Anna opened her satchel. "Let me get you a fresh bandage."

"Thank you," Eliza said.

Anna's breath caught, acutely aware of Eliza's eyes on her as she applied the bandage with slow, deliberate hands. If she didn't focus, there was no telling what she'd do with them. She wanted to place her palm on Eliza's shoulder, or maybe tug one of the curls around Eliza's face to see if it bounced.

Eliza seemed to follow the same train of thought, placing her hand over Anna's and holding it against her skin. "You don't understand—*thank you*. You saved my life."

"And you saved mine."

Eliza gripped Anna's hand tighter and caught her gaze. "You touched my heart."

"Actually, the knife missed your heart and punctured your lung instead."

Eliza placed a finger beneath Anna's chin. "You touched my heart, Anna Thatcher, long before you touched my skin."

For a breathless moment, Anna considered fleeing from the room and from their future. She ignored her instinct to run and let her lips meet Eliza's.

It was like falling in a dream, with a rush of adrenaline and air, waiting for the single moment of thrilling terror before she'd wake, head against the pillows. Only, Anna never wanted to wake. She wanted to drown in the dream of Eliza's lips, always falling, never landing.

When Eliza finally pulled away, one hand in Anna's hair, the other low on Anna's back, she wore a loose smile and a mischievous sparkle in her eye.

"Nathaniel's asked to break off our engagement."

"Is that so?" Anna fiddled with the collar of Eliza's robe, the silk smooth against her fingers. Why were they talking now when they could be kissing?

Eliza plucked Anna's fingers from her collar like they were flowers in a garden, examining them with her own. "Nathaniel deserves to be free to make his own choices, and I deserve my chance at love."

Anna found it suddenly difficult to breathe. How could her hands be so steady holding a scalpel but so shaky now?

Eliza slid her hand around to Anna's waist, gripping the cloth of her shirt and sending a ripple up Anna's spine.

"So," Eliza said with smile as warm as a summer afternoon, "how are my chances?"

Anna could have done the math, but instead she answered with another kiss.

CHAPTER FORTY-SEVEN

It began with the earth. Eliza knelt, elbow deep in the freshly turned dirt, brown and soft and cold to the touch. If anyone saw her in this state, it would be very grave indeed.

To think, a war had been waged over this planet, blades drawn behind a curtain of secrecy, a veil of whispers, yet neither side had truly won. Both commanders lay dead and buried, a mountain of crimes the only blanket for their final rest. They'd wanted Earth Adjacent, the ground beneath Eliza's knees, the dewdrops seeping into the rich fabric of her dress, and so they'd have it.

So many people had fought for the planet. The Queen and the Commissioner had died for it.

In a way Eliza didn't yet understand, she herself had *killed* for it.

They'd clashed over an entire world, a future for humanity. Eliza ought to have been humbled by the enormity of it all, but a part of her still battled even though the war was over.

From the folds of her skirt, Eliza withdrew the long silver blade, pressing the dirt on her hands against the hilt. There'd been a time when polishing the metal until she could see her reflection had been the one true joy in her life. Now she let her eyes drift, sending the world out of focus, unable to bear the thought of her round face forming a perfect iris for the eye on the pommel.

This dagger had been her war, not the planet. Eliza had never cared if humanity descended from the Tower in her lifetime. In fact, she'd always found more solace among the stars, as if they could somehow see her better than all the eyes in the world. No, for Eliza, everything began with the blade.

It had taken the Queen's face, her skin, her eyes, her life.

It had winked in starlight, calling Eliza like a siren, making her want with everything she had, compelling her to give up a love she could barely recall.

It had become her, twisting metal through her veins and around her heart until Eliza was no longer herself, until *Eliza* was but a distant memory.

The Queen had given her a home and a job and a knife, and Eliza had stripped herself of the past, tearing herself like cloth, spinning herself like thread, sewing herself back up in a patchwork imitation of a girl.

She was the smoke, not the fire; the footprint, not the leg; the wound, not the weapon.

She was adjacent.

Just like the world.

But somewhere in the depths of Eliza's hollow heart, she'd hidden herself away, the girl she'd been before she became the Queen's Eyes, the girl who'd belonged only to herself—the girl who'd lived without the weight of the Queen's ambition.

It began with the earth, and it could end there, too.

Eliza lowered the blade into the Queen's grave. She'd no need of eyes except her own.

CHAPTER FORTY-EIGHT

Nathaniel sat in his father's chair, at his father's desk, but he'd never felt less like the Commissioner. He'd explained the situation to the council, told them about Mechan and the cure, but even after disclosing every detail, they'd miraculously agreed he should succeed his father. He was only an eighteen-year-old boy who possessed little experience with governing and certainly no endorsement from his father, but he had a plan, and the council seemed to respond to it.

He'd work with transparency instead of secrecy, with compassion instead of control. He'd never be the man his father wanted him to be. Nathaniel had only wanted his father's approval, but Oliver Fremont was dead, and it was time to start wanting more.

Nathaniel wanted to abolish the Tech Decrees. He wanted to open the Settlement's gates. He wanted more open communication and discussion in creating new laws. But first, he wanted peace with Mechan.

Anna's grandfather was as different from the fiery Technician as could be. He was tempered where she was rash, collected where she was dramatic. He'd already given Nathaniel valuable counsel, and Nathaniel hoped he'd agree to more.

"What can I do for you, Commissioner-elect?" Thatcher asked upon entering the office.

Nathaniel gestured for him to join him at the desk, acutely aware of the violence that had occurred there only days ago. At first, he'd thought to close the office off and start fresh, but the past couldn't be forgotten, only covered up. It would be a disservice to them all not to acknowledge it, remember it, and promise to do better.

"I'm glad you could join me," Nathaniel said.

"This house still holds unpleasant memories for me; I'm afraid it has me a bit on edge." Thatcher eyed the corners of the room as if he were checking for unobserved guards.

Nathaniel nodded. "This government and my father treated you and your family in an inexcusable manner. I cannot apologize enough for what you've been put through in the name of the law."

"Apologies are ineffective."

"I know—nothing can make up for what he did."

Thatcher shook his head. "No—I mean apologies are something you give to make yourself feel better. Rarely do they come from a selfless place. It's best to skip them entirely and get on with it."

"Right." Nathaniel suppressed a smile, remembering how Anna had lectured him about forgiveness. Perhaps the Technician and her grandfather were not so different after all. "Well, onward. I find myself in need of excellent counsel. I want better counsel than my father had, different counsel. The advisors I have can tell me everything I need to know about law and policy, but I don't need more of that. What I need is someone who can help me understand what the people need, what *your* people need. I want to do a better job for everyone on Earth Adjacent."

Thatcher frowned. "That's all well and good, but the Settlement isn't home to a lot of us anymore. You can be as inclusive as you like, but you'll be hard-pressed to convince most of us to come back."

"Who said anything about the Settlement?" Nathaniel tried to hide his smile. "My first act as Commissioner-elect will be to officially recognize Mechan as its own city."

"The people of Mechan won't bow to you, TICCER or no."

The Thatcher before him was different from the one he'd met in his father's prison. That man had been defeated yet hopeful. He'd been willing to give up everything for his granddaughter, willing to help Nathaniel save her. Now he was terse and defensive—and perhaps rightly so.

"You didn't let me finish." Nathaniel pushed a document forward, spelling out the details of his proposal. "This document, once I sign it, gives Mechan governing power. I don't want to rule over the people of Mechan; I want to work with them."

Thatcher made a noncommittal sound as he scanned the paper. "Mechan doesn't have a governing body."

"And that's up to Mechan. I don't want to enforce unwanted restrictions. But I *do* want a relationship. I want to work with Mechan's people to amend my father's laws and to produce more of the vaccine. Anna mentioned you might have an alchemist or two who could assist with deciphering my mother's notes."

"I can't speak for Mechan, but I'll ask Ruby to help with the vaccine." His finger traced the line at the bottom of the document. "There are two lines here."

"Ah, yes." Nathaniel picked up a pen and handed it to Thatcher, his hand shaking. "Part of the agreement is cooperation from Mechan on one point."

Thatcher didn't take the pen. "And what is that?"

"I'd like to be kept informed and advised by a member of your town. I'd like a representative from Mechan to join my council." He pushed the words out in a single stream.

Thatcher laughed.

"What?" Nathaniel asked, taken aback.

"If you think you need my permission to ask Anna anything, then you don't know her at all." Thatcher pushed the document back toward Nathaniel.

"No, I don't mean her." He swallowed. It felt bizarre justifying his decision to her grandfather of all people, but he plowed on. "She's like me more than a little, and I need someone with more experience."

"Ah, you mean someone older."

"I'm young, it's true. I know that many will see me as too inexperienced to run the Settlement, but I think with the right advisors, I can do a good job—a great job. I want you to be one of those advisors."

Thatcher eyed him warily. "And how do I know you'll keep your end of the bargain? You'll stay out of Mechan's business, you say, but you have more military power, more governing power. We're just a small village."

Nathaniel bowed his head. "I know it isn't easy to trust, when all the Settlement's ever done is cause you pain, but if there's one thing I've learned over the past few days, it's that trust is essential. Anna and I—if we hadn't trusted each other, none of this could have worked." He paused, his hand on his heart. "Even if you can't trust me or the Settlement, know that I trust you. You helped me once when I was only an infant, and again when I thought I couldn't be helped. I ask you to find that same compassion now."

Thatcher grunted. "I'll consider it. Have to ask the rest of Mechan first, anyway." He folded the paper and slipped it into his pocket.

"Thank you." Nathaniel let out a long breath, not caring that his relief showed in every inch of his face.

Thatcher wheeled his chair toward the door, but paused at the threshold. "Be better than him."

"I will." Nathaniel hoped with every essence of his being that it was the truth.

Dusk had fallen by the time Nathaniel had a free moment, and there was only one person he wanted to talk to. She wouldn't answer back, but that was okay.

It had been a long time since Nathaniel had ventured out to the cemetery to visit his mother's grave. His father's world had excluded her, and so, too, had Nathaniel. How much of that was his own doing, he'd never truly know, but he was tired of blaming his father for everything.

It was there that Anna found him. "She'd be proud of you, I think," she said from the tree line.

Nathaniel glanced up to see her leaning against a pine, framed by the tree's branches. "She can't be proud of anything. She's dead."

"You can still try to do right by her." Anna crossed over to stand beside him. "She doesn't have to know what you've done in order for it to matter."

Nathaniel nodded slowly, his tongue dry in his mouth. It felt too late for tears, like he should have shed them years ago, and now they wouldn't count. He'd seen Eliza on his way there, staring down the freshly turned earth over the Queen's body. She hadn't cried, either; only buried her eye-tipped dagger and walked away.

"Do you think the Queen really hated my mother—and my father—so much?"

"I don't know," Anna replied. "I doubt we'll ever know for sure. There are two sides to every story."

Just like with theirs. Anna was the girl who'd brought so much destruction into his home, but she was also the girl who helped him see the wrongness around him. She helped him find his legs and stand up for himself. Nathaniel's breath hitched in his chest. Who was he in her eyes?

Anna continued, "Sometimes it isn't the sides that count; it's where they intersect." She swayed back and forth with the breeze. "I think somewhere, deep down, both of your parents—and maybe even the Queen—would be proud of what you've become."

Nathaniel grimaced. "And what is that? I don't even know who I am."

"That's all right." Anna laughed. "None of us do."

"Who am I?"

"You're you."

"What is that supposed to mean?" Anger peppered his voice. "I've never been anything other than young Master Fremont, the Commissioner's son. Can I really be anything else?"

Anna nodded in understanding. "You aren't the same anymore. You're not the scared boy who defended his father's ideas, who let me and Eliza sway him to our plans. You're a leader now."

"I didn't want this," he whispered. "How did this happen?"

"It didn't just *happen*. I know you've always had power handed to you, but that isn't how it usually works. Power's something you have to take. And you did."

Her words dug under his skin. "I'm still me, right?"

Anna cracked a smile. "I don't think that means much to either of us."

Nathaniel looked up from the grave to stare at her. She looked the same as always, freckles like secrets dotted across her skin, jaw jutted forward in a defiant overbite, and hair pulled tight with rebellious curls escaping from her braid—but her eyes weren't narrowed anymore.

She'd changed, too.

"How did everything go so wrong?" he whispered.

"Did it? I rather think everything went right. You're a leader now."

"I don't feel like one." Nathaniel felt like a child—made smaller by the shoes he had to fill. Even with his father removed from office, even with him dead, Nathaniel shrank beneath the weight of the title.

Anna cocked her head. "It isn't how you feel that makes you a leader; it's what you do."

It was like they were back in the abandoned building where she'd first told him about his TICCER, about how her world and his clashed. She seemed to know just what to say, even if it pained him to hear it.

"I want you with me," he said without thinking, letting the truth govern his words rather than logic. She and Eliza had stood by him while they took the Commissioner down notch by notch, unraveling his claim to power. He hadn't acted alone, and he hoped he never would again. "I want you with me on my side. Working with you to"—he gestured aimlessly around—"achieve all this, that's the most alive I've ever felt. I want to keep feeling that way."

"That's called friendship, Nathaniel. That's what friends do for each other."

Nathaniel's smile widened. *Friends.*

"Now . . ." Anna said matter-of-factly, steering him back toward the manor. Eliza, who'd waited for them at the edge of the clearing, linked her arm through Anna's as they made their way across the garden. "In Mechan we like to honor the dead by eating a lot of pie and telling stories about them."

Nathaniel frowned. "Really?"

Anna wrinkled her nose. "Yes—well, no. Not the part about pie. I'm just hungry."

Eliza gasped, feigning shock. "That's a terribly rude lie, Anna."

Anna pursed her lips, clearly fighting a smile. "But we do tell stories. It helps, I promise. If we remember the ones we love, it's like they're never truly gone." She tightened her grip on Nathaniel's arm, but her eyes drifted toward a darkening sky.

Nathaniel followed her gaze, unsure if he hoped to find some comfort among the stars, not invisible, and not yet bright. They shone feebly, like half-lidded eyes watching through the purple sunset. Perhaps his mother saw him, too, cloaked in that secret place between night and day where stars hid from the world.

They paused at the edge of the manor to watch stars fall from the sky, silver slingshots carrying the nobles of the Tower. Soon the eastern fields would be speckled with Bullets, and the Settlement would welcome the Tower's elite. They would leave their titles with their ships; the Settlement had no use for lords.

Nathaniel, too, would start fresh, leaving his grief in the garden behind him.

He had no stories to tell about his mother. He couldn't even remember her. But he would make sure no one forgot her.

"Isla," he whispered. "That's what we'll call it."

"Call what?" Eliza asked.

"The Settlement." Nathaniel crossed his arms, standing straighter. "I've been trying to think of a new name for it—it sounds so militant, so like my father. *The Settlement.*" He spoke the words through tight lips, doing his best impression of his father. "Besides, we're a fully planetary society now. Everything is a settlement. It's time to give ours a name."

"Isla," Anna repeated thoughtfully. "I like it."

"Really?" Nathaniel asked, turning on her, eyebrow raised. "You don't think naming an island city Isla is a little, well, like naming a cat Cat or a piece of tech Tech?"

"Oh, it definitely is." Anna nodded.

"The Commissioner would hate it," Eliza added, grinning.

"You're going to have to find something else to call him." Nathaniel grinned back. "I'm the Commissioner now."

Six months later . . .

Anna didn't like the color red. It was the blood on her clothes and her hands that took her minutes to wash off, but hours to feel clean, and it was the clock tower that chimed loud bells through her thoughts with the same consistent rhythm of her heart. But most of all, it was the color of the uniform spread out across her bed.

Nathaniel had updated the military uniform so as to start anew. The old maroon and gray symbolized fear for many of the citizens of Mechan, as well as the Settlement—newly renamed Isla—and Nathaniel was determined to put his father's reign behind him. The new uniform was a striking red and black, well designed and liked by most.

But Anna couldn't seem to put it on. She'd agreed a few months back to join Nathaniel's militia as a tech expert, but with each day that brought her closer to her induction, she regretted that decision. To go from the Technician, Isla's most wanted, to a uniform-wearing officer felt wrong.

Besides, red clashed terribly with her hair.

That was how Anna found herself dressed in one of Eliza's gowns again—far too elegant and several inches too short. It didn't suit her in the slightest, and the rich fabric swishing against her legs made her self-conscious; someone would notice she didn't belong. But really, she didn't mind so much with Eliza's hand in hers.

"Where's Thatcher?" Anna asked. "He should be here, too."

Eliza searched as well, but it was no use. Anna was taller by six inches at least, and even from her vantage point she found nothing.

As the room fell silent, Anna's gaze snapped to the dais where Nathaniel stepped, looking like a massive ladybug in his red and black—a *regal* ladybug.

"By order of Commissioner Nathaniel Fremont," he said, his voice cracking ever so slightly over the name. "In the year 2893, human-augmentation technology will no longer be prohibited."

It was over in seconds. The councilor handed him the paper, and he signed it. The crowd roared with approval and then dispersed.

Anna knew it was only the beginning. It would be an uphill battle to undo the years of legislation put in place by Nathaniel's father.

This was only the first step—a good step.

"Well then. Time to celebrate!" Eliza wrapped her arm around Anna's waist and squeezed.

Anna returned the gesture, locking them in a walking embrace. "Do we really have to go? I don't fancy rubbing elbows with Nathaniel's advisors over wine I'm not allowed to drink. Besides, no one will miss us."

"Nathaniel will miss us." Eliza nodded up toward the dais. "He's been working hard—it's not all speeches and signing documents, being Commissioner. He deserves a break."

Anna sighed, letting her free hand tangle with Eliza's curls. "We deserve a break, too." But Eliza was right. It was Nathaniel's day, and it was a day worth celebrating, even if Anna's definition of celebration involved fewer strangers and more comfortable clothing.

"In good time. I promise." Eliza stood on her toes to plant a kiss on Anna's temple. "Perhaps we'll finally get a chance at that dance you've been promising me."

Anna groaned. Eliza might have spent hours watching Anna deftly piece gears together with her nimble fingers, but if she saw how disconnected her feet were, whatever fantasy of fluttering gowns and swooping music Eliza had concocted would truly be shattered once and for all.

"Fine," Anna grumbled. "But only if you promise not to laugh."

"How about a promise to make you laugh along with me?" Eliza's eyes glittered, and she stole a kiss.

As they exited the hall, a gentle pinging sound filled the air. Anna had, after much convincing, obtained the Commissioner's old holocom and replicated the device, giving one to Thatcher and keeping one for herself. It was to facilitate easier communication between Mechan and the Settlement—or, rather, Isla.

Withdrawing the holocom from her dress pocket, Anna answered the call.

"Anna," Thatcher wheezed. He wore grubby trousers and a soiled apron—not at all appropriate attire for attending the Commissioner's party

"Where are you?" Anna asked. "The ceremony's over."

"Mechan. Ruby's gone into labor. You won't want to miss this."

Anna let go of Eliza's hand. "Give Nathaniel my regrets?"

Eliza nodded and squeezed her shoulder. "I'm sure he'll understand. Go be with Ruby."

And without a moment more, Anna hitched up her skirts and broke into a run.

When she reached Mechan, Anna entered Thatcher's home—barely lived in since Thatcher had started working on Nathaniel's council. Anna, too, had spent increasingly more time away to see Nathaniel and Eliza as much as she could.

Inside, Ruby lay on the bed in the patient room, screaming bloody murder.

Anna slipped inside and stood in the corner, watching from as far away as she could. Though she'd observed countless surgeries, they all paled in comparison to the violence of birth. Anna hoped she would go all her life and never witness another.

When the baby's first cries hit the air and Ruby fell back against the pillows, Thatcher waved Anna over. She held her breath, afraid to hope for a healthy child.

Handing her a stethoscope, Thatcher smiled and said, "Listen."

And Anna listened.

There was nothing quite like the first beat of a new heart.

ACKNOWLEDGMENTS

We say words matter, and never have words mattered to me more than when it comes to identity. I was given the gift of vocabulary—the words *asexual* and *aromantic*—by the brave authors who came before me, putting words to a feeling or lack thereof; you made this book possible. Thank you to everyone who pushed me to write my truth and to be myself. Your permission has been a blessing, and I cherish each and every one of you who helped make this book a reality.

Thank you to Saba Sulaiman, my fearless agent, who never ceases to be my hero, as well as the whole Talcott Notch team. I am forever grateful to have found such a genuine, savvy, and delightful advocate. You make this industry a joy even when it's The Worst.

To my editor, Orlando Dos Reis, without whom *Tarnished Are the Stars* would have a lot less Eliza. Thank you for truly understanding this book in ways I could never have anticipated and for always pushing me to make it better. Your guidance and faith in this story mean the world to me. To the entire Scholastic team as well, thank you for your hard work to make this book happen: Josh

Berlowitz, Yaffa Jaskoll, Annika Voss, Shannon Pender, Jackie Hornberger, Elisabeth Ferrari, and Debra Latour.

Linsey Miller, who believed in this book before I did—thank you for being right All The Time. I'm so glad you made me rewrite this book and then rewrite it again—I am a better writer for it. You are the best mentor I could have asked for, my writerly Uncle Iroh. Thank you to Pitch Wars for bringing us together and K. Kazul Wolf for pushing me to enter in the first place (and for the puns!). To my fellow 2016 pitch warriors as well, without whom publishing would be a much lonelier place. Ian Barnes and Jen DeLuca, y'all make me laugh way too much!

Infinite thanks to Elizabeth Fletcher, who suffered through the worst drafts of this book more times than I can count and still told me to keep going. Also to Wordsmith Workshops for bringing Elizabeth and me together, and for your wisdom, advice, and snacks. Thank you to Beth Revis for your support and for breaking my brain over and over, to Cristin Terrill for your advice and guidance with navigating the publishing industry, and to Lynn Moor for the best-timed cup of tea in the history of the world.

Al Graziadei and Marisa Kanter, thank you for being on this journey with me for (by the time this is published) ten whole years! I can't believe we made it this far, and I'm so glad to be going through all this with you two by my side. And thanks to Alexa Donne, Emily Duncan, Rory Power, Christine Lynn Herman, Kevin van Whye, June Tan, Deeba Zargarpur, and Emma Theriault for the knife-reacts and for putting up with my bad puns.

I am so grateful to my early readers who helped shape this book from the beginning: Anna Bright for your insight back when this book was a complete disaster; Carly Heath for your support and camaraderie; Rachel Griffin and Jenny Howe for encouraging me when I feel lost, even when I'm actually not; Sasha Nanua for your help with my pacemaker research; Taylor Brooke for our daily screaming sessions; Bea Conti for loving this book and yelling along with me; Kim Smejkal for your thoughtful feedback and encouragement; Rachel Lynn Solomon for all your publishing wisdom; Alexa Donne for your realness and advice; and Sarah Harrington for being the second goat in my boat.

Thank you Claire Murphy and Faye Jones for sticking with me through the ups and downs of life and being the best of friends. Thanks for never laughing at me when I got Serious and Writerly when we were youths. Thanks also to Mandy Vincent, April Wong, Stephen "Phteven" Weltz, Lance Armstrong, Dante Quazzo, and Daniel Merritt for supporting me along the way; to Sabreen Lakhani for taking my picture in the snow and also your invaluable coffee knowledge; to Andrew Sunada, for your incredible friendship and dedication to bettering yourself—you inspire me to do the same; to Colleen Crook, thank you for putting up with my messy-deadline-self and for listening to pub gossip about people you don't know—so glad to run through life holding left hands with you; and to the rest of my IRL writing group: Sarah Burton, Emily Toohey-Andrews, and J. S. Fields.

I would not be where I am without the support of my family. Mom, thank you for encouraging me to be creative and for giving every fairy on my posters a backstory. Dad, thank you for getting a master's degree and then deciding to build harps instead. Your commitment to your craft is inspirational, and I never would have believed I could be successful doing what I love without your example. Sorry I didn't turn out to be a harpist, but hopefully this will do instead.

Lastly, hugs and cookies to Tess, the love of my life and doggo extraordinaire, who patiently bore my endless deadlines and only whined about her lack of walkies a little bit.

ABOUT THE AUTHOR

Rosiee Thor began her career as a storyteller by demanding that her mother listen as Rosiee told bedtime stories instead of the other way around. She lives in Oregon with a dog, two cats, and four complete sets of Harry Potter, which she loves so much, she once moved her mattress into the closet and slept there until she came out as queer. Follow her online at rosieethor.com and on Twitter at @rosieethor.